THE

CRYSTAL

SHORE

BOOK ONE OF THE **TEMPERED SOUL** SERIES

To the person who picks
this up at Levenshulme
station, enjoy the adventure!

8th May 24

THE
CRYSTAL
SHORE

Copyright © 2022 by Jo de-Lancey

First paperback edition July 2022

Cover Art: Thea Magerand
Illustrations: Thea Magerand
Editing: Lesley Jones and Natalia Leigh
Book Design: Greg Rupel at Enchanted Ink

ISBN 978-1-7399566-0-8 (paperback)
ISBN 978-1-7399566-1-5 (ebook)

WWW.JODELANCEY.COM

For my big brother, Dan de-Lancey.
I won the bet for both of us.

KILLIAN O'SHEA

'YOU NEED A KILLIAN
O'SHEA RIGHT NOW, AND
UNFORTUNATELY FOR YOU,
I HOLD A MONOPOLY.'

CAPTAIN
LILY ROTHBONE

'I CAN DUMP THE TWO OF
YOU IN THE SEA, BLEEDING
FROM YOUR GUTS, IF I WANT.
IT'S YOUR CHOICE, KILLIAN.'

REN THORNCLIFFE

'HE'S THE ONLY PERSON I
HAVE IN THE WORLD, AND . . .
AND I'M WORRIED WE'LL BE
TOO LATE.'

NESTA

'ONCE YOU GO IN, THERE
IS NO TURNING BACK. YOU
FINISH, OR YOU DIE. DO YOU
UNDERSTAND?'

CHAPTER
ONE

REN THORNCLIFFE THOUGHT HE SAW A SMILE flash across Killian O'Shea's face, but he couldn't be sure. Blinking, he dismissed it as a trick of the light in the murky glow of the tavern and went back to studying the drink in front of him. He needed to ask O'Shea something, but not yet; he would wait for the right moment to present itself. Everything had to be perfect.

He glanced up at Killian and saw him take a hearty swig from his mug of ale. Feeling somewhat inferior, Ren reached for his own and took a sip. It was disgusting, bitter and tart, and his tongue recoiled in his mouth. With trembling fingers, he placed the mug back down. He quickly stuffed his shaking hands inside the pockets of his fine jacket to hide them. Cowardice was second nature to him, but he didn't need it on display for all to see. His gaze flicked to the man before him again, and to his dismay, he found he was being stared at.

Ren shuffled awkwardly beneath Killian's glare, searching for words. He swallowed. Despite the ale, his throat was as dry as a bag of sawdust. This was not going to plan; he hadn't thought this far ahead. After considering his beer mat from all angles, he decided that excusing himself and leaving was probably the best idea. That perfect moment clearly wasn't going to arise tonight. Perhaps he could come back tomorrow and try again. As he grabbed his scarf, Killian finally broke the silence.

'Jilt?' he asked.

'Pardon?' Ren's voice came out slightly higher than he'd have liked.

'A game of cards,' said Killian. He ran his hand through his chestnut-brown hair, tucking the remains of a long-forgotten fringe behind his ears. 'They do know how to play cards in Chazza, don't they?'

Before Ren had time to answer or even acknowledge the insult to his hometown, the cards were before him.

'You familiar with jilt?' asked Killian as he rearranged his hand.

'Oh, er . . . yes.'

'A little wager then?' Killian added, putting some coins on the table and giving Ren a wink.

'All right,' Ren said, adding his own coins to the pile.

A roar of laughter from the bar made him jump, and he looked around to see a group of hard-faced fishermen swilling tankards of ale, froth clinging to their unkempt beards. They were chatting with the barmaid, who was joining them in drinking and smoking. Ren shuddered and tried to ignore them; he wasn't used to being in such places. Woodsmoke from a crackling open fire filled the room and his lungs. It would have almost been comforting if it hadn't been for the underlying reek of tobacco that accompanied it.

'Are you playing or what?' Killian's impatient tone caught his attention.

'Oh, yes. Sorry,' Ren mumbled back.

As he looked at his cards, Ren felt an excited thump in his chest. His hand was so good there was no possible way he could lose. If he could beat Killian at jilt, then maybe he would feel obliged to help him. He watched his opponent take a long, carefree draught from his jug and lean back in his chair. There was an aura of relaxed calm about him, which gnawed away at what little confidence Ren had. He averted his eyes from his opponent and studied his cards again. *They* wouldn't make him feel insignificant or small. They were going to help him win. He'd win all that money on the table, and then with the respect he'd earned, he'd ask Killian for help. This was his new watertight plan. It wouldn't fail. It couldn't fail.

'So, Thorny – I can call you Thorny, can't I?' Killian said without giving Ren time to respond. 'Have you come here just to play me at cards? Is that it? Am I right?'

Ren's mind raced as he mulled over tactics. It looked like he could most definitely win, but *should* he win? If he won, Killian might refuse to help him out of pure spite. However, if he lost, Killian would think he was a pushover. Ren found himself at a tricky impasse. He picked a card from his hand and gazed at it, silently promising himself to ask for what he needed on his next turn.

'Quiet, aren't you?' Killian said airily.

Ren snapped back to reality. 'Sorry?'

'I said you're quiet.'

'Just trying to focus, that's all.'

Killian shrugged, cleared the deck and threw down his three remaining cards. Ren's mouth dropped open.

'Good try.' Killian smiled as he scooped up his winnings, his brilliant azure eyes twinkling mischievously in the flickering gloom of the tavern. 'I like it when someone puts in the effort.' He turned to grab the long brown coat from the back of his chair.

Ren thought fast; if he let him go now, he might not get the chance to ask him again. 'Another game?' he blurted out before he could stop himself or at least think of any other excuse to keep Killian there.

Killian raised an eyebrow. 'Only if you're sure ...'

Once more they tossed some coins into a wager, and once again Killian won. Ren still hadn't plucked up the courage to ask him for the Favour, so they played again, and again, and again. As the night wore on and the other punters staggered home, the contents of Ren's purse decreased and his frustrations increased. His opportunity was slipping away, and if that wasn't bad enough, Killian was fleecing him of his money. He'd known the miscreant wasn't to be trusted as soon as he clapped eyes on him – the stubbly beard, the obvious drinking problem, the careless slouch. It all screamed *scoundrel*, and now Killian was robbing him, and there was nothing Ren could do about it. Killian laid down his cards and won again; he wasn't even bothering to hide that devious lopsided smile now. Ren ground his teeth and plunged his fist into his purse. When it dawned on him that he hadn't enough left to rent the room above the tavern for the night, let alone make another bet, his misplaced rage boiled over.

'You thief!' he snapped. 'Were you going to play me down to my final coins?'

'Sore loser, eh?' Killian sported a cocky grin, clearly unaffected by Ren's furious, threatening behaviour.

'How dare you! That was my final wage packet! My final wage packet from my honest job! Do you even know the meaning of the word *job* – or *honest*, for that matter? You swindling b—' He paused and took a deep breath; he did not intend to shame himself or his family name. 'You are a despicable human being.'

'You're the one who insisted on all the games. I did try to warn you. You've only got yourself to blame.'

That was the limit for Ren. He scowled at Killian, threw down his cards and stormed out of the tavern.

KILLIAN smirked as the tavern door whimpered shut with the most pathetic attempt at a slam he'd ever heard. A sense of smug satisfaction rose up inside him, and he reached for his drink. It felt good to have taught that pasty man from Charrington a thing or two about life outside his cosy hometown. Maybe he'd learn something from it. If not, at least Killian had had some fun. He downed the remains of his ale and pocketed his cards, then slung on his coat, picked up his mug, and ambled to the bar.

'Please don't scare my customers away with your antics, Killian.'

'I was only having a bit of fun, Rubes.'

Ruby let out a deep sigh and pushed her blonde fringe from her eyes.

'I could take offence to that attitude,' said Killian.

'Good.' She reached out and took his mug from him. 'Another drink?'

'Nah, not tonight. I'm done. I was bringing it back, like a good patron.'

'Thank you, Killian.' There was a hint of sarcasm colouring her tone.

'You're welcome.'

He raised a hand in farewell, stepped out into the night and was greeted by a thick rasping sound. Ren Thorncliffe lay sprawled on the ground a few steps in front of him, and the awful guttural noises were coming from his throat. Above him, three shadowy figures loomed.

'Get his purse an' shut him up,' one of them growled.

Killian had to do something. It was bad enough that he'd swindled him out of his money; he couldn't leave him like this too. He stepped away from the tavern door and into the dim light of the wall-mounted oil lamps.

'You won't find anything; I've already taken it all.' Killian slipped his hands inside his coat and ran his fingers over the cool hilts of his swords. 'How about you try to rob me instead?'

He quickly unsheathed the swords. His right flashed out, knocking the knife from the assailant's hand. He took a swift step forwards and threw the man to the ground. Swinging with his left, he cracked another attacker hard in the face with the hilt of his sword. He dodged a clumsy lunge from the final man and dealt him a sharp blow to the spine with the other hilt.

Ren's attackers scrabbled to their feet and stumbled off into the night. Pleased with the encounter, Killian sheathed his weapons.

'Yeah, you'd better run!' he called after them, pushing his hair back and laughing to himself. He turned to the figure slumped on the cobbles. 'It's all right, you can get up now, Thorny.'

There was no reply.

Killian unhooked a lamp from outside the tavern and held the light over Ren's body. An expressionless face with sightless white eyes stared back at him. Shuddering, he looked away from the haunting visage and examined the wound in Ren's shoulder by the light of the lamp. The gash from the knife had already begun to putrefy. Thick yellow pus and a strange black liquid seeped out and ran down to the cobbles.

Killian eased Ren up onto his feet, supporting him with his shoulder while whispering words of encouragement. Holding the gravely injured man tightly, he sped off into the dimly lit night.

It wasn't long before the burst of invincible energy born of an evening of drinking wore off, and Killian struggled to haul the stricken Ren down the silent lamplit streets. His mouth was filled with ale-flavoured saliva, and in the chilly air he felt like he was inhaling salty serrated knives. His heart pounded in his head, making his brain throb. If this continued, he'd be hung-over before he'd had the luxury of passing out first.

Ren dangled limply off his shoulder, his semiconscious breathing weak and catching in his throat. His jaw was slack and his mouth hung open, crimson blood dripping and splattering onto his shirt. It oozed from his nose in two ghastly streams. He coughed violently, projecting a spray of red-stained froth.

They reached the town square and turned left, heading south towards the beach. Ren fell silent – a bad sign. He didn't have much time left. Killian stumbled over the uneven cobbles, cursing under his breath. Sweat poured down his brow as he lugged the deadweight along. He didn't want to think about what had spurred him into action or why he was carrying someone he hardly knew through the dark streets of Brackmouth. He shook his head; he was going to ignore it, like he did with most things. Shove it down into the lower recesses of his mind where it belonged.

Finally, they reached the beach. The crescent moon hung low in the sky, its reflection glistening silver on a black sea. White-crested waves collapsed on the shore with a breathy moan, small pebbles and shells rattling in the surging backwash. The fresh cool air rolling in from the sea was tinged with a briny odour.

Killian's legs shook beneath him. He unburdened himself, laying Ren on the sand as gently as his trembling arms would allow. Staggering, he fell to one knee, his body burning up and his heart beating so fast he thought it might explode. He shrugged off his coat, letting it fall to the beach, and breathed deep to staunch the fire in his lungs.

Nothing like a scrap and a jog to sober you right up.

Looking towards the frothy shore, he spied his target: a lone figure, knee-deep in water, dancing wildly in the moonlight. Cylus. He was as predictable as the tides.

'Cylus,' Killian called out, his voice hoarse with exhaustion. He got to his feet and cleared his throat. 'Cylus!' He rested his palms on his thighs and hung his head, his shirt plastered uncomfortably to his back with sweat. 'Oi, here!'

The figure sloshed out of the surf and danced towards him; there was a distinct lack of rhythm in its cumbersome movements. It slowed as it reached Killian and stood before him, swaying.

Even the pale light of the moon couldn't disguise the hideous sight of Cylus Turner. His clothes were dirty and shabby, his shirt ripped and his trousers torn. From his neck hung clusters of wooden beads and a string of fish bones. He clutched a rusted sword that looked like it couldn't slice through a soap bubble. A dolphin skull covered his head like a macabre helmet; a thick mass of reeking seaweed was attached to the base of it and poured down his back like an overgrown drain.

With a groan, Killian straightened up and pushed his hair out of his face. He grabbed Cylus's bag from his shoulder, almost stealing his balance.

'Hey,' the dolphin skull burbled, the stench of stale alcohol wafting from its beak as it spoke, 'what d'you think you're doin'?'

Killian ignored the slurred ramblings and rummaged through the bag. Inside were seashells, dried-up starfish, slimy seaweed, miniature glass bottles that clinked together and other things he didn't care to think about. At last he found what he was looking for: a small bottle of liquid giving off a faint amber glow.

'What're you up to, l-l-laddo?' stammered the dolphin. 'I'll 'ave you for robbery. Bloody thief.'

'Take off that pissing skull and drink this,' Killian ordered, pushing the amber bottle firmly into his free hand.

Cylus clumsily removed the skull and gulped down the liquid. The drunken sway of his body eased, and his gaping jaw tightened up as the vacant expression left his face.

Killian regarded the old man in front of him, his face so wrinkly it looked as if the lines had been ploughed into his head by an overenthusiastic farmer. His hair was short and grey, and his eyebrows, wild and untamed, curled down towards his shadowy deep-set eyes.

'How many fingers am I holding up?' asked Killian, waving his hand.

'Three,' Cylus answered correctly. Then, indicating Ren's deathly still form, he whispered, 'Here, laddie, what should we do with the body?'

'Look,' said Killian shortly, anxious that they were wasting time, 'you were drunk, and I had to sober you up – again. This guy's been stabbed and probably poisoned. It's sort of my fault, and you're the only person I know who can help. So . . . help!'

Cylus squatted down and examined Ren. He reached into his pocket and pulled out a match, then struck it and held it over the body. The light shone over the oozing wound, and he shook his head grimly. The black liquid was flowing freely from Ren's shoulder.

'Laddie,' Cylus said to Killian, sitting back on his heels and tossing the match away. 'It's poison all right. Can't do nothin' here. Best lug him to mine.'

Killian nodded and put his coat on. The heat had drained from his body, and the cool wind was rapidly turning his sweat into a layer of thin ice. He scooped up Ren's lifeless body again and returned Cylus's bag to him. The dishevelled man snatched it back with a glare, promptly opened it and spent some time meticulously checking the contents. When he was satisfied, he shut it and slung it over his shoulder. Finally, he bent down to pick up his skull and sword and dusted off his clothes.

'Are you quite ready?' asked Killian, his frustration mounting as he staggered under Ren's weight.

'Aye, come on, lad. I'm waiting for you!'

Killian swore under his breath and started towards the cliffs.

They marched a good way up the beach, then turned off onto a path hewn from the rocks. After a brief altercation, Killian persuaded Cylus into sharing the load. They carried

Ren between them as they scrambled up the rocky hills that lined the coast. The higher they climbed, the narrower the path became, until they were forced to go single file.

'Sorry, laddie,' said Cylus as he tossed Ren's limp arm from his shoulder. 'Path's too narrow for the both of us, and what with my back and everythin', he's all yours.'

'Thanks,' muttered Killian, scowling into the darkness.

Cylus marched in front, using his rusted sword as a walking stick. Killian lumbered behind, struggling under Ren's weight, which seemed to grow heavier with every step. Finally, they reached a weather-beaten door set back in the rocks and overlooking the sea. Cylus pulled out his key and unlocked it.

'I don't know why you lock it,' Killian grunted from under his heavy load. 'I can't see anyone trekking all the way up here just to break into your shack.'

'Better to be safe, laddie, better to be safe. There's always unsavoury types about,' replied Cylus, glancing shadily to his left and right before going inside. 'Watch your step.'

Killian stumbled down into the shadowy moonlit darkness of the hollow. Cylus was already busy lighting oil lamps so he could see what he was doing. He hurled a bundle of sticks into a hole in the wall and produced two bottles from his bag. He opened the first and poured the contents over the wood, then stepped back and launched the second into the fireplace. The bottle smashed, and the bundle burst into flame with a flash of purple. It quickly died down to a steady blaze.

'Lay the boy down here, laddie.' Cylus indicated a threadbare rug next to the fire.

Killian laid the young man's body down and took a step back. By now, Ren's breathing was barely audible. His vacant white eyes stared lifelessly at the ceiling, and blood was crusting around his mouth. Killian folded his arms tight across his chest. He didn't want this man to die; he *couldn't* die. If he did, it would be all his fault, and he'd have to live with it. A dreadful chill crept up his spine. He wouldn't be able to live with it – not again. The sound of Cylus smacking his lips as he inspected the patient wrenched Killian from his racing thoughts.

'Very nasty poison indeed,' Cylus muttered half to himself, half to Killian. He leant over Ren and took a swab of the black liquid that seeped from his laceration.

Killian hovered over him, frowning. He took a deep breath and steadied his voice before speaking. 'Are you sure you know what you're doing? Are you still drunk? Don't let him die, Cylus.'

'Hey, lad, have faith,' Cylus replied, getting up. His bones crackled as he shuffled to a cupboard in the corner of the room.

He pulled an armful of different potions out and mixed them together, adding the swab from the wound. Killian sat down on the chilly stone floor next to Ren. He was so still, he looked dead. Concerned that Cylus might already be too late, he put a finger under Ren's nose to check he was still breathing. Thankfully, a faint breath blew against his skin.

'Nasty, nasty poison that,' Cylus mused as he continued to mix up an antidote. 'From a mushroom, you know,' he enthused over his shoulder. 'Local to these parts. You gotta grab 'em at midnight. That's when they're strongest. You boil 'em up for a few hours and extract the gloop. Let it cool and thicken, and there you have it, death in a jar. It's one of my best sellers!'

'Best sellers! I'm feeling guilty for letting this guy get poisoned, and you're the one who made it?'

'Hang on. They might have brewed it themselves. They could easily have,' Cylus said defensively.

'Unbelievable. Are you done yet?'

Cylus shot him a withering glance. 'Aye.'

He ambled over with a bottle containing a dark purple liquid. Kneeling down next to Ren, he poured a little of the liquid around the blackening wound, then tipped the remains into his blood-encrusted mouth. The young man's body reacted instinctively, and he swallowed the mixture. A pair of bloodshot eyes rolled back into their sockets, and he blinked. One last pitiful convulsion coursed through his body, and then he passed out.

CHAPTER
TWO

REN'S EYES FLUTTERED OPEN. HE PULLED BACK a thin knitted blanket and slowly pushed himself up to sitting. His body ached all over; it felt like one giant bruise. His lips were dry, and he could feel a crusty residue around his mouth. He wiped it away with the back of his hand. There was a horrible musty smell in the air. Where was he?

The floor was flat grey rock, which continued up the wall on one side of the room, meeting crude wooden beams and a rough slate roof. The opposite wall was built with rocks and held together with mortar. A small round lead-lined window let in a little daylight. Ren squinted in the gloom and tried to look around. Attached to the walls were exhausted wooden shelves bowing in the middle from the weight of books and bottles. Small wooden cupboards hung on the wall. One had swung open, revealing glass jars of coloured liquids and powders. Ren strained his ears and could just about hear the sea, but other than that it was silent. He definitely wasn't in the town anymore.

Warily, he got to his feet and stretched. A sharp pain pierced his shoulder, and he winced and staggered. The night's events came back in disjointed flashes. He tried to piece it together, but it was all a haze. He remembered an attack, but everything else descended into a blur. What had happened after he'd hit the ground? Had they dragged him off? Was he being held prisoner? A dull ache rippled through his brain, and he swayed slightly. He put out his hands to steady himself, then sat back down and pulled the blanket around his shoulders to keep out the wintry chill. Where was his shirt? And his jacket, his fine jacket? He screwed his eyes up and pinched the bridge of his nose against the pain growing behind his eyes.

Where was he? It smelt like an old chapel, dusty and disused with the slight hint of decay, but all those suspicious coloured liquids that leered at him from the dilapidated cupboards suggested somewhere altogether more sinister. Ren's train of thought was interrupted by a disgruntled noise coming from under a blanket draped across a shabby moth-eaten couch. The blanket moved, and a man peeled it back. He lay still for a moment before sighing and rubbing his sleepy eyes with the heels of his hands. Presently, he swung his legs around and sat up.

'Morning, Thorncliffe,' he said gruffly, squinting at Ren through his partially open eyes.

'Who? You're . . .' Ren frowned.

The man pressed a hand to his chest and shook his head. 'I'm hurt,' he exclaimed, his tone drenched in faux sadness. 'I'm Killian, remember? Your new best friend.'

'Killian . . . Killian,' Ren murmured, rubbing his dry, itchy eyes as he thought. Then everything fell into place. Killian was the one he had been sent to find, the one he needed. He opened his mouth to speak, then quickly shut it. Killian was also the one who'd swindled him of all his money. Ren looked at him again; the thief was casually leaning back, his hands knitted together behind his head. Clearly, he hadn't a care in the world. He wasn't to be trusted. Ren scowled at him icily. 'What are you doing here?'

Killian huffed and sat forwards, easily holding Ren's glare. 'You're lucky I *am* here. If it weren't for me, they'd be chipping you off the cobbles this morning.'

'If it weren't for you, I wouldn't have been out on the street at all, you thieving cheat. I bet that was part of the scam, having your mates hang out around the corner to win you the dregs.'

'Hey, I beat you fair and square. If I'd known you were gonna be so unappreciative of my services, I wouldn't have bothered – and why would I be sat here if I'd tried to rob you?' He snatched his shirt from the arm of the couch and slung it on. 'Anyway, I'm not having this argument. I didn't have to help you, and I'm starting to regret it.'

Ren grunted disapprovingly, but Killian ignored him as he continued his tirade. 'You're a bad loser, you're rubbish company, and you can't fight, but you're good at getting beaten up and poisoned.'

'Poisoned!' Ren exclaimed.

'Yep,' said Killian. He'd clearly had enough and was ferreting about for the rest of his effects. 'I brought you here. My friend Cylus healed you.' He pulled on his coat and tucked his swords into their sheaths at his sides.

'You fended off my attackers?' Ren asked slowly.

'Yep.'

'I suppose I should thank you.'

'You certainly should; it was very traumatic. I might have nightmares. Not to mention what you've done to my clothes.' Killian adjusted his blood-smeared shirt as he spoke.

Ren stood up again. He still felt dizzy, but the room had regained its proper perspective, at least.

'Here.' Killian tossed him his shirt and jacket.

Ren gingerly put them on, taking care not to disturb his tightly bandaged wound. 'How did you know I was being attacked, and why did you help me?'

'I didn't know. I just followed you outside. A young man like you storming into the night – anything could happen, and it did. I suppose, technically, I made you storm out. If I hadn't, well, you know, you wouldn't have been stabbed, and so on, and . . . look, can we just leave it and get some food? I'm starving.'

Ren didn't respond. Perhaps the perfect moment to ask for the Favour would present itself over breakfast.

'My treat,' said Killian, patting his coat-pocket, which jingled with the winnings from their ill-fated card games.

'All right,' said Ren, finding his voice. 'But I'd like to thank this friend of yours for saving my life before we go.'

'That might be a bad idea. He's not a morning person.'

The words had barely left his lips when Cylus came staggering out of his bedroom. Dark rings encircled his bloodshot eyes. He blundered through the room, oblivious to his house guests. There was a heavy thump as he slumped to the floor in what Ren assumed was his bathroom. Ren made to check on him, but Killian held him back. The muffled sounds of coughing and retching were the perfect cue to leave.

Killian led Ren down a rocky path. It snaked precariously around gorse and brambles as it taunted the edge. It was a clear, crisp day, and their breath hung in the air in front of them. The sea sparkled a brilliant blue, reflecting the colour of the sky, and the low sun shone brightly, giving the illusion of warmth.

They came down the hillside to the powdery white sand of the beach and the tranquil calm of the waves lapping the shore. The sound of the morning gulls and the gentle hubbub of the town filtered softly through the wind. Killian turned off the beach and led Ren through cobbled streets lined with ramshackle stone houses. Ren tensed, almost expecting to get stabbed again. He kept himself in Killian's shadow. The man was clearly a rogue, but he trusted him more than anyone else in the town right now. After all, he had saved his life, which appeared to be a profitless, selfless act.

As they got closer to the town centre, the sound of people grew louder, and the buildings increased in size and stature. When they reached the square, Killian turned right and headed up the hill. The main street was full of market stalls set up by local farmers selling their various wares. Jostling bodies bartered and bickered while children wailed and laughed around their feet. The noise had sounded almost comforting as it drifted across the beach, but now Ren wished they would all just shut up and go home. It amazed him how people could get so worked up about the price of a cabbage.

'Here we are,' said Killian at last.

He stepped into a small stone building, quickly ducking his head as he entered. Being almost half a foot shorter, Ren had no need of such an action. A sharp pang of inferiority struck him as he followed his companion. Killian was far better built than he was; his shoulders were broader, his legs were longer, and even his hair was healthier and stronger. The man had carried his unconscious body up the cliffside the previous night, so he clearly had muscle strapped to his lean frame. But Ren was a good man who had an honest job; surely that made him better than this borderline felon? *Looks count for nothing,* or so he'd been told by his father countless times.

The rich, fatty smell of frying foods halted Ren's train of thought and ignited the fires of hunger within his stomach. He'd not eaten since lunch the previous day.

The breakfast rush had died down, so the teahouse was relatively quiet. Pockets of elderly people sat nursing mugs of tea over empty plates. Two women busied themselves behind a counter. One was skinny and young, her hair tied out of the way in a bouncing ponytail. The other was middle-aged, and she beamed when she saw Killian.

'Killian, my handsome,' she said, giving him a tight hug and a kiss on the cheek. 'You don't come round often enough. What can I get you? On the house, of course.'

'Ah, Stell, you don't have to do that. He's paying.' He motioned to Ren with a wink.

'I don't, but I will. And who's this fine young man?' She turned to Ren.

'This is Thorncliffe,' Killian said before Ren had a chance to answer. 'He's my charge for the day.'

Ren held out his hand, realising much to his embarrassment that he was trembling. 'Hello, it's Ren, Ren Thorncliffe, miss,' he said quietly.

'Oh, my poor dearie!' she exclaimed, clasping her warm hands tightly around his. 'You feel like a bundle o' bracken wrapped in wax! Sit down, and you too, Killian. Rose and I'll sort you a decent breakfast. We can't have you going 'bout like that.' With a smile, she went back to the counter.

The two men moved over to a table in the corner. Ren hung his coat on the back of the chair and sat down; his weary body was grateful for the rest.

The teahouse was small but cosy. Large grey flagstones lined the floor, and the walls were of stone, roughly plastered and painted terracotta. Wooden beams ran across the ceiling, from which oil lamps hung. A crackling fire burned in the wall, its fierce tendrils reaching hungrily up the chimney. A blast of cold air rushed in as a group of five people entered. They strolled up to the counter and ordered some food.

Killian frowned. 'I'm so hungry.'

'Me too,' Ren mumbled. 'She seems nice,' he added, half-heartedly attempting conversation.

'Who?' asked Killian absently.

'Stell.'

'Estelle,' Killian corrected him, 'and she is.'

Ren surveyed the flaking paint above the fireplace rather than attempting further conversation, feeling like he'd been scolded for the crime of using the incorrect name. A few minutes later, Estelle wandered up to their table with two plates and set them down. She'd cooked them a feast of eggs, bacon, sausages, mushrooms and fried potatoes with bread and butter. Rose dashed out from her shadow and nervously deposited two cups of tea on the table, then scuttled off to the kitchen without a word.

'Enjoy,' said Estelle.

'Thank you.' Killian caught her hand and pressed a silver coin firmly into her palm. She tried to give it back, but he refused.

'You're a silly boy.' She ruffled his hair as she put the coin in her apron pocket.

Both men were so hungry that they ate in silence for most of the meal. The hot food quickly helped Ren regain his strength, and he mused over his mission. He desperately needed Killian's help, but how could he go about asking him? He ran through his speech in his head; it sounded pathetic. Killian would laugh in his face. Perhaps the money would be enough – that and the watch, which by some miracle hadn't been destroyed or stolen during the antics of the previous night. Killian cleared his plate and breathed out a sigh of satisfaction.

'So,' he started, 'you didn't answer me last night. What brings you to Bracky? I'm pretty sure it's not your card skills.'

'No,' said Ren. Nervously, he glanced at their tea. He had been waiting until they'd finished that before broaching the subject. However, now that it had been brought it up, he may as well get it over with. Tensing his shoulders, he readied himself for disappointment.

'Thought as much.' Killian smirked and raised his eyebrows in question.

Ren took a deep, shaky breath. 'My father is dying.'

Killian's smile dropped to a tight line, and his eyes briefly wandered to the table.

'And I . . .' Ren's mouth dried up. He glanced at his teacup, but he was too tense to pick it up. He'd rehearsed this speech over and over in his head; he had got it down to a fine eloquent art. But now that it came to actually saying it, the words seemed to evaporate in his throat. He put a hand over his mouth and coughed. Was he choking? Was he choking on words? Was that even possible? A burning sensation streaked across his skin. He was dying – no – he was panicking. He looked at Killian, and with his hand still clamped over his mouth he said, 'I need your help.'

'Yeah, I'll get you some water.'

'No.' Ren moved his hand away, embarrassed. 'I mean . . . I need you to help me save my father,' he mumbled, his carefully prepared speech now just a blank page lost in his jittery mind.

'Me?' The front legs of Killian's chair clacked on the stone floor. 'You're winding me up?'

'No. I . . . you can help me,' Ren blurted out. 'My father said you could help. He said you, by name. I don't know how he knows – he was delirious – but it's all I have.' He fell silent. Once again, he felt his skin burning, and he couldn't bring himself to look into Killian's eyes.

'What do you mean?'

'There's a relic crafted by an ancient civilisation,' Ren said, his gaze fixed on the table before him. 'The Gramarye. It can save him.' He paused to swallow the lump in his throat. 'It's in a temple on an island. My father told me . . .' As much as he tried to, he couldn't shake the defeated tone from his voice. 'He told me that you can help me get it.'

Killian nodded, looking slightly bewildered. 'I see.'

'You don't believe me, do you?'

'Well, would you?'

Ren's eyes stung as all the hope was sucked from him. 'W-we can pay you,' he stammered. 'Father's life savings are waiting for you. He was an accountant, and he saved well. His inheritance, he's never touched it . . . and mine too, all yours.'

Killian cocked his head to the side. 'How much?'

'A fortune. Enough for you to live comfortably for the rest of your life.'

Ren looked hopefully towards Killian, yet he appeared unmoved. He didn't want to reveal what he deemed his deal-breaker just yet, but he could sense the attention of his audience waning. 'I have a small down payment with me.'

'I hope you're not referring to my winnings from last night.'

'No, I . . .' Ren pulled a pocket watch from inside his coat, almost dropping it on the table in his nervous haste.

'Not bad,' muttered Killian.

'It's gold.'

'Thanks for pointing that out to me.'

'And' – Ren ignored Killian's sarcasm as he popped it open – 'there's a diamond at the centre.'

Killian's expression remained indifferent towards the small fortune in front of him, but he held his hand out for a closer examination. Ren gently placed the watch in his palm. It was an exquisite piece, something that had been in the Thorncliffe family for three generations. Ren winced as he watched Killian turning it over slowly in his hands. The thought of this man being gifted this heirloom – then no doubt selling it to spend on ale and whatever other debauched things he was into – was almost too painful to bear.

'And there's more than this to follow?'

'Yes, certainly, much more. You have my word. I know what I've said sounds ridiculous, but—'

'Shh, let me think,' Killian said.

Ren nervously obeyed.

Killian frowned, ran a palm across his stubbly face and gazed off towards the fireplace. A creeping dread clasped itself around Ren's heart as he sat waiting for an answer. He reached for his teacup and sipped at the cold remains in an attempt to remain calm. Everything hinged on this moment. His father's life was now linked to this man's choice, his next words. The watch sparkled seductively in Killian's hands. Ren hoped that had been enough to sway him – that and the promise of money – but he couldn't tell; Killian's face was unreadable. It didn't surprise him though. He knew professional card players (if he could call Killian professional) had to keep their emotions hidden for as long as possible. It almost felt like they were playing again, and last time that hadn't gone very well for him. He drained the remains of his tea and waited.

'I guess you'll be needing a ship,' said Killian, slipping the watch inside his coat. 'To get to this island,' he added when his statement was met with silence.

'I . . . yes.' Ren fumbled in his jacket. 'The island – it's not far, but it's not on any maps. You see, my father gave me a chart that—'

'Leave it in your pocket,' Killian said abruptly. 'I'm not a navigator.'

'Yes, okay,' murmured Ren, heat rushing into his face. 'Are you saying that you'll . . .'

'Help you?' Killian finished for him. 'Yeah, why not? I've got nothing else to do today, and, y'know, debts to pay, fine wines to drink, new beers to sample.'

A wave of relief washed over Ren. 'Thank you,' he said, his voice barely audible.

'Right.' Killian slammed his fist into his palm. 'Let's get off to Bracky Island and have a little word with Captain Rothbone.'

A hard spike of ice crashed into Ren's spine at the mere mention of that name. 'Won't that be dangerous?' he asked in a whisper.

Killian shook his head in exasperation, then stood up and walked out the door. Ren hurried after him.

CHAPTER
THREE

KILLIAN WATCHED REN PULL HIS COAT TIGHT
about his body and hunch up in the back of the
small rowing boat. He looked a miserable, pathetic sight. Short waves of limp blond hair clung
to his face, and his chocolate eyes were dull despite his
youth. His skin was so pale it bordered on translucent, and
his muscle mass was almost non-existent. There was an unhealthy look about him. Killian wondered how he'd managed to walk from Charrington to Brackmouth all by himself without any help. It wasn't an easy hike; there were steep
inclines and winding paths. He was moderately impressed
Ren hadn't tripped up and tumbled off the cliffs.

A dramatic, morose grunt from his shipmate snapped
Killian out of his musings, and his back bristled. Part of him
wanted to kick the little wretch overboard and row away
with the watch right there and then, but if he did that, he'd
never get the rest of his payment. He also couldn't help but

feel a little sorry for him. They were, after all, rowing directly into the territory of a notorious pirate queen.

Captain Lily Rothbone was one of the most – if not *the* most – feared pirates on the seas. Mystery and legend surrounded her like a suffocating fog. She was known to be a fierce, callous woman who had traded her humanity to an ancient god for a chest of gold, feasting on the souls of her victims to sustain her unnatural good luck. It was said she had charmed a powerful one-eyed demon into her service, its hideous face blackened by tattoos. Killian narrowed his eyes. He knew her, of a fashion, and was sure that most of the legends – if not all of them – about her were complete rubbish.

'I'll speak to her,' said Killian as he rowed.

'Sorry?'

'I'll do all the negotiations. Lil and I go way back, and you . . . well, I don't know you that well, so I may be way off, but I'm assuming that crafting an alliance with a nasty pirate is probably beyond your capabilities?'

Ren nodded.

'Thought so.'

Ren truly was hopeless. Should Lily agree to help them, Killian had the feeling he would be spending most of their trip keeping an eye on Ren, making sure he didn't fall overboard or get himself killed. If that happened, he could kiss his promise of a fortune goodbye.

He followed the current down the river, through the mouth, past the short stone pier and out onto the open sea. Behind him loomed Brackmouth Island. Considering its small size, the island rose a good number of feet into the air. From sea level in the tiny boat it was quite intimidating. It was covered mainly with a dense forest of dull evergreens, and a long sandy beach gently sloped to the sea. Moored offshore was a brigantine, its white sails tightly bound to the masts. Between the beach and forest stood a grey stone castle with four battlement-adorned turrets stretching up towards the sky.

'Look, Killian, are we . . .' Ren stared at him, his eyes glistening with fear. 'Are we going to die?'

Killian glanced at Ren, then back to the sea. He wasn't going to indulge his paranoia; he could just sit and stew in silence. A tiny smile battled its way onto Killian's lips. He dropped his head and focused on the oars to hide it. Tormenting Ren a little could prove to be amusing.

The waves lapped thickly against the hull, and the distant caw of the gulls drifted on the breeze. The air was sharp and fresh, easily blowing away any fog that had built up in Killian's mind. It could almost have been classed as a moment of peace – if they hadn't been skirting pirate territory. He rowed as close as he could to the shore before jumping out into the frothing surf and dragging the little boat up the beach to set it down in the sand. The island was eerily quiet.

Killian at last acknowledged Ren's ashen face and calmly said, 'No, we're not gonna die. Just leave everything to me, and it'll be fine.'

Those reassuring words lost their effect immediately as a crossbow bolt sang through the air, neatly piercing the sand between Killian's feet. Both men turned to see a band of pirates marching towards them. The pirates came to a halt a few feet in front of them, and their leader regarded them coldly.

'Yer trespassin',' he remarked in a voice that sounded like he gargled whisky and razor blades every morning for breakfast. A thick jagged scar ran down his left cheek and onto his neck, disappearing from view under his shirt. His head was covered by a bizarre skintight leather cap, part of which contained a monocle that hung over his right eye. Tormented wisps of hair peered suspiciously from beneath it.

'Something wrong with your hearing, boy? I said yer trespassin'!'

Killian took a slow step back, brushed his coat to the side and overtly laid his hands on the hilts of his swords.

'We've come to see your captain.'

The crowd of pirates had already doubled in size, but he remained calm, confident in his own abilities. If one of them challenged him, taking them down would be easy and would hopefully earn him an audience with Rothbone.

'You threatenin' me?' the pirate growled, drawing his sword with one hand and simultaneously twirling a dagger in the other.

'I don't think I did, but if that's what it takes to speak to your captain, then yes,' said Killian. Feeling a surge of adrenaline, he drew his weapons and dropped into a low fighting stance.

The pirate swung his sword menacingly and lunged. Killian dodged, blocked him with ease, and then retaliated by cutting a small gash on his arm. The pirate recoiled with rage and spat in the sand.

Killian swung his swords backwards and forwards, grinning. 'We can stop now if you'd like. I only want to speak with Rothbone, so all this is unnecessary.'

The pirate rushed him again. Killian stooped down and struck him hard in the stomach, winding him. He gasped in pain. Killian leapt from his low stance and struck the pirate hard in the face with his knee, causing him to drop his weapons. He grabbed his opponent by the arm and bundled him roughly to the ground. He pressed his blade against the pirate's unscarred cheek and raised his eyebrows.

'Now,' he said politely, 'can I please see the captain?'

The pirate grimaced and stared defiantly up at his victor, white light reflecting off his monocle. The beach was silent apart from the soft breaking of the waves and the rustle of the wind in the trees.

Killian sighed. He was wasting his time. 'Look, just submit, or I'll give your scar a companion. You could do with some symmetry on a face like that.' He pressed his sword a little more firmly against his cheek.

The pirate growled, and his lips pulled back into a sneer. 'I'll kill you.'

'Is that a promise?'

'One day I'll gut you – you cocky piece of shit.'

'Why wait for one day?' Killian took a step back and picked up the pirate's sword. He offered the weapon to his fallen opponent.

Ren gasped behind him, and there was no doubt in Killian's mind he was concocting numerous awful scenarios in his head. This made him smile to himself. Provoking a possibly dangerous enemy and tormenting Ren in one move made him glad he'd got up that morning. Now all he needed to do was infuriate a certain pirate queen, and his day would be complete. He held the weapon tantalisingly close to the defeated man.

'No?' He made sure his tone was full of mockery. 'You don't want to fight?' He tossed the sword to the side and stood over the pirate. 'You're wasting my time,' he said, his voice now cold and threatening. 'Go and get me your captain, and I won't—'

'Anybody care to tell me what the hell's going on?'

Killian looked over his shoulder, and his gaze fell upon Captain Lily Rothbone. A fitted black doublet layered over a lacy white shirt showed off her athletic body, which perfectly complemented the small arsenal that hung from her belt. In contrast, her trousers were simple, black and slightly baggy and were tucked into a pair of black knee-high boots covered with buckles and laced tight.

Captain Rothbone glared at Killian with all the intensity he expected from the feared pirate queen. Without breaking eye contact, she slowly placed her hands on her hips and remained silent, allowing her authority to be soaked up by the gathered crowd. Her long wavy hair fluttered just above the soft curve of her waist, the only motion offered from her otherwise statuesque body.

Nobody spoke. To ease the tension, Killian smiled at her, but it did nothing to move her.

'Killian, let him go,' she said at last, her tone devoid of emotion. 'Morton, get up.'

Killian stood aside, and Morton rolled to his feet, fuming. He picked up his blades and returned them to his belt. He turned and stared at Killian, his eyes brimming with hate, then melted into the gathered crowd. Lily turned to her crew and nodded once. They understood and dispersed quickly. A young pirate looked eager to stay, but a tall lean woman clamped him on the shoulder and steered him away.

Killian heard a laboured breath that indicated Ren was still alive. Lily approached Killian, her face twisted with anger. He rolled his shoulders back and readied himself for her onslaught.

'What brings you here, you filthy rat?' she snarled through clenched teeth.

'Filthy?' said Killian incredulously. 'That's rich coming from someone who spends months on end stuck on a floating heap with no baths, you stinking pirate!'

'Better to be a stinking pirate than a rotten, cheating thief.'

'That's low. I never cheat. I'm just good. And I'd like to point out *I've* never stolen from *you.*'

A pair of emerald-green eyes set within smooth olive skin flashed at Killian from beneath the shadow of a tricorn hat.

There was a long silence. Lily stood tall, rigid and spiteful as a frost-hardened tree. Killian casually stuck his thumbs through his belt loops and ignored the short series of gulps coming from Ren. A gentle gust of wind picked up Lily's long ebony hair and blew it across her face. The silence was almost unbearable, but Killian waited. He knew what the pirate queen was doing. She wanted him to know that she was in control, that she held all the power and he was beneath her. As frustrating as it was, he knew he'd have to go along with it. Lily's eyes gleamed as she stared at him, unblinking.

'Killian,' she eventually said, curling her lip into an ugly sneer as she said his name. 'Why have you come here?'

'To beat up your men,' he replied. He could play games too. 'Seriously, Lil, if that was the guy I had in charge of my security, I'd be worried.'

'Do you honestly think I need protecting?'

'I suppose not.'

'You suppose right. Now, you're trying my patience. You've got exactly two minutes to get the fuck off my island before I call Raven to show you the way. And take that craven little bitch with you!'

With that, the pirate captain turned on her heel and marched away.

'Ah, c'mon, Lil, I've not even told you my proposition yet,' Killian called after her, unfazed by her aggression.

She stopped walking but kept her back to them.

'An O'Shea scheme. How delightful,' she said flatly. 'You now have *one* minute.'

'All right,' Killian began, 'this craven little bitch is Thorncliffe, and his dad's dying. There's a thing in a temple on some island that can save him. We need a ship to get there.'

'How does that benefit me?' was Lily's curt response. 'Thirty seconds.'

'Calm down, I'm getting to that part.' He'd got her attention, and now he could appeal to her greed. He was the one in control now. 'Okay, this temple,' he went on. 'Not only does it contain the thing Thorny needs, but it's loaded with treasure.'

Behind him, Ren scuffled his feet nervously in the sand.

'Treasure, you say?' said Lily with an air of nonchalance.

'Yep, belonging to the guys who made the thing – a lost civilisation's stash of loot. Any treasure in there is all yours, minus my cut and Thorny's device, of course. Just think about what you could do with all that. You could retire . . . again.'

'And just where is this magical, mystical treasure chest of an island?' asked Lily, ignoring Killian's snipe.

'It's not far. Thorny has the charts. We'll turn them over to you if you agree to help.'

Lily turned to face them, her eyes glittering with unnerving curiosity. She placed her hands on her hips and rapped her fingers on her doublet, keeping her gaze fixed on Killian. He felt a distinct frustration run through his body, knowing she was once again displaying her power and there was nothing he could do except ride it out. It irked him that she could make him feel this way, but he needed her. Without her aid, he didn't stand a chance of getting his reward – or making up for his past. A gentle stab of pain pressed into his chest. He gritted his teeth and forced it away. Lamenting about either of those would certainly not help now. Narrowing his eyes, he glared back at the pirate queen, hoping to see some sort of emotion flicker across her face. No such luck.

She spoke. 'All right. You're lucky because I've been contemplating stretching my sea legs for the past few months. I doubt you'd have experience of this, but owning your own island can become rather dull at times. So I'll give you food and lodgings and let you tag along for the ride, but there is a little something I ask of you in return.' She removed her hat and thrust it into Killian's hands. 'My hat, what's wrong with it?'

Killian turned the emerald-green hat over and over, but he could find no fault with it. He looked back at her with a blank expression.

'Er, you don't like the colour?' he asked.

'Of course I like the colour, you cock!' she snapped. 'Look! It hasn't got a feather. A hat – especially a captain's hat – should have a feather.'

Killian nodded, slightly puzzled, and murmured his agreement.

'I thought that would be obvious even to a cretin like you. Now the colour of the feather should complement it appropriately. You probably aren't aware, but there are no wild birds that fit the bill in these parts. But as luck would have it, I hear that a certain citizen of Brackmouth owns a bird with a fantastic array of colours in its tail.' She put her hand thoughtfully to her chin and mused out loud. 'Hmm, maybe I should have blue . . . no, that's a ridiculous idea. Green, definitely green – or even red. No, no, not red, just plain green, or perha—'

'Sorry to interrupt, oh benevolent Lily. You wouldn't be talking about the tropical bird as owned by Jack Sullivan, would you? Because if you want me to break into that nutter's house for a bloody feather, you can forget it. I'd rather take my chances with the sharks and sea demons and swim to the island myself.'

'Fair enough,' said Lily, sweeping her hat out of his hands. 'Bye.' She took a step backwards and was turning when Ren shouted.

'Wait! Please, we'll get it.'

'Speak for yourself,' Killian hissed through his teeth. 'I'd rather keep my insides *inside* if it's all the same to you.'

'But please,' Ren begged. 'Father says you're the only one who can help me. The only one. Please don't let me down.'

Killian shuffled his feet awkwardly.

'You're the only person who can help him?' Lily chuckled at Killian. 'Oh dear,' she added through an infuriatingly smug grin.

'Okay, all right,' said Killian, trying to salvage a shred of dignity. 'I'll do it, I'll do it, I'll get your damn feather from the crazy man's bird. What colour would you like, your most royal highness?'

'Red, actually, no . . . green.'

CHAPTER
FOUR

I T WAS LATE AFTERNOON WHEN THEY TURNED into the harbour. The tide had been against them, and Killian didn't seem to be in the mood for exerting himself more than was necessary. As a result, the return journey had been a long one of silent contemplation. Ren had attempted conversation, with old classics such as the weather and the sea. He'd received a couple of grunts and a *hmm*, but it had been primarily a one-sided affair. Eventually he'd tired of the venture and occupied himself with the dull horizon.

Back on dry land, Killian located Loris, the old dockworker he'd hired the boat from, to claim back his deposit.

'Back in one piece, eh?' said Loris as he opened his knapsack.

'Physically, yes,' said Killian, glowering at Ren as he pocketed the coins.

Loris nodded and raised his hand, then crouched to secure the boat.

Killian seized Ren roughly by the arm and hauled him down the quayside. He was livid and walking with such speed that Ren was finding it difficult to keep up. They turned off the quay and into the street. Ren stumbled over cobbles and tripped himself up, but Killian didn't seem to notice.

'Please stop!' pleaded Ren, grabbing Killian's arm with his free hand and bringing him to a halt. 'Will you stop being so moody and tell me what's wrong? Are you really so scared of this Jack Sulli . . . whatever he's called?'

'No, I am not!' said Killian defiantly, effortlessly twisting his arm from Ren's desperate grasp.

'So what is it then?'

'You,' he seethed, pointing a finger at Ren, 'should have left all the negotiations to me. I told you to, but did you listen? No. You had to come barging in saying we'll do anything, making us look like a pair of snivelling worms.'

'Oh,' said Ren, moving uncomfortably from one foot to the other. 'I thought if we just did what she wanted and th—'

'And what? We're right under that cackling sea monster's claw. Now she can get us – and by *us*, I mean me – to do whatever she wants.'

'Oh, I didn't think . . .' said Ren.

'Now I've got to break into a house just to get a bloody feather. Tell you what, Thorny, if it weren't for your dad's savings, you'd be on your own.'

'I could try an—'

'No, you couldn't.'

'You're right.'

A chilly breeze swept through the streets as they aimlessly wandered through the town, their shadows elongating as the light faded.

Ren wrapped his arms about his chest. He couldn't believe he'd already infuriated Killian. Why was he so useless? He should have kept his mouth shut. What did he know about dealing with pirates? *Nothing, that's what.* He glanced over at Killian; there was definitely a scowl on his face. He had to smooth things over somehow. He needed him on his side, and at the moment he was the only person he knew and could almost trust. Perhaps he could find some common ground in a mutual dislike of Captain Rothbone? It was worth a shot.

He drew a deep breath and broke the silence. 'Are you annoyed because she laughed at you? Because I thought that was rather mean of her if I'm honest.'

Killian stopped walking and turned to stare at Ren. His blue eyes frosted over. 'If you want my help, Thorncliffe, you'd better watch yourself because you're right on the precipice. I don't have to put up with this. I could refuse to help you. I know that would mean saying *bye* to a lot of money, but I'm wondering if putting up with your tedious company is even worth it. You need a Killian O'Shea right now, and unfortunately for you, I hold a monopoly. So I'd keep my flapping mouth shut if I were you.'

Ren averted his eyes from Killian's chilly glare and decided not to press the issue, feeling like he was back at school and had accidentally dropped his pen in a silent classroom. Killian turned a corner and stopped in front of the Laughing Swan.

'I need a drink,' he announced.

Ren silently agreed. It was easier that way.

The Laughing Swan was just as quiet as the streets. It was too early for the serious drinkers and card players to be out, yet much too late for the afternoon crowd. Drinking at this time of day was reserved for the depressed and ambitionless. A barely conscious barfly was slumped on a stool, a thin stream of drool dangling from his gaping mouth. Two other men in similar states were strewn across a table, and an old man was huddled next to the fireplace, trying to draw warmth from its dying embers as he read his way through a massive tome, a tankard of ale at his side.

The blonde barmaid from the previous evening was the only member of staff in the tavern. She'd been so kind to Ren when he'd been unsure of which ale to order; it wasn't something he'd had much experience with. She hadn't made him feel stupid or awkward, and for that he was grateful. He approached the bar, leant against it and left Killian to do all the talking.

'Hey,' she said softly. 'What'll it be?'

'A couple of tanks please, Ruby,' said Killian.

She smiled, yet it was distant and forlorn. She lowered her pale green eyes and pulled the pump.

'Nice necklace,' Killian said as she passed him the drinks. It was a small disc of polished amber that shone like a sunrise in the afternoon gloom. 'From anyone I know?' he added, a playful glint in his eyes.

'Oh, no, no one you know,' she said, smiling bashfully, but there was a touch of sadness in her voice.

'Looks expensive.'

'It does, doesn't it?' she replied absently. 'Enjoy your drinks.' She set about cleaning down the already spotless bar, making it clear that the conversation was over.

Ren followed Killian to a table in the corner and sat on a rickety wooden chair opposite him.

'Right,' Killian said in a hushed whisper. 'We'll wait here till nightfall.'

Ren glanced over his shoulder. Ruby was cleaning. In the opposite corner sat the two incapacitated men. The old man was still hunched over his book and didn't appear to have turned a page since they'd entered. That only left the barfly. Ren swivelled to look at him; he looked unconscious, his tatty jumper damp with dribble, but maybe he was just really good at acting. Ren didn't trust him. Surely no one could emanate that much despair; he had to be some kind of spy, or a sentinel – maybe even one of the king's own black sentinels. He didn't want to die. He was only stealing a feather; it wasn't much of a crime. But it was a crime. That feather didn't belong to him. He was breaking the law. His body flushed hot. If a cleanser got hold of him, he'd wish he were dead. Whether he was a mage or not, they wouldn't care. He was a lawbreaker, which made him as bad as a mage to them. He winced. He would be an outlaw, a thief. His life would be over. He'd have to live in hiding forever.

'No one's listening,' said Killian, interrupting Ren's internal panic. 'There's no need to be neurotic.'

'Why are you whispering then?'

'I'm being cautious,' said Killian. He took a draught from his tankard.

'So am I.'

'Yeah, but my caution is subtle. You're making us stand out like a pair of lacerated thumbs,' he muttered. 'You might as well raise a flag that says "Dodgy dealings this way."'

'You might be comfortable with breaking the law, but I am not,' Ren said in a tight whisper.

'We're nicking a feather. It's hardly raiding the king's personal vault.'

'It's still a crime,' Ren murmured, gazing desolately at his drink. 'I'm a criminal.'

Killian sighed and rubbed his forehead. 'Look, if something happens, I'll go down for it. I'll get you away so you can save your dad, all right?'

'I couldn't ask you to do that.'

Killian shrugged and took a casual drink. 'Just make sure you pay me what you owe me when I get out of jail. That's only fair.' He held his jug up, and Ren reluctantly clinked it with his. 'Right, here's the plan,' Killian continued, lowering his voice. 'We go to Sullivan's when it's dark. I break in and get the feather while you stand guard. Anyone comes, you give the signal and we scarper, with or without the bloody feather. You got it?'

'Got it,' said Ren, keen to prove his worth.

'You better have,' said Killian. 'I've grown attached to my kneecaps.'

'I've got it,' said Ren, the enthusiasm already sapped from his voice. He took a swig, his tongue curling at the taste. Ale wasn't something he usually drank, especially dark ale; it was too rich and bitter. He let out a morose sigh as he set down his jug, and his shoulders slumped.

Killian grunted. 'What's up?' he asked.

'I've just never committed a crime before and . . .'

'And?' Killian prompted. 'Don't keep me in suspense.'

'What are we going to do when we get to the temple and there's no treasure in it for all those pirates?' The corners of his eyes prickled with hot tears.

'Who's to say there won't be?' said Killian with a wolfish grin. 'You don't know, I don't know. Just relax and focus on the matter at hand, okay?' He drained the remains of his drink and leant back in his chair, his arms encircling his head. 'Don't let your jittery mind get too crammed with worries. It's not healthy.'

'You're right, I'm sorry. I'm just a bit nervous.'

'You'll get over it,' Killian said, closing his eyes.

Ren very much doubted that. He grabbed his tankard and took another sip. Despite the harsh tang, there was something about it that relaxed him. He took a swig, allowing the liquid to remain in his mouth for some time before swallowing. It was comforting, like being wrapped in a blanket and sitting next to a fire with a bowl of hearty stew. He glanced at Killian. His eyes were still closed, his head back; he was the perfect image of nonchalance. Ren took his time emptying his jug and set it down, feeling light-headed. That must've been Killian's secret: dark ale. Maybe if he drank more and always had dark, he'd be as blasé as him.

Killian rocked forwards to rest an elbow on the table.

'Another?' he said, indicating Ren's empty jug.

'Erm . . . no thanks,' was Ren's juddering reply.

Killian sucked his bottom lip. 'Yeah, you're right, you shouldn't. Doesn't mean I can't though,' he added, getting up.

Ren watched him as he walked to the bar. He moved with a slight swagger in his step. Deals with murderous pirates, breaking and entering – nothing fazed him. He had a consistent air of bravado about him that Ren couldn't help but admire, as much as it pained him to do so. Killian was definitely not the sort of person he would choose to spend his time with, but desperate times called for desperate measures. If saving his father meant allying himself with the local gambling slacker, then that was what he had to do.

He shifted his attention to the wall on his left. A low shelf ran along it, filled with moth-eaten volumes. He picked one up to examine it. It looked ancient and was missing the final ten pages, but on inspection of the cover notes, he found it to be just five years old. He replaced it and picked up another, glancing over at Killian as he did so. He was having a lively conversation with the man at the end of the bar, who had apparently roused himself. Ren felt a stab of dread. *Sentinel, cleanser, spy?* He sucked in a deep breath. *He's a drunk, Ren. Stop being a fool.* As he released the breath, he scrutinised the book in his sweaty hands. It was in a similar condition to the others and also bereft of its conclusion. *Disgraceful.*

Killian sauntered back, placed his drink on the table and slumped in his chair. He looked at Ren and frowned. 'You all right?' he asked in a tone that suggested he didn't really care.

'I'm fine.'

'Good.'

Outside, the long afternoon shadows melted away as they were swallowed up by the darkness. Softly burning oil lamps cast a warm orange glow into the dark night as they gently swung in the breeze. The tavern was slowly filling with punters. Lively conversation sprang up, chasing away the gloom of the afternoon. The barfly had long since crawled away, making way for the more respectable night-time drunks. Ruby relit the fire, filling the room with a welcoming warmth. At the bar, a raucous guffaw signalled the start of the evening staff's shift.

Ren and Killian had been playing jilt without a wager for some time now. Much to Ren's annoyance, he hadn't won a single round. What riled him even more was the lack of attention Killian was giving to the game. Half the time he seemed to put cards down without even looking first. It was no wonder Ren had lost all his money to him. He laid his hand on his purse; he wouldn't let that happen again. Killian looked out of the window, downed the remains of his drink and shrugged his coat on.

'Let's get this done,' he said to Ren as he put the cards in his pocket.

Ren nodded, buttoned up his jacket and followed him out into the night.

Killian walked at a swift pace. Ren stole a glance at him; his face was set, totally unreadable. Wall-mounted oil lamps battled the murk of the evening as the pair walked up the hill. What few people they did pass were too busy either getting home or getting to the Laughing Swan to give them a second glance. They walked by Estelle's shop. Ren took a mental note of its location; if they somehow got split up, he'd head back there. At the end of the road was Skevington's Weaponry. A pristine iron sign with beautiful cursive lettering hung above the shop frontage, its detail apparent even in the dull, cloudy night.

Killian turned left down another street, which was lined either side with narrow terraced houses. He turned again and again. All the streets looked the same to Ren, and he was mildly impressed that Killian knew where he was going. Killian turned once more and slowed his pace. Most of the houses were in darkness; a handful beamed with the pleasant glow of oil, but only one was lit with the eerie flicker of candlelight. Killian stopped walking and spat out a curse when he saw it. He put his arm around Ren's shoulders, pulled him in close and hunched over.

'That house there.' He indicated with a terse nod in its direction.

'He's still up,' whispered Ren. 'There's a light coming from inside.'

'I'm glad I have you here to tell me these things, Thorn-cliffe,' said Killian in a hushed voice. 'But it changes nothing. Now, do you remember my plan?'

'Yes, you break in and get the feather, and I am the look-out. If anyone comes or if I see him, I alert you and we're gone, with or without the feather,' Ren reiterated. 'What's the signal?'

Killian narrowed his eyes. 'Just be an owl.'

'An owl?' said Ren. What type of owl? There were many owls, all with different calls. Some shrieked, some cooed, some howled.

'Yes, an owl,' said Killian mordantly. 'You do know what an owl sounds like, don't you?'

'Yes, yes . . . of course. I'm sorry.' Ren lowered his eyes, wondering if it was possible to feel more pathetic than he did. 'I'm sorry. I'm just—'

'Nervous,' Killian finished for him. 'Well, you don't need to be. I'm here.' He slapped Ren's shoulder in a gesture of friendly reassurance.

'I know.'

'So, owl?'

'I've got it. I know.'

'Excellent.' Killian pressed his hands together. 'Whatever you do, though, don't shout my name, all right?'

'Oh, come on,' said Ren sharply. 'I'm not that stupid.'

Killian rolled his eyes and shrugged.

Ren watched him slide up to the front of the house, vault over the fence and disappear from view.

KILLIAN landed softly on a lawn of springy grass. Keeping as low as possible, he stealthily slithered around the walls until he reached the back door. He got down on one knee and pulled a thin metal rod and a hooked tool from inside his coat-pocket. He pushed the hook into the keyhole, quickly finding the lock. Holding it in place, he slipped in the thin rod, gently moving it from left to right until he heard a click. A rush of excitement surged through him; it had been a long time since he'd done something like this.

The door creaked ajar. He allowed it to open just enough to squeeze his body through. The air was heavy with the revolting smell of month-old sweat and sour milk. His stomach roiled; he knew Sullivan was insane, but surely even he knew basic hygiene.

As he slunk around in the gloom, searching for the bird, soft rhythmical snoring drifted to him from the next room. With his mind distracted by what he was looking for, Killian carelessly stepped forwards and struck his shin on a chair. His teeth automatically sank into his tongue so as not to swear out loud. He froze on the spot and listened. It was too quiet, way too quiet. Time drifted by for an eternity, his skin growing clammy with sweat as he waited. The snoring resumed unaffected and continued its winding path through the shabby furniture. He sighed with relief, pushed his hair back and looked up to see a polished silver cage glinting in the pale cloud-smothered moonlight. It hung from a hook next to the door leading to the sleeping lunatic.

He sneaked up to the cage and carefully lifted the clasp. The door swung smoothly open on well-oiled hinges. The bird roosted silently on its perch; he could make out its outline, but in the darkness it was impossible to tell one colour from the next. He pulled a pack of matches from his pocket and lit one. The bird's tail cascaded over the perch like an iridescent waterfall, sparkling with all the colours of the rainbow. He reached into the cage and softly put his fingers around a red feather, holding it still as he prepared to pull it out.

Wait, did she want red, or was it green? Red to go with green, or green to go with green? Green . . . it was definitely green.

He let the red feather go and grabbed a green one instead. During his dilemma, the flame had craftily approached his hand, and the instant he caught hold of the feather, it playfully licked his fingers. He cursed sharply and threw the match to the floor, rousing the bird with a start. It leapt from the cage and flapped about the room while Killian desperately held on to its tail. The bird lurched around frantically, pulling him into various items of furniture until he could get a firm hold of its body with his other hand. He held the angry flapping mass still and yanked the feather out, and it let out the most hideous wail he'd ever heard. It sounded like a hundred burning cats spitting out their final chorus of misery. Shocked by the noise, he stumbled backwards and fell over a chair, the bird still struggling and screaming in his grip.

The door to the other room swung open, revealing the menacing silhouette of Sullivan. Killian quickly sprang to his feet and launched the bird at his face. Sullivan blundered about in the dark, swearing and trying to remove the shrieking, clawing creature. Seizing his chance, Killian bolted out of the door.

OUTSIDE, Ren ran towards the house, his body having somehow taken over his mind. He opened his mouth to shout something – he'd decided on a tu-whit, tu-whoo. Then he heard a loud thump, swiftly followed by Killian's ungracious figure tumbling over the fence.

The thief landed roughly on the floor, rolled to his feet and, keeping low to the ground, ran. He grabbed Ren firmly by the arm and almost pulled him over as he went by. 'Run!' he growled urgently.

As they hurtled down the road, a new voice joined that of the bird.

'I's kills ya!' it wailed. 'I's comin' ta kills ya!'

The front door of the house swung open violently, splintering as it slammed against the wall.

'He's coming, he's coming,' Killian said over and over again as they ran through the streets. 'Faster!'

Ren's legs had never moved so fast. His heart hammered in his ears, and his body was drenched with sweat. He wasn't used to such physical exertion. The cold air made his lungs burn. Killian bounded through the streets a good few paces ahead of him; he seemed like a man accustomed to running away from trouble. Ordinarily such thoughts would have made Ren tut in disgust, but right now he didn't care. As long as Killian got him safely away, he really didn't care.

They tore down the main street, past the weaponry, past Estelle's. All the buildings blurred into one as Ren's eyes watered in the wind. He wiped his face with his sleeve to see a group of men clustered on the corner, wisps of smoke around them. Surely they'd help them, would stop this madman.

'Ay! Killian!' one called out.

Yes, thought Ren. *He knows him. Glorious help is at hand!*

'Bit busy, Barrington,' Killian shouted as he raced by.

They dashed past the Laughing Swan and darted over the town square. Killian abruptly turned left, snatched Ren's arm and pulled him into the twisted complex of terraced fishermen's houses. Killian's grip tightened as they ran through the darkened alleys. The houses were incredibly close together. Ren felt like they were leaning in towards him, threatening to topple over and crush the life from him. Narrow cobbled walkways with a smooth network of gutters separated the houses from one another. Their tired footsteps echoed off the walls, betraying their position.

'I's 'ears yer!' Sullivan screamed. 'I's 'ears yer little booties!'

Killian yanked Ren this way and that through the maze of houses. Ren had no idea where they were. It was so disorientating. Whitewashed walls, grey cobbles and limp nets merged into a messy smear before his eyes. At last they came out in the open, and everything took shape again. Killian let out a stream of profanities.

'Shit,' he panted, releasing Ren's arm to lean forwards and rest his hands on his thighs. 'Wrong way.'

They stood still, vulnerable and exposed outside the deserted fish market. Their rasping breath and Sullivan's aggressive footsteps were the only sounds to pierce the crisp night air.

'Now what?' gasped Ren between deep, hoarse breaths.

'I'm thinking,' said Killian brusquely. 'Don't hustle me.'

Ren scanned the marketplace for anything that could possibly help them. He wasn't going to die. He couldn't die. He glanced at Killian; he'd straightened up and folded his arms. He didn't even seem that bothered. How did he do it? It just wasn't fair. Then he saw something – the silhouette of a large box, large enough for two. Now it was his turn to seize Killian.

'I've got an idea.'

'Oh really,' said Killian, pulling free from Ren's clutches.

Ren ignored his tone and indicated the box.

'I's comin' to get yas, ya scabs!' roared Sullivan. He was getting closer by the second.

Ren urgently pulled the top off the box and instantly wished he hadn't as his nasal receptors were assaulted by a putrefying reek.

'You do know what that is?' Killian asked, his voice deadpan.

'Yes, it's fish guts,' said Ren.

'I was being rhetorical.'

'Just what we need when there's a raving madman coming to skin the pair of us – a good dose of rhetoric. That'll get him. Let's get in, shall we?'

'What?' said Killian in what was rapidly becoming more than a whisper. 'There is no way in the world that I am getting in a tub of rotting blood and guts with you.'

'It's not that bad,' said Ren, desperation taking hold.

'Not that bad!' snapped Killian, his voice rising an octave in exasperation. 'It's the most disgusting thing I've ever smelt. Can you imagine what we're going to smell like after being in there? Bad, that's what, bad.'

'Bad like two men who've been sitting in a tub of fish guts?' said Ren, fighting to keep the nervous quiver from his voice. He had to sound confident; he had to sound like Killian.

'Exactly, just imagine what Li—' He stopped speaking and didn't finish his sentence. 'I'm not getting in.'

'Think of the alternative. That mad whatever-he-is is going to find us and—'

The words had barely left his lips when the scream rang out again; he was close.

'I can take the bird-fucker,' said Killian confidently, reaching in his coat for his swords.

'And I don't doubt that one bit,' said Ren. 'But he seems like the kind of person who won't stop until he's dead. Do you really want his death on your hands? For a feather?'

'All right, all right, you've made your point. You win. Happy?'

'Not really.'

As quickly as they could, they lowered themselves into the box of squelching fish guts. They were soft and slimy. Killian recoiled in disgust as rotten scales and spiky bones touched his body. Ren carefully pulled the lid on top, and they both hunkered down in the putrefying remains. The stench was repulsive; they held their hands over their noses and mouths in a vain attempt to keep out the rotting odour.

Sullivan's incoherent mutterings could be heard from inside the box as he paced around the empty marketplace. Ren's stomach lurched. He couldn't stay in there much longer; he had to breathe. There was a guttural growl of defeat followed by low heavy footsteps fading into the night.

As soon as it was apparent the threat was gone, Killian lifted the lid off their hiding place. He flopped over the side of the box, gasping for air. Gingerly, he heaved his body out and slumped down in a heap on the floor.

Ren quickly followed suit and scrunched himself into a ball. 'I'm going to be sick,' was all he could manage to say. He promptly retched onto the ground.

'At least I got the feather,' Killian said to his vomiting companion as he produced their spoil of war from his pocket. 'She probably won't even want it now.'

'Great,' Ren grumbled back.

'Come on!' Killian grabbed the back of Ren's jacket. 'Let's go night swimming.'

Ren shakily got to his feet and staggered after Killian, who had already hurried to the quay – his coat alive with the motion of stringy entrails that hung from it like little tassels – leaving a trail of blood and scales in his wake. Without saying a word, Killian threw himself into the icy river.

'Thorncliffe, you not coming in?'

'No. I'd rather stink than freeze.'

'Come on in, the water's fine!'

'No thanks.'

'Suit yourself. Do me a favour while you're up there and untie a boat. We'll go and see the sea-crone now.'

CHAPTER
FIVE

L ILY SLOUCHED IN A BEAUTIFULLY CARVED wooden chair; the arms were fashioned into the shape of a pair of leaping dolphins, the legs were twisted and pocked to give the appearance of octopus tentacles, and the back was etched with thousands of tiny seashells. She was at the head of a long table that spanned the entire length of the great hall. A handful of pirates remained, playing cards and dice, though the majority were slumped around a roaring fire. The lucky ones sprawled in soft cushioned chairs, the others content to spread out on the thick blue rug. The clamour of drunken men and women filled the air, their voices merging into one as they echoed about the high ceiling.

The pirate captain swirled her untouched red wine round a large crystal glass and stared absently in front of her. Tomorrow was the dreaded day, the day she'd grown to despise the most: her birthday. She had never celebrated it. To her it wasn't the glorious anniversary of her birth but a sad reminder of mortality and weakness. She released the glass, pushed it away and rested her hand on the wooden dolphin, drumming her fingers on its head.

She'd spent years carefully constructing a wall around her emotions, had numbed her feelings and made herself stronger. She'd become a fearsome pirate queen, a dominator of the oceans. She grabbed the glass again and ran her fingers slowly up and down its delicate stem. But now Killian threatened to upset the balance, and the thought of it sickened her. Why couldn't she have gone the rest of her life without seeing him again? That would've suited her fine. Why did he have to show up now, at this time of the year, just before the only day that ever made her feel vulnerable? She should have said no and sent him away. She should have got him out of her life forever. But she hadn't. She'd allowed herself to be pulled in by his lure. She gripped the stem firmly between her thumb and forefinger and frowned.

Someone sat next to her, bringing her awareness back to the present.

'You're not drinking tonight?' asked a soft voice.

She sighed heavily, releasing the glass. 'I never do much around my birthday. I—' She stopped abruptly and changed her tone. 'I'm sorry, Raven. I'm pretty wretched company tonight.'

'Never mind. Maybe I can cheer you up,' he replied. 'Fancy some cards?'

At first she hesitated, but after he'd dealt her his best forlorn look, she found she couldn't resist. She turned her chair to face him and gave him a weak smile.

Raven shuffled the deck, the cards moving between his hands with mesmerising liquidity. His unusual deep violet eyes were locked in concentration as his deft fingers twirled.

He was her oldest friend and most trusted crew member. She could confide any secret she wanted in him and knew it would go no further. He was the calm amid her often stormy life. He'd always supported her and never asked for anything in return. She still looked back fondly on the days when her crew had consisted of her, Raven, and no ship. Life had been simple – no responsibilities, nothing tying her down – yet she hadn't been content to remain like that. She had been reborn in the oceans, so it was only natural that she was drawn back to the waves. Her gaze wandered about the hall; she wouldn't have had any of this – her own mini-army of loyal cut-throats, an island and a castle, the respect of everyone who sailed the seas – if she'd remained tied to the land and its restrictions. She probably wouldn't have met Killian. She grimaced. There he was again, invading her thoughts.

Raven cut the deck and traced his tattoo with his finger while he waited for Lily to draw her cards. It began at the corner of his left eye, an intricate pattern in black ink that curled and twisted its way down to his jawbone.

Lily wasn't paying full attention; she was attempting to concoct a way to excuse herself. She just wanted to go to sleep and be alone so she could shut her thoughts down for the night. Tomorrow she'd awake refreshed, strong as ever.

'Raven, I—'

'Sorry to barge in, Cap'n!' Tom, one of her gunners, interrupted her. 'But that guy's back.'

'Are you sure?'

He nodded.

She let out a deep theatrical groan and got to her feet.

'He could have waited till morning,' she muttered under her breath. 'I'll take care of this.'

She swept up her long green coat, buttoned it to the top and marched out of the room with a disgruntled look carefully arranged on her face.

The night was still and calm, the soft lapping of the waves on the beach a peaceful accompaniment. The moon was still obscured by a thick blanket of clouds, its dim silver glow bleeding into them, giving them the appearance of giant floating mountains. Lily held up her lamp and squinted; she could just make out two staggering shadows stumbling up the shore. As they drew closer, she heard them arguing. She put her lamp on the ground, placed her hands on her hips and arranged her body in a lofty position. Killian and Ren stopped a few feet away from her.

'I've g-g-got your feather,' said Killian through furiously chattering teeth.

'Bring it to me,' commanded Lily. 'And it had better be the right one,' she added for good measure, smirking to herself in the darkness.

As they stepped into the light, she had to stifle a bout of laughter. Killian was soaked, his wet clothes plastered to his body like a second skin, and he was shivering so much it surprised her he could speak at all. He folded his arms tight across his chest and glared up at her from under his dripping wet hair. Ren was a horrendous sight; he was covered from head to foot in blood and absolutely reeked. Killian delved inside his coat-pocket and pulled out the green feather, sodden with seawater and with more than a faint whiff of fish. He reached out with a trembling hand and offered it to Lily. She swiped it from him in disgust.

'New fragrance, Killian?' she said.

'Is th-that the b-best you c-can come up w-wi-with?' Killian stammered, rubbing his arms.

She winced at his pathetic attempt to warm himself. It would never work. 'I see you lent it to your friend too. What is it? I can't quite put my finger on it.'

'Rotten f-f-fish.' He sounded resigned.

'Ah, yes, that's it.' She turned to walk away. 'Are you coming or not?' She smiled as she heard their grudging footsteps trailing after her.

KILLIAN let out a soft grunt of satisfaction as he shut his eyes and lay back in a tub of hot steamy water. The heat felt so good against his numb skin. His body gradually ceased its trembling, and he regained some control over his muscles. He lifted a leg out of the bath and slowly moved his foot backwards and forwards. He repeated this with his other foot and then sank back into the water. Jumping into the river had seemed like a good idea at the time, but as soon as his feet had broken the surface, he'd known it was a horrible mistake – not that he'd ever admit that to anyone. The freezing winter waters were not the place for a spot of night swimming.

He sat up and had a quick glance around the room. It was small yet lavishly decorated. The walls were plastered smoothly and painted with swirls of blue and green paint. Gold paint had been sprayed arbitrarily in patches over the green and blue; it shimmered as he looked at it. There was an ornately carved marble fireplace in the middle of the back wall, in which tiny flames puckishly flickered. The polished copper tub he floated in was about two feet away from the fire. Directly opposite was a lockless door, which made him nervous. He wished he'd shoved something under the handle.

Next to the door was a small wooden cupboard with delicate designs of sea creatures and shells etched into it. Looking at all the fine detail, Killian guessed it must have taken someone months to carve it. A mirror edged with a twisted golden frame rested on top. The floor was covered entirely with a huge woven green rug flecked with strands of silver yarn. It looked very expensive.

Good steal.

He lifted his hand out of the water and observed his pruned skin. *I wonder how long it would take for my whole body to—*

His thoughts were cut off as the heavy wooden door creaked open and Lily walked in. Killian splashed about, trying to submerge as much of himself as possible without drowning.

'Excuse me!' he said sharply, trying desperately to cover himself.

'Oh, come on, Killian. It's nothing I've not seen before.'

'Not on me you haven't.'

'Have you got something to hide?' she asked, playfully cocking an eyebrow.

'It's a question of privacy,' he seethed, glaring furiously at her, hoping it would compensate for his lack of clothing.

There was an uncomfortable length of silence between the two of them before Lily took charge.

'Here,' she said, throwing him a towel and a bathrobe. 'Thought you might want these. I'll have your clothes washed for you . . . unless you'd rather I had them burned?' She wrinkled her nose at the sight of them. 'Just leave them in here. I'll send someone to take them away.'

'Thank you,' said Killian, trying his best to get the perfect balance of gratitude and disdain in his tone.

'Not a problem.' Lily smiled, but there was a distinct air of mockery in her manner. She took a step closer, and Killian sank deeper into the water. 'So, are you looking forward to our little trip together?' she asked, her eyes locked on his.

Killian tutted; what was she doing to him? 'Yes, I am, but not because . . .' He shook his head. 'I'm in it for the money, that's all. Thorny and I have a deal.'

She raised her eyebrows. 'And here I was thinking you were doing it out of noble sentiment. You disappoint me again, Killian.'

'I like to be consistent,' he said sardonically.

Lily grinned slyly and took another step forwards.

Killian plunged his hands beneath the water and glowered at her. 'Are you done?' he snapped.

She chuckled and moved back. 'Most definitely. When you get out, turn left. Two doors down on your right is a spare room and a couple of beds. I think your mate Ren is already there.' She turned around and walked away. 'Goodnight,' she added with her back to him.

'Night,' he replied shortly.

She shut the door firmly behind her and was gone. Killian listened attentively as her footsteps faded down the corridor. He let out a relaxed groan and rocked back in the bath.

He glanced at the fire; the flames were dying down, and the bathwater was beginning to cool. He briefly toyed with the idea of adding more hot water, but that was too much effort, and he was tired. It had been a long day, and as much as he didn't want to, it was time to get out. He quickly stood up, wrapping himself in the towel in one swift movement. The shock of the cold air struck him immediately, and he stood shaking, dripping water all over the rug. When he became accustomed to the chill, he rubbed himself dry and put on the robe. He picked up his swords, which he'd scrubbed clean before he'd even washed himself, and left the room.

He found the spare room and slowly pushed the old wooden door open; he was disappointed to find Ren sitting on one of the beds. He was wearing a robe similar to Killian's and nursing a steaming cup of something hot, which emitted a pleasant sweet smell.

'Hello!' he said, sounding pleased to see him.

'Hey,' said Killian wearily as he walked over to the other bed and slumped down. 'What're you drinking?' he asked, vaguely interested.

'Oh, it's hot milk, honey and rum. I got a bit lost looking for this room and accidentally wandered into the kitchen. The cook was there. Very friendly chap, only got one eye. Anyway, he was making himself a nightcap and offered me one to help me sleep. Fancy a sip?' He offered it to Killian.

'Go on then,' said Killian, taking the cup.

He took a long swig of the warm, soothing drink. The sweetness of the honey and fiery kick of the rum instantly relaxed him. He took another, leaving a thimbleful in the bottom, which he passed back to Ren.

'That's good,' he said, satisfied with Ren's hurt expression as he surveyed the barren wasteland that had been his drink. He lay down and pulled a thick woollen blanket over himself.

'Uh-huh,' agreed Ren, and he drained the pitiful remnants. 'Killian?'

'Not now, I'm going to sleep.' He had no interest whatsoever in listening to Ren's latest anxiety. He rolled onto his side. 'And blow the candle out. You're closer.'

CHAPTER
SIX

IT WAS THE COMFORTING SMELL OF COOKED bacon that roused Killian from his heavy slumber. He peeled his eyes open, blinked a few times and lay still, staring at the ceiling. He yawned and stretched, letting out a loud grunt of contentment. Lazily, he rolled onto his side to say something to Ren, but he wasn't there. For a few seconds, his hazy mind pondered Ren's where-abouts until he drew the obvious conclusion that he'd gone for breakfast without him.

Feeling a little betrayed, he swung his legs out of the bed and tentatively placed a bare foot on the cold stone floor. He forced its brother to join it and sat up on the edge, wrapped up in his blanket. Scanning the room, he caught sight of his clothes, pleased to see they hadn't been burned. They'd been cleaned and left in a pile by the door. By the side of his bed lay his two beautiful swords, sheathed and attached to his belt. He swung an arm down and picked them up. Gently, he pulled one out and examined it. He held it as if it were made of glass and turned it over slowly. The blade was thick and over two feet long; it was sharp on both sides and glowed a brilliant silver in the morning sunlight. The hilt, which shone brighter than the blade, was etched with intricate designs of stars and moons. Curious twisted shapes weaved in between the astrological carvings. He'd had them for so long now that they almost felt like a pair of extra limbs, and in a way they were. He had a connection with them, a deep bond that transcended their function. Slowly, he ran his finger along the hilt, transfixed by the otherworldly lambency that emanated from the metal as his skin glided across it.

He slid the sword back into its scabbard and set the pair of them aside. His stomach growled violently, reminding him of its existence. With great effort, he forced himself off the bed and threw his clothes on, briskly running his fingers through his dishevelled hair.

He wandered down the long corridor he'd navigated the previous night, following the clamour of voices until he came to two ornately carved wooden doors, which opened out into the great hall.

It was a large room with a lofty ceiling. A wide pair of glass doors overlooked the calm blue sea, letting in the morning light. The room was painted in a deep rich red, giving it a warm and cosy atmosphere despite its size. The walls were punctuated with nautical paintings, each one a souvenir from a ship raid, no doubt.

A vast mahogany table spanned the length of the hall, surrounded by hordes of pirates noisily stuffing themselves. There was such a cacophony that no one batted an eyelid when Killian slipped in.

He scanned the room for Ren or Lily amongst the

throng of pirates, but hunger got the better of him, and he decided to pick a seat at the table and help himself. He sat down next to a woman and immediately recognised her from the beach the day before. Her distinctive face housed a collection of scars. A deep, thick one extended from her bottom lip to her jawbone, another was streaked across her left cheek, and a final one ran down her neck. She looked up as Killian sat down.

'All right,' she said in a gruff voice. 'It was you what kicked ten shades of shit outta our quartermaster yesterday, weren't it?'

'Erm . . . yeah,' Killian answered warily, unsure of the consequences of his response.

'You wanna be careful with that one. He's got some weight around here, and he's respected. Y'know what I'm sayin'?' the pirate grunted back. 'Finn,' she added, extending her hand.

'Killian,' he said, cautiously taking it.

Finn yanked him closer, jerking his body forwards. She pressed her mouth to his ear. 'Don't you go tryin' any of them fancy tricks on me,' she growled in an aggressive whisper, her hot breath burning his skin. 'Or you'll be coasting the beach lookin' for your missing limbs. Got it?'

'Er, yeah, got it,' said Killian, wriggling out of Finn's strong grip. She was strong and her sudden mood change slightly scary. He mentally added her to his ever-growing list of people not to piss off. He picked up a plate and reached for the bacon, watching her suspiciously from the corner of his eye.

'Is that it?' asked Finn, a hurt tone to her voice.

Killian stopped piling his plate with bacon, which by now was stone-cold anyway.

'Is what it?' He gave a short unconvincing laugh; it was probably better to humour this maniac than cause a scene.

'I thought you might put up a bit of a fight, you know, to brighten up me morning, or do you save all your abuse for our cap'n?'

'What?' He was still too sleepy to be dealing with this.

'I heard you and the cap'n going at it.'

'You heard all that?' He was so hungry he could almost hear the mournful elegy of his stomach.

'Aye.' The pirate grinned maniacally as she pulled a roll-up from behind her ear and clamped it between her teeth. 'I've got ears and eyes everywhere, so here's a hint, and I'll say it only once.' She struck a match on the lapel of his jacket, lit her cigarette and took a short drag. 'Watch what you say round here.' Smoke tumbled from her mouth as she spoke.

'Okay,' said Killian, wishing she would leave him alone to eat his breakfast.

Finn gave Killian the sort of menacing grin a shark would give to a swimmer and swung at him, striking him on the shoulder.

'I'll be seein' you later,' she hissed through her teeth as she stood up to leave.

'Yeah,' said Killian, rubbing his shoulder in bewilderment, which disappeared as soon as he started eating.

He furiously chewed his way through a heap of bacon. He was about to reach over and grab a plate of mushrooms when, out of nowhere, Ren sidled up next to him and sat in the vacant seat.

'Hey, Killy,' he said in a nauseatingly enthusiastic voice. It was too early to sound like that. 'I—'

'It's Kill-ee-an,' Killian said sharply; all he wanted was his breakfast in peace. 'Not Killy, ever. Got it?'

'Yes . . . Killian,' said Ren meekly.

Feeling a slight shred of guilt for his abrasive tone, Killian decided to give Ren another chance. 'What are you so happy about anyway?' he asked as he picked bits of bacon out of his teeth. 'And why didn't you wake me up for breakfast?'

'I'm sorry. There is cutlery, you know,' said Ren, glancing at Killian's greasy fingers. He hastily changed the subject on receipt of a murderous glare. 'Guess what?'

'What?' said Killian, already bored and his guilt forgotten.

'This morning, the captain is going to announce about our expedition,' Ren enthused. 'She told me that we can leave the day after tomorrow. First we'll have to get provisions and sort the ship out, then do all the other stuff that needs to be done. You know, Killian, I really feel that—'

'When exactly did you talk this all through with her?' Killian said, shocked by the jealous tone in his own voice.

'Last night while you were washing. She demanded to see the charts. She'd heard rumours of the island – seafarers call it the Phantom Island – but she'd never seen it marked on a map. Her sailing master, I believe he's called Jarran, confirmed the charts are authentic,' said Ren sheepishly. 'I was going to tell you, but you fell asleep.'

'All right,' muttered Killian. He picked up a cold rubbery mushroom and crammed it into his mouth.

All at once, everyone fell into respectful silence. Killian looked up, sucking the grease from his thumb – he should have used the cutlery – to see Lily standing on a chair at the far end of the table.

'All right, you foul sea dogs, can I have your complete and undivided attention please?'

It was an unnecessary line; the hall was already in silence, and all eyes had turned to her. She was merely asserting her authority, which made Killian bristle.

The captain was dressed in her three-quarter-length emerald-green coat and black trousers topped off with her tricorn hat, now adorned with a large glittering feather. Killian was taken aback that she'd cleaned the thing up; it was almost like she actually wanted it. She stepped from the chair onto the table and placed her hands on her hips, pulling her shoulders back. She narrowed her eyes and stared down at her crew.

'Now,' she began, 'this may just be a personal opinion of mine, but I think we've got a little bit lazy of late. In fact, I can't remember the last time we sailed the *Tempest*, and we call ourselves pirates? Quite frankly, I'm ashamed. It's pathetic.' She shook her head.

A ripple of agreement ran through the crowd.

'Wouldn't you say,' she continued, her voice getting louder, 'that it was time we got off our arses and did something?'

The pirates responded with a unanimous, 'Aye!'

'Shouldn't we be out exploring new lands?'

'Aye!'

'And taking what is ours?'

'Aye!'

'Okay,' she said, lowering her voice to a speaking level. She paced up and down the table as she spoke. 'Now, a genuine chart pinpointing the exact location of the Phantom Island has neatly fallen into my lap. I've been reliably informed' – she shot Killian a split-second glance – 'that there's a temple on the island loaded with the treasure of a lost civilisation. Now I think it's a damn shame that all those poor jewels and gold pieces are locked away, imprisoned against their will. Wouldn't you say it was about time that somebody liberated them?'

'Aye!' yelled the pirates in unison.

'And shouldn't that be us?'

'Aye!' cried the pirates.

Excited talk rippled through the crew. Lily watched them for a few moments, then drew a gun from a holster at her side and fired a shot out of an open window. The pirates fell silent.

'That's better,' she said calmly. 'Our ship will be seaworthy and stocked in time to make way the day after tomorrow. Morton will be organising maintenance and supplies.' She shifted her gaze to the quartermaster. 'Everyone is to do exactly as he says, so apologies to those of you who will be careening. I want swift, efficient work from all of you. We all work together, we all have our share of the loot. Any questions?'

She was answered by silence.

'Good.' She bent down and picked up a metal jug from the table. 'Now get to it!' She crushed the jug with her bare hand.

The squeaking of chairs filled the hall as the pirates got to their feet and flocked to Morton for orders.

Ren gasped with disbelief. 'My word! Did you see what she just did?'

'Standard theatrics,' said Killian. He, for one, was not impressed by blatant pirate trickery. 'Right, I've got some stuff to do. I'll be back tonight or tomorrow. We'll see.'

'What? Wait! Where are you going? What are you

doing? Can I come with you?' asked Ren, a look of desperation in his eyes.

'No,' replied Killian shortly.

Before Ren could protest, Killian got up and left.

Killian rowed across to the town, the late-morning sun glinting off the tiny wave crests. He was feeling emotionally ambiguous. On one hand, he was excited about the prospect of an adventure and the pile of loot waiting for him at the end, but on the other, he was feeling a slight sense of foreboding, the cause of which he was unable to ascertain. Maybe it was Ren's own brand of insufferable optimism mixed with ineptitude getting to him, or perhaps it was just Lily in general. Whatever it was, it was unsettling him. As he did with most of his problems, he resolved to ignore it; he believed thinking about something would make it so. He moored the boat and set about finding Loris. After a brief walk along the quay, he found him sitting on a three-legged wooden stool with his back to the wall. He was intently resurrecting an exhausted fishnet.

'Where's your little matey today?' Loris remarked, looking up.

'Careening, hopefully,' replied Killian with a sly grin.

'Cap'n Rothbone off on her travels?'

'For a bit.'

'She best not be gone long.'

'She won't.'

Loris grunted. 'You pay for that?' he asked, nodding in the direction of the boat.

'Hey, give me a chance,' said Killian defensively. 'It was an emergency.'

'Aye,' Loris agreed, 'knowing you, it was. Long as you pay, there's no problem.' He picked up his net again.

'Thanks,' said Killian as he walked away.

The quayside was busy; many vessels were still unloading the morning catch. Killian swiftly marched towards the town centre, skilfully avoiding the ruddy-faced fishermen who ambled along the quay, bent double with their heavy loads. He cast a guilty eye towards the open box of fish guts. A group of men were standing around it shaking their heads and muttering about cats. As he walked through the noisy streets, he gave small smiles and nods to anyone he recognised, almost as if he were running on automatic. The streets were heaving with people, and he had to dodge them or face being knocked over by the shoppers at the market stalls.

After a few near misses with the aggressive shoppers and even more aggressive vendors, Killian reached his destination: Skevington's Weaponry. The heavy wooden door easily swung open on freshly oiled hinges, and a dainty bell chimed somewhere in the shop. Killian closed it and leant back, relieved that the noise of the street was staunched by the thick wood.

'Who is it?' asked a light, friendly voice from another room.

'Only me, Geoff,' answered Killian.

'Ah ha, be with you in a jiffy, lad.'

The shop was small, fusty and dark. The faint scent of gunpowder with an underlying tang of varnish drifted in the air. It was extremely cluttered. Weapons seemed to be clamouring for space everywhere. There were axes, maces, lances and staffs. Some hung from the ceiling, and others sprawled across the sturdy wooden shelving that encompassed the shop. The walls were covered with all sorts of swords and daggers. Killian brushed a few whips out of his face as he carefully made his way towards the back. Mounted on the wall behind the wooden glass-topped counter was a plethora of guns of different sizes and shapes – single barrels, doubles, triples. Beneath them hung a row of vicious-looking gauntlets. Killian reached over, lifting a pair off a hook. He eased his hands into them; they were a snug fit. The metal fingers extended a good inch over his own and culminated in a vicious point. The interlocking metal plates clacked against each other faintly when he flexed his hand. He ran his finger along the edge; it was razor-sharp.

'Nasty things, those,' said a voice from behind him.

Killian gasped and started. 'Hey, don't sneak up like that!'

'You knew I was there,' said Geoffrey. 'Righto.' He swooped under various hanging implements and settled behind the counter. 'What can I do for you?'

Geoffrey Skevington was in his early sixties. He wore his silvery grey hair swept back, and his thick moustache curled into two points. He clasped his scarred hands together and rested them on the glass top.

'Do you like the look of my gauntlets?' he asked.

'No thanks,' said Killian, taking them off and handing them back. 'Not really my style.'

'They're pretty horrible things, though the craftsmanship is most excellent if I do say so myself,' said Geoffrey, placing them back on their hook. 'I sell the occasional pair, so it's best to keep some in. In fact, I sold a set to some fella just last week. Off they went, out of my shop. Do you know what I always wonder?' Before Killian could interject, he continued. 'I wonder what happens to my stock once it's been sold. Where does it go? What do my customers do with it? Is it looked after? You know what I mean?'

Killian raised his eyebrows and blinked his dry eyes. He should have slept in this morning and made Ren errand-boy.

'Let's see your swords then, lad.'

Killian unsheathed his swords and handed them over. This had become a tradition. Geoffrey took them and turned them over critically in his hands before handing them back.

'Good stuff, Killian,' he said as he always did. 'Nice to see you look after them. You can tell a lot about a man by the way he treats his blades, did you know?'

'Yes.' Killian nodded. He was growing impatient, but he didn't let it show.

'Some of the awful blades I've seen,' said Geoffrey, a far-away look in his blue-grey eyes. He paused, then sighed. 'Nothing saddens me more than a neglected weapon. Remember the state of yours when you brought them to me? Blades had rotted away and everything. Their previous owner must have been a real careless bleeder.'

Killian nodded again.

Geoffrey shook his head. 'I don't know, lad, I don't know. Righto then, what can I do for you?'

'A bag of your special bullets please,' Killian blurted out before Geoffrey could embark on another lengthy digression.

'Right you are,' said Geoffrey, opening a drawer under the counter. 'Doing anything exciting?' he asked as he rummaged.

'I'm going treasure-hunting with Lily Rothbone and her crew.'

'Hmm,' Geoffrey mused. His tone indicated that he was smiling. 'Going off with Miss Rothbone, eh?'

'And?' said Killian irritably.

'Miss Rothbone, eh?' Geoffrey chuckled. 'If I were thirty years younger ... well, she'd probably kill me.'

'Yes, well, I'm just using her and her ship for a friend, all right?' said Killian, folding his arms tetchily. 'Have you got those bullets?'

'No need to be so defensive, lad. I'm just teasing you.' Geoffrey smiled and handed him a small leather pouch that jingled as he took it. 'There you go, lad. My finest bullets, just for you.'

'How much do I owe you?'

'For anyone else it's ninety, but for you, sixty-five.'

Killian handed over the coins and stashed the leather bag in his coat-pocket. 'Cheers.'

'No problem, lad. Now you have fun off adventuring or whatever it is you're doing with those buccaneers. I want to know all about it when you're back.'

'Okay,' said Killian, and he turned to leave. 'Thanks again, Geoff.'

'Take care,' Geoffrey called after him, 'and give my love to Lily.'

Killian grunted once he was outside. Geoffrey was mentally exhausting. He couldn't quite decide which was more stressful – the busy street or listening to him waffle on. It was difficult to keep up the pretence of interest whenever he went off on a tangent, but he did his best; he didn't want to hurt his feelings. Geoffrey had given him his first and only job after he'd finished his Estelle-enforced schooling, and he always gave him some kind of discount. In his youth, Geoffrey had been a high-ranking black sentinel until the death of his father forced him to quit and take over the family business. When he took Killian on, he taught him everything he knew about combat, which had got him out of more tight scrapes than he cared to remember. So the very least he could do was tolerate his ramblings. Cylus was his next port of call, and his gaze drooped at the prospect. Cylus was worse than Geoffrey, but for different reasons.

Killian marched through the town once more, careful to avoid the shoppers who seemed sorely lacking in spatial awareness. He walked past the turn that would have taken him to his flat and made a mental note to go there at the end of the day to grab some spare clothes before heading back to the island. The spring returned to his step, and he felt a warmth within his body. He was looking forward to returning to the island, though he couldn't determine why. It was nothing to do with Thorncliffe – it was liberating not to have him ducking in and out of his shadow all day – and it definitely wasn't anything to do with that cantankerous, supercilious pirate. The thought of her immediately crushed his spirit. His shoulders tensed, and he shoved his fists into his pockets.

He arrived at the town square. As usual, it was full. There were street entertainers telling stories, playing instruments, breathing fire. A crowd was gathering outside the church waiting for the orator, and a vendor had set up a stall selling mulled wine; its sweet spicy scent clung to the cold air. As he picked his way through the clusters of people, a familiar voice drifted within earshot.

'So where next, Seth?' asked Ren eagerly.

Killian swore; his frustrations were about to increase tenfold unless he could successfully disappear. Ren crossed the square, helping a one-eyed man pull a small trailer. They were on a direct collision course, and after the vocal deluge that was Geoffrey, he couldn't take any inane chatter from Ren. Glancing to his right, he saw a group of people in road-worn clothes, clearly a party of travelling pilgrims who were no doubt disappointed by Brackmouth's shambles of a church. He discreetly edged along until he was level with them. He slowed his pace to match theirs, angled his head down, hunched up his shoulders, blended in with their group and ignored their discussion. He slipped past Ren unnoticed. When he reached the other side of the square, he disengaged from the group and pressed on in the direction of Cylus's house.

Killian gave the rotten front door a sharp knock and heard a muffled grunt from inside, which he translated as 'Why hello, come in and make yourself at home.'

Cylus was sitting on his couch, leaning over a small wobbly round table, dropping multicoloured slugs into a jar with a pair of tweezers. He mumbled a rough acknowledgement towards Killian but didn't look up.

Killian knew the only thing he could do was wait for him to finish. He stuffed a hand in his pocket and idly fiddled with the bullets, their smooth metal casing clacking satisfyingly. He looked about the room for something to occupy his eyes with. As usual, Cylus's home was a mess. Bottles of liquids littered the work surface next to the tired cupboards, shards of glass lay in a heap on the floor, and some of the flagstones were stained a deep purple colour. The room smelt faintly like burnt hair. Killian glanced at the clock that hung just above the fireplace, but it didn't seem to be working. He grunted under his breath. Cylus picked up the last slug, a bright orange one, and released it into the jar. Only then – after what seemed like hours – did he face Killian.

'Hello, laddie,' he said, seemingly oblivious to his own ignorance. 'What'd you want?'

Killian launched into an explanation about Ren, Lily and the Gramarye, but it became clear from the old man's vacant expression that he wasn't listening.

'Oi!' snapped Killian. 'Are you even listening to me?'

'Ah, sorry, lad,' said Cylus, rubbing his forehead with a grimy palm, streaking it with glistening orange slime. 'Start again.'

Killian opened his mouth to speak, but as he did, Cylus detached himself from the couch and shuffled into the kitchen, wrapping his ageing dressing gown tightly about himself.

'It's cold out, ain't it?' His voice carried from the kitchen.

Killian stood alone in the lounge, tapping his foot on the hard stone floor in annoyance. Eventually, Cylus returned with a hunk of dried bread and a lump of crumbly cheese.

'Can't do anythin' on an empty stomach, lad,' he said, apparently unaware of Killian's mounting frustration.

This was it. This was the limit for Killian. He'd had enough of waiting around and being tolerant of others' idiosyncrasies. It was time to get to the point, get what he wanted and leave. 'Cylus,' he said, exasperated, 'can I buy some potions and antidotes please?'

'Sure thing, lad,' said Cylus, setting his food down next to the slug slime. 'Is it another poisoned matey?'

'No,' said Killian through his teeth, 'but don't tempt me. I'm going away, and I want some precautions.'

'Ah, good lad. You can't be too careful in these parts. You never know who you'll run into. Unsavoury types . . .'

Cylus opened his cupboards and groped around, muttering the end of his sentence. Killian couldn't catch what he said, but he knew most of his ramblings by heart now and was willing to bet he wasn't missing any major revelations. The old man turned around with an armful of potions and set them roughly on the table, slopping one of them over his bread by mistake. He read the label of the offending brew before putting it back and taking a bite.

'Here you go, lad,' he said through churning food. 'These should do you.' He picked up four bottles and handed them to him. 'Red one is good against poisonin' from beasts, yellow's good for most plants. If you're still dyin', try the green one. Might work.' He shrugged. 'Might not. These things tend to need specific brews. These are only general cures, so don't come crying to me when you're dead.'

'I won't,' said Killian, taking the assortment of bottles and packing them into a satchel.

'The blue one is best for healing, should sort out infections too. If not, try hackin' off the rotting bit.'

Killian's gaze was drawn to the three-fingered grip Cylus had on the bread. 'How much do I owe you?'

'Fifty'll do if you got it.'

Killian paid him and turned to leave. He paused at the doorway and said, 'I'll see you in a couple of weeks then.'

'You off somewhere, lad?'

Killian opened his mouth to explain but saw that Cylus was washing his bread and cheese down with whisky.

'Never mind,' said Killian, shaking his head.

After stopping by his flat for a quick nap and to pick up some spare clothes, Killian ambled towards Estelle's shop. The frantic crowds had subsided and left empty dishevelled stalls with battle-weary owners in their wake. Estelle's shop was warm and comforting. It was quiet inside, a welcome end to a frustrating day. Rose sat behind the counter while Estelle leant against it, her back to the door; both women were holding cups of tea and idly chatting. Rose looked up.

'Hello, Killian,' she said shyly.

'Hey, Rosie,' he replied with a smile that seemed to silence her.

Estelle turned.

'Killian, my handsome!' she exclaimed. 'Sit down, darling. I'll fix you up a drink and something to eat.'

'That's nice, Stell, but I'm fine,' he lied politely.

'Nonsense, nonsense. Look at you. There's no meat on you. Sit down.'

Killian took a table by the window, putting his feet up on the chair opposite. He wrapped his arms about his head and leant back, gazing lazily out the window at the slowly darkening sky. He'd spent a whole day chasing around town, and now he could sit and relax. He could really do with a drink. Brackmouth Island would be able to help him out there. Pirates and booze went hand-in-hand, everyone knew that. After a few minutes, Estelle came over with a steaming bowl of rich beef stew and knocked his feet off the chair with a playful flick of the wrist. She sat with him.

'Not joining us, Rose?' she called to her assistant.

'No, I'm fine,' said Rose, nervously fiddling with her apron strings.

'Come on,' said Estelle. 'Come and put your feet up.'

Rose took a nervous step forwards, glanced at Killian and shuffled back, her skin crimson. 'Oh no, Estelle, really, I'm fine. There's still some tidying to do. I'll sort it.'

'If you insist.' Estelle turned her attention to Killian. 'So, my love, anything new to tell me?'

Between bites of food, Killian told Estelle all about Ren, Lily, the Gramarye, the island and the pirates. As he spoke, the expression on her face wavered between concern and interest. The colour slowly siphoned off her cheeks.

'Well,' she said once he'd finished, 'now that is a tall tale, and I suppose you're going through with it?'

'Yeah,' said Killian, dropping his spoon and rocking back on his chair.

Estelle stayed silent.

'Stell, you all right?'

'Yes. No.' She shook her head. 'A thing that powerful, something that can bring someone back from death's embrace.' She leant forwards, her eyes serious. 'Killian, are you sure you should be messing about with something like that?'

'I wouldn't exactly call it "messing about."'

'I can see you want to do the right thing, but it frightens me. If something were to happen to you . . .'

'Ah, Stell,' he said, smiling, 'don't worry about me. I can look after myself.'

'I know, but . . .'

He dropped forwards on his chair and put his hand on top of hers, holding her gaze. 'Nothing is gonna to happen to me. I'll be careful, I promise.'

'All right, go.' She sighed. 'But I ain't happy about it.'

'I'll be fine,' he insisted. He looked towards the counter. 'Tell her, Rosie. Tell her I'll be fine.'

Rose froze; she looked like a startled rabbit. 'He'll be fine,' she murmured.

'See,' said Killian triumphantly. 'There's no need to worry.'

Estelle smiled weakly and shook her head.

'Right, I'd better head back,' he said, getting to his feet and shrugging his coat on. 'I left Thorny on his own all day with pirates – now there's someone for you to worry about. He's got all the backbone of a slug.'

She chuckled. 'Is he that bad?'

'Worse.'

She stood up and gave him a firm hug. 'Be sure to come see me tomorrow before you go.'

'I promise,' he said, gently breaking free from her grip and leaving.

CHAPTER
SEVEN

LILY SAT ALONE ON THE SOFT SANDY BEACH OF her island, her legs scrunched up, chin resting on her knees. She reached a hand up and removed her hat, plucking the feather from its top. She turned it over in her hands and ran its silky smooth edge back and forth across her cheeks. It caught the waning sunlight as it moved and shimmered like a precious stone. She bent it into the sun and watched the light play across its surface. Slowly, she moved it towards her face, put it up to her eye and stared through its barbs. Her vision glowed with an emerald tint. It brought a tiny flicker of a smile to her otherwise solemn face.

A chilly sea-breeze whipped up her hair and blew it around her. Irked by its intrusion, she angrily stabbed the feather into her hat and shoved it back on. Shuddering and scowling, she wrapped her arms around her body and pulled her coat together to keep out the oncoming cold. She looked out over the sea and spied Killian's small rowing boat approaching the shore. Her stomach lurched, and her temperature rose. She let go of herself and permitted the cold wind to blow into her coat, cooling her down. Looking at him a second time sent a surge of anger rippling through her. Why did he do this to her? It must've been the time of year. She dug her fingers into the sand as she fought to regain control. *I will be civilised,* she told herself. *I will not let him get to me.*

She watched him jump from the boat and into the surf, hauling the boat out of the sea and up the beach a little way. A satisfied smirk formed on her lips as he struggled against its weight. Even with the dying sunlight in her eyes she could see he was trying to ignore her presence, his head turned away from her. He set the boat down and casually sauntered over to where she sat. She looked up at him as he drew closer, and they exchanged acknowledging glances. He flopped down next to her, and they both stared out to sea.

'Nice of you to lend a hand.'

'Mmm,' she replied through a contented smile.

Killian huffed and shook his head.

They sat together, quietly watching the sun in its leisurely descent to the horizon. The sky was splashed with shades of blue and orange. Thin wispy clouds shone bright pink against a deep purple background.

'How's the ship?' he asked.

'Fine,' she replied absently. 'We're on track.'

'Good.'

Silence fell again. She caught a glimpse of him in her peripheral vision; he was turning towards her. This was not what she wanted. He might start asking her questions she didn't want to answer; she had to make him back off. She moved to look at him, and he quickly averted his gaze to the sea.

'You all right, Lil?' he said in a nonchalant tone.

'Yeah,' she lied and stood up, knocking the sand from her clothes. 'I'm fine. Come on, we'd better go in. Seth's laying out a massive spread.'

'Okay.'

She held her hand out. He took it, and she pulled him up.

'Thanks,' he said.

The sun turned from orange to blood-red and sank below the horizon, leaving a shifting marbled sky as its epitaph.

KILLIAN picked at his food and pushed the meat idly around his plate. He wasn't hungry, and he didn't need to be here. It hadn't been long since he'd left Estelle's, and he was too deep in thought to enjoy food anyway. He needed to plan his escape, he needed another drink, and he needed to stop thinking about Lily. Ren sat next to him, talking incessantly about his day with all the gusto of an old lady describing a shopping trip, but with fewer laughs. Killian made sure he nodded and agreed or disagreed in all the right places. After all, Ren couldn't help his great ardour. Every moment brought him closer to saving his father than he'd ever dreamt possible. Killian ventured a subtle glance at Lily; she still wore a thinly veiled look of sadness on her face. He shook his head, picked up the goblet of wine in front of him and unceremoniously downed the remains. Why should he care if she seemed to be having a bad day?

'Are you going to eat that?' asked Ren, staring down at Killian's plate.

'No, I'm not hungry. I saw Stell, and you know what she's like,' he mumbled back. 'Here, you have it.'

'Thanks, I'm famished.' Ren pounced on Killian's food like a starving alley cat.

While Ren was occupied with devouring his overloaded plate, Killian switched their goblets. It was a fair trade in his opinion. He slumped back in his chair and enjoyed Ren's wine. Once he'd drained it, he placed the empty goblet back on the table and leant forwards, supporting his chin with his fist. He felt much better.

After the meal was finished, Lily stood on the table.

'Well, you bunch of rotters,' she said to her crew. 'I'm impressed. We'll be ready to sail the day after tomorrow as planned. Well done on your swift, efficient work. To show my appreciation for all your efforts, you may help yourselves to the liquor and ale in the stores. Start a fire, start a riot, I don't care – just get down to the beach and enjoy yourselves, you filthy pirate scum!'

'Aye!' they shouted back in unison, raising their goblets to the captain.

Chairs scraped and groaned as the pirates got up and headed down to the beach. Killian glanced at Ren; he was frowning at his goblet.

'Something wrong?' he asked casually.

'No, no. It's just I thought I only had a sip.' He shrugged and stood up. 'You coming?' he asked when Killian didn't move.

'Yeah, yeah, I'll be down in a minute. Get me a drink, something strong.'

'But, Killian, I—'

'You'll be fine without me for a minute. You managed today on your own, didn't you?' He looked up at Ren's pale face and shook his head. 'Look, just bang a couple of shots to take the edge off, and I'll be down to rescue you before you know it.'

Ren nodded meekly, stepped back and melted away into the hordes making their way to the beach.

Killian stood up and idly admired the paintings and furnishings until everyone had left, except for Lily. She was standing by the window, watching her crew run down the beach with bottles in their hands, her fingers knitted together behind her back. Killian made his way over to her and stood behind her. She remained silent and still, not even acknowledging his presence. The fresh herbal-citrusy scent of her skin drifted towards him; it was intoxicating. His body tensed in response. Perhaps he shouldn't have drunk that wine so fast. He was fine with ale and spirits, but wine was a different story.

'Do you want something?' she eventually asked.

'You sure you're all right?'

'I'm fine.' She shrugged and turned to face him.

'If something's bothering you, Lil, you can tell me.'

'Thanks,' she said. 'It's stupid really. It's nothing.'

'Go on.'

'No,' she said, her quiet voice laced with her familiar stubborn tone.

'Fine then,' he said, holding his hands up in defence. 'I don't know. I try to be nice, and she just throws it in my face.'

Despite Lily covering her mouth with her hand, a chuckle escaped. 'When are you ever nice?'

'Sometimes.' He rolled his shoulders. 'Tonight.'

'All right, I'll tell you.' She seemed to hesitate momentarily. 'Today is my birthday.' She looked over her shoulder out of the window. 'Not a word to anyone. Only Raven knows.'

'My lips are sealed.'

'Thanks.' She turned back to face him.

'So . . . only *Raven* knows, eh?' He cocked an eyebrow.

'Killian O'Shea! If you're implying what I think you are, then you're sadly mistaken. Raven and I are very close, but we're nothing more than friends. Not that I wouldn't be tempted if I'd just met him – he is impossibly beautiful,' she added with a smirk. 'But it's not like that. We're just friends.'

'I wasn't implying anything. No need to get so defensive.'

'Whatever you say.' She grinned and gave him a gentle push on the shoulder. Almost as swiftly as it had arrived, her grin faded. She snatched her hand back from him as if touching him caused her pain, and her face became blank and unreadable. 'You'd better get down to the beach before everything's drunk dry.'

'Yeah, you coming?'

'I doubt it.'

'You should.'

'No.' She shook her head. '*You* should.'

'Is that an order, Captain?' he asked.

She nodded tersely.

'Well, I'll follow it just this once, but don't expect me to make it a habit.' He turned and walked towards the door.

'Killian,' Lily called after him.

He paused in the doorway. 'Yeah?'

'Thanks.'

The pirates had wasted no time in getting drunk. By the time Killian made it down to the beach, most of them were already inebriated. A towering bonfire blazed and crackled, throwing bright orange light and searing heat amid the revellers. They were everywhere, playing cards or dice, telling stories, playing instruments, dancing, sparring or slumped in arbitrary drunken heaps. Killian scanned the shadowy firelit faces for Ren. He felt responsible for him. He was young and more than a little naive; someone was probably already extracting the rest of his money from him. Killian narrowed his eyes. It was difficult to pick out individual facial features – in the flickering light, everyone seemed to merge into one.

He weaved his way in and out of groups of drunken pirates gambling with cards and dice, slurring to one another. The thick smoke billowing from the wild bonfire made his eyes sting. As he blinked away the tears, he caught a glare from Morton that could have skinned a kitten at fifty paces. He'd have to keep his eye on him; having a member of the crew with a grudge like that was not a good start.

A clanging of metal rang out through the night, and Killian turned to see a familiar face approaching a small battleground. He anxiously pushed his way through the swaying crowd, but by the time he reached him, it was already too late. Ren, who judging by his pink cheeks had taken his advice and banged a few shots, was preparing for a duel, a borrowed bent-up sword clamped in his right hand.

'Thorny,' said Killian as he walked up to him and put a firm hand on his shoulder, causing him to rock dangerously.

'Hello . . . Shhhkillian,' said Ren.

'So . . . duelling?' Killian asked in a stern whisper.

'I'll be fine,' he replied, brushing the hand away and patting Killian on the chest.

'But you don't know how to fight,' said Killian, 'and you're battered.'

'It's all fine, Killian, 's all fine,' Ren drawled. 'This guy I'm fighting's so drunk . . . I can't lose. Don't you worry about me, I've got the advantage.' He tapped the side of his nose in case Killian revealed this by mistake and blew his cover.

Killian considered arguing about the logic of that statement but decided against it. Ren could learn from his mistakes like everyone else.

Ren turned to face his opponent. He took one step forwards, and his sword was sticking out of the ground. He turned to look at it and was floored.

'This is a man's game, boy!' His opponent laughed, standing over him.

Ren, bright pink, scraped himself up and gave the pirate a coin.

'Hey, I'll give you a go. Double or quits?' said Killian.

'Sure thing, lad,' said the pirate. 'As long as you're good for it.'

'Don't worry about that, he's paying.' He nodded towards the humiliated Ren.

They faced off and drew their swords. The pirate lunged for Killian, trying the same move as before. Killian neatly sidestepped out of the way, catching the pirate's wrist as he did. Using his momentum to disarm his opponent, he swept his legs from beneath him and knocked him to the ground.

'So . . . are *you* good for it?' said Killian, sheathing his swords and offering the defeated pirate his hand.

'Fair's fair, boy,' grumbled the pirate as Killian helped him up. He handed him the money he'd won from Ren plus some extra out of his coat-pocket.

Killian swaggered up to Ren, who wore a look of drunken wonder on his face. He grabbed the bottle of ale from his hand and took a long swig, then slung a sympathetic arm around him and had another draught.

'Don't worry, Thorny,' he said, putting all the winnings in his own pocket. 'I'll teach you a few tricks tomorrow.'

'Really?' Ren gasped.

'Of course. I've got to protect my investments.'

'Thanks,' said Ren humbly.

'Nice fightin',' said a husky female voice from behind them.

Killian turned around to see Finn. With her were two others.

'I know. He's a one-man army, our Thorncliffe,' said Killian, still a little unsure of how friendly Finn was.

'Very droll.' Finn smirked. 'But let's see if you can drink as well as your mouth flaps.' She opened her long leather coat to reveal rows of bottles.

'Have you got a licence for that coat?' said Killian.

'Let's have a lock-in,' she said, a wicked gleam in her eyes. 'Tom, Blake,' she said to the two men by her side, 'this is Killian Shithead and Ren Thorncliffe.'

They sauntered over to the fire and sat down, the wind conveniently taking the smoke in the opposite direction.

'Cheer up, Ren,' said Tom as he lay down on his side. He ran his hand over his closely shaved head and pulled a deep red bandana from his pocket. 'I'm useless with a blade too – 's why I stick to guns.'

'You're useless 'cos you never practice.' Finn grunted, lighting a roll-up. 'It'll catch up with you one day, Tom. Just you wait and see.' She rocked her head back and blew out a cloud of smoke.

'Bollocks!' Tom cackled and tightened the bandana around his head. 'Who needs blade skills when you're a crack shot?'

'Maybe if you *were* a crack shot then you wouldn't need them,' said Blake, filling his pipe with sweet-smelling tobacco. 'But you're not, are you, Tom?'

'Get out of it. I'm better than you.'

'Care to prove it?' asked Blake.

'Not tonight,' said Tom quickly. 'Ren needs cheering up. My gun skills will only make him feel worse.'

Blake chuckled and lit his pipe.

'Thanks . . . I think,' murmured Ren.

Finn handed him a bottle from the depths of her clinking coat. 'There you go, Ren. That'll make you forget everything. Your name, your hometown, how to walk . . .'

It only took one sip to send Ren into a violent coughing fit. Killian was not at all surprised by his reaction; he doubted the young man had ever tasted real pirate grog.

'That's the stuff!' Finn laughed, slapping him on the back. 'Say, Killian?'

'Yeah?'

'You're a pretty good fighter for a floppy-haired shithead. How'd you get so good?'

'Natural talent,' said Killian. He took a swig from a bottle. 'Shithead?'

'That's what I said,' said Finn, pulling that evil grin again. 'Wanna make something of it?'

Killian shrugged. 'I'd rather be a shithead than a mindless drone like you. I'm surprised you can dribble out a sentence without someone moving your mouth for you.'

'You know what? You really piss me off,' Finn snarled through her teeth. 'I see your face, and it fills me with rage, uncontrollable rage.'

'And what are you gonna do about that?'

Finn lunged for him, pinning him down. Killian didn't know what to do. Finn was clearly a tough, battle-hardened pirate, but she was still a woman. He couldn't hit a woman, could he? She drove her knee into his gut and grinned at him.

'Come on! What's up with you?' she heckled.

Killian saw this as an open invitation to fight back, and soon the two of them were rolling around punching each other, kicking their heels in the sand. Killian pushed her back and thumped her hard on the arm.

'Scum!' Finn yelled dramatically.

Killian dived on Finn, and she punched him back, chuckling evilly. He dodged her pounce and struck her in the side, knocking her to the sand. Seizing his chance, he leapt on top of her and attempted to pin her with his knees. A waft of sweet smoke from Blake's pipe drifted in the air; it was delicious. Finn squirmed beneath him and rocked him off balance. Now it was Killian's turn to tumble face-first onto the beach.

'You're gonna get it now!'

Killian rolled onto his back and held his arms up. 'Mercy. Stop. You win!'

'Pathetic!' Finn jeered as she approached him.

Killian turned his head to the side to hide his inevitable smirk, then grabbed her ankle and flipped her over.

'Cheating bastard!' she raged.

'Did you expect any less?'

Finn snorted in answer.

They soon shook hands and carried on drinking, covered in sand. Killian lay on his back, his arms wrapped behind his head as he searched the stars. He caught Ren in his peripheral vision; he seemed a little more relaxed, though that was probably a result of whatever it was Finn had in her bottles. Every now and then, though, he seemed to frown and sneer, almost as if wrestling with something. Killian rolled his eyes. *You can take the boy out of Charrington.* The posh little dick was probably disgusted with himself for drinking scummy pirate booze – only the finest wines and ales for the folks of Charrington. Or maybe he couldn't stand the fact that someone as worthless as Killian could help him. That would sting anyone.

'You all right, Ren?' asked Tom, whose rich dark brown skin glowed in the warm light.

'Sorry . . . I was just thinking.' Ren stumbled over his words.

'What?'

'Well, I was sort of wondering . . . how you all ended up on this island.' He was a bad liar, Killian noted.

'Blake,' said Tom, turning to the dark-haired pirate. 'Will you do the honours?'

'As ever,' said Blake. He took a quick shot from his bottle.

'Hey, Blakey,' said Finn quietly. 'No smoke tonight.' She nodded towards Ren.

'Killjoy,' Tom muttered.

Killian rolled onto his side, propping his head up with his hand. 'Go on then, tell us the tale I've been told a thousand times,' he said.

'You might have to go a bit slower for shithead here, and use small words,' said Finn, baring her teeth at Killian.

Killian wrinkled his nose; Finn fought back with a menacing glare.

'Okay,' said Blake. He coughed once and cleared his throat. 'About a hundred years ago, some rich fella called Lord Aberwithe moved into this castle. He was one of those paranoid types, always worrying about thieves and the like, so a castle on an island was ideal for a guy like him. His wife died not long after he moved in, yet he happily stayed here, pottering around, adding to his study . . . before the sickness set in. At first it was little things – insomnia, no appetite, normal stuff. Then the voices began.' He paused to puff on his pipe. Ren was staring at him, open-mouthed. Blake took a long swig from his bottle, which allowed the tension to build before he continued. 'His servants would catch him having a conversation with an empty room. At night they'd hear him shouting at someone in his bedroom, but he slept alone. As time went by, he became frail and withered. His cheekbones were sunken, his eyes blackened, his hair falling out in clumps.

'One day his servants heard a blood-curdling scream erupt from the study. Concerned for their master, they raced into the room. They burst in to find him looking towards the door, one hand extended and his lips pulled back into a horrific grin. He never moved from that position. They tried to shift him but couldn't. It was like he'd become part of the floor. After a few days, his body began to rot and smell, so they had no choice but to bury him. They had to remove the floorboards to get him out. You can see for yourself if you go in the old study; there're two boards, a shoulder width apart, that don't match the others. Some said he tried soul binding with his wife, and it was her voice whispering in his ear that drove him to madness, but I—'

'What's that?' Ren said in a quiet voice.

'Someone dies, you cut your skin in a particular way, do a little ritual – candles, words, whatever – and their soul enters your body through the cut to live within you,' said Blake. 'It's banned and risky, so I doubt some rich lord would try it. Most people came to the conclusion that the castle was cursed. The building was quickly deserted by all who lived and worked there, and it was left lonely and vacant for years. Its reputation for madness and misery kept away any potential dwellers.

'As fate would have it, a certain fearless pirate and her motley crew happened upon the building some years later and decided that it would be perfect for a base of operations, and the rest is history.' Blake drained the bottle next to him and sat up.

'What?' Ren gasped in astonishment. 'Is that it? What about the madness? Did anyone else go mad? Will I go mad? What if someone binds my soul? I don't understand.'

'It's just a story, Thorncliffe. Relax,' said Killian, shaking his head.

'But what if something gets me while I'm here, while I'm sleeping?' Ren protested.

Killian sighed laboriously.

'Ren, nothing's going to get you,' said Blake.

'Are you sure?' Ren asked.

'Positive,' Blake replied firmly.

'How can you be?'

'Because we live here, and the only things that go bump in the night are drunken pirates looking for the lavvy.'

Tom leapt out from behind the fire with a scream, grinning dementedly and waving his arms. Ren squealed and cowered on the beach. The pirate stood in front of him with one arm extended. Ren's shriek trailed off, and the crackling of the fire filled the deathly silence. The look of pure terror on Ren's face made Tom lose his composure, and he crumpled to the ground, tears of laughter streaming down his cheeks.

'That . . . that was mean,' rasped Ren.

Tom giggled. 'Ah, Ren, Ren, Ren, you should have seen your face.' He twisted his expression into one of horror. 'You're too easy.'

'But it was scary – I was scared,' said Ren.

'Ah, come on,' said Tom. 'It was funny.' He hurled a bottle at Ren, who awkwardly caught it. 'Friends?'

Killian winced as Ren remained silent for a few seconds too long, his expression wavering between fear and disgust. Charrington, one of the more favourable seaside towns in Vermor, was his hometown. It was a place where being an acquaintance, much less a friend, of pirates would be frowned upon. After living that way for years, breaking free of that mindset would be difficult for anyone.

'Okay,' he said, though his tone lacked some sincerity.

Tom punched the air in mock celebration. 'Yes!' he yelled. 'You really know how to build up the tension. I thought you were gonna tell me where to go.' He chuckled. 'Then I'd have had to get Finn to slit your little chicken neck.'

Finn slowly drew her thumb across her throat, her stony eyes not leaving Ren's terrified face.

At this, Tom burst out laughing again. 'That ... that was a joke, Ren!'

CHAPTER
EIGHT

REN WOKE UP FACE DOWN ON A DAMP PILLOW and grimaced as daylight poured through the window. He pushed himself up onto his elbows. His stomach undulated dramatically. A minute, perhaps two, passed before he felt safe to move again. With a cold trembling hand, he detached his sweat-matted hair from his cheek.

He'd never felt like this before. He was cold and hot, his head ached, his eyes throbbed, his mouth was dry, and he felt monstrously sick. Was this his punishment for drinking pirate liquor? A pang of shame shot through him. His father was dying, slowly and painfully, while he was supping alcohol with a bunch of lawbreakers. This was not how he'd been brought up; his father must never find out.

He heard a moan and looked to the other bed to see the blankets moving.

'Thorncliffe?' Killian croaked weakly. 'How much did we drink last night?'

'Not . . . sure.'

Killian sat up slowly and held the blanket to his chest. 'Ugh, I feel like my brain's been embedded with rusty shards of metal. It's like they're scraping off bits of my skull.'

'Thanks for the image.'

Killian groaned again. 'Come on, Thorncliffe, get up.' He got out of bed. 'We'll feel better after some food. I've got to show you some moves today. I can't bail you out all the time.'

Ren rolled out of bed and got dressed. The last thing on his mind was learning how to fight. Even the tiniest movement was a vomit-inducing nightmare. 'But I feel horrible.'

'Well, you've only got yourself to blame. And Finn, the walking bar, I suppose.'

The hall was awash with hung-over pirates. They moved lethargically, slowly drifting about the room with gentle footsteps. Some were strewn across the table, eating in an attempt to dispel their headaches; others had given up on food to seek solace by the fire. There was a peaceful stillness in the air despite the number of crew in the hall. Those who were talking did so in low voices, and the familiar scrape of knives on plates was respectfully absent.

Ren and Killian flopped down in the first two seats available and ate whatever was within arm's reach. At the opposite end of the table were Tom and Blake, who seemed to be suffering a similar plight.

'How did we get back to our room last night?' asked Killian between mouthfuls.

'I don't know,' said Ren slowly. He was finding eating dreadfully taxing. He knew the food would make him feel better, Killian had told him, but he was terrified his stomach would reject it. As a result he ate painfully slowly, chewing everything numerous times before swallowing. Every few bites his skin burned up and his mouth watered; he tensed and willed the food to stay down. He grabbed a pitcher of water, filled his tankard and gulped it down.

'I remember drinking a lot,' said Killian thoughtfully. 'After that it's a blur. I can't remember walking back here at all.'

'It's a good job we made it back,' said Ren, glancing out of the window at the icy morning.

'Yeah,' agreed Killian. 'I'm never drinking again,' he mumbled. He sucked the grease from his fingers, much to Ren's disgust. 'You done? We should get going.'

'Now?' Ren whined. 'But I feel so rotten. I don't even think I can keep this food down.'

'Well, your enemies aren't gonna care if you feel rotten or fine,' said Killian. 'They'll only care about cutting you up.'

'Point taken. Let's go,' Ren grumbled, defeated.

As they got up to leave, Finn shuffled over, a tatty shirt half hanging off her shoulder and a smouldering roll-up dangling from her mouth. It took all Ren's will to not roll his eyes at the state of her. He wasn't sure whether to be terrified or appalled – perhaps both would suffice.

'Oi, shithead,' she said throatily to Killian. 'What you two up to today?'

'Killian's going to teach me how to defend myself,' said Ren flatly.

'Better you than me, Killian,' said Finn, looking Ren up and down. 'It's gonna be a long day.'

'Why is it always the shit days that are the longest?' Killian sighed. 'We'd better get to it. Come on, Thorny.' He grabbed hold of his arm. 'Catch you later.'

'Will do. You out on the beach then?'

'No, I think Thorncliffe's exhibition career will be put on hold for a while. We're off back to town. We'll practise somewhere away from prying eyes.'

As they left, Ren glanced over his shoulder and caught a man with a black pattern tattooed on his face looking at him. The man gave him a hint of a smile, which sent a chill coursing through his body.

Killian led Ren briskly through the town and up towards the sullen hills that overlooked Brackmouth. He walked swiftly, strongly, as if his hangover was already a distant memory. Ren was still suffering an ache in his brain; he wasn't used to drinking so much, or so many different things. He took a deep breath; the crisp morning air slowly helped revitalise his numbed senses.

'We'll go up in the meadow, just through the wood,' Killian explained. 'There's loads of open space up there.'

'Uh-huh,' Ren said half-heartedly. He was far more concerned about his pounding head and the churning in his stomach than how much room he had to swing a sword in.

A thin mist hung in the air, and the sun was low in the sky, like it was too lazy to bother rising properly. Its pale light shone dimly through the murk. Ren followed Killian through a small wood. The branches of the trees and the fallen dead leaves were outlined in white from the morning's frost. The wood was dense, the frozen trees standing stock-still as if they were paralysed by the cool air. The frosty ground glistened with tiny beads of ice that flashed like stars and crunched like broken glass underfoot. In the middle was a small clearing defined by a pond that glistened silver in the shadowy light.

'Have you seen that odd-looking fellow?' Ren asked. He kept his eyes focused intently on watching his footing on the increasingly slippery ground.

'You'll have to narrow it down a little.'

'Strange eyes.' His foot slipped. He quickly put his arms out to steady himself and, much to his own surprise, saved himself from falling. 'A weird marking on his face.'

'A tattoo,' said Killian.

'Yes, one of those,' Ren said.

'Yeah, what about him?'

'He doesn't seem normal,' said Ren. 'Who is he?'

'How should I know?'

Ren frowned. 'I thought you said that you and Captain Rothbone go way back?'

'I did, and *we* do,' said Killian. 'I don't go way back with her crew though.'

'Oh,' Ren muttered.

They continued the rest of the way in silence, Ren feeling somewhat irked that Killian couldn't answer his question. They emerged from the wood to the verdant meadow on the other side. The long green grasses rippled in the breeze. Seagulls wheeled and dived above them, screeching to one another boisterously. Ren couldn't help but feel they were laughing at him.

'Okay, here you go,' said Killian, tossing him a sword. He drew his own, which twinkled softly in the pale sunlight. 'Right, some people fight with one. I prefer two.' He whipped his swords back and forth, slicing the air as he spoke. 'You're best starting off with just the one.'

'Okay,' said Ren, his hand already feeling clammy.

'Right then, come at me. Don't hold back. Give it everything you've got.'

Ren charged at Killian with all the aggression he could muster, only to find himself disarmed and on the ground in a matter of seconds, Killian's sword pressed to his throat.

'Dead,' said Killian, raising his eyebrows. He removed his blade from Ren's jugular, held his hand out and pulled him to his feet.

They tried this several times, and each time Ren found himself on the grass with a cold sharp edge to his throat, his clothes rapidly becoming soaked with dew.

'I'm useless,' he cried, defeated.

'Ah, come on, you're not that bad.' Killian was almost certainly lying. 'Let's try something different. I'll come at you, and you defend yourself.'

'I don't know,' said Ren, feeling embarrassed by his pathetic fighting skills. Killian made everything look so easy; it was depressing.

'Exactly, you don't know,' said Killian cheerily. 'Defence could be your strong point.'

'Perhaps,' said Ren. He felt his resolve tighten and readied his stance.

Killian rushed him and once again disarmed him. Ren fell to his knees and groaned.

'Argh! This is pointless!' He slapped the grass in front of him. 'I'm never going to get any better.'

Killian rolled his eyes and muttered something under his breath.

'Look,' he said, picking Ren up, setting him on his feet and putting his sword in his hand. 'If I lash out long like this, you should try and dodge underneath and come up at my side.' He held his arm out and mimed ducking below it.

'A good blow in the side, between the hips and the ribs, can easily knock someone down. Ready to try again?'

'Sure,' said Ren, staring at the ground.

'I'll move a little slower this time. Try to do what I said.'

Ren held his stance firmly, his sword gripped tight in his hot, sweaty hand. Killian lunged at him slowly. This time he managed to duck under the strike and dealt him a swift blow to the side with the sword's pommel. Killian crumpled onto the ground. Seizing his chance, Ren put his sword to Killian's throat and allowed himself a small smile.

'All right, all right.' Killian coughed as he got up and rubbed his side. 'You've got it. We'll try it at full speed, but don't crack me quite so hard this time. I don't wanna get broken.'

After a few more failed attempts, Ren was on first-name terms with the damp grass, but he got to grips with it eventually. They moved on to something else.

'This is a good one,' said Killian, flapping his long coat open. 'Take my gun.'

'But I don't know . . .' Ren started.

Killian pointed to the gun at his hip. 'Look, you know where it is. Even if you couldn't see it, you'd know where it was, so take it.'

Ren gingerly approached Killian and pulled his gun from its holster. It was cold, heavy and felt like death. He turned it over in his hands.

'See, easy,' said Killian.

He held his hand out. Ren passed him the gun, and he slipped it back in the holster.

'Turn around.'

Ren obeyed.

'I'm gonna grab you from behind, and you'll be able to feel where the gun is. I want you to take it.'

'All right.'

Killian grabbed him, and he felt the cold metal press into his lower back. Ren wiggled and squirmed until he could reach an arm backwards, and after some clumsy scrabbling he managed to pull the gun free and break out of Killian's grip.

'Pretty good,' said Killian. 'We can work on this so you're less wriggly.'

For the next few hours Killian worked Ren hard in the ways of defence. When he was convinced he could smoothly take his gun from him, he moved on with other lessons. He showed him how to dodge and counter-attack, how he could guess an enemy's next move by the angle of their arm – but that he wasn't to rely solely on this technique – and a number of ways to disarm an opponent. Eventually, Killian nodded and declared Ren adequate, which was good enough for him. They slumped down on the cool ground to rest.

Ren stretched his legs out before him. The wet ground was refreshing after all the hot, sweaty fighting.

'Say, Killian?'

'Uh-huh?'

'Want to tell me how you and Captain Rothbone know each other?'

'No,' Killian said bluntly.

'Why not?' asked Ren, running his fingers through the wet grass.

'Because.' Killian paused as if for dramatic effect, and on cue a light gust tousled his hair. 'It's too painful.'

'I'm sorry.' Ren focused on the sparkling dewdrops that surrounded him. 'I'm such an idiot. I should have worked it out.'

'Worked what out?'

Ren looked at Killian and attempted to arrange his face into a sympathetic expression. 'She broke your heart, didn't she?'

'No,' Killian snapped, and Ren flinched. 'You wanna know about me and Lil? You really wanna know?'

'I don't know if I re—'

'Well, I'll tell you. She stole from me. She stole from me – can you believe that?'

Ren shook his head. 'What did she take?'

'Just some necklace I was gonna sell,' said Killian, sitting up and drawing his knees into his chest. 'And I'll be damned if I don't swipe it back as soon as this is all over.'

'Please do it when I'm not around.'

Killian laughed. 'Come on, we've got to go see Stell. She asked me to drop in before we left.'

'Okay,' said Ren, disappointed that he had to get up; he was beginning to ache.

'You did well today,' Killian said, giving him a friendly slap on the shoulder. 'You might survive on a ship full of pirates yet.'

AS soon as they entered Estelle's shop, she pounced on them like she always did, fussing over how they looked tired and half-starved. She insisted on getting them something to eat despite their polite protests about being fine.

'Rose, could you sort these boys out a meal?'

'Of course,' said Rose, her gaze to the floor and her skin flushing.

'Killian, my handsome,' said Estelle, taking off her apron. 'Will you come with me please?'

Killian nodded and followed Estelle through the kitchen and up the steep uneven staircase to her flat.

'Wait here,' she told him as she went into her bedroom.

Estelle's flat was small and cosy. The walls were made from the same grey stone as her teahouse, but years ago she'd adorned them with red and orange drapes to brighten the place up, having long given up on Killian's well-meant promises to paint them for her. She had two soft dark red couches, and the floor was completely covered by a burnt-orange rug. Next to her smouldering fireplace was a hefty wooden trunk with chunky roses and spiky thistles carved into the lid.

Killian slumped down onto the comfortably familiar couch and stretched his feet out underneath her coffee table. It was a dainty thing made of dark wood and etched with designs of flowers and birds. He used to love those birds; he frowned as he tried to remember the names he'd given them as a child. There was definitely a Victor and a Fallow, but the other two eluded him.

'I have this nasty feeling, and I can't ignore it,' said Estelle as she emerged from her room clutching a purple pendant. 'I'd feel much better if you took this charm with you.' She dropped the necklace into his palm and closed his hands about it. 'You can only use it once, mind, but it'll protect you when you ask.'

Killian pursed his lips thoughtfully and hung it round his neck. 'Thanks, Stell,' he said, not wanting to question her further. The less he knew about certain things that might incriminate those he cared about, the better. 'And don't worry yourself about me. I'll be fine.' He flashed what he hoped was a roguish, confident smile.

'I know,' she said.

He pulled her into his arms, held her tightly and kissed the top of her head. 'I'll come back, you'll see.'

Rose was sitting at a table talking to Ren, twiddling her golden hair between her fingers and giggling. She stood up when Estelle and Killian returned, then politely excused herself and went to fetch their food from the stove in the kitchen. Ren looked relaxed for the first time since he'd arrived in town. Killian smiled. It was good he was enjoying himself; he made less noise. Killian sat down, and Rose brought them a couple of steaming pasties. She gave Ren a smile, ignored Killian and hurried back to the kitchen.

'Steady on, you sly philanderer,' said Killian with a wink. He dug into his pasty, gravy and meat oozing all over the plate.

Ren flushed scarlet and said nothing.

'I think she likes you,' said Killian quietly.

'She does not.' Ren scooped a forkful of pasty into his mouth and chewed it slowly. He glanced over his shoulder in the direction of Rose before leaning towards Killian. 'She spent most of our conversation talking about you.'

'Well, I am an interesting topic.'

Ren lowered his gaze and dug his knife into his food. 'Women only like me when they squint,' he mumbled.

Killian looked at him and narrowed his eyes.

Ren put his head down and shovelled the food into his mouth, making it quite clear that their conversation was over. Killian followed suit. Sometimes he could be such hard work. As soon as he'd finished eating, he stood. He'd had more than his fair quota of Ren for the day.

'We'd better head back to the island,' he said, throwing his coat on.

'I guess so.' Ren got up. 'Thank you very much for the food, Estelle. Bye, Rose,' he added politely.

'My pleasure, my love,' said Estelle, smiling. Rose waved timidly from the counter.

'See you when we get back, Stell,' said Killian.

'Take care,' she said.

By the time they got back to the island, all the preparations for the ship had been completed. Groups of pirates were scattered all over the beach, sitting amid clouds of smoke and piles of coins. The sun had been swallowed by the horizon, and the first of the stars were scattered across a deep blue sky.

As he paced across the beach, Killian felt an icy chill creep up his spine, freezing it one vertebra at a time. He was sure he was being watched. He glanced into the woods, but there was nothing there.

'Are you okay?' asked Ren.

'Yeah, I'm fine, just tired. Gonna go in and have an early night.'

Killian became aware of a presence behind him and turned round to see the man with the tattooed face. He took a small step back, startled by his unexpected appearance.

'The captain would like to see you. She's waiting in the hall,' the man said softly.

'All right,' Killian said abruptly. 'Thanks.'

A ghost of a smile flickered across the man's unusual face. He nodded and walked away.

'Best see what she wants,' Killian grumbled, half to Ren, half to himself.

He left Ren on the beach and headed towards the castle.

Inside, it was surprisingly quiet. Most of the pirates were outside or resting after a hard day of hung-over work.

When he entered the hall he found Lily in her usual position, staring out of the window across the beach, hands on her hips.

'Lil,' he said, strolling over to her. 'You called?'

'I did indeed, slug-lips,' she said sharply, turning to face him. She folded her arms across her chest and glared at him intensely. Her lips were together in a tight line; she was crushing him with her authority, yet again.

Well, she's back.

'And?' he prompted, frustrated. She'd managed to single-handedly destroy his mood. 'I wasn't planning on standing here staring at you all evening.'

'You need to show some respect to your captain!'

'I don't have a captain.'

'Enough,' she growled, sweeping her arm in front of her. 'Contrary to what is going through your tiny mind, I don't want to waste my evening staring at you either.'

'What *do* you want then?'

She took a step towards him, placing one hand on the curve of her waist. 'I had a little loyalty problem with one of my crew members a while back. He stole something from me and sold it on. For his efforts, I stole his life.' Her eyes were hard and unfeeling as she spoke. 'Tomorrow evening, we'll be docking at Plyton, and I have a little task for you. My item has resurfaced there, and you are going to steal it back for me.'

'More breaking and entering.' Killian shook his head as he spoke. 'Come on, it's not my scene anymore.'

'Well, you'd better make it your scene,' she said flatly. She moved closer to him, glaring, everything about her cold and callous. 'If you don't do this for me, the deal's off. Understand?'

Killian grimaced. She was using him, and as much as it pained him, he knew he couldn't refuse. He was using her, after all. 'All right, you win. I'll do it.'

'Thank you very much, Killian,' she said, turning her lips up into an approximation of a smile.

'Whatever the lady wants.' He returned her smile with a mock bow. 'Can I go now?'

She nodded, and he left. Killian paced towards his room, cursing himself for slipping under her power. It didn't agree with him, and he was glad it was just for a couple of weeks. As soon as he got to his room, he flopped down on the end of the bed. In less than a minute she'd managed to totally drain his spirit. He rested his chin in his hands and closed his eyes, letting himself drift away, his breathing slow and gentle. He couldn't let her get to him. He wouldn't. If he did that, she'd win.

He lifted his head, opened his eyes and sat looking vacantly at the wall. He hated what she did to him. He took off his shirt and trousers, leaving them in a crumpled heap at the foot of the bed, and crawled under the covers.

CHAPTER
NINE

KILLIAN WAS LOST SOMEWHERE WITHIN A DEEP, comfortable slumber when a hand on his shoulder gave him a gentle shake. With his eyes still closed, he brushed it off and rolled over, grumbling a bunch of half-baked profanities into his pillow. But there was no escape from the hand. It came back and gave him another shake, this time with more force.

'No,' Killian moaned into his pillow. 'Not yet, a minute...'

'We haven't got a minute, Killian,' said Ren urgently. 'The captain said they're going to leave, with or without us.'

'Let 'em go.'

'I'd rather go with them if it's all the same with you,' said Ren in one urgent breath.

'All right,' Killian groaned. 'I'm up.'

He sat up and rubbed the crusty sleep from his eyes, then yawned and stretched his arms towards the ceiling. 'You worry too much, Thorny. They won't leave without us.'

'I wouldn't be too sure.' Ren pointed towards the window.

Killian glanced out to see Lily and her crew boarding the ship in the distance.

'Why didn't you say they were boarding?' he shouted as he leapt out of bed and tossed his clothes on. He had another look out of the window. 'Shit. We'd better run!'

They bolted out of the castle and thundered towards the jetty, Killian trying to do his shirt up as he ran. They tore across the beach, leaving small clouds of sand in their wake, Killian's running hindered by his incessant fumbling with his flapping shirt. The wind blew his hair into his eyes, making it difficult to see where he was going.

'Leave your shirt alone!' Ren shouted into the wind.

'Easy for you to say. I have a reputation to keep,' Killian gasped between laboured breaths as he battled to make himself remotely presentable.

Lily was standing tall at the top of the gangplank when they reached the ship, arms crossed, shoulders back.

'So, you decided to join us after all.' She beamed at the two breathless men, a look of smug satisfaction radiating from her.

Her large bright eyes were edged in black eyeliner with a neat flick at either end, and her full lips were given just enough colour to emphasise them without overpowering her face. Thick ebony hair tumbled over her shoulders in glossy waves. She looked good – even Killian had to admit that. No doubt she'd risen early to craft herself into the perfect pirate queen.

Killian scowled back, searching for something witty to say, but he came up with nothing. He looked with contempt at Ren in his neatly brushed coat and perfectly aligned shirt; he smelled faintly of soap. Who was he trying to impress?

'Are you getting on board or not?' she asked and turned to walk away.

Begrudgingly, Killian stomped up the plank, the slow realisation that he'd missed his only opportunity for a bath for some time dawning on him as he went. Ren trailed closely behind. As soon as they set foot on deck, two crew members darted out from behind the captain and heaved the plank back on board.

Lily stared at Killian from under her hat, the green feather rippling in the breeze. It was clear that they were the last aboard. He glared back at her defiantly.

'Look, I don't have anything specific for you pair to do on board, and I wouldn't trust you to do it properly if I did. So do yourselves a favour – don't get in the way of my crew, and keep out of trouble.'

'Isn't that the same thing?' said Killian, tightening his sword-belt.

'And if you try to smart-mouth me on my own ship,' she said impassively, 'I'll turn that flapping tongue of yours into fish food. Now, both of you, report to Finn for your quarters and stay out of my sight until this evening.'

She turned, looking down over the main deck towards her expectant crew, and shouted to set sail. There was a tremendous roar, and the ship became a hive of activity. The anchor was hoisted, the sails were released, and with a reluctant creak the ship moved slowly out to sea. The crew let out a whoop of delight, ecstatic to be back on the open waves, on their way towards more fortune and adventure.

'I'm going to try to find Finn,' announced Ren.

'All right,' said Killian. 'I'll catch up later. I'm gonna have a mosey.'

'You'll lose the top bunk.'

'I certainly will not. You'll sleep in the bottom one out of respect.'

'Yes, of course, I'm sorry,' said Ren, his cheeks colouring. 'I'll see you later.'

Killian ambled around the deck, watching the seamen work. He had no idea how to run a ship and was glad Lily had told him to stay out of the way – an order he'd happily follow. The crew bustled backwards and forwards doing various things that looked important, mainly involving ropes.

Someone roughly barged into his shoulder from behind. He staggered forwards, but the sway of the ship helped him to maintain his balance. A familiar figure was striding in front of him. His assailant was none other than Morton. Even though he knew it would only stoke Morton's grudge, Killian couldn't allow him to walk off without confronting him.

'Hey, watch where you're going!' he shouted, unfazed by the aura of hatred emanating from the rigid back.

Morton stopped dead in his tracks, spun round on one foot and faced Killian.

'Have you got a scratch on your lens or something?' asked Killian.

'Ya best learn to stay out me way, or else,' Morton hissed through clenched teeth. 'I got authority 'ere. You may have bested me on the beach, but you won't 'ere. There's rules to a ship – ya best learn 'em.'

With that, he continued on his course, barking orders at anyone who got in his way. Killian didn't follow; another encounter might've ended badly. He turned and looked over the bulwark at the water below. It rushed against the side of the ship; ice-cold waves crashed on the wooden structure to release a potent briny aroma with each break. Out of the freezing foam leapt a dolphin, followed by two more. The weak winter sunlight dashed off their grey skin, highlighting them with shimmering streaks of silver. Killian watched them thoughtfully as they played in the surf, racing the ship and clicking to one another in their own incomprehensible language. He smiled, letting his arms hang over the side and allowing his mind to be carried away with the churning waters.

TOM was draped across a cannon, his arms and legs dangling off either side. Every few seconds he adjusted his position, spat on it and polished it with his sleeve.

'I think it's clean now,' said Blake, who was sitting with his back against the quarterdeck, lackadaisically unpicking the knots from a long thick coil of rope.

'Almost,' he replied, giving it yet another determined rub.

'You wanna use that thing as a bloody mirror?' grumbled Finn. She stuffed a paper with tobacco.

' 'Course – there's nothin' else better to look at.' Tom grinned.

'So, what do you fellas . . . and lady' – Ren corrected himself, his skin instantly burning at his clumsy use of words – 'do on the ship?' He squatted down next to Blake; he'd decided he was the least intimidating of the trio.

'We're gunners. We sit about and keep the guns in

shape. Not a lot really,' said Tom, his eyes fixed on the shining black metal of the cannon beneath him. 'Unless there's a battle, of course. Then we get serious.'

'That's not exactly the truth though, is it, Tom?' said Blake.

'Yeah, it is,' Tom muttered.

'We have other duties too, Ren,' Blake explained. 'On long voyages Tom and I are shoved up the rigging to give the others a break. Finn's the one who sits about all the time doing nothing.'

'Ay!' snapped Finn. The roll-up parked in the corner of her mouth moved as she spoke. 'I have a responsibility.'

'Yes,' said Blake with a sly grin. 'Finlay Todd, master gunner, gunpowder sifter extraordinaire.'

Blake, like Tom, looked to be in his early twenties. His hair was roughly cut and often flopped in front of his face. It was so dark it was closer to black than brown, a stark contrast to his incredibly pale skin. A strong jawline shaped a youthfully handsome visage. He had a gentle, well-spoken voice, which helped to put Ren at ease.

'Hey!' growled Finn. 'It's an important job.' She pulled the cigarette from her mouth and blew out a long plume of smoke. 'If it weren't for me, none of you lot would have decent guns, the cannons would be in a shoddy state, and as for gunpowder, don't get me started. Also, none of you would be able to shoot straight. I trained the lot of them, Ren, all twenty-odd of the wasters.'

'Yeah, thanks to her I'm the best shot on the ship!' Tom boasted.

Finn glared, and her eyebrows knitted together.

'Not this again,' muttered Blake.

'Well, it's true,' said Tom.

'I hate to disagree, Tom, but I think you'll find you're not.' Blake tossed his rope aside and wiped his grimy palms on his trousers.

'Blake's right,' said Finn, stubbing out her roll-up. She put the remains behind her ear. 'I'm the best shot.'

'Strong words, Finn. Want to put it to the test?' Blake said.

'Let's do it!' replied Finn, her dark grey eyes glittering. 'Ren! Stand over there with this bottle on your head.'

'I'm not sure I like that idea. Couldn't we just put it on the side of the ship or something?' said Ren, getting to his feet and gingerly taking the bottle from Finn.

'Nah, it'd fall in the sea, and we'd have no target then. Besides, half the fun is trying not to kill the stand.'

'Stand?' Ren broke into a cold sweat. He was doomed. Where was Killian?

'She means you,' said Tom, his tone deadly serious. 'Go on, stand by the bulwark with the bottle on your head. That way any mess will land in the drink and not splurge all over the deck.'

'Splurge . . . what's a bulwark?'

'The rail at the edge of the deck, Ren,' said Blake. 'Go on, let's get this competition going. I've got important stuff to do; rope won't unknot itself.'

'I'm not sure about this at all,' said Ren. He edged towards the rail and balanced the bottle on his head. 'What if you miss?'

'Ren, we're professionals,' said Finn as she pushed her fringe back and adjusted her blue bandana.

'And besides,' Tom added, 'if we miss, you won't know about it anyway.'

Ren stood quivering on the edge of the ship with his back to the sea and a bottle perched on the top of his head.

The three pirates loaded their weapons, got into position about ten feet away from him and took aim. His eyes scrunched up in terror. He wanted to take the bottle off and run, but doing so would only highlight him as a victim, and it would ruin their competition. He'd take the possibility of getting shot over that.

'Right, you first, Blake,' said Finn.

The report of the weapon resounded around the deck and was swiftly followed by the tramp of several pairs of feet. It sounded as if the whole ship was gathering to watch his humiliation. Terrified and trembling, Ren screwed his eyes up tight to block out everything and everyone. The bottle jiggled about on his head like a fisherman's float.

'Ah, that's a shame, Blake!' said Finn, her voice strained as if she were trying not to laugh. 'Maybe Tom'll have better luck.'

'Luck? I don't need luck. This is Thomas Gainsborough you're talking to. Gentlemen, gentlewomen, stand back and watch the master at work.'

A loud crack rang out as Tom fired. Ren flinched within the darkness. By now he was shaking uncontrollably with his eyes shut tighter than ever, willing it all to be over one way or another.

'Oh no, Tommy boy! It looks like you ain't as good as you think!' said Finn with mock dramatics. 'It's up to me to claim the title.'

Ren's stomach dropped away; this was it, his final chance at survival. Surely Finn, the master gunner, would knock the stupid bottle clean off in one shot, and then everyone could just go about their day as normal. He heard someone clear their throat, and with that, the atmosphere completely changed. There was a hasty shuffling of feet followed by a painful silence.

Ren summoned the courage to open his eyes to see Lily standing with the gunners. He wasn't sure what frightened him more, being shot at by three trigger-happy pirates or being within breathing distance of the captain.

'And what, pray tell, is going on here?' asked Lily, her voice stern.

'Just a bit of target-practice, Cap'n,' said Finn. 'Ren here said we couldn't hit that bottle off his head. We were just proving a point.'

Ren opened his mouth to protest, but Lily silenced him with a point of her finger.

'We weren't gonna hurt him,' said Tom, a barely suppressed grin on his face. 'We didn't even put any shots in the guns.'

Upon hearing that revelation, Ren felt as if he were going to collapse with relief. He still had the bottle on his head and was beginning to feel a bit silly.

'I see,' said Lily, raising her voice. 'Well, I'd expect this kind of behaviour from you three, but from you, Ren, after all we're doing for you – taking you to your island, putting ourselves out for you – you should be ashamed of yourself. You will spend the rest of the day assisting Seth in the mess. Do I make myself clear?'

'Yes, miss, I mean Captain,' said Ren, wondering how he could be so ungrateful. He moved to take the bottle from his head, but Lily clicked her fingers, rooting him to the spot.

'One second.' Her flintlock leapt from her holster to her hand as she spoke.

Ren's gaze became lost in its foreboding triple barrel. He took a sharp breath, and his body went rigid. There was a loud crack from above his head, followed by a distant splash. The bottle. The bottle was gone. She'd shot him!

Was he dead? He staggered back against the bulwark, grasping it with trembling hands to keep from falling. It took a moment for him to remember how to breathe.

'I don't want to hear of any more shenanigans from you, Ren.' She said it like nothing had happened, like she'd not almost killed him.

'Yes, miss . . . Captain. I mean Captain,' he squeaked pathetically.

'Now get down there and get out of my sight,' she said.

Ren nodded feebly and scurried towards the stairs. As he descended, snorts of laughter drifted to him from the captain and her gunners.

KILLIAN was still staring down at the choppy sea. The dolphins had long since departed. He'd heard a commotion at the other end of the deck but felt he was above investigating piratical disputes, and besides, it was probably just Morton causing a ruckus. Hopefully he was on the receiving end of the gunshots. He took a deep breath, filling himself with the refreshing scent of salt and timber, closed his eyes and relaxed to the steady momentum of the ship. He felt oddly at peace. A soft breeze ruffled his coat, and he knew instantly someone was behind him, but he sensed no danger. The person stood next to him but remained silent.

The sun shone steadily, bathing the ship in its golden embrace. The colour gave a sense of warmth but was betrayed by the freezing wind that buffeted the pair as they stood.

'Beautiful, isn't it?' asked a gentle voice.

Killian glanced to his side, noting the distinctive black tattoo on the man's face. 'The sea?'

'Yes. Vast, unconquerable, mysterious.'

'Mmm.' Killian eyed him suspiciously.

The unusual man rested his arms on the bar in silence, his strange eyes fixed on the gold-tipped crests rising and falling. 'Raven,' he said, turning to offer his hand.

'Killian, but I've the feeling you already knew that.'

'Mm-hmm.' Raven smiled. 'Yet we have had no formal introduction.'

'Nope,' said Killian, taking back his hand.

So this was the man privy to all of Lily's secrets. Killian rolled his shoulders and did a swift reconnaissance of him. There was something bizarre about him – and not just the tattoo; there was something else, something that didn't feel human. Raven had an undeniably attractive face, a rich tan and ethereal purple eyes. But Killian, he was ruggedly handsome, wasn't he? She'd prefer that. He frowned. What was he even thinking? His back bristled.

'I should probably get back to my post. I can't claim the position of lookout if I'm down here,' said Raven, almost as if he sensed Killian's discomfort.

'All right,' said Killian.

With that, Raven walked away in the direction of the main mast. Killian's gaze followed him briefly, then he returned it to the sea. A cold uneasiness settled over him. He shuddered, feeling as if he could no longer be on his own. He needed the company of someone who didn't make him feel on edge and inferior, so he resolved to find Ren.

It wasn't long before he located the three gunners. Tom was lying across a cannon, half-asleep. Finn and Blake were playing dice for coins. Ren was conspicuously absent. As Killian walked over, Finn looked up.

'Ay! It's pretty-boy shithead.' She grinned. 'Why'd you have to bring your annoying face over 'ere?'

'Move over, scumbag,' he said. They shifted over, and he joined them on the floor.

'Want to play?' asked Blake.

'Nah,' he replied, 'not really my thing – no skill involved. Where's Thorny?'

Finn smirked. 'He had a bit of a disagreement with the cap'n. Now he's peelin' spuds for the day.'

Killian smiled. 'Oh well, it'll probably do him good. Besides, he's less likely to cause any shit down there. I'm sick of bailing him out all the time.' He pulled his swords out and critically examined them in the sunlight.

The two pirates continued their game, the brittle rattle of bone on wood followed by the clink of exchanging coins.

'What do you know about Raven?' Killian asked, mindful not to look from his blades as he spoke to keep the pretence of nonchalance.

'Not a lot,' said Blake. 'He keeps to himself. The captain knows him better than anyone; they're very close.'

'So I've heard,' muttered Killian.

'Why do you ask?' said Blake.

'I don't know, he just seems kinda strange.'

'Him and the cap'n were a team long before this crew got together; s'why he's first mate—'

'He's first mate?' Killian asked. 'But he just said he was the lookout.'

Finn laughed. 'The lookout. The bloody lookout!'

'Someone sounds jealous,' Tom drawled, apparently awake enough to join their conversation now it had turned to mocking Killian.

Finn carried on. 'Normal rules don't apply to him. I

seen him cut all over, but a day or two later there's not a mark on him – don't know why. Maybe the cap'n does, but she's as tight-lipped as him. Make a good pair, them two. I've been on the ship about ten years, and he's never looked any different – hair, face, nothin' changes. He's an odd one, that's for sure, but a good one. Still, some of the crew are scared of him. You know, superstitious crap. Load of bullshit if you ask me.' She pulled the remains of her cigarette from behind her ear and rolled it between her thumb and forefinger. 'But I tell you what. I've been in more than a few scrapes with him, and I'm glad that I fight with him, not against him. Know what I'm saying?'

'Yeah,' said Killian. Now he had more questions than he'd started with.

'Good,' said Finn. 'Come on, Blakey boy, let's see you lose some more.'

Confused, Killian sheathed his swords and leant back against Tom's cannon, then watched Finn and Blake as they continued with their game. The sea air and the gentle rocking of the ship had a soporific effect, and he felt his eyes closing. He had nothing better to do, so he allowed himself to drift away.

For the rest of the afternoon Killian floated between worlds. The odd snatch of conversation filtered into his broken dreams, always accompanied by the sweet smell of Blake's pipe. It was only when Finn roughly shook him awake that he became fully conscious.

'What do you want?' Killian said gruffly, clearing his throat.

'Raven's been by, said the cap'n wants to see you in her cabin,' said Finn.

Killian eased himself to his feet and rubbed his aching limbs.

'Cap'n wants you in her cabin, eh?' said Tom, sensuously grinding his hips against the cannon. 'I'll bet that's not all she wants you in.'

'You've got a one-track mind, Tom,' said Blake, pushing his fringe from his eyes.

'Hey,' retorted Tom. 'It's at least two! Food, guns, women, booze – yeah, there you go, four!'

LILY stood by the window, a large panoramic affair that stretched the full width of her cabin. She'd watched the island until it disappeared from sight, her smile growing the smaller it became. It was good to be out on the open sea again. It felt less claustrophobic out here, which was odd seeing as she was stuck on a ship. She hadn't realised how much she missed travelling. Spreading her arms wide, she took a deep breath and soaked up the endless view of the gold-splashed waves. She felt as if she were welcoming old friends home; it was glorious nostalgia. A sharp knock at the door disturbed her.

'Who is it?' she asked despite knowing exactly who it was.

'You should know. You sent for me,' said Killian through the door.

'Come in, Killian,' she answered, keeping her tone tight and abrasive.

Killian opened the door and entered, but Lily kept her back to him. A tiny ripple of joy ran through her as she forced him to wait. Keeping the balance of power between them tipped in her favour was as essential as it was enjoyable. After what she deemed an adequate waste of his time, she turned around.

He was standing with his hands in his pockets, looking glum and staring at a painting on the wall to his left. It was a unique piece depicting a seaside town tumbling precariously around a craggy cliff face bathed in the warm rosy glow of an autumn sunset. The houses were all different pastel colours and seemed to blend into one another as they scrambled for space on the rocks.

'You know why you're here,' she said after an extended dramatic pause.

'Yep,' he replied curtly.

'Great.' She grabbed a tattered piece of paper from the writing desk and handed it to him. It was a crumpled street map of Plyton, a black circle drawn around one of the houses.

'That,' she said, pointing to the circle, 'is your destination. The contemptible fool has a treasure-room somewhere in his house, and we both know how good you are at finding things.'

'Well, that's something we can agree on,' said Killian, grabbing the map and shoving it in his pocket.

'Don't get cocky. I'm sending you because I can.'

'Can you?' he said, his tone playful.

'I have Ren's chart. I can dump the two of you in the sea, bleeding from your guts, if I want. It's your choice, Killian.'

'All right, no need to get nasty,' he said, holding his hands up and stepping back. He raised his eyebrows and cocked his head. 'We're all friends here.'

Lily felt her lip curl and her fists ball up. She was about to speak, but Killian beat her to it.

'You've yet to tell me what it is I'm after. I need to know what I'm looking for, and in as much detail as possible. Colours are useful.'

'A small oaken casket with an octopus carved on the lid. It's lined with green velvet.' She held eye contact as she spoke. 'Inside the box is a pearl-coloured spindle shell, the end of which tapers into a mouthpiece. Bring both to me.'

'Is that it? Is that really it?' His eyes grew wide with disbelief. 'I'm risking my neck for a shell? First a feather, now a shell.'

'And a box.'

'Okay, yeah, and a box.'

'Believe me, that shell is worth a lot more than your neck.'

'And the box?' he asked.

'It's something to keep the shell in.'

Killian put his hand on his forehead and groaned. 'All right, whatever you say. At least I know how much I'm worth to you.'

'Good, I'm glad you've worked that out.' As she looked at him, she felt a warmth inside her, something she'd not felt for years, something foreign. It felt safe, comforting, and she didn't like it. It wasn't natural. It wasn't her. It was him; he was doing it. He was playing with her emotions, and it disgusted her. He had to leave. She hardened her voice before speaking again. 'You can use one of my lifeboats to get to the harbour. Now get going, and don't mess it up.'

He nodded sarcastically and left, shutting the door behind him. Lily paced back to the window and breathed out the entire contents of her lungs. The sun was dipping below the horizon, a deep orange sea hungrily consuming it.

She put her warm hand against the cool glass and shook her head. 'Idiot,' she whispered to herself.

CHAPTER

TEN

THE TIDE WAS WITH HIM, SO KILLIAN HAD NO problem rowing into Plyton. As he moored, the sun disappeared and the first stars pricked the sky. The quayside was deserted, which suited him just fine. A handful of dilapidated ships bobbed on the waves, creaking their sad lament of loneliness. He pushed back his hair and decided to head for the nearest tavern he could find.

He was only a few paces away from the quay when he found the Whispering Mermaid and slipped inside out of the chilly evening air. The familiar warm draught of a friendly pub was conspicuous by its absence; in fact, he'd felt warmer on the street. He breathed out, and his breath clung to the icy air and scattered when he passed through it towards the bar. There was no homely roaring fire like the one in the Laughing Swan. The place was dingy, depressing and dull. Even the patrons seemed to be brushed with varying shades of grey. The air was thick with suffocating damp and reeked of mould. Killian was about to leave and find somewhere more appealing, like a tanning yard, when he caught the barman's eye.

'What'll it be?' he asked in an unfriendly tone.

Killian scratched his arm and looked about in the vain hope that he was addressing someone else.

'Oi! What do you want?' the barman asked again, his voice gruff and menacing.

It was too late to escape now, and the proprietor didn't look like he'd take too kindly to a lost tourist routine followed by a swift exit. Killian confidently marched up to the bar and leant against it.

'A mug of ale please. Dark.'

The barman grunted in answer and poured the drink, snapping the pump backwards and forwards with short aggressive movements, like having to do his job was of great inconvenience to him. He was a short, stocky brute with oversized lips and a bulbous red nose scrawled with spidery purple veins. Bloodshot eyes were hooded by sagging, fleshy eyelids and flanked by an array of grimy deep-set wrinkles. He slammed the chipped misty glass down on the bar, slopping the pasty-looking ale all over Killian's hand.

'Three,' he grunted.

Killian put his sticky hand in his coat, retrieved some coins and handed them over. The barman took his money with another grunt. Killian half opened his mouth to say thank you but couldn't bring himself to dignify this man with his gratitude and instead slunk away to a quiet shadowy corner to consume his drink.

The tavern was dead. A few drunken men lay slumped across the tables, half-asleep. Two women, daubed in make-up and wearing low-cut tops, were steadily making their way through a line of shots while they eyed up the locals, and a few shady characters exchanged whispers and suspicious looks to each other in another corner. The air in the bar was still. Killian felt a pang of loneliness that was swiftly replaced by the pleasant realisation that he wasn't surgically attached to Thorncliffe.

A deep depression loomed within the bar. It was infectious; he could almost hear his own cells dying as he sat there. He rocked the glass from side to side, watching the measly layer of foam sway to and fro, then took a long swig and shuddered. It tasted like it looked. He sat back in his chair but kept his gaze on the glass; he hadn't the time or the patience to make eye contact with any of the locals. The scant bubbles drifted idly through the ale and burst when they reached the surface. Against the protests of his tongue, he grabbed the glass and drained his drink in three large gulps.

He placed his glass on the table and stood up to leave, keen to get away. His chair creaked loudly, and he winced as an imaginary spotlight centred on him from above. All eyes snapped to the stage as he walked hastily towards the exit. One of the women gave him a slow kohl-coated wink. The other licked her lips. He cursed inwardly and returned the smile; he knew he'd cause more of a commotion by ignoring it. As he passed their table, she grabbed his coat and pulled him towards her.

'Ain't seen you before,' she remarked in a gravelly tone, the stench of despair radiating from between her greasy lips. She pulled him closer and whispered, 'Come find me if you need a hand, darlin'.'

'I've got my own, thanks.' He grinned, twisting free of her grasp.

She laughed, a low crackling sound. 'Naughty.' She winked.

Killian smiled, nodded and headed for the door.

Outside, the blackness of a winter night had settled over the town like a discarded cloak. He let out a deep sigh, and his hot breath lingered on the breeze. The air seemed impossibly sweet after emerging from the hole. He pulled the map from his pocket and held it up to the lamp outside the tavern. The house Lily had highlighted was on the other side of town, which made him grunt with frustration.

He pocketed the map and started down the street. The tall narrow buildings were bathed in a bright glow from the multitude of street lamps. They were crafted from black metal which split into two branches halfway up. A glass ball dangled from each branch and pulsed with light. They were rather flamboyant for their one purpose. That was one thing Plyton had going for it – it was much better lit than Brackmouth. A much larger and more prosperous town, he wouldn't have expected any less, but it was a shame they didn't put more effort into their taverns. He sucked his bottom lip; he could still taste that vile ale.

The brighter the lights, however, the deeper the shadows. As he navigated through the sparse clusters of people hurrying by, he noted the alleys lining his route and gave them a wide berth. Every now and again, a cough or a chuckle emitted from the gloom. He upped his pace and rested his right hand on his sword hilt; he could see why the streets were mostly deserted. A long groan drifted from a blackened alleyway, followed by heavy laboured breathing. Killian couldn't tell whether someone was really enjoying themselves or being brutally murdered. Either way, he wasn't going to investigate. What a wonderful place she'd sent him to! He pondered over whether she genuinely wanted him to get hurt. It wouldn't surprise him; it seemed like the sort of thing she'd get a kick out of.

Eventually, the street opened out into a square with a church not unlike the one in Brackmouth, though strangely smaller. It was choked from the skyline by tall, imposing buildings with slate-covered roofs, which leant towards it as if leering and mocking it amongst themselves.

He paused to have another glance at his map, then turned off the main square and headed up a side street, keeping an eye on his surroundings to make sure he wasn't being followed. It seemed like the sort of town frequented by muggers, and he wasn't in the mood for fighting. Get in and get out were the only thoughts running through his mind. As he walked, the buildings gradually became more extravagant and the pedestrians more respectable; some even went so far as to smile and nod at him. It felt like he'd somehow wandered into a different town. He was more at ease passing the alleys, which were lit to reveal nothing sinister. He stopped, checking his reflection in a shop window to see if anyone was following him. Satisfied he wasn't about to be jumped, he relaxed a little and gave sentry duty to his ears.

He passed a tavern and peered in as he walked by. The suited patrons were busy chattering between guffaws and sups of rich, frothy ale. He counted three roaring fires and a jolly landlord sharing a joke with a buxom barmaid; it was a stern reminder of the value of reconnaissance. It did not help his mood. He turned off the road and into a residential area; the houses increased in size and stature the farther he got from town. He passed large well-lit houses, turned down one more street and found himself at the foot of a long winding carriageway leading up to a mansion.

He took a step back and pulled the map out again to double-check the location.

'Crazy pirate,' he muttered to himself as he stared at the building.

There seemed to be an unusual amount of light emanating from it, accompanied by the distant sounds of clamouring voices.

Staying in the shadows, he navigated the edge of the carriageway until he reached the house. It was surrounded by a large grey stone wall pierced by a huge elaborately designed wrought iron gate. The house itself was a grand affair, a mammoth white building that glistened in the moonlight as if made from precious gems. The front door was dressed with two sparkling and totally unnecessary marble pillars. The building was punctuated with an overabundance of windows, each one decorated with a twisted wrought iron frame matching the design of the outer gates.

He crept up to the gateway and peered through its bulrush-and-lily-pad design. To his annoyance, there appeared to be some kind of function in progress. People were milling about in the garden and walking in and out of a side door. He could hear the distant throb of music mixed with loud drunken banter.

Of all the days to throw a party.

He slunk around to the back of the house, clambered up the stone wall and vaulted over the top. He landed on soft grass, his right hand on the ground for support. Keeping himself low, he darted behind a bush and peered through the branches towards the house.

Luckily for him, the large glass doors of the conservatory were wide open; at least he had easy access to the inside. Unfortunately, there were unavoidable pockets of revellers scattered about the garden between him and the doorway. He cursed to himself and hunkered down to watch them. Most were staggering about, drinks in hand, talking in loud, uneven voices.

They were all wearing costumes, some in suits of armour, others in masks. There were even a few pirates dotted about. He watched as a man cartwheeled across the garden dressed in the tight red-and-yellow harlequin costume of a jester. He managed three rotations before collapsing to the ground in a giggling heap, much to the delight of a huddled group of women, all of whom had shimmering iridescent wings and glittering wands. A man dressed in a fur-lined cloak sporting a tidy beard, crown and sceptre strutted up to the women and said something that made them burst into laughter. He helped the wobbly jester to his feet and handed him a drink. The king and the jester clinked glasses and downed the contents. The group of fairies surrounded the two men and ushered them in the direction of a small fire-pit, which was fashioned in the style of a mini-turret complete with battlements. They formed a tight circle around the flames.

Killian chewed his bottom lip. He was in no doubt that he'd stumbled into a raucous costume party in full swing. He looked down at his rather ordinary clothes; if he'd known, he'd have at least borrowed Lily's hat for the occasion. *Well, I suppose I could pass as a thief.* With his watertight plan in place, he stood up, dusted himself down and swaggered out from behind the bush.

He strode across the lawn, expertly dodging a man who'd lost the use of his legs and was now lying on the cold, damp grass, blathering to the stars or whoever had the capacity to listen. Every few steps a slurred voice garbled a cheerful greeting in his direction, and he gave them an acknowledging look as if he'd known them for years. He skirted around the fairies, one of whom was now wearing the king's robe while the king himself did his best to look chivalrous, but his blatant shivering undid his heroic farce.

Killian kept eye contact to a minimum as he approached the door. He was almost there when a large flabby hand clamped him firmly on the shoulder.

'Tarquin!' boomed a jolly voice.

Killian turned around to see a rotund old man dressed in a fitted blue suit. He had a patch over one eye and a piece of wood tied to his left leg. Presumably it was supposed to be a peg, but because he was using both his real legs it jutted out from his knee at a ninety-degree angle, narrowly missing people as he turned.

'All right, mate?' said Killian, a forced smile strapped securely across his face.

'I'm grand, lad, just grand! Now, as I was saying the other day, about my land,' the old man rambled, his bushy moustache moving like a hungry caterpillar as he spoke.

'Oh yes, of course,' replied Killian.

'Should I sell it to your father?' The old man's breath was noxious; it billowed from his mouth in great steamy plumes, condensing in his thick moustache.

'Well,' said Killian. He paused and furrowed his brow. 'Do you need it?'

'I wouldn't be selling it if I did, would I? The point is, I want to get a good price for it, but I want a quick sale. If I wait for the market to improve, I might get more money, but it could be years, and your father's willing to give me a decent price now. Besides, I've known him a long time.' A guttural laugh burst from his lips. 'So I know he won't try to rip me off!'

'I think you've answered your own question.'

'He's a good man, your dad,' said the old man, squeezing Killian's shoulder a little too tightly. 'Let's hope you follow in his footsteps, eh?'

'I'll certainly try. Hard act to follow, though, by any standard,' said Killian, failing in his attempt to shrug off the man's hand.

'So, what are your plans with the family business once you take over?'

'Upward and onward, build on his legacy. No point in sitting around twiddling thumbs. You've got to grab the bull by the horns, strike while the iron's hot, you know?' Killian was beginning to enjoy himself.

'You're my kind of guy, Tarquin,' said the man. By now moisture was dripping from his moustache, but he didn't seem to notice. 'Grab 'em by the balls, I say!'

'Hear, hear!'

'Heavens, boy!' the man exclaimed loudly, making Killian jump. 'Here's me wittering on, and you're without a drink! Excuse me while I resolve the situation, and we will continue this conversation anon.'

With that, he released Killian's shoulder and staggered off into the house, barking drunken greetings to whoever crossed his path. Killian rubbed the spot where the man's firm grip had been and breathed a sigh of relief. He waited until he'd lost his bulky frame amongst the crowd before he entered the house. The conservatory was edged with exotic-looking plants, some of which were flowering even though it was winter, but its centrepiece was clearly the tacky indoor fountain. A naked woman with glistening golden skin reclined on a black rock as a white marble man with a narrow face and ratty ponytail poured an endless jug of water over her arched body.

The conservatory seamlessly blended into another huge room, which appeared to be where the majority of the guests were. It was lavishly decorated. Colossal crystal chandeliers hung from the ceiling, and massive blue marble pillars lined the room, stretching up to the roof. Looking down at the floor, Killian saw it was also made from solid marble; he tapped it with his heel instinctively. The right wall was almost entirely glass, intricately etched with flowery patterns. *I wonder how much of this place I could buy with Thorny's cash.* A bar was located at the far end, and just to the right of it sat a band, its members attired in smart black suits.

The occupants were dancing, drinking or talking over one another in loud voices. The sheer number of bodies made Killian feel uneasy, but for the purpose he had in mind, the more the merrier. All the commotion would make it easier for him to sneak around and seek out Lily's prize. He just had to locate the treasure-room and hope it wasn't filled with amorous revellers.

He did a swift scan of the room and noted at least three doors. He was drawn to the one on the far left in particular and watched it for a moment; nobody seemed to be going in or coming out. Rocking his shoulders back, he marched towards it confidently, bobbing between partygoers and politely declining any drinks the harassed-looking waiters were offering. Drawing closer, he slowed his pace until he came to a halt a few feet away from it. He spun around to face the room, folding his arms while he swept the vicinity with his gaze. No one was even giving him a second look. A grin tugged at the corners of his mouth. *Easy, in and out.* His smirk beat a hasty retreat as he spied a blonde woman in a silver mask and tiara marching towards him. There was an aura of determination in her stride, and her glistening dress rippled like water as she swayed her hips. She stopped in front of him and smiled.

'Do I know you?' she asked.

'No, I don't think so,' he replied.

'Are you quite sure?'

'Certain.'

'I'd like to know you.' She took a step closer, arching her back slightly to throw out her chest.

'So it would seem.' This was not what he needed right now.

'Well,' she said softly, pointing a silver fingernail at him. 'Now that you've caught my attention, mystery man, I just can't let you slip away.'

'That would be a shame.'

She chuckled and pouted her red lips, eyeing him up and down. 'Tragic. What's with your costume anyway?'

'What do you mean?' he said. 'It was very expensive.'

'What are you supposed to be? You just look like . . . like a man.'

'I am a man.'

She threw him a flirty frown.

'I'm a thief,' he said, using a slightly mysterious voice to arouse her imagination. 'That's why I'm dressed as a normal man, so I can move amongst all of you unnoticed.'

'Very clever.' She laughed and put a hand on his chest.

'And what are you? You just look like a woman.'

'Is it not obvious? I'm a princess,' she said, removing her hand and reaching up to tilt her tiara. 'I'm Princess Allura, my beautiful sneaky thief. And what, pray, is your name?'

'A good thief never tells.'

'Intriguing – you certainly know how to raise an air of mystery,' she said, laughing again and taking a step closer. 'I must say, you don't have the face of a thief.'

'That's why I'm so good.' He took a step back only to discover a wall. 'They never suspect a thing.'

'I always imagined a thief to be a rather disgusting-looking character. You know, wretched face, rotten teeth, all over hives, but not you.'

'I thought I'd leave the make-up and just go with the clothes. I didn't have that much time to prepare.'

She took another step closer and softly pressed herself against him, pinning him to the wall. Like the old man, she reeked of tobacco and stale alcohol.

'I never thought I'd be attracted to a good-for-nothing thief,' she purred. 'But maybe I'm a rebel princess who likes a rough man, a man who's beneath me.' She removed her mask with a flick of the wrist to reveal a large pair of brown eyes.

'Maybe you are.'

'So, what are you going to do about that?' she whispered, her lips brushing his ear as her soft womanly body squeezed against him.

There were clearly only two answers to that question, but all he wanted to do was push her off and get out of there before someone noticed him. Although he couldn't deny this woman was attractive, he had work to do. He had to find a way to get rid of her without causing too much offence or disturbance. He looked over her shoulder and saw the old moustached man, drink in hand, searching the crowds for him. *Well, I suppose she's the lesser of two evils, and definitely the more desirable.*

He put his arm round her waist and pulled her tight against him. She gasped with pleasure, tilted her head up with her mouth partially open and caught his lips. She kissed him with a fiery, aggressive passion, clamping her hands firmly around his back. No escape.

As he kissed her, he slyly opened his eyes to see the old man making his way outside and engaging another poor unfortunate soul. She twisted, and her arms entwined around his neck, her grip tightening like she would never let go. He shut his eyes and tried to think of something else, anything other than her stale tongue forcing its way into his mouth. She released an arm from his neck and placed her free hand on his thigh with a loud slap. Her nails dug in. Her hand snaked up his leg, moving further into the middle as it went. *I've got to stay cool. I'm ice. I suppose it has been a while . . . No, mustn't think that. It won't help.* He opened his eyes as she reached her target. With a little bit of subtle wriggling, he managed to dislodge her prowling hand and slid out of her grasp.

'It's nice to see a lady like you stoop to someone as low as me,' he said breathlessly.

'Sometimes I surprise myself. Shall we find somewhere more private?' She ran a finger across her lips.

'Now there's an offer I can't refuse. How about you wait here, and I'll go find us a nice shady secluded spot?'

'Perfect,' she said, putting her mask back up. 'I'll be waiting with bated breath.'

That's definitely not how I would describe it. He edged along the wall until he reached the door. He slipped his hand behind his back and tried the handle. It was locked. Keeping her gaze, he dropped a lockpick into his hand and dexterously released the catch without looking. He hit her with a seductive wink and slipped through the door.

He closed the door behind him, relocking it. He shook his head, grunted and turned to walk down a long poorly lit corridor. There were a lot of offers coming his way tonight. The women in the bar had only been doing their job, but he was sure Allura wasn't of the prostitute persuasion. It had been a while – he didn't want to work out how long a while was, exactly – and she was attractive, but she just didn't do it for him. She wasn't his type. But what was his type? What was he even thinking? He had a job to do, and thoughts of past and future sex were doing nothing to help him.

He crept around in the shadows, listening for any activity behind the doors he passed. He was close enough to Lily's shell to locate it now, so he slipped his hands inside his coat, felt for his swords and grasped the hilts firmly.

Killian shut his eyes and thought of the box, the octopus carving and the green velvet, then the shell, the mouthpiece and their connection to Lily. A bright silver light raced through the blackness of his mind, creating a jagged glowing pathway. It moved erratically, zigzagging and turning back on itself before coming to rest in the form of a star, which flashed once and disappeared. The sword hilts dropped in temperature and felt heavy. Using them to locate something always fully drained them of their power until the next sunrise. He'd have to avoid all card games until they recharged unless he wanted to tarnish his reputation. He let go of them and opened his eyes. At least he knew exactly where to go.

He scurried up the corridor, opened the last door on the left and walked into the entrance hall, a vast airy space covered with white marble. His light footsteps echoed hauntingly around the room as if he were exploring a vacant cathedral. The massive wooden front door was barred, chained and secured with a padlock. He cursed with frustration; he'd have to think more creatively about his escape route. A wide carpeted staircase ran up the centre of the room, at the top of which hung a portrait. The subject appeared to be attired in relatively fashionable apparel, so it was safe to assume this was his host. He wondered about the type of man who would have an eight-foot rendition of his face at the top of the stairs that stared down at him every time he climbed them.

He padded up the stairs without giving the portrait a second glance. There was another door in front of him, but not the one. He turned right down a red-carpeted corridor. The walls were covered with lavish golden wallpaper and adorned with the occasional painting or mask; he wrinkled his nose at the gaudy taste of his host. He stopped when he got to a corner and, keeping himself flat to the wall, peered around. It was another corridor with a single door at the end, guarded. He ducked back behind the wall and pinched his cheeks to add some colour to his facade for an authentic drunk look. After taking a deep breath, he lurched from his hiding place.

'Hey!' shouted the guard, alarmed by his presence.

'Terribly sorry, old bean,' Killian slurred in his best refined accent. 'But can you help me? I'm a tad lost, you see.'

Without waiting for an invitation, Killian moved forwards. He made a very good show of staggering and stumbling across the carpet – he'd had plenty of experience. Occasionally he stopped and leant against a wall to steady himself before lumbering on.

'You're drunk!'

'I certainly am not,' Killian drawled. 'I'm just lost.'

He came to a halt in front of the guard but continued to sway on the spot. The guard was dressed in a fine red suit buttoned up to his neck. He was in his forties with slicked-back dark hair. Through his clothes Killian could see the outline of a muscular physique.

'You are drunk, sir,' said the guard. 'You're not supposed to be here.'

Killian chuckled to himself at the thought of being called *sir*. 'What's in there, squire?' he asked, pointing to the door.

'Nothing to concern you, sir. Now if you turn around and head back the way you came, I'm sure you'll find your way back to the party.'

'Show me.'

'No, sir, I cannot abandon my post,' the guard replied firmly.

'No, no . . . show me what's in there. Go on, be a sport.'

'Sir, this room is off limits.'

Killian heaved a great sigh of disappointment. 'Drats!'

'Now turn around, sir, and go back the way you came.'

'All right,' said Killian, taking a wobbly step backwards. 'I just want you to know that I'm truly sorry.'

'For what?'

In answer, Killian punched the guard hard in the face, knocking him unconscious. He caught the limp body as it fell and soundlessly lowered it to the floor. He slipped his hand under the sleeping man's coat and groped around for his keys. They were hanging from a belt by a chain, and he allowed himself a small smile as he took them in his hand, a smile that promptly disappeared when he realised they were secured to the belt. He didn't have time to wind each key from the ring, so he did the only thing he could – he removed the man's belt. It was an odd experience, undressing another man, an alien process, like trying to tie someone else's shoelaces or tie, things you take for granted until you have to do them backwards. He slid the belt from its loops and glanced down the corridor, relaxing slightly when he saw there was no audience; he had no idea how he would talk his way out of this one.

He hurriedly tried three keys, and on the fourth, the lock popped. The room opened out into a study, a small cube packed to the ceiling with raggedy old books and manuscripts. The quarter moon beamed in through a window, illuminating the room with its silvery glow. He turned around and stooped to pick up the guard, dragging the unconscious body in with him and shutting the door. The study smelled musty and old, and everything was smothered with a thin layer of dust. Directly ahead was another door. He walked over to it and curled his lip in annoyance when he realised that none of the keys would fit. The lock looked complex and would require more than his simple pick. He rubbed his hands together, dropped to his knees and removed his locksmith kit from his coat. He set to work, jamming one pick in the top part of the lock and feeding a more slender one in below. After a minute or so, it popped and the door swung open, its hinges groaning their objection.

The other side housed a private museum full of glass cabinets containing various artefacts. There were ancient sceptres, small carvings of animals, various necklaces and bracelets all embedded with charms. *Quite the collection,* thought Killian as he surveyed the room by the lucid moonlight. It was clinically tidy; surfaces shone with a pristine radiance and smelt vaguely of citrus, contrasting sharply with the adjacent room.

The lines of treasure ignited his dormant passion for thievery, and he was tempted to return with more than he'd come for. The charms on the jewellery glittered seductively. He rested his hand on a glass cabinet and peered in at a silver necklace bearing a star-shaped purple stone. He squinted, studying it, and then stifled a quick snigger; it was a fake. Even in this light he could make out a moulding seam on the pendant; the metal coating was wearing away where the chain-links met it. It was a good effort, but it had done ir-reparable damage to his host's reputation. This was clearly a man with far more money than sense, although Killian hoped he would not get the chance to argue the point.

After a swift methodical search interspersed with stern critique, he found the box he was looking for. It was tucked away, hidden behind some particularly ugly bracelets on a bottom shelf. He reached in to take it and set it on a low table, opening it to check the contents. Sure enough, it contained a shimmering conical shell about four inches in length, the narrow end fashioned into a crude mouthpiece. He took it out and examined it, frowning at its insignifi-cance before returning it to the box, slipping it inside his coat and heading for the door. He ruled against taking any-thing else. There were treasures in the collection, but they were so gaudy the only way to shift them would be to strip them down and sell the raw materials.

He gently shut the door behind him and surveyed the situation. It would be best to leave the unconscious guard locked inside the bookroom; someone would be along at some point to let him out. He stepped over the body and, feeling a pang of guilt, mouthed a silent apology to the sleeping man. As he went to the door, it swung open of its own volition, and he leapt back in shock. Standing outside was another guard, this one short and stocky. His brow was furrowed with confusion, and then he saw his unconscious colleague slumped on the floor. His small brown eyes fixed on Killian and then moved south to the belt he was still car-rying.

'Look,' said Killian, giving the guard a friendly smile. 'It's not what you think.'

'I'm not sure what to think,' said the guard. 'And I think I'll be the judge of that.'

'Look, you've caught me, fair enough, but I'm not going without a fight, and if we do fight, I'll win.' Killian kept his tone light. 'It would save us both a lot of hassle if we just go our separate ways and forget all about this.'

'Oh, I don't think so, you dirty little thief. I'm gonna enjoy this.'

'Why do people always assume that thieves are dirty? I wash every day, which judging by that smell is more often than you, and as for little, come on. I'm at least a foot taller than you. Unless you mean little in the horizontal sense because yes, you definitely win on that front.'

'You won't be being so clever in a minute,' snarled the guard, cracking the knuckles on his bloated sausage fingers one by one.

Killian heard the first guard groan behind him as he slowly regained consciousness. He sighed. 'I don't have time for this.'

'Don't worry, I'll be quick.'

'So will I.'

Before the guard had even moved, Killian had buried his fist in his stomach. As he bent over in pain, Killian met him on the way down with a knee to the face, knocking him out. He grabbed the guard's body, his knees almost buckling under the weight, and awkwardly shoved him into the room with his now semi-conscious partner.

'I really am sorry,' Killian said to the dazed and confused guard, who was struggling to sit up.

He shut the door, dropped the belt and proceeded along the corridor at a swift pace. By the time he reached the entrance hall, he was running. He gave the creepy portrait a two-fingered salute and bounded down the stairs. Once he was back on the ground floor, he scuttled down the corridor, gradually slowing his pace and respiration. One minor piece of role-play and he would be on his way.

He reached the door, took a deep calming breath, flicked the lock and casually entered the marble room. As he made his way through the throngs of people, he caught fragments of conversations. He kept hearing the words *break-in* and *thief*, or at least he thought so. He wasn't used to this kind of subterfuge; he was more the quietly-break-through-the-window type. Despite his rising fear, he held a flawless composure, smiling at guests as he passed. He was focused on the conservatory when an arm flowed up his back and down onto his chest. Panicking, he thought it was a guard, then quickly realised it was a very unorthodox restraining hold. He was spun around and came face to face with Princess Allura.

'So,' she said quietly. 'Have you found us a spot?' She pulled him close again, thrusting her hips into his.

'Yeah, about that, I had a bit of a look around and—'

'Attention, everyone!' shouted a loud nasally voice. 'I do believe that it's time to thank you all for coming. This has been a fabulous party, and I'm so glad to have shared it with you. Here's to you all!'

The room erupted with jubilant cries, and everyone took a drink.

'I'm so lucky to have such wonderful friends,' the man continued. From his tone and the way he was stumbling over words, it was obvious he was drunk. 'I'm sorry, I'm not very good at this sort of thing, but go, carry on drinking, enjoy yourselves . . . I know I am!'

'He's great, isn't he?' the woman whispered to Killian.

'Yeah, great,' he agreed, looking from the door to the host and back again.

'Why so tense?'

'I'm not tense.'

'You are,' she murmured, slowly grinding herself against him. 'Let's go somewhere private, where I can relieve you of all this pent-up tension.'

'I think a drink and some fresh air will do the trick,' he said, taking a step back to break her hold.

'Okay.' She caught his hand. 'I can wait.'

Killian ground his teeth. He didn't want to knock her out too – that would probably be considered bad form, especially at a party. He glanced at the host again.

'What's he supposed to be anyway?' he asked.

'Mr Volkert can be whatever he wants; it's his party.'

'Come on, you moaned about my costume. Look at his.'

Volkert was dressed in a well-fitting smart white suit edged with gold. His long blond hair was scraped back into a waxed ponytail. Killian noticed a rapier at his side; he wondered if the man could use it or whether it was just for show. Judging by its jewel-encrusted scabbard, it was probably just for show.

'Mr Volkert is a man of style,' said Allura.

'It looks like he's gone for style over dress code. That's a bit rude at your own party. It's quite clear that he wants everyone else to look ridiculous so he can sweep in wearing his dapper suit and have the pick of the women.'

'Well, he won't get me.'

'Lucky me,' Killian muttered under his breath. 'Hey, you know what they say about a man in a white suit?'

'Pray tell.'

'What a dick.'

Allura giggled; she certainly didn't need another drink. Killian decided to abandon the drink plan and head for the exit. He squirmed out of her grip and shimmied through the crowds of sprites, witches, warlocks and knights who had inconveniently gathered for Volkert's heartfelt speech. He saw a thin rat-featured guard march up to the host and lean into his ear. Volkert's expression changed from jolly drunk to irrational raging drunk in less than a second, surely a new record. Killian's heart took off like a wild horse. If he ran now he might get away without too much of a scuffle.

'What's wrong, daaarling?' Allura slurred, grabbing his arm.

'I have to see someone outside.'

'Who is she?' she demanded, stamping her foot.

Before he could answer, his host was shouting again.

'No one can leave here! We have a thief in our midst!' he screeched at the peak of his register. 'Nobody move!'

Volkert leapt onto a table and surveyed everyone gathered in the room, staring ferociously at his wonderful friends through suspicious eyes. He pulled out his rapier and sliced the air in a threatening manner.

'Everyone, remove your masks!' he demanded. 'I want to see your faces.'

'This is exciting,' Allura whispered to Killian. 'A real thief at the party. I bet he puts you to shame.'

If only you knew.

Volkert scanned the crowd for unfamiliar faces. Every now and then he'd stop and ask someone who they were, often with embarrassing results. He seemed like the vacuous sort; he'd probably have asked his own mother who she was. He was getting dangerously close to Killian, who was sweating a little.

'What is wrong with you?' drawled Allura.

'Nothing, just a little warm. I need to go outside.'

'You need me to calm you down,' she purred, resting her hand on the top of his thigh.

After what seemed like an eternity, Volkert came to Killian.

'You,' he said menacingly. 'I don't know you. I don't know your face. Who are you?'

'I-I'm,' Killian began. He stopped and thought. Who was he?

'Look,' said Allura abrasively, 'just because he's dressed like a thief doesn't mean he is one. He's with me.'

Volkert ignored her and stared at Killian. 'I don't know you,' he repeated.

Killian stared back at him, the fear steadily rising in his body. A deadly silence crept into the room, and all eyes turned towards him.

'What am I going to do with you?' Volkert sneered, pointing his rapier in Killian's direction.

Killian whipped a sword from under his coat and held it to Allura's throat, to the sound of many gasps.

'You're gonna let me leave quietly, or I'll spill this lovely lady's blood all over the place. It's your choice. Just imagine all that sticky red blood over this exquisite marble floor.'

'You *are* my dashing thief,' she whispered romantically.

'Told you I was good.' He smirked.

'You'll never get away with this!' Volkert shouted furiously.

'I will, and am.'

'How dare you ruin my party. Do you know how much this cost?' he shrieked, waving his rapier uselessly above his head.

'Some coins? Anyway, I've hardly ruined the party. I imagine this will be the most memorable party you ever throw. I should be collecting my entertainer's fee right about now. Oh, wait – I already did!'

Everyone moved as one as they backed away, creating a neat pathway to the conservatory door. Maybe it was the adrenaline, but Killian had the sudden urge to laugh maniacally as he walked through the crowd with Allura. From the way everyone was positioned, it looked like they'd just got married and he was leading her down the aisle. It was probably too much to hope for confetti and a carriage to be waiting at the gates.

He edged past the hideous indoor fountain, the hard stone eyes of the marble Volkert glaring at him with impotent rage. He passed over the threshold and backed across the garden, keeping his sword close to her throat. The crowd followed in total silence, some kind of stunned fascination leading them on. From across the garden he heard a familiar voice.

'Tarquin!' called the old man. 'You jolly good, boy?'

'I'm fine, thanks. You?'

'Oh, I'm just dandy, lad! I've a drink for you,' he said, hoisting a squat tumbler skywards.

'Thanks, but you have it. I've got my hands full, and I'm on my way now.'

'A man of impeccable taste! Until next time,' he bawled, nodding to Allura and giving Killian a thumbs up.

When he reached the perimeter wall, Killian released the sword from his hostage's neck and pushed her away from him. As he'd predicted, as soon as he let her go two burly men from the crowd ran at him, and he knocked them out cold with a few deft manoeuvres. He addressed the remaining revellers, twirling his swords casually as he spoke.

'I'm going to leave now. It's been fun, but I think I've overstayed my welcome. However, if any of you want to continue the party, then by all means follow me. If you're lucky, you'll end up like these two cretins here.' He looked down at Allura, who was sitting on the grass, her dress spread about her like a silver puddle. 'Sorry, darling, it would've never worked,' he said, giving her a friendly wink.

He looked up and bowed for his audience before leaping over the wall.

A pair of purple eyes looked down at Killian from the ship. Even in the dark of the night they twinkled with an otherworldly glitter. Moments later a rope ladder was tossed over the side. Killian grabbed it and climbed up. After hauling himself over the edge, he collapsed onto the deck. He lay on his back, breathing heavily and gazing up at the shadowy moon.

'You'll be all right . . . getting the boat up for me . . . won't you?' he rasped between painful frosty breaths.

'I'll be fine.' Raven was already pulling it up.

'Thanks,' said Killian.

When Raven had finished with the boat, he knelt beside Killian and placed a hand on his shoulder.

'Come on,' he said, putting his hands beneath Killian's arms and pulling him to his feet. 'You'd better see the captain before you go to sleep.'

'I suppose I had,' he murmured.

Killian was once again knocking on Lily's door. This time, instead of shouting, she answered it herself.

'Killian,' she said, failing to hide her mirth.

'Lil,' he said. He reached into his coat and pulled out the box. 'For you.'

She took it from him. A grin spread across her face as she opened it, saw the contents and snapped it shut.

'A job well done. Thank you. Have a good night.' She went to shut the door.

'Hey,' he said, stepping forwards. 'Is that all I get?'

'What?' she asked with a mischievous tone to her voice.

'I mean, I've just risked my life for that thing.' He paused. 'Look at me.' He held his arms out. His body was still trembling from the rush of energy, his skin clammy and damp, and he felt his sweat-slicked hair sticking to his face. He knew he looked a mess. No, not a mess, rugged; there was a difference.

'I'd rather not.'

'And this is all the thanks I get?' He folded his arms across his chest. 'Well done, thank you, goodnight?'

'Do you want a medal or something?' she asked, cocking an eyebrow.

'Yes, yes, I would, actually! I would like a medal that says "I've been screwed by Lily Rothbone . . . yet again"!'

'Well, I'm sorry, my dashing hero saviour, but I'm fresh out of those. You'll just have to make do with food and accommodation for the next two weeks. Do you think I reward every crew member when they do something for me?'

'Well, no, but—'

'Exactly. Goodnight, Killian.'

'Well, goodnight then.'

'Dinner, tomorrow night, my cabin,' she said as he turned away.

'And that's supposed to be a reward, is it?' he said.

'Take it or leave it. I'll even let you have some fancy wine. I think it's a pretty good reward myself.'

'Well, I guess if that's all that's on offer—'

'Yep.'

'All right, it's a date.'

'No, Killian, it's not a date. It's a grudging acquaintance. Now get out of here before I change my mind.' And with that she shut the door.

Killian breathed out a sigh of relief as he ambled along the moonlit deck towards his cabin; he was beginning to enjoy their little talks.

CHAPTER
ELEVEN

B Y THE TIME KILLIAN AWOKE, THE SHIP HAD
left Plyton far behind and was on course for the
island. He sat up in his hammock and pulled the
cover around his chest; the door was ajar and admitting a salty chill that was scouting the area for any pockets of resistance. The others had already gone. They must
have deliberately left him asleep knowing he'd endured a
late-night adventure. He rubbed the sleep from his eyes,
eased himself out of the hammock and gathered his discarded clothes from the crumpled pile he'd left them in.
He got dressed, clipped on his sword-belt and ran his hand
along the hilts. They felt like his once again, having fully recharged with the rising sun. There was always a niggling fear
at the back of his mind that one day they wouldn't return to
normal, but they hadn't let him down so far. He tossed his
coat on and headed out to secure some breakfast, then to
locate the others.

It took him over an hour to track down a lacklustre bowl of cold lumpy porridge, after which he wandered the ship until he found Tom and Blake lazing in the early afternoon sun. He told them of his previous night's antics and instantly regretted it as Tom hit him with a barrage of questions, jealous of his nocturnal activities.

'So you didn't get up to any mischief then?' Tom asked, sounding disappointed.

'No, I was on business, and I had to kiss her.'

'I bet you did.'

'I did,' said Killian defensively. 'It was a touchy situation.'

Tom burst into laughter. 'I bet it was!'

'Oi! I'm not some kind of promiscuous man slag.'

'I don't see why not,' said Tom, stretching his arms up to wrap them around the barrel of his cannon. 'If I'd been there, I'd have given her what she wanted and the rest.'

'If you'd been there, you'd have been caught.'

'And it would have been worth it for a sly shag with a rich bit.' He looked up to the clear blue sky with a wistful gleam in his eye. 'Ah, Plyton, the party town.'

'Not from where I stood. With the exception of the actual party, it was a bit of a hole.'

'Are you blind? I was there, 'bout a year ago now, staggering from bar to bar, chatting to the ladies.'

'Oh please, not this again,' grumbled Blake.

'You're just jealous,' said Tom.

'Jealous of your overactive imagination?' Blake retorted. He raised one eyebrow.

'Pah.' Tom waved off Blake's comment. 'Now where was I? Oh, yes, ladies. I was too pissed to get back here, so I had to rent a room, and let's just say I had company.' He paused and narrowed his eyes. He slowly got to his feet and mounted his cannon, drawing his fingers over its shimmering black surface. 'Me and five girls – I was up all night if you know what I mean.'

'Where's Thorncliffe anyway?' Killian had switched off from Tom's sordid tale.

'Oi!' snapped Tom. 'Are you even listening?'

'Off with Finn somewhere. She's teaching him about guns and stuff,' said Blake, completely blanking Tom.

'That's good. It'll keep him out of my hair for a bit. Fancy a game?' Killian asked as he produced a pack of cards from his coat and waved it in Blake's direction.

'Go on then. No stakes though. I've been told what you're like.'

'I'm in,' said Tom, sliding off the cannon to seat himself next to Blake.

They played late into the afternoon, Killian winning every game. Tom and Blake stared at him, puzzled.

'How do you do it?' Tom asked in disbelief.

'Skill,' said Killian with a grin.

Blake shook his head. 'Tom, sit this one out, will you? Watch him and see if he cheats.'

Tom nodded and focused on Killian. He won once again, without cheating at all.

'I don't understand,' said Blake, squeezing the bridge of his nose.

'Understand what?' rasped a gruff voice.

'All right,' said Killian, looking up to see Finn outlined against the late afternoon sun.

'How he wins all the time.' Blake indicated Killian, who grinned smugly and folded his arms. 'We've been playing for hours, and he always wins.'

'He does,' agreed Ren as he squatted down next to Tom. 'I should know.'

'I don't always win. I have to throw a few now and then or no one will play me,' said Killian.

'Come on then, pretty-boy,' said Finn, slumping down and pulling out her smoking pouch. 'Let's 'ave a go.'

'So, Thorny,' said Killian as he dealt the cards. 'Learn anything fascinating?'

'I know how to fire and reload a pistol,' said Ren proudly.

'You didn't let him fire one?' Killian gasped.

'No.' Finn struck a match and lit her roll-up. 'A ship at sea ain't no place for foolin' about with guns. A slack shot is a dangerous thing.'

'A Thorncliffe is a dangerous thing,' said Killian, holding his cards in a carefree one-handed grip.

Ren's expression wavered between upset and joy, then finally settled on a neutral blank. After ten minutes of playing, Finn was swearing.

'How the hell do you do it?' she snapped, breathing smoke through clenched teeth, her nostrils flared like an angry dragon.

'Skill,' Killian answered simply.

'Come on, you floppy-haired shithead. Deal 'em out!' Finn growled.

The gunners crowded around, each determined to beat Killian just once. Eventually their frustrations melted away and they gave in to the ludicrous hilarity of the situation. Even Finn laughed as they were defeated yet again.

'I don't get it.' She hung her head, beaten. 'I just don't get it.'

'It's skill,' repeated Killian.

Everyone was so wrapped up in the games that nobody noticed the sun slip below the horizon. Pastel pink-and-peach crystals glowed all around the deck, providing enough soft light for those outside to see what they were doing. Some were mounted on the sides of the ship like torches, and others lined the walkways so crewmates could easily pick a clear path in the dark.

'What are those?' asked Ren, pointing at the glowing rocks with a look of childlike wonder.

'Sunstones,' said Blake. 'Captain Rothbone got a load last time we were in Santonos.'

'But what *are* they?'

'They're rocks from the Santonos islands. They absorb the sunlight in the day and glow at night. A pretty good alternative to oil lamps.' Blake lit his pipe and had a puff. 'Less of a fire hazard too,' he added with a grin.

'They're amazing,' said Ren with a soft gasp.

'Right, I think that's enough for me,' said Killian, standing.

Finn groaned. 'Oh, come on, one more game.'

'I would, but I've got a prior engagement.'

'What?' asked Ren.

'Who?' asked Tom, leering.

'Dinner with Lily, reward for getting that thing for her last night,' said Killian, being careful not to make eye contact with any of them. 'I risk my life, again, and as a reward I have to spend the evening with that miserable crone in her cabin.'

'Oh yeah?' Tom smirked. 'One night not enough, eh? Now she wants you for dinner in her cabin. What's next? I bet you wish you'd heard my story now. You might have learnt something. I could give you the odd pointer before you go, set you in the right direction.'

'I'm perfectly capable without the help of your pointer,' said Killian flatly.

Ren sniggered behind his hand, which only encouraged Tom, who puckered up his lips.

'Oi!' snapped Killian. 'Knock it off. It's just dinner.'

'Yeah, all right, whatever you say. What's for dessert, fruits of the forest?' Tom grinned.

'Well, whatever it is, it'll be better than your weevils on toast,' said Killian. He turned on his heel and left.

'Ay! I'll tell Seth you said that!' called Finn.

Killian was standing outside Lily's cabin once again. A soft pang of apprehension shot through him as he looked at the sturdy door in front of him. He balled his fists up and rapped on the wood. There was no answer, so he knocked again, a little harder this time.

He moved closer and cleared his throat. 'It's me,' he said through the door.

'Come in.'

Killian opened the door and hastily closed it behind him.

'Good evening,' said Lily from her position at the end of the bed, her large green eyes fixed on him. 'Please, have a seat.' She indicated the table and chairs in the middle of the room.

Killian slipped off his coat, hung it on the back of a chair and sat down, looking anywhere but at her. His fiery mood from the teasing by Tom had quelled, leaving nothing but an awkward nervousness in its wake. His gaze wandered over a robust chest of drawers scattered with various brushes and a small amount of make-up. Next to it stood a writing desk covered with parchment and a collection of pens, and above ran two shelves filled with books. He noted her room also had a hammock; surely the queen of the sea demons wouldn't slum it in a hammock like a common sailor?

Lily got up from the bed and made her way to the table, the scent of rosemary and citrus drifting from her as she moved. She picked up a bottle of red wine and filled their glasses.

'Thanks,' he said. He took a large gulp of the crimson liquid, thankful for the distraction and the mild wash of courage that swept through him as the wine took effect.

'I asked Seth to prepare us a little selection from my personal stores,' she said as she lifted the cover off a large square plate. It was covered with an array of food: olives, bread, cheeses, sun-dried tomatoes and an assortment of meats and fish. 'Help yourself.'

Killian picked up some bread and cheese, which he washed down with generous slugs of the bold fruity wine. Lily kept his glass full as he drank, and the atmosphere relaxed after the first bottle had been emptied.

'So,' said Killian, 'you enjoying our little excursion?'

'I am,' she said as she twisted a corkscrew into a fresh bottle. 'It's nice to get away from the island. It can get pretty boring at times, and I don't get to the mainland much.' The cork came out with a loud pop that resounded about the cabin.

'Yeah,' he agreed. 'Been digging a rut myself lately too.' He paused to take more wine; it made him feel deliciously warm and confident. 'I'm not surprised you don't get to the mainland much. You are a pirate, after all.'

'Am I?' Lily laughed. 'I've heard the locals rather like me. I keep trouble away, or so they say.'

'They don't know you very well,' said Killian. He picked up an olive and chewed it, wincing at its tangy flavour, which he swiftly washed away with more wine.

A sly grin formed on Lily's slightly red lips, almost as if she were laughing at her own private joke. 'So, how much is Mr Thorncliffe paying you for your services?'

'Not enough. I have to put up with him, this ship, Tom and hi—'

She chuckled. 'It's not that bad!'

'I hadn't finished. Him, this ship, Tom and his tales.' He paused and levelled his slightly drunken gaze with hers. 'You.'

Lily smiled. It was a sweet, genuine, playful smile, and the whole cabin seemed to light up with it. She reached over the table and prodded him in the chest.

'You are nasty,' she said, jabbing him once for each word.

A flash of warmth rippled through him as she touched him, but he shoved it away and tried to ignore it. He'd had a lot of wine, after all. Her hand moved, and she wrapped her fingers around the pendant he wore, the purple stone softly clinking against the thick band of her ring.

'What's this?' She rested the back of her hand against his chest and stared at the stone that lay in her palm. 'It's new.'

'I didn't realise you were so observant of me.' He didn't know how, but he managed to force out a confident smile.

'I'm not,' she replied bluntly. 'I notice change, however subtle.'

'It was a gift from a friend, a lucky charm or something.' He shrugged.

She cocked an eyebrow. 'I reckon you'll need it.'

'Me too.'

With a smirk, she sat back down, finished the food on her plate and drained her wine glass. After a few beats of silence, she got up from the table and walked over to her bed.

She slumped onto it and lay on her front, her arms under her chin.

'I'll tell you a secret if you want,' she said over her shoulder.

'Go on then,' he said, getting up and realising how much he'd drunk; no wonder his thoughts were trying to betray him.

'I love lying here and watching the stars come out across the sky. It's been so long since I've done this.'

Killian sat ungraciously on the edge of the bed, his back to Lily, cupping his glass as he fought to stop it from slopping onto the covers.

'Funny, you don't strike me as the sentimental type.'

'It's just so beautiful,' she said softly. 'All those tiny silver lights glimmering against the black. You know, some people say each star is a lost soul.'

'Do you believe that?' He turned to look out the window with her.

'If that were true, we'd have to look for the patches of black amongst all the silver.'

He was unsure of what to say or do next. She wasn't being her usual caustic self, and he found it rather disconcerting. He swallowed more wine, which helped spur him into action. He set the empty glass on the floor and lay down next to her, mimicking her pose. They lay together in silence and watched the stars light up the night sky.

As the stars flitted playfully on the waves, Killian unwittingly moved closer to Lily, the soft mattress drawing them into its middle. He felt her hips brush against his and turned to her; the starlight and soft lamplight illuminated her face.

'Thanks for dinner. It was ... different.'

'Thanks for getting my shell back. You don't know what it means to me.'

'Not a problem.'

Killian tried not to stare, but he couldn't help himself. There was something undeniably beautiful about her, as much as it irked him to admit it. The scent of her perfume clung to the air around them. It was like a fresh herb garden after a summer rain and did nothing to help him allay his growing desires.

'You're not just in this for the money, are you?' she asked.

He rolled onto his side and rested his hand in his hand. 'What makes you say that?'

'Because I don't think you're like that.' She kept her eyes fixed on the view from the window.

'Really? What do you think I'm like?' Ordinarily he never would have asked; he didn't even feel like he had asked. The wine was doing it for him.

She shrugged. 'I honestly don't know. I've not met anyone like you before.'

'A compliment?'

'Take it how you want.' She pushed herself up onto her forearms. Her movements were sluggish and uncoordinated, giving a fair hint as to just how drunk she was. She glanced at Killian. 'But for what it's worth, I think it's really decent of you to do all this for Ren.'

'I'm not doing it for him. I'm . . .' He paused, stared at the ceiling and collapsed into the bed. He breathed in the fresh scent of the silky sheets, then came up on his elbows and turned to look at her. 'Maybe I feel a little sorry for him. Maybe I just want to help him. Maybe . . . maybe he happens to have a load of cash that makes me feel even sorrier for him.'

'So it really is all about the money, eh, Killian?'

'It helps.'

'So you're the bad guy, the villain?'

'If helping someone for my own financial gain makes me a bad guy, then I guess I am.'

'It certainly does. It's disgusting behaviour. You'd never catch me doing anything like it.' She gave his shoulder a gentle shove. 'So, if you're the villain and I'm your exact opposite, that must mean I'm the hero.'

Killian had to stifle a laugh; it wasn't often he saw Lily's humorous side.

She stared at him through narrowed eyes. 'And if you're the bad guy,' she said, her voice cold, 'then I'll have to take you out.'

Before Killian could do anything about it, Lily had landed a punch on his arm. It left a sting. She smiled, shaking her head and tutting. She was mocking him. He glared at her, wordlessly accepting her challenge, and pounced. They quickly fell into a rough yet playful scuffle. All the barriers that were usually so apparent between them melted away. They punched, slapped, kicked and laughed. They rolled about the bed, getting sweatier and more breathless by the second. Killian eventually got the better of Lily. He caught her wrists in his hands and forced her down onto her back. He straddled her body and held her arms above her head.

'Submit,' he panted, leaning down towards her.

'Never!' She grinned, defiant. 'Not to you.'

'Submit,' he repeated, his voice a little stronger.

Lily's struggling wrists fell limp. Their eyes locked, and they stared at each other in complete silence. Killian shifted his body and slowly moved down towards her. He stopped an inch from her face, his lips trembling, his heart thumping. She tensed beneath him, and her legs moved to coil around his thighs. They were warm and strong; it was like she wanted to keep him there.

The space between them was infinitesimal. Killian took a deep breath, and a hot, pleasurable rush ran through him; her body pressed firmly against his. Everything seemed right, and yet a seed of doubt planted itself in his mind. What if this was a mistake, a huge mistake? It would only lead to hurt and disappointment. He breathed out slowly, and instead of closing the gap, he sat up and slid off her.

'I'm sorry,' he said. 'I shouldn't have done that.'

'It's all right,' she said absently, sitting up. 'No – I mean, what the hell do you think you're doing?' Her belated scolding had lost its impact.

'Right,' said Killian, looking anywhere but at her. 'I should probably leave now – big day ahead of us and all that.'

'Yes.'

He got off her bed and clumsily went about putting his coat on.

'Thanks for dinner,' he said.

'Bye,' said Lily, her voice devoid of emotion.

He paced back to his cabin as fast as he could, the soft crystal lights guiding him. The cold night air helped douse the aching embers of arousal that lingered within him. When he got back, he was relieved to find the others already asleep. He slipped off his clothes and stealthily climbed into his hammock. For a while he lay on his back staring at the ceiling, unable to sleep. *Bloody red wine.*

CHAPTER
TWELVE

KILLIAN KEPT A LOW PROFILE FOR THE NEXT few days. He certainly didn't want any unplanned run-ins with Lily. After all, what would he say to her? He lay in his hammock, swinging gently from side to side. Maybe he was blowing this out of proportion. *I'll just make out like nothing happened. Anyway, nothing did happen,* he justified to himself for what must have been the hundredth time. *Two friends – no, acquaintances – got a bit battered, but nothing happened.* He had nothing to worry about. Those feelings hadn't been real; they couldn't have been. He'd been way too drunk to think coherently that night. It was definitely the wine. It seemed to have the uncanny ability to turn his most rational thoughts into oozing pulp.

He stuck his leg out of the hammock and pushed it against the wall. He looked about the cabin. It was basic. There were five hammocks for sleeping, and one hammock – which happened to be below his – was a dumping ground for stuff. Guns, belts, spare blankets, dice, an odd bottle and pouches of tobacco all fought for space on the net. The door had two hooks, which were forever obscured by a sea of coats. A weather-beaten wooden chest lay just to the right of the door; it was a home for spare clothes and Finn's fishing equipment, which she seemed to check daily with military efficiency.

Killian wrapped his arms around his head and grunted; he'd been trying to avoid his roommates since his dinner with Lily. He'd had the odd conversation with Ren and Blake so they wouldn't get too suspicious. It was Tom who bothered him. He was convinced he'd say something that would force him to spill the whole ugly truth – not that he had anything to hide. Nothing had happened, nor did he want anything to happen. *This is pathetic. I'm pathetic. She's making me pathetic.* He sat up and slid out of the hammock. *What's the worst that could happen?*

After sauntering around the deck for some time, Killian decided to face whatever comments would come his way and meet up with the others. He was bored, and isolating himself so much was beginning to agitate him. He spied them straight ahead; Tom was standing and leaning against the rail. His head turned as Killian approached, and a broad grin split his face.

'Here he is!' Tom shouted.

Killian scowled at him. The plan to blend in and hope they hadn't noticed his absence over the past few days had already been foiled.

'Thought you'd dropped overboard or something,' said Tom. 'I was worried,' he added insincerely.

'Finally dragged your lazy arse on deck,' grumbled Finn, a smouldering cigarette clamped firmly between her teeth.

'I have been on deck,' Killian protested.

'I've not seen you,' said Ren.

'Shut up, Thorncliffe,' said Killian sharply. 'And I have been on deck, just not round here. I've been busy.'

'Busy?' asked Ren.

'Yes, busy, doing stuff.' Killian had to force back the urge to snap at him again.

'Yeah, hammock stuff,' said Tom, elbowing him in the ribs. 'After all you've been through lately, I'm not surprised. Only so much one man can take. Don't worry, mate, I've been there a thousand times.'

'And what's that supposed to mean?'

'Well, you know,' said Tom, grinning. 'You're bound to be worked up – that woman at the party, dinner with the cap'n, and still no release . . . unless you and the cap'n—'

'Piss off!'

'I'll take that as a no then.' Tom smiled smugly.

'Want me to split your jaw?' Killian grumbled as he slumped to the floor next to Blake.

'A little touchy, aren't we?' said Tom. 'You'd think after two solid days of hammock time you'd be all relaxed.'

Killian huffed in response; he should have stayed hidden.

'Ignore him,' said Blake. 'He'll give up sooner or later.'

'Later,' said Tom, grinning evilly as he ambled to his cannon to drape himself over it.

Killian sighed and leant back against it, taking his swords out and polishing them with the end of his coat. He heard Tom stifle a giggle from above, but the pirate kept whatever seedy thought he had to himself. Finn, Blake and Ren were sitting on the deck dicing for coins.

'You in?' asked Blake.

'I'm fine. I'm not into dice.'

'I like dice,' said Ren. 'Sometimes I win.'

'Of course you do. The result is entirely random. You could play using your mouth and still win this game. There's no skill involved whatsoever.' Killian sheathed his swords. 'Is it always this bloody boring?'

'Would you rather we were in a raging storm fightin' for our lives?' Finn asked flatly as she rolled her dice.

'Well, no . . .' Killian stopped and thought. 'Yes, actually, I think I would. That'd be preferable to lying around here, getting bombarded with suggestions from the bald-headed voyeur up there.'

Tom chortled. 'Bald-headed voyeur,' he repeated softly. 'Thank you.'

'Not a compliment,' said Killian sharply.

He put his head back, gazed at the cloud-smothered sky and listened to the waves crash against the ship. Every few minutes he heard Finn swear, followed by a chuckle from either Ren or Blake. He shuffled uncomfortably against the cannon and tried to make his body relax – a difficult task with a cold lump of metal pressing against his back. He was so tense that all his muscles felt as if they'd locked. With a grunt, he reached up his left arm and rubbed his aching shoulder.

'I bet you could get the cap'n to do that for you,' said Tom.

'Get the captain to do what?' asked a stern voice.

Killian knew that voice; he knew there was no escape from her. Now he'd have to face up to any fallout from the other night. He looked up. She was standing perfectly straight, glowering in Tom's direction with a look that could've soured honey.

'Well?' said Lily impatiently.

'Um, get him some ointment for his stiff shoulder,' Tom lied.

'Do I look like a chemist?'

'No, Cap'n.'

'Do I look like a masseuse?'

'No, Cap'n.'

'Well, next time you have inappropriate thoughts about your commanding officer, have the sense to check she's out of earshot before you voice them. Okay?'

'Aye, Cap'n, it won't happen again.'

'Good. A gunner's position is a privilege, not a right, after all. I could snap it away from you in an instant.'

She swept past Tom and turned her attention to Killian.

'Does it hurt?' she asked sharply.

'It's not too bad,' said Killian, taking his hand away from his shoulder. 'It's just a bit stiff, that's all. I must have slept on it funny last night or something.'

'Are you dying?'

'Erm, no,' Killian replied, shaking his head dumbly.

This was not how he had envisaged their next encounter. She seemed so blunt and detached; it was as if that night had never happened. She made him feel like he was nothing, utterly worthless.

'So you'll live?'

'I should think so.'

'How unfortunate,' she said brusquely, then turned to address the others. 'We'll be docking just off the coast of the island tonight, should Ren's chart be accurate.' She looked

at Ren, who instantly shrank under the power of her glare.
'Tomorrow we'll go ashore, and the five of you will be present. Spend the evening as you wish, but keep clear heads for
tomorrow.'

With that, she turned sharply and left. Tom waited until she was a safe distance away before commenting.

'Mate, what did you do to her?' He grinned impishly.

'Shut up,' said Killian.

'You must have really messed something up. I ain't seen
her that moody in a while.'

'Shut up.'

'Don't you ever learn?' asked Blake.

'Nope,' said Tom.

'You'd better watch it.' Blake grinned up at Tom from
under his dark fringe. 'She was livid. Get caught again and
you'll be deck scrubbing for months.'

'Pah! A bit of scrubbin' might do the rank-minded git
some good.' Finn stubbed the remains of her roll-up out in
her palm.

'All the soap in the world ain't gonna clean my mind,'
said Tom with a slimy smirk.

'That's it, I'm gonna go see Seth,' said Finn, getting up
and rubbing her hands together. A fine dusting of ash fell
from them. 'Shit's sorted for tomorrow. We may as well get
pissed early.'

'Hey,' Ren piped up, 'aren't we supposed to be keeping
clear heads? You know, for tomorrow, for the island? Won't
Lily – I mean the captain – be annoyed?'

'Ah, Ren.' Blake sighed. 'As long as we can walk, she'll
be fine. I'll come too. With any luck you'll need a hand carrying it.'

'In a bit,' said Tom sleepily from the cannon.

Blake and Finn swaggered off down the deck. Killian once again got out his swords and polished them along to Tom's soft snores. Ren sat at the foot of the cannon, glancing up and down the deck, then took to picking at his scarf. They stayed like this for almost an hour, in comfortable companionable silence.

Raven's voice boomed across the deck, shattering the peace. 'Land ho!'

Ren sprang to his feet and raced to the side of the *Tempest*. Killian followed, and looking towards the bow of the ship, he saw the island looming in the distance. It was covered almost entirely with dense pine forest – a featureless hump of dark green against the slate of the sea. There didn't appear to be a temple or construction of any sort.

'So that's your island then,' said Killian.

'Presumably,' said Ren, sounding distracted.

Killian pursed his lips thoughtfully. The wind rushed in, blowing his hair around his face and forcing his coat to flap open.

'What if it isn't there?' said Ren, his voice low and full of worry. 'If it's been there for hundreds, maybe even thousands of years, why has no one taken it? Surely somebody else would have stumbled upon it before us.'

'Don't worry, it'll be there,' said Killian.

'And what will we do if there's no treasure for these pirates?' whispered Ren.

'You've got to stop worrying. I've got it all under control,' Killian lied. He felt slightly guilty about taking advantage of Ren's naivety, but there was no point in panicking him, amusing though it might've been.

'But if it's not there, I'll have failed my father. I'll be a failure. If he dies, I'll have nothing. And you, what about you? If there's no treasure, what will they do to you? What will they do to me?' He slumped forwards and groaned. 'I'll die, you'll die, we'll both die.'

'Look, Thorny, just relax a little. Breathe.' Killian patted him on the back as he spoke. 'You're letting your thoughts take you away. We're here, and that's all that matters. Look, if it makes you feel better, I promise, hand on heart, I'll get you out of this alive. Whatever happens, you *will* survive. I'll make sure of it. Okay?'

'But what about you?'

'I think you already know I'll be fine.'

'Yeah,' said Ren, managing a tiny smile.

'Feel better now? Calmed down a little?'

'I do feel a little better. Thanks, Killian.'

'You've got me on your side,' he said. 'You've got nothing to worry about.'

'You're right.'

'I always am,' said Killian, flashing a lopsided grin. He stepped forwards and rested his elbows on the bulwark. 'Just try not to have an episode like that in front of the others. It's not a good look.'

Ren nodded. 'I don't know what I'd do if I lost him.'

'Your dad?'

'He's always been there. I don't know how I'd cope without him.' He tightened his scarf and pushed his blond hair from his face. 'Do you know what I mean?'

'No,' said Killian blankly. He lowered his eyes to the choppy white-edged waves below and waited for the tangled feeling of nausea, sadness and anger to pass before he spoke again. 'I never knew my dad. He left before I was born.'

'I'm sorry.'

'I'm not.'

'And your mother?'

Killian dropped his chin into his hands. 'She died when I was six, so Stell took me in.'

'I'm so sorry,' said Ren, his cheeks reddening.

'That's okay,' said Killian.

'I'm really sorry. I'm sorry, so sorry. I can't believe I asked. I shou—'

'Thorny! It's fine, don't worry about it. I don't.' The magnitude of that lie would be lost on anyone but Killian.

'My mother ran out on us when I was a boy. She was having an affair with some man. My father . . . I'd never seen him so upset. It was awful. That day I promised myself I'd always look after him.' He smiled thinly.

'Parents, eh?' said Killian, lightening the mood.

'Yeah.'

The sound of clinking glass mixed with Finn's gruff complaints made Killian and Ren turn around. Finn and Blake were ambling up the deck, a drunken sway in their step, laden with bottles. Blake gave Tom a playful kick to wake him. He sat up looking groggy, his red bandana half covering his face. He pushed it back, and after a few blinks, the look of confusion on his face melted away to one of awe as he laid his eyes on the alcohol.

'Nice one, guys!' He grinned, swiping a bottle out of Blake's hand.

'Come on,' Killian said to Ren as he grabbed him by the coat.

'Killian, I—'

'Shh. No more worries, no more talk of death – past, present and impeding – and no more apologies. Got it?'

Ren nodded and followed Killian towards the others.

Killian sat on the cannon next to Tom. He snatched the bottle from him and took a long swig. It was watered-down rum, spiced with cinnamon and cloves and a hint of sweet vanilla, and, like all good alcohol, was a fantastic sedative.

'Oi!' exclaimed Tom. 'You can keep that one. I don't know where your mouth's been.'

'More places than yours will ever be allowed.'

'Yeah, yeah.' Tom shrugged.

Ren sat next to Blake, who promptly handed him his bottle. He took it politely and, much to Killian's surprise, immediately had a swig.

'So, are we going to sit out here all night and drink?' Ren asked tentatively.

'Yup,' said Blake. 'You all right with that?'

'Yeah, that actually sounds quite good,' said Ren.

'You've changed your tune,' said Tom.

'Uh-huh,' murmured Ren. He took another deep draught before handing the bottle back to Blake.

A sense of calm descended over the five friends as they drank and smoked, watching the day rapidly melt into night across the sea. Deep orange gave way to a stormy blue. Flocks of seagulls, brilliant white flecks against the dull sky, raced towards the island to roost, filling the air with their doleful wails.

'There you are,' said a mellifluous voice from the shadows.

Killian recognised it straight away as belonging to Raven.

'What does she want now?' he asked, trying to sound as deflated as possible.

'The captain?' said Raven, stepping out of the dark. 'Nothing,' he added after a short pause.

'Oh, good. That's good,' said Killian, shrouding his disappointment in a cloak of insouciance.

Raven stretched his arms above his head, the gentle light of the sunstones illuminating his body. There was no doubt about it – he had an enviably impressive physique. His toned muscles were encased in strikingly smooth, deeply tanned skin. That alone was enough to turn any man green with envy, but coupled with those otherworldly eyes, he was a thing of beauty, a work of art.

'I've been stuck up there all day.' He nodded towards the mast. 'Mind if I join you?'

'Feel free,' said Finn, tossing him a bottle of his own. 'Nice to see you cuttin' loose for once.'

Raven smiled softly and sat on the deck next to Ren. Ren's gaze flicked towards the enigmatic man and then quickly dropped towards the deck. It was as if he were afraid of him.

' 'Ere, Killian,' Tom drawled, leaning over to poke him in the ribs. 'How about you let me have a go of that fancy gun of yours? I've seen it. You've tried to hide it, but you failed. Nothing gets past my peepers.'

'Do you have any idea how much the bullets for this thing cost?' said Killian firmly as he pulled his gun from its holster and held it tantalisingly close to Tom.

'No,' said Tom.

'A lot, at least a lot,' Killian said, trying his best to sound serious.

Tom laughed and slapped him on the back. 'Come on, Killian, give us a go.'

'No.'

'Please! I've had my eyes on it ever since you turned up. I just want a quick go, a quick blast. You won't even know it's gone.'

'Nope,' Killian said as he slid the gun back into the holster.

'At least let me hold it,' Tom pleaded.

'Why? That's just weird.'

'I just want to feel it in my hands, against my skin, to—'

'It's a bleeding gun, Tom, not a woman,' snarled Finn.

'I do know the difference, Finlay!' Tom snapped back, and then he softened his tone. 'Please, Killian, just a little hold.'

Finn growled and curled her lip.

'All right, all right.' Killian sighed, finally worn down. 'If it will shut you up.'

He pulled out the gun and passed it to Tom. The pirate held it as if cradling a newly emerged butterfly, like it could break in the slightest breeze and he had to defend it at all costs.

'Come on, Tom, you cock. You don't have to hold it like that,' said Finn. 'It's made outta metal, not sunbeams and spiderwebs.'

'It's a delicate piece of art, Finn!' Tom protested.

Finn slapped her forehead and dragged her hand down her face, groaning in despair.

'I've never seen anything like it. It's amazing!' Tom gaped as he ran his hand delicately along the barrel, working his fingers over the vines and leaves moulded into the metal.

'Yeah, it's pretty good,' said Killian indifferently.

'Pretty good!' Tom echoed incredulously. 'It's a work of art, a beautiful work of art.'

'I wouldn't go that far,' said Killian.

'I would,' said Tom, popping the barrel out and spinning it around. 'I've been saying we need to get some of these for ages. Our guns are shit. Shot, powder, shoot, repeat. It's a waste of time. You're dead before you've even reloaded.'

'S'why you need to learn to fight too.' Finn scowled.

'Nah, not if I had this.'

'I'd like to see you get one of them,' she said. 'Actually, how'd you get your dirty hands on one, shithead?'

'I have my ways, my contacts,' Killian replied.

Tom reluctantly handed it back. 'Please, Killian, just let me have a go, one go, one shot, maybe two, to get the feel of rapid fire. Please?'

'Maybe later,' said Killian. He slipped the gun away.

Tom smiled and took a swig from his bottle.

Ren cleared his throat and turned to the mysterious man sitting to his left. His bizarre purple eyes let off a gentle glow, cutting through the gloom of the evening. 'Well, Raven,' he began, 'it's pleasant to have you down here with us.'

'Thank you,' said Raven. He took a sip from his bottle. 'It can get lonely up there, by yourself.' He paused as if he'd been interrupted by a distant thought and stared at the sky momentarily before he continued. 'So I thought I'd reintroduce myself to civilisation.'

'Wouldn't call us civilised.' Tom laughed.

'Speak for yourself,' said Blake, his mouth around his pipe.

'Oh fnar, fnar, Blakey, fnar,' mumbled Tom.

Blake smiled in response, his pipe turning upwards with his mouth.

'Are you coming to the island tomorrow?' asked Ren, a slight tremble in his voice.

' 'Course he is,' said Finn. 'Cap'n won't go anywhere without him.'

Raven nodded as he swept his long purple-black hair out of his face, revealing his devastatingly handsome features. Killian gave him a glare, which he concealed behind his bottle as he took a swig. No one should look like that; it just wasn't fair.

'I hope you find what you're looking for tomorrow,' said Raven.

'Me too,' said Ren. He took a long gulp. 'Thank you.'

They drank in silence, each lost in their own thoughts.

Killian's mind kept drifting back to Lily. As much as he tried to dull his thoughts of her with alcohol, she was ever present, and it was really starting to get to him. That feeling he'd had in her cabin, was it real? He'd never felt anything like it before. It had shocked him, had made him feel vulnerable. He closed his eyes. It must have been the wine. It was strong, and it was red. Was he even interested in her? Was she even bothered about him? The way she'd acted today suggested she didn't care, and that hurt.

A firm intrusive poke to the ribs snapped him sharply back to reality. He jolted and turned to face Tom, who opened his mouth to speak, but Killian stopped him before he could get a word out.

'All right,' he said, defeated, and offered him the gun. 'Fire away, not that there's anything to aim at now.'

Greedily, Tom snatched it from his hand and staggered to the edge of the deck. He straightened himself, placed one hand on the bulwark and took a wobbly aim at the island.

'Killian, what do I do?' he asked pathetically.

'It's a bloody gun. Just pull the trigger. But remember, you don't have to reload. You can just fire the next bullet straight off. But d—'

Before he could finish, Tom fired. The noise drowned out Killian's pleas for him not to empty the whole barrel. With each shot he fired, Tom's laughter became more uncontrollable, and soon he was barking like a drunken madman. A pitiful squawk rang out after the final shot was fired.

'I think I got a gull,' he slurred as he turned around and

casually blew the smoke from the barrel. He tottered over to his friends, sloppily sat himself down on the cannon and passed Killian his gun back.

'You shot all my rounds,' muttered Killian. 'Do you know how much they cost?'

'Erm,' said Tom, rubbing his eyes. 'At least a lot.'

'No,' said Killian, but try as he might, he couldn't keep his stern look together, and his face cracked into a wide grin. 'Yes,' he drawled. 'They are – were – at least a lot, but don't worry about it. I'll take it out of your share of the loot.'

'Fair enough.' Tom shook Killian's hand to seal it.

Between swigs of alcohol, they engaged in merry conversation, which none of them would remember by dawn. The soft lull of the waves and the gentle whisper of the sea-breeze was the perfect complement to their chatter. One by one they fell asleep on the deck. Ren was the first to go, swiftly followed by Tom, who was draped awkwardly across his cannon, as usual. It wasn't long until the late night and excessive consumption of alcohol also claimed the consciousness of Finn and Blake. Killian glanced around at his sleeping companions and realised that he was the only one left awake, except for Raven. He slid his body down to the floor so that he was on the deck and facing him.

'Looks like we're the only ones left.'

'It does.' Raven smiled. 'Perhaps I've met my match.'

Killian nodded slowly. He brought his bottle up to his lips for only a few drops of liquid to fall into his mouth, then put it down in disappointment. He considered Raven through half-closed eyes and then ventured to talk to him.

'Raven, you're not like everyone else, are you?'

'What do you mean?' Raven asked, seeming amused by Killian's drunken questioning.

'You're different. Your eyes, your tattoo, everything. You're different. Hope you don't mind me saying,' he added quickly. 'I don't want to offend you or anything.'

'Not at all.'

Killian sat up straight, and the world wobbled. He pressed his palms into the deck, keeping his arms rigid to regain some sort of equilibrium. 'What I'm saying is, it's not bad, it's just I'm just curious about you. Let's start simple. Where are you from?'

Killian pulled his legs up to his chin, wrapped his arms around them tightly and stared at Raven over his knees.

'Well,' Raven began. 'That, my friend, would be quite a tale, and I doubt you would still be awake by the end of it.' He paused before adding, 'To be honest, even if I told you now, you probably wouldn't remember it in the morning.'

Killian chuckled. 'You're right. You are right.' He sighed, leant against the quarterdeck and relaxed his legs to the floor, allowing his body to go limp. 'Another time, eh?' he murmured.

'Another time.' Raven smiled back.

Feeling more than satisfied with that response, Killian allowed his eyes to close.

Killian's eyes fluttered open. There had been a change. The air was different, musty and stuffy. It was much darker. He moved, and his body swayed with the rock of his hammock. It creaked in the quiet. He hadn't walked to the cabin, had he? He didn't remember walking. What did it matter? He was in bed now. His eyes shut once more, and he drifted into a deep sleep.

CHAPTER
THIRTEEN

KILLIAN STOOD ALONE ON THE SHORE OF A
vast silver lake; he pulled his coat close to keep out
the chilly breeze blowing across the water. The
endless night sky glistened above with thousands
of stars pulsing with silvery light. They seemed to move,
drifting about one another like languid fireflies. The wind
rustled in the tall silver grass behind him. He glanced over
his shoulder; he was alone. Tiny waves lapped at the shore,
bringing his attention back to the lake. The place exuded a
deep feeling of loneliness, yet there was something familiar
about it, like he belonged here.

His mouth filled with the taste of metal, and the
strength left his legs. He slumped to his knees, leaning forwards on his hands for support. He hung his head. The sand
beneath him was covered in rubies. He ran a hand over
them, and they smeared. Blood. He looked at his body. His.
Droplets of crimson rained onto the shore from a myriad of

deep slashes across his body. He panicked and tried to get up, but something was oppressing him. A presence loomed over him, something sinister and foreboding.

'. . . live with this,' a voice whispered darkly.

He awoke with a start, his heart thumping, and sat up to examine his body only to find nothing, not a mark. He lay back and breathed out slowly; he often had vivid dreams, but this one had been different. There was something about it. *Come on, Killian, get it together! It was a bloody dream.* He sat up and rolled out of his hammock in one smooth motion. As usual, Ren was already up and gone, as were Finn, Tom and Blake. *This is their job, I suppose.* He turned and gazed lovingly at his comforting hammock – still swaying slightly from his departure – and considered returning to its warm embrace, but his thoughts were interrupted by a sharp knock at the door.

'Who is it?' he asked groggily.

'Blake,' came the voice through the door. 'Captain sent me. She wants you up on deck pronto. We're going ashore.'

'All right,' said Killian. 'Gimme a few minutes.'

Blake's muffled footsteps faded down the corridor. Killian rubbed his stubbly face, muttering curses as he hastily dressed himself, disgruntled about being forced away from his bed by her. He set about attaching his weapons and cursed again as he reached for his gun, remembering that Tom had fired off a whole barrel the night before. He popped it open and refilled it, slipped his swords into their scabbards at his sides and ran an unenthusiastic hand through his hair. *That'll do.*

UP on the deck, Ren shuffled from one foot to the other. The palpable tension in the air was adding to his neurosis, and as Killian's companion he felt he would be held personally responsible for his punctuality. In a way, it was his fault. He knew what Killian was like in the morning; he should have woken him. He glanced at the pirate queen, her body statuesque and her face emotionless. Shuddering, he looked away. She cut a terrifying figure. Killian strolled onto the deck, his carefree grin at odds with the foreboding atmosphere.

'I hope you didn't rush on our account,' Lily remarked flatly.

Ren winced internally, already dreading Killian's inevitable sarcastic reply. From what he'd learnt of him over the past few days, the man seemed to have little to no regard for his own safety, or perhaps that was the kind of thinking that went hand in hand with reckless swaggering self-assurance. Ren didn't know; his mind actively repelled any thought remotely related to confidence.

His gaze wandered towards the island, and his heart thumped. He was only a boat ride and a hike away from saving his father. Soon everything would be over. He could go back to his normal life, beg for his apprenticeship back and forget all this had happened. That was providing the Gramarye really existed and there was something for the pirates on the island. His blood instantly frosted, and he shot a sideways glance at Killian. He'd save him, he'd protect him; he'd promised he would. Despite it being the promise of a lawbreaker, Ren desperately clung to it. It was all that was keeping him remotely calm. For a felon, Killian didn't seem that bad. He had already saved his life once, without even knowing there was anything in it for him. He could have left him dying in the street. Ren felt a pang of shame; would he have done the same? Probably not.

A salty breeze swept through the ship, and the sails flapped obnoxiously in the tense silence. Ren's attention was brought back to the deck and the immediate matter at hand.

'You best keep yourself and yer mouth in line today,' Morton grunted. 'I don't be wanting any more fightin'.'

Much to Ren's surprise, Killian nodded in silent agreement.

RAVEN and Finn heaved the small boat onto a deserted beach of fine white sand and came to join the rest of the hunched-up landing party. The wind picked up, and the temperature dropped.

Killian pulled his coat tight and nudged Ren in the ribs. 'You couldn't have dragged us out to a nice tropical island, eh?'

Ren nodded numbly.

'Come on then!' Lily snapped. 'It's freezing. Let's get a move on.'

'We even know where we're headin'?' grumbled Morton.

'Well,' said Killian. He felt he needed to redeem himself for his previous silence. He sauntered towards the quarter-master, stopping just outside striking distance. 'My guess would be through these woods' – he pointed through a gap in the trees as he spoke – 'and up to that temple.'

Morton's eyes flashed dangerously, and he snarled. Killian knew that look all too well; he'd seen it before, dozens of times – the frustration in his eyes, the determination in his grimace. He was clearly planning his demise. Killian was glad he'd be off the ship and back to his normal life soon. Any longer with the crew and he'd feel the knife in his back. Either that, or Morton would feel his sword in his chest. Neither of them was a good option.

'Right then, the sooner we get going, the sooner we get the loot,' said Tom cheerfully, clasping his hands together greedily and inadvertently breaking the tension.

'And the sooner I get your carcass off my boat,' Lily muttered at Killian. She took charge and led her small band through the woods.

From the way the trees grew, it was clear there had once been a path leading up to the temple. Thin streams of daylight trickled in through the thick dark canopy at irregular intervals, highlighting patches of dirt and rock amid the gloom. There was an eerie, suffocating silence about the place that did nothing to help the general mood of the crew. The smell of damp, soggy earth rose from beneath their feet and mingled with the crisp scent of the pines. Rigid dead twigs and pine needles littered the forest floor. Every time someone stepped on a twig and cracked it, Ren jumped.

'A bit nervy, aren't we?' Blake commented.

Ren looked sheepishly up at him but said nothing.

The path inclined rapidly, and Killian's thighs let him know about it. It was hard going for everyone except Raven, who didn't break a sweat.

'You know,' said Tom, wincing as his uneven voice thundered through the silence. He lowered it accordingly and continued. 'It's hard to believe anyone ever lived here.'

'What're you blatherin' about?' groaned Finn.

'This place seems so dead. Well, not dead. I mean, there's plants and shit . . .'

'I know what you mean,' said Blake, glancing up. 'It's unnaturally quiet, like the birds are afraid to make a sound.'

'Probably because Tommy Dick-fingers shot 'em all last night,' said Finn.

Killian shot Tom a glare, then lowered his head and pressed on. He felt bitter and angry; he slashed aggressively at any branch that dared cross his path. Frustration coursed through him, though he couldn't quite ascertain why, which only served to incense him further. Maybe it was Ren.

'Thorncliffe! Will you stop jumping at your own shadow? It's pissing me clean off,' he snapped, his tone laced with acid. That was it.

Ren mumbled a weak apology and continued walking.

The trees grew denser as the path became narrower and zigzagged tightly up the steep incline. The ground was dry here, and the needles crackled beneath Killian's boots. Thick foliage choked the sky from view, but there was no undergrowth to impede his path, so he slipped his swords into their scabbards. The way became apparent here, bordered by large stones marking the route to the top. The slope was covered with steep crags and overhangs that he passed beneath as he walked. Earth-covered roots dangled above him. He could never see more than a couple of turns ahead, and the summit was obscured by dense woodland.

The trees thinned out as he climbed higher, taking with them their pine needle carpet. The path could be seen here – huge ancient stones set into the hillside with channels for water running down each side. He caught glimpses of the temple as the path coiled closer to its zenith. Sweat trickled down his brow, and he wiped it away with the back of his hand.

The coils ended abruptly and were replaced by a flight of steps leading up to the temple. Raven hung back, allowing Lily to take the lead. She powered up the archaic stairs two at a time. Killian followed with similar haste.

The temple shrank as he approached. It had appeared enormous from the glimpse offered on the beach but now looked small and insignificant. It was a squat cube with four blank flat walls and no windows or designs. A path of large stones led up to it and continued around in a circle. Running along the edge were the remains of a half-hearted attempt at a wall.

The building was flanked by a collection of stone statues standing a few feet away from the walls. There were fifteen in total, all crudely humanoid. They were skinny and about eighteen feet tall, with long spiky limbs. Like the temple, they looked as if the work to complete them had been rushed; many didn't have faces, and those that did were haunting to behold. Their expressions were carved into looks of permanent agony and despair, their eyes unseeing black hollows.

'They weren't very arty,' chirped Tom.

'It looks like this was put up in a hurry,' said Raven. 'I wonder why.'

'Come on,' said Lily, marching forwards. 'We didn't trek all the way up this hill just to gawp at it.'

Tentatively, the rest of the party followed her towards the temple.

'Raven,' she ordered, 'have a scout and see if there's an easy way in.'

Raven nodded and disappeared around the side of the building.

'It doesn't look like there's a door,' Killian said, staring at the blank wall in front of them.

'Thank you, Captain Obvious,' Lily muttered, sitting down on the low crumbling wall.

'It's a bit eerie up here,' Killian said as he sat down next to her.

'Scared already?' she asked with the faintest smile on her lips.

'No,' he said, perhaps a little too defensively. 'I just don't like those lanky statues staring at me.'

She laughed. 'That's right, Killian, they can't take their eyeless sockets off you.'

He shrugged and bit back a retort. Raven returned from his search, a troubled look on his face.

'There's no way in,' he said. 'No door, no hidden trapdoor, nothing. The building can't even be touched.'

'Can't be touched?' said Ren, flustered.

'Yes, I tried to scale the sides, but it repelled me. It seems to have some kind of protective seal around it. Powerful magic.'

'But there must be a way,' said Ren. He looked desperately at Lily, his shimmering eyes pleading with her. 'We've got to get in.'

'Calm down,' said Lily sharply. She stood up. 'Let me think.'

Killian saw something horrific from the corner of his eye. He leapt to his feet and pushed her to the ground. He lay there, shielding her with his body as the ruined wall collapsed behind them, covering him in dust. Swiftly, he rolled off and pulled her to her feet.

'Lil,' he said, drawing his swords, unable to shift his gaze from the terrifying thing that watched him. 'We have a problem.'

The wall where they'd been sitting was now no more than a pile of rubble. Standing behind it was one of the statues, its faceless head turned in her direction. The other statues were slowly creaking to life, dust cascading from their limbs as they stumbled towards the party.

'Right!' she shouted, her voice strong and even. 'Everyone, back to the ship. Get her ready and go! Don't look back, just go. I'll try to distract them. Raven, stay with me. I may need you.'

'But, Cap'n, we can't jus—' Tom began.

'Shut it! Don't question me! Get going!'

Killian stood firmly by her side.

'Killian, go, please,' she said in an unusually soft tone.

'And miss all the fun?' He flashed her a crooked smirk.

'I'd hardly call being crushed to death fun.'

'You clearly don't know what I do for fun.'

She cracked an unexpected smile. 'All right, stay . . . if you want.'

'Thanks.'

'Killian!' Ren wailed.

'Go!' shouted Killian. 'I'll be fine. Finn, look after Thorny. He may need a change of underwear.'

With the statues edging closer, the party turned and ran back down through the forest. Raven, Killian and Lily positioned themselves facing the enemy.

'Have you got a plan?' Killian asked, pushing his hair back.

'Not exactly,' Lily admitted. 'Call me reckless, but I hadn't prepared for this particular turn of events. They're solid rock, so our weapons will be useless. We should just try to distract them long enough for the crew to set sail.'

'Okay, that's good enough for me.'

'We need to keep them up here for as long as possible,'

said Raven. 'If they make it to the beach with the ship moored so close to the shore, they could destroy it.'

'Agreed. Let's split,' said Lily. 'Raven, try not to get injured. Killian . . .' She took a deep breath. 'Don't die.'

'I'll see what I can do,' said Killian. He sheathed his swords, tensed his body and turned to her. 'I told you they were looking at me,' he added with a wink.

The monstrous statues advanced with irregular, spasmodic movements, their blank or agonised heads jerking erratically left and right, up and down. They emitted a sickening hiss as they chased the three interlopers. Raven ran to the first statue that moved, flipped himself from the ground onto its chest, pushed himself off, twisted in the air and landed on its head.

Killian narrowed his eyes and focused. He couldn't allow himself to dwell on Raven's sudden superhuman agility; that could wait. He had to stay cool, which usually wasn't a problem, but he wasn't usually being hunted down by gigantic statues. He blew out a long calming breath and ran towards the legs of the nearest statue, crouching down at its feet and biding his time. As soon as it moved to strike him, he dived out of the way. Looking back, he saw its face. It had wide holes for eyes but no pupils. A pointed nose was crudely chiselled out of its head, and its mouth gaped open as if expressing horror. It was like something from a grotesque nightmare.

He looked to his left and saw he'd attracted the attention of two more, which were making their erratic way over to him. Their long angular limbs sliced through the air with sporadic movements. He put his head down and ran. Blood rushed into his brain as his heart went into overdrive. It was dizzying and confusing. His vision blurred, and he staggered back against the perimeter wall. He only needed a second or two to catch his breath, yet they refused to give him that. A huge fist thundered towards him. He leapt out of the way but caught his foot on a malicious root and stumbled to the ground. He rolled onto his back and found himself cast in the looming shadow of the statue.

Holding his arm up in a feeble defence and gritting his teeth, he prepared for the inevitable. A flurry of black and green appeared in front of him. Lily was there. She turned and winked at him, then faced the statue and put her fists up. Lily and the statue threw their punches simultaneously, striking each other with an earth-shattering crash. They were knocked back in opposite directions amid swirls of gravel and dust.

Killian watched in horror as she collided with a stone wall. His stomach dropped away into a well of emptiness, but no sooner had she hit the ground than she was back on her feet again. He frantically scrambled to his feet and raced over to her.

'Wh-what,' he rasped, 'was that?' She should've been dead, or at least broken in some way, but she seemed fine. 'Are you . . . ?'

'It was nothing. I didn't even feel it,' she said, calmly dusting down her coat. 'But thanks for rescuing me earlier. The thought was there.'

Killian felt his skin flush; hopefully he was already red from exhaustion or he'd never live it down. 'I wasn't rescuing you.'

'What a coincidence. Neither was I.'

'Hey, you two!' Raven called from above. He was straddling the shoulders of a statue and riding it as it flailed uselessly, trying to dislodge him. Dust clouds exploded all around him as the arms connected with the heads of other statues. 'Shall we leave?'

'I reckon so!' Lily yelled back.

Raven dived from his angry perch and joined Killian and Lily on the ground, and the three of them turned to run. Estelle's charm slapped against Killian's chest, reminding him of its existence. Without much thought, he ripped the pendant from his neck and launched it at the abominations. When it hit the ground, it erupted into a thick mist of purple smoke, shafts of deep blue lightning flashing and cracking within the cloud. The statues screamed, thrashing around frantically, blindly searching for the intruders.

'What the hell was that?' asked Lily as they reached the edge of the clearing.

'No idea, but it should buy us some time,' Killian said, gasping.

They were at the wrong side, away from the steps, which were now barred by the writhing statues. They had no choice but to hurtle blindly through the woods. Sharp twigs and branches tore at their clothes and skin. Much to Killian's vexation, Lily and Raven appeared unfazed by this, so he treated them to constant updates of his condition.

'Shut up,' Lily snarled. 'It'll heal.'

'That's easy for you to say,' Killian spat between hoarse gasps. 'I could lose an eye next.'

He frightened himself with this statement and put his hands in front of his face. The branches glanced off his arms, and thorns ripped into his shirt, tearing his skin. With his vision hindered, he failed to notice a sudden steep decline and stumbled forwards. He had no idea where he was falling and couldn't stop himself. There was a dull pain, and everything went black.

Killian gasped. 'What happened?' he asked, disorientated. He sat up, his head throbbing. Warm blood trickled down the side of his face.

'You knocked yourself out on a tree,' said Lily, deadpan.

'Ah ... I did a Thorncliffe,' he muttered.

'Luckily Raven was here to rescue you. He shouldn't have bothered though.'

'Thanks. That's nice. You really know how to make someone feel special,' said Killian.

'Look behind you, Killian. They're following us. They'll be here in less than a minute, and the ship is way out there.'

The forest splintered and groaned as it was torn asunder by the relentless surge of enchanted stone. Killian watched as the trees were mown down, creating a great brown trench through the deep green of the forest. He turned to stare out to sea. The ship had weighed anchor and was a good way off. He blinked a few times and waited for reality to set in before he spoke again.

'We're fucked,' he said.

'Well, Raven and I might be all right, but you're fucked,' she said.

'Thanks again.'

The roar of falling trees and creaking stone grew louder, and with a great crash, the first of the statues emerged from the woods. It raced towards them in its nauseating, strobing fashion.

'Nobody is going to die,' said Raven, calmly rising to his feet. 'Grab on to me. Quickly!'

Killian and Lily stood and grabbed Raven; he held them under his arms and ran towards the sea. The shoreline drew closer. Was he going to charge directly into the sea? Smashed to pieces by the rocky statues or a mercy drowning by Raven – it wasn't much of a choice. Killian shut his eyes tight and braced for whatever was to come. The ground dropped away, and a weightless sensation took over his body. Forcing his eyes open against the roaring wind, he tried to work out what was happening. Through his tear-blurred vision he could see they were impossibly high above the sea and heading rapidly towards the ship. He glanced at Raven and for the briefest of moments thought he saw two huge black feathery wings outlining his body. He caught a look from Raven and guiltily closed his eyes. Was he supposed to see that?

His stomach lurched as they began their descent. The buffeting winds steadily subsided, and Killian felt lighter, almost as if he were floating. He dared to look, keeping his eyes fixed below. The deck was coming closer; they were drifting towards it. *Impossible.* Things were getting too strange.

'Brace,' said Raven.

Killian tensed, shut his eyes again and clung on even tighter. They landed as softly as a feather in a cotton field.

'You can . . . let go now,' Raven wheezed to his passengers.

Lily had already let go by the time Killian opened his eyes. His heart was still pounding as he released his grip and took a tentative step forwards. Raven crumpled and fell towards the floor. Killian lurched back and grabbed him before he hit the deck.

'You all right?' he asked.

'Fine, just need a rest.'

'Come on.' Killian pulled Raven's arm around his shoulder.

'Thank you,' Raven whispered, leaning heavily on him.

Killian became aware of the whole crew staring at the three of them, open-mouthed.

'Come on,' Lily snapped, drawing the crew's attention away from Raven. 'Get on with it.'

'With what, Cap'n?' Tom asked hesitantly.

'We're going home.'

'Is that it? Are we abandoning the mission?' Tom said what Ren would be afraid to ask.

'Certainly not,' said Lily defiantly. 'I'm not letting a brainless pile of stones keep us from our well-deserved loot. But we need a plan or some help, and we won't get either from mindlessly sailing round this shitty island scratching our heads. Now let's get going.'

She marched through her crew, barking orders and sending them scurrying off in all directions. While everyone was distracted by Lily's aggressive tone, Killian slunk off, hauling Raven below deck.

'Nice work back there,' he said.

'Don't mention it.'

Killian wanted to ask how the three of them had managed to soar through the sky, but it wasn't the time. Raven was clearly exhausted. He needed to know about the black wings. Had they really been there, or had they been a mere product of his harassed mind? The more he thought about them, the more he believed he'd imagined them; he had taken a pretty hard knock to the head. But if he had imagined them, how had they made it back to the ship? He reached Raven's single-man cabin and pushed the door open, pulling him inside.

'Raven?'

There was no response. He carried him over to the hammock in the corner of the room and laid the peaceful figure into the gently swinging net. Killian loosened Raven's belt and removed his shirt; he held it up and frowned. The back was completely shredded. Had it been like that before? It could have been the branches. He decided it must have been the branches as he tossed the shirt to the floor. As he rolled Raven over he noticed two thick blackened scars running behind each shoulder blade. It was all getting too weird – mysterious scars, wings, shredded clothes, gigantic leaps. Killian shook his head and pulled a thick woollen blanket over the first mate.

CHAPTER
FOURTEEN

THE GOLDEN LIGHT OF DAWN SHONE THROUGH the chink in Killian's curtains, its concentrated beam falling upon his face and searing his unwilling eyes open. He sat up and yawned as he ran his hand over the rough stubble that had gathered on his chin. He pushed his hair out of his face and looked through the crack in the door towards his couch. Ren was still slumped across it, asleep. Relief washed over him. Ever since they'd returned, Ren had done nothing but mope, and it was really starting to grate on him.

He heaved himself off the bed, threw on a pair of trousers and made his way to the bathroom, mindful not to wake Ren. They'd been in Brackmouth for three days now, and the ground finally felt steady beneath his feet. He hadn't realised how long it would take for the rocking sensation of the sea to wear off and for his equilibrium to return completely. He hated ships, everything about them – their smell, the way they moved, the way there was nothing to do. But most of all, he hated their captains.

He fleetingly contemplated having a bath, but the effort it took to heat that much water felt beyond him. A wash and a shave would be enough for now. His thoughts drifted to Lily as he filled the sink and swirled his hand through the water. There was more to her than she let on; she couldn't be hurt – that was obvious – and she was strong. Scarily strong. He picked up a razor and set to work deforesting his face. She'd punched that statue and knocked it back; he'd seen it with his own eyes. It didn't seem possible, but it had happened. It had been an incredible sight, one he wasn't likely to forget. With strength like that, she could have easily overpowered him that night in her cabin, but she hadn't.

He brought a handful of water up to his face and washed away the stray hairs and grime. These thoughts weren't helping; he needed to get his mind back on task and away from her. He stared into the mirror as he worked and considered his options. He'd asked Estelle about the temple and statues, but she'd been unable to help. Either that or she was reluctant to help. Killian couldn't decide. He'd known her all his life but still couldn't read her. Maybe it was the mother–son thing they had going on clouding his perception of her. It struck him that he'd never learnt much about her past. He'd guessed that she dabbled in the arcane – a glance around her flat told him that. With mages outlawed, it was an incredibly dangerous thing for her to do, but she wasn't exactly a mage; he didn't think so anyway. There were no laws against studying, after all, only practising. Since the island, though, he'd wondered about her. She obviously knew more than she was letting on about the arts. The pendant she'd provided had given them time to escape. Without it . . . well, it was tight anyway.

He wiped his face with a towel and wandered back into his room, where he flopped onto the bed. He glanced at the bag slumped on his bedside table. It still hadn't been unpacked, but he didn't really have much need for Cylus's potions in his day-to-day life. He was struck by a notion; he hadn't asked Cylus about their problem. Feeling revived and almost hopeful, he got up and rummaged around for the rest of his clothes. He toyed with the idea of waking Ren but decided not to. If Cylus was as clueless as Estelle, he certainly didn't want to bring Ren along with him. No need to dash his hopes any more than necessary. He scribbled a note on a scrap of paper and left it on the table next to him.

'Eh, laddie! Not seen you 'bout in a while,' exclaimed Cylus as he opened the door, dry bread crumbling from his mouth.

'I've not been about. Can I come in?' Killian asked.

' 'Course,' said Cylus. He chewed and swallowed. 'You didn't say you were going away.'

'I'm pretty sure I did,' said Killian, deadpan, as he walked into the cave.

'I must be gettin' forgetful.'

'Either that or you're an ignorant old git.'

'Eh?'

'Forget it.'

'Drink?' Cylus offered.

'Bit early.'

'Tea, I mean tea. What d'you think I am?' Cylus laughed as he ran his finger across the many earrings that adorned his large fleshy ears.

'An alcoholic,' said Killian. 'Go on then, my throat's parched.'

As Cylus went off to the kitchen, Killian surveyed his surroundings. As always, it was a mess. Strange-coloured liquids in bottles were everywhere. There were papers full of notes, hairy half-eaten sandwiches and empty cups scattered about. Bunches of herbs hung from a long bar over the hearth, their fresh, tangy scent overruling the usual frowsty smell of Cylus's home. A collection of fungi reclined lazily before the smouldering fire, basking in its heat. On the table in front of him was a strange bottle, tall and thin with a kink in the neck. Varying shades of purple swirled in the liquid whenever the sunlight caught it.

'Somethin' to eat too?' Cylus called from the kitchen.

'No thanks, just a drink's fine,' Killian answered hastily, glancing at a moulding chicken leg and half expecting it to crawl towards him.

'Suit yourself.'

Killian put his hand on the bottle. Its surface was smooth and cold to the touch; it felt good against his skin. He pursed his lips and narrowed his eyes thoughtfully as he gazed at the violets, mauves, plums and lilacs.

He wandered over to the couch, the one he'd slept on the night he met Ren, and slumped down. It creaked aggressively and tossed a cloud of dust on him in protest. He wiped his trousers and put his feet up on the small round table in front of him. With a restful sigh, he wrapped his arms around his head and looked towards the broken full-length mirror on the far wall, its shards still clinging desperately to the bulky wooden frame. Something warm slopped onto his foot, drawing his attention away from his multiple reflections. He glanced down to see Cylus attempting to cram a mug between his feet. He could have moved them, but the moment had passed. Instead, he rocked his head to the ceiling and pretended he hadn't noticed while he waited for Cylus to finish with his crockery and foot arrangement.

'So,' said Cylus, sitting down on a rickety chair and cradling a mug without a handle with both hands. 'What brings you here?'

Killian explained the situation from the beginning. He told Cylus of Ren and his plight, of Lily and the pirates and, most importantly, of the island and the statues.

'So you see,' he concluded, 'we're a bit screwed. Any ideas? For my sake as much as Ren's – his miserable face is driving me insane. I swear if I hear one more exaggerated sigh of despair from him, I'll be the next person buying poison from you, and I won't be needing the antidote.'

'Ha! Feeling a bit guilty, are we?'

'No, why should I?' said Killian shortly. For someone who spent most of their time drunk, alone or both, Cylus could be irritatingly perceptive. 'I need to do this or I won't get my payment, and I've already made plans for that cash. In fact, if anything, he owes me more. I saved his bloody life. That must be worth something.' He took a swig from the cup; it was chipped, and the tea tasted more of unwashed pottery and slightly sour milk than anything else. 'And he's still not thanked me for that, the ungrateful cretin.'

'Not everyone knows how to say thanks,' said Cylus, slurping from his cup as if to make a point.

'You'd think a Chazzer would though,' Killian grunted, ignoring Cylus's thinly veiled gibe. The tea, if it could be called that, deserved no thanks. He took another courtesy sip before placing it around the side of the couch, out of sight.

'So it's all about the money with you, eh?' asked Cylus.

Killian turned his head to the side. He took a silver coin from his pocket and rolled it across his knuckles. 'I don't know. Yes.' He sighed. 'I suppose I do feel sorry for the little nob as well.'

'You're not as nasty as you make out,' said Cylus.

'Maybe . . . maybe I just want to . . .' Killian couldn't finish his sentence. He turned to Cylus. 'But I didn't come here to talk about me, as fascinating as I am. Can you help us or not?'

'Lad, you shoulda told me where you were going. Could've saved you the trip.'

Killian felt a strange cocktail of frustration, anger and hope combine within him. 'I—forget it. What do you mean? Is there no way in?'

'No. S'ancient magic. I doubt there's a man alive who could break that spell—'

'Not even a mage?' Killian said. He pocketed the coin and stretched his arms around the back of his head.

'Do you know any mages?'

'Nope.'

'You wanna get caught with one?'

'Nope.'

'There we go then. Anyway, like I said, I doubt any mage, however powerful they might think they are, would be able to break that seal. Not in this day and age. But there may be a way you could cheat.' He narrowed his eyes, which became lost in wrinkles and a mass of wiry eyebrows. 'Ever heard of the Demon's Drop?'

'The Demon's Drop,' repeated Killian thoughtfully.

'Some call it the Hole in the Sea, or just the Drop.'

'I've heard of it in stories. Mum used to tell me about it,' said Killian, puzzled. 'Isn't it supposed to be down in the south?'

'Ain't supposed to be. It *is* in the south.'

'It's just a myth,' replied Killian. He was wasting his time here. He glanced at the vile cup of tea lingering by the couch.

'Rubbish!' snapped Cylus, making Killian jump. 'Ain't no myth, lad! It's there, a gigantic circular waterfall in the middle of the ocean.'

Killian stared at Cylus. 'All right, if there is a gigantic circular waterfall in the middle of the ocean, why is there still an ocean? Surely it would have all disappeared down the hole by now.'

'That's where the geyser comes in.'

Killian groaned. This was becoming tedious. 'Oh, the geyser, of course,' he said, unable to disguise the cynical tone in his voice.

'Aye,' Cylus continued despite the waning attention of his audience. 'It fires the water that falls down the hole back out.'

'You seem to know a lot about this, Cylus,' said Killian.

'I do have other interests besides saving your dyin' friends,' Cylus replied.

Killian nodded slowly. He watched Cylus slurp away the remains of his tea and wondered if the man knew what a real cup tasted like.

'All right, let's say you've convinced me and there's a hole in the sea. What's that gotta do with anything?'

'Beneath the hole lives a race of strange creatures skilled in the mystic arts,' Cylus said. Killian gave a sarcastic groan, but Cylus proceeded with his story. 'These creatures are capable of magic more powerful than you could imagine. Few have travelled down the Demon's Drop, seeking their power and wisdom. Only one has ever returned to my knowledge.'

'That sounds about right. Throwing yourself off a waterfall isn't the safest of pastimes, but a waterfall in the middle of the sea? You're not gonna come back from that in one piece,' Killian said.

'True, you could drown or get crushed, and there must be plenty of shipwrecks that'll slice you to ribbons. But if you live through that, the rewards will be rich.'

'How do you know all this?' Killian asked.

'Years ago I knew a guy called Eros, and we did some travelling. He was a powerful mage, obsessed with the idea of going down the Drop. He thought whatever was down there could make him stronger. I told him not to go, but he didn't listen to me. He went down, and I waited for him, hidin' in a cave on that geyser. A day went by, and I was convinced he was dead. Then he returned with nothing. He wasn't worthy of their magic. He was livid. He'd tried to fight them, but they were too powerful, so he legged it. After that we drifted apart. He weren't no fun anymore.'

'How did he make it down and back again without dying?'

'He used the wind to help him – almost killed him, but he did it. He was unconscious for most of our trip back. Come to think of it, I never saw him wield magic again after that, not even a little gust. Must 'ave burnt him out permanently. Shame you can't do nothing like that.'

'A real shame. Just as well I have Raven and Lil,' said Killian.

'So, you'll send the demon or a pirate down to do your job?' Cylus frowned.

'I'd rather not send either. I'd rather not go to this fucking hole, but it looks like I don't have a choice,' said Killian. 'See, Cylus, you managed to convince me it's real. Well done. Anyway, Raven and Lily. I've seen what both of them can do, and they can survive just about anything, so I'd gladly hand my job over to them.'

'Wasn't Ren sent to find you?' asked Cylus.

'Yeah, and I'm sure he'll still pay me if they go instead.'

'That's not what I was gettin' at. I thought Ren was sent to find you – not Rothbone, not Raven, but you.'

'That's a minor technicality,' said Killian, waving away his comment. 'Don't get pedantic, Cylus. It doesn't suit you.'

Cylus sat forwards, and his chair squeaked with joy. He glared at Killian, his expression cold. 'Eros was denied, probably because he was a power-hungry bastard. I doubt they'd look too highly on a pirate or a demon either.'

'And if I made it there still breathing, who's to say they won't tell me where to go too?' said Killian. 'What's your point?'

'You got a better chance than either of them, and besides, Ren was sent to find you. His dad sent him to you,' he said seriously. 'You ain't that bad, you know.'

Killian hung his head. Why did everything have to get so complicated? He couldn't deny that Cylus had a valid point. Ren had been sent to him, but surely a suicidal leap of faith wasn't the answer. He didn't want to die; he really didn't want to die. 'So you're suggesting that I throw myself head first into certain death?' he said without looking up.

'I'm tellin' you that you're the one who's gonna help Ren.'

'And by doing that I risk my life? Cylus, you've made some sick jokes in your time, but this?'

'Fine then, you win! If that's the way you feel, get rid of the boy and carry on with your life knowin' that you've failed the only person who's ever asked for your help. Oh, and you'll be skint too, a skint failure. How's that sound to ya?'

'Don't put it like that.'

'It's the truth,' said Cylus bluntly.

Killian pressed himself into the couch and glared at his feet. It wasn't just the money that motivated him, and he knew it, but admitting that to himself was hard enough; he could never voice it. Redemption was being offered to him on a silver platter, and all he had to do was risk his life. He grunted in his throat.

'All right,' he said slowly. 'Suppose there's something wrong with me, as in mentally, and I do see your point, and as a result I leap to what could well be my death. What the hell do I do when I'm down there?'

'That, lad, I don't know. Eros never found out. They just said no, right from the off. Suppose they just give you something, perhaps.' Cylus shook his head. 'Come to think of it, probably best not to mention Eros to them.'

Killian pressed his lips together so firmly they started to sting. He chewed the inside of his mouth while he pondered the option Cylus had given him. 'Reckon I'll die?' he asked.

'Nah, you'll be fine, lad,' Cylus said with a wink.

'That's comforting,' muttered Killian.

Killian headed back to his flat before going to see Lily; he wanted Ren to hear the 'good' news as soon as possible. He turned the key in the lock and entered. It was dark inside. Ren still hadn't opened the curtains – another of the annoying habits Killian had come to detest.

'Thorncliffe?' Killian called out as he walked around letting the daylight in.

The flat was small and cosy. Surprisingly, it wasn't a cluttered place. As messy and careless as Killian was, he kept his flat in some kind of order. This was mainly due to not having many things in the first place. He checked the couch in the lounge and found it had been vacated; perhaps Ren was in the bathroom.

'Thorny?' he said softly against the door. There was no response. 'You in there?' he asked.

Once again, his question was greeted with silence. Feeling somewhat concerned for Ren's well-being, Killian opened the door and prepared himself for anything he might find. Much to his relief, Ren wasn't inside.

Outside, the clock tower chimed twelve. He'd taken longer than he thought to walk to Cylus's and back. He slung his coat on and was about to leave in search of Ren when his stomach growled. Ren was big enough to look after himself for an hour or so.

He lit the stove, ready to make himself a pan of porridge. As he mixed the oats and milk, he pondered what Cylus had said. It sounded plausible, or at least Cylus had been good at making it sound plausible. Anyway, it wasn't like he had another option; there was no way in. This was the only way – throwing himself into certain death.

He transferred the porridge to a bowl and carried it and a pot of honey over to the couch. Slumping down, he brought his legs up under him. If he did this for Ren, not only would it redeem him, but it'd also give his life purpose, meaning. He wouldn't be just a card-playing swindler – this would prove it to everyone and, most importantly, to himself. He balanced his breakfast on his thighs and dripped a spoonful of honey into it. As he twisted the spoon, creating intricate designs on the surface of the porridge, his thoughts drifted to Estelle. He wasn't going to tell her – he couldn't tell her; she'd only go out of her mind with worry. He didn't like to keep secrets from her, but it was better than lying to her. If she found out what he was planning, she'd probably tie him up, gag him and lock him away out of sight until everything had blown over. He'd tell her when he got back. If he got back.

A cold wind whistled through the streets, and Killian shoved his hands into his armpits. Without the market it was a quiet and peaceful little town. Some quayside workers drifted about, their heavy boots clipping on the cobbles. Colonies of seagulls clustered together on the dark slate rooftops, chattering amongst one another. The scent of salt and seaweed wafted on the breeze, but it was tainted by an underlying rotten stench that could only mean the tide was low.

He'd given Brackmouth a good half-hour patrol, but there was no sign of Ren. He'd avoided checking Estelle's; he didn't think he could bring himself to outright lie to her face. If he didn't see her, he wouldn't have to lie. There was one other place Ren could be, though Killian was doubtful. Ren wasn't exactly the tavern-dwelling type. He rounded the corner and looked at the wooden sign creaking above him. The painting of the chortling swan wearing an orange-and-blue jester's hat never failed to make him smile.

'Hey, Rubes!' he called out as he walked into the Laughing Swan.

'Killian, what'll it be?' Ruby asked. She beamed at him from behind the bar.

'Nothing. I'd lost something, but I think I've found it,' he said, walking towards Ren's comatose body.

'Ah, yes.' She frowned. 'He's had quite a few.'

'More than one?'

Ruby giggled.

Ren's mouth hung open; a thin stream of saliva dripped out and oozed all over his jacket. Quiet rhythmical snores drifted from his gaping maw. He stank of stale alcohol and unwashed clothes. What a disgrace.

'Do you think you can take him away?' Ruby said.

'Sure,' said Killian. 'Thorncliffe.' He poked Ren firmly in the shoulder.

Ren didn't stir, so Killian changed his pokes to shakes. He grabbed Ren's arm and yanked it, calling his name at the same time, but his eyes didn't even flicker.

'He's out cold,' said Ruby, coming out from behind the bar. 'But I do have a cure for that.'

'You do?'

She picked up a jug of water. 'Sorry, Ren,' she said without a shred of sincerity.

She tipped it up, pouring the contents all over Ren's face. Ren's eyes instantly sprang open. His arms flailed about in the air, and he fell off the back of his chair. He hit the floor hard and lay on his back for a few seconds before sitting bolt upright.

'I'm drowning!' he gasped, terrified.

Ren sat on the flagstones, shivering in a puddle of cold water. He looked up at Killian and Ruby from under a mass of limp hair.

'I'm wet,' he said pathetically, 'and cold.'

Killian snorted a laugh; Ren looked so pitifully bedraggled. Ruby stood above him with her hands on her hips.

'Ru—' Ren managed to say.

'You're a nasty drunk! You know that?' she snapped.

Ren hung his head like a scolded child and said nothing.

'What's he done?' asked Killian.

'He's been a vile brat,' she said. 'The nob called me a

harlot. Can you believe that? I was being nice, and he threw it all back at me. He can't take his drink. It's pathetic.'

'Thorncliffe,' said Killian, glaring at him. 'Don't be a nob to my friends.'

'I'm sorry, Killian,' he mumbled, lowering himself to the floor.

'It's not me you should be saying that to.'

'I'm sorry, Ruby,' he said, lifting his head to look at her. 'I'm really sorry. I'm not normally like this. I was brought up better.'

She crouched next to him and put a hand on his shoulder. 'Thank you, Thorncliffe. I suppose I can forgive you.'

'Thank you,' he mumbled.

'Come on,' said Killian, reaching down and pulling Ren to his feet. 'Let's get you out of here. You're making the place look a mess.'

CHAPTER
FIFTEEN

KILLIAN UNCEREMONIOUSLY DUMPED REN ON the couch. The young man landed face down in the soft cushions and groaned.

'I feel wretched,' he moaned.

'I'm not surprised.' Killian removed his coat, tossing it over the chair to his right.

Ren groaned again.

'Do you want me to feel sorry for you or something?' Killian asked, still angry about his treatment of Ruby. Someone with the professed airs and graces of Ren should've known better than to insult a lovely woman like her.

Ren muttered something inaudible into the cushions.

'Because I won't,' he continued. 'All this is self-inflicted, so shut up and deal with it.'

'I know,' Ren grumbled out of the side of the couch. 'But that's why you should feel sorry for me.'

'That makes no sense.'

'It's all your fault.' He rolled over and pointed a wavering finger at Killian.

'My fault,' said Killian, offended. 'How'd you work that out?'

'If you'd done what you were supposed to, I wouldn't be in this mess,' he drawled. 'You were meant to help me. I was told to find you and you'd help me, but you can't because you're useless.'

'You might wanna cut back on the insults, Thorncliffe.' He didn't have to deal with this – he *shouldn't* have to. He should kick him out, send him back to Chazza empty-handed and get on with his life. Maybe he could deal with being a skint failure; after all, he wasn't that hard up anyway – he got by. And yet Ren was his ticket to redemption. He wouldn't be able to live with himself if he passed up this opportunity: save a life to repay a lost one . . . or two. This gave his life purpose and meaning. Did that make him selfish? Was he really the bad guy?

'Everything was for nothing. There's no point anymore.' Ren groaned quietly.

'You're a depressing little man, aren't you, Thorncliffe?' Killian sighed.

'What do you expect? Everything's gone now. I've failed, you've failed, it's all empty and hollow. No point.'

'Come on, it's not that bad.'

'You wouldn't understand,' he said bitterly. 'I love my father. It's impossible for you to know what that feels like.'

Killian bunched his fists, took a deep breath and spoke calmly. 'I still love my mum, and it's been over twenty years since I lost her. I know what it feels like to lose someone you care about, and I'm gonna fix it so you don't have to.'

'Killian, I . . .' Ren mumbled. 'How?'

Killian rubbed his face and ran his fingers through his hair. Dredging up painful memories was never a good idea. He worked so hard to keep them buried. Whenever he let them resurface it was like a punch to the gut. Hopefully, when all this was over, he'd be able to face the past without the pain. He dropped his arms to his sides and banished the sullen expression from his face.

'I've sorted it,' he said simply.

'What?'

'I've found a way in.'

'Really? How? Tell me,' Ren exclaimed, rolling over and propping himself up on his arms as if he'd already forgotten his previous disgrace.

'While you were out drowning your sorrows and staring hopelessly into the void, I was doing some research,' Killian announced proudly. 'I saw old Cylus Turner. He told me there's a way to get in.'

'Cylus?' muttered Ren.

'Yes, and don't interrupt.' Killian flopped down onto a chair and rested his feet on the table, deliberately keeping Ren in suspense as punishment for his actions. 'You heard of the Demon's Drop?'

Ren nodded meekly.

'Well, under it lives a race of creatures. Cylus said they can help. We just need to get there and go down.'

Ren stared at Killian, his eyebrows raised and his mouth hanging open. 'You sound ridiculous,' he said.

'Take it or leave it. It's the only option.'

'It made you look stupid too.' Ren rolled over as if all the hope had been sucked from him once more.

Killian slid his legs off the table and stood up. He glared at the back of Ren's head and gallantly fought off the overwhelming desire to punch it. 'Listen, you ungrateful little cretin,' he seethed through clenched teeth. 'Cylus knows what he's talking about.' *I think.*

Ren stayed silent.

'He's been there,' Killian continued. 'He watched somebody go down and come back. The creatures are real. It's all real. Put it this way – do we have any other choice?'

Again he was faced with silence.

'I don't know why I bother.' Killian shook his head. 'I'm starting to wonder whether your cash is worth all this bloody hassle.'

'I'm sorry.' Ren's voice was low and tinged with regret. 'You're right, we don't have a choice.'

'Thank you,' said Killian, feeling smugly satisfied. 'Before you ask, I'll go,' he added, almost as if it were a blasé afterthought. 'You were sent to find me. Maybe this is the way I help you.'

Ren turned to face him, his eyes wide. 'You can't do that,' he spluttered. 'You'll die.'

'We'll just have to wait and see, won't we?' said Killian, shrugging. He swept his coat from the chair and slipped it on. 'I'd better go and see the pirate then, eh?'

'Killian, wait for me,' said Ren weakly. He moved to get up but collapsed onto the couch again. 'The world won't stop spinning.'

'You stay here. The state you're in, I doubt she'd agree to take you anywhere.'

The door opened, and for at least half a second Lily looked pleased to see him. Her eyes shimmered, and a smile even threatened to take up residence; however, it was soon beaten into submission by a hard grimace.

'Killian, to what do I owe the pleasure?' From her tone, it sounded like his presence was anything but pleasurable. 'Come in.'

Killian strode in. The first thing that hit him was the fresh smell of perfume. It was light, breezy and didn't quite fit with the stern look on Lily's face. The room was very much like her room on the ship but larger and more lavishly decorated. A thick red rug covered the floor, and the walls were smoothly plastered and painted white. Her bed, all dark mahogany and silky red sheets, took up a large portion of the room. Behind it, as on the ship, was a sprawling window. The glass reached down to the floor, and there was a door on the left leading out to a half-moon balcony. Taking up most of the wall space was a gigantic painting, a night-time countryside scene. A snaking silvery river cut through a beautiful landscape of fields and forests, the night sky full of glowing stars cleverly reflected in the water. Its style closely resembled the one in her room on the *Tempest*.

'Pretty, isn't it?' Lily remarked.

'It's not bad. Reminds me of the one on your ship,' said Killian. 'Where'd you steal them from?' he added.

'I didn't steal them from anywhere,' she said sharply. 'Raven painted them.'

'A man of many talents,' he huffed. He shifted his gaze to her more mundane writing desk, its surface choked from view by heaps of books and rolls of parchment.

'He is indeed, but I'm sure you didn't come over here to talk about my painfully handsome, artistic first mate.'

'No, I didn't,' said Killian, trying to salvage his dignity.

'Well, out with it then.'

'I've got an idea.'

Lily looked at him and raised a quizzical eyebrow.

'No need for that condescending look,' he said flatly.

'I wasn't giving you a condescending look.'

'You were.' He glared at her.

'Does it matter?'

Killian didn't dignify her with an answer and instead launched into the tale Cylus had told him. He looked at her after he'd finished. She was staring at him with disbelief written all over her face.

'Killian, are you feeling all right?' she asked with a smirk. 'Are you sure you didn't smash your head a bit too hard on the island? You've not been drinking, have you?'

'I knew you'd react like that.' He folded his arms sulkily.

'Little absurd, don't you think?'

'Yes,' he agreed, 'but so are walking stone statues, a woman who can't be hurt and a man who can leap hundreds of feet in the air.'

Lily was silenced. She sat down on the edge of her bed and drummed her fingers on her knee.

'So what you're suggesting is that I round my crew up and we all set sail, again, to possibly the least ship-friendly place on the planet, so someone can jump overboard and converse with the magical pixies at the bottom of the sea?'

Frustration mounted within him. He composed himself before speaking again. 'Yes. That's exactly what I'm saying.'

Lily looked at him and chuckled, which sent another pulse of irritation through him. She always managed to find some petty way to grind him down.

'I can't believe this. This is ridiculous,' she muttered, shaking her head and standing up. 'So.' She put her hands on her hips, a patronising smile smeared all over her lips. 'What idiot is going down when we get there?'

'Me.'

Lily's smile melted immediately. He'd known she would expect him to shower her with praise and ask her to go, or at the very least ask to borrow Raven and his many talents. Nominating himself was showing her a different side to him, a side he often kept guarded behind a wall of shrugs, smirks and winks. He waited as she stared at him, her eyes searching his.

'You could die,' she said.

'I don't care about that.'

'And neither do I, but what I do care about is inside that temple. If you die, I won't get what's mine, what's owed to me. What a waste of my time and effort that'll be, which is why Raven or I should jump down there. You'll die. We won't. End of.'

'That's not it. It's . . .' He paused. He had to make it sound as if it were his idea all along. He inwardly cringed as he spoke – mawkish sentiment wasn't usually in his repertoire. 'For once in my life I feel like I have a purpose, like I can do something worthwhile.'

'You're doing it for a wedge of cash, aren't you?'

'Well, yes, that too,' Killian said, hoping it wouldn't lessen the impact of what he was saying. 'But Thorny and I have a deal. I help him, he pays me.'

'And you've helped him. Now we can take over.'

'No,' said Killian firmly. He needed Lily on his side, and telling her that she couldn't go because the sea pixies would most likely turn their noses up at her and send her packing probably wouldn't end with her agreeing and lending her ship and crew. 'Out of all the people in the world, Thorncliffe was sent to find me – *me*. If he'd been sent to find you or Raven, then fair enough, but he wasn't. I think there's a reason for that.'

'Maybe you've played your part.'

'And what was that? To fleece him of all his money and then almost get him killed five minutes after he set foot in town?'

He'd backed her into a corner, and he knew there was only one way out. He patiently waited as she collected her thoughts, allowing his gaze to once again rove around her room. Breathing deep, he took in her scent; it filled him with a familiar comfort.

'All right,' she said eventually. 'I'll sort out the crew. Be here at sunrise the day after tomorrow, with Ren.'

'You'll see I'm right.'

'Killian . . .' She paused, folded her arms and hardened her glare. 'This better not be another waste of my time and resources.'

'It won't be,' Killian said confidently.

'If you die down there, it bloody well will be.'

'Well, I'm not gonna die, so don't worry about it.'

'I'm not worried,' she replied a little too quickly. 'Now out. I've stuff to do.'

CHAPTER
SIXTEEN

K ILLIAN HAD NO SYMPATHY FOR REN, WHO WAS
curled into a tight ball on the deck and clearly still
hung-over from his drinking binge two days pre-
viously. The gut-churning sway of the ship probably wasn't helping his delicate stomach either.

'Best off lying flat,' said Finn.

'Sorry?' asked Ren feebly.

'If you're feeling shit, lie flat on your back. It'll help.'

Ren did as he was told, stretching himself out along
the deck, which unfortunately left him open to the full onslaught of the rain. He shifted himself as close to the body of
the ship as possible in a pathetic attempt to escape the wet
and closed his dark-ringed eyes.

'You're a mess.' Tom grinned, his peridot eyes obscured
by a large pair of goggles.

Ren made a weak groan in response.

'Where'd you get those from?' Killian demanded from under his sodden hair.

'My pocket,' drawled Tom.

'You're a dick.' Killian scowled, glaring at Tom and folding his arms slowly. He immediately unfolded them as his wet clothes pressed uncomfortably against his cold skin.

Tom beamed, gladly accepting the insult as a compliment.

'They're for when it's pissin' it down,' Finn grunted. 'Helps you see where you're going.'

'They help you see underwater too,' added Blake, his face hidden within the hood of his dark purple cloak. 'Actually, you could probably do with a pair, considering where you're going.'

'Brilliant,' Killian grumbled back.

'I'll go and find you some.' Without another word, he paced away and disappeared behind the mainmast.

'Bastard!' exclaimed Tom as Blake left.

'What?' Killian asked, deadpan. He didn't really care about what had irritated Tom and instantly regretted asking him.

'I was gonna go,' Tom groaned. 'I'm so bloody bored.'

'Cut your damn moanin',' growled Finn. She was hunched over, shielding her roll-up from the driving elements. Her mousey-brown hair hung loose and glistened like a wet sheet over her back. She wore her bandana, as usual, but the rain had fused her fringe to it. 'I ain't puttin' up with weeks and weeks of your bitching.'

'Come on,' Tom groused. 'What's not to moan about? It's raining, it's horrible. I'm cold and wet. Surely that's a bad omen.'

Killian shuddered at that thought. Ordinarily he wasn't bothered by talk of superstitions, but something about the thought of throwing himself to what could easily be his doom was bringing out a strange side of him. He didn't like it; he was usually in control of his own thoughts and emotions. *It's raining today. That doesn't mean I'm gonna die in a few weeks.* His stomach tensed. He could die, he could easily die. Drown, bleed to death, be crushed . . .

'Only thing bad about it is your bloody whingin',' Finn snapped, thankfully interrupting Killian's morbid thoughts. 'Tell you what, Tom, when you're like this, you grate me like a tub o'bairns.'

Tom rocked back onto his soaking cannon and turned towards Killian. 'So,' he said, grinning at him, droplets of water dripping from his nose. 'You really gonna chuck yourself down the Drop?'

'Yep,' said Killian, not caring to elaborate. He drew his knees into his chest and wrapped his arms about them, hoping Tom would take the hint. He didn't want to talk; he especially didn't want to talk about his imminent death. Casting his gaze to the wet deck, he watched the bloated raindrops as they exploded on impact. It wasn't imminent; he wasn't going to die. He couldn't think like that. He had to stay positive, but the odds of survival – his shoulders locked – were slim. How had he ended up in this ridiculous situation? His desire for money and an easy life, his pathetic quest for self-worth, his need to prove he was more than just a card-playing swindler. It was as if his mind were conspiring against him, and there was nothing he could do about it.

'You're mental!' blurted Tom.

'Thanks,' Killian muttered robotically.

'You should send Raven or the cap'n,' Tom said, pressing on. He was either oblivious to or didn't care about Killian's discomfort.

'Nope.'

Tom chuckled. 'You're insane, in a good way . . . sort of.'

'Thanks.'

'I couldn't do it. For what it's worth, I think you're equal parts brave and mental.'

'Thanks,' Killian mumbled again, wishing Tom would close the subject.

'I've had enough,' grumbled Finn, crushing her soggy roll-up in her fist. 'I'm going below deck for a nap. With any luck someone'll have cut off his flappin' mouth by the time I get back.'

'Don't go, Finn,' Tom pleaded. 'What if something mad kicks off?'

Finn flicked her wet fringe.

'You know, we might get attacked, and you'd miss it all if you were asleep.'

'Thomas, can you even remember the last time we were attacked?'

Tom's blank expression answered Finn's question.

'Exactly,' she said, her point proven. 'And even if we were, which we won't be, I think I'd wake up for it.'

'Ah, but Finn, what if—'

'One more word from your gaping muller and I'll punch your tongue into the back of your skull.' With that, Finn turned on her heel and left them.

'Is she all right?' Killian asked as he watched Finn clomp away.

'Ah, don't worry about her. She won't admit it, but she hates the rain more than a girl in a white blouse,' said Tom. He ran his hand over his shaved head and grinned sleazily to himself.

Blake trudged up to the dwindling group, keeping one hand on his hood as he hunched his shoulders into the driving rain.

'Here you go,' he said, handing a pair of goggles to Killian.

'Cheers,' said Killian.

They had a thick brown leather strap, which could be adjusted by a large buckle on the back. The eyeholes were oval pieces of glass set into the leather and backed with rubber seals. He put them on. The rubber felt slimy against his skin, and the leather was smooth and worn. They smelt fusty from age, but it was the tart smell of the black rubber that was the most overpowering. He fiddled about with the buckle, trying to get the right fit. After a few size changes he got them to sit comfortably on his face.

'They take a bit of getting used to,' said Blake. 'And don't worry about the smell. The wetter they get, the more it fades.'

'And you'll be getting them pretty wet,' added Tom.

'I found some for Ren too.' Blake glanced at Ren's still body.

'Thank you,' Ren croaked, his eyes opening to thin slits.

'It's awake?' Tom gasped.

Ren shuffled to a seated position, leaning his back against the quarterdeck for support. 'I've not been asleep. I've been . . . drifting.' His shoulders slumped, and his body trembled, his breathing coming out in short sharp bursts.

'How're you feeling?' Killian asked.

'Terrible.'

'Here,' said Blake, offering him the goggles.

Ren took them with a trembling hand, unable to hide a wince as his fingers grazed the slippery leather. He thanked Blake politely and rammed them into his coat.

'Where's Finn gone?' Blake asked.

'Nap,' Tom said, pulling his goggles down around his neck and spitting in them. 'Had enough of the rain.' He rubbed the inside with the corner of his coat and put them back over his eyes.

'Getting out the rain doesn't sound like a bad idea,' said Killian.

'Yeah,' Blake agreed. 'Why exactly are we sat out here?'

Tom sat up straight and stared at Blake. 'In case anything happens. You never know what will happen at sea,' he added, lowering his voice in an effort to seem mysterious.

'You're forgetting that I do know what happens at sea,' replied Blake. 'We get cold, wet, bored and miserable, and then . . . nothing happens. Sorry, lads, but I'm going below deck with Finn.'

'Oh, aye!' said Tom, giving Killian a nudge. Killian brushed him off. He was freezing, soaking and quite possibly heading to his death, so he was certainly not in the mood for Tom's awful attempt at a joke.

Blake turned to leave.

Tom quickly grabbed his arm as he went by. 'What if something happens?' he protested. 'We'll need to sound the alarm.'

'Why do you think we have Raven up there?' said Blake, shaking him off. 'He's not there for decoration. I'm cold, wet and tired, and I'm going below deck. I'll see you lot later.'

Killian looked up at Tom, and without saying a word he got to his feet.

'Not you too,' moaned Tom.

Taking this as a cue to leave, Ren heaved himself up. He tottered backwards, putting his arms out to keep steady.

'Ren, come on. Don't you want adventure and excitement?' said Tom.

'Erm, a little, I suppose. But I don't want to miss them by getting ill from sitting outside in the rain.'

'Ah, you're all too soft.' Tom groaned and slid off the cannon to join them.

They traipsed along the sodden deck, past groups of bedraggled, drenched sailors. Killian watched them as they pulled ropes this way and that, fiddled with knots and pulleys and glared at the sky accusingly, grunting words to one another. He strained to hear what they were saying over the patter of the rain and the breaking waves, but it was impossible. Most of them were wearing goggles to keep the lashing rain out of their eyes. He was impressed that Lily had chosen to fit her crew out with them. It was a simple yet effective solution to working in the elements. The ship dipped, and he staggered slightly.

They approached the companionway at the centre of the ship. It was covered by a wooden awning, saving the stairs from the worst of the rain. Before going down, Killian glanced up at the crow's nest. He could just make out Raven's dark silhouette against the livid skies.

The first level was lined with cannons. They were set up in pairs with a store of cannonballs sandwiched between. The distinct scent of gunpowder mixed with sweat and weather-worn timber lingered on the clammy air. A low murmur of voices drifted around the wooden interior. The pirates seemed to treat this room almost like a common room. Those who weren't battling the elements out on deck or resting in their hammocks were gathered amongst the cannons, playing cards or dice around piles of coins. Killian noticed the playing circle closest to him shrink as soon as his presence was noted, and he smiled to himself. Out of the corner of his eye he saw Finn swiftly duck down.

'I'm gonna hang about in here for a bit,' Tom announced, eyeing up a rather tense game of dice. He removed his goggles and stuffed them in his pocket.

Killian was sure he heard a forlorn moan drift out from Finn's bolt-hole.

'Right then, I'm off for a wander. I didn't look around before,' said Killian. 'I may as well soak up all the glorious sights,' he added sarcastically.

'I'll stay here. It's close to the deck, and I still feel delicate,' admitted Ren. His pallid skin and sunken eyes suggested he was feeling more than delicate.

'I bet you do.' Tom grinned. 'It's nice that you've recovered enough to keep water down.'

'Yes,' said Ren, shuddering.

'You off to harass the cap'n then?' Tom asked.

'No,' Killian replied flatly.

'Don't lie,' he said, giving Killian a seamy wink. 'I know exactly what you meant by *glorious sights.*'

'Tom, I'd rather gouge my eyes out with salt-laden spikes than be in the same room as that woman.'

'All right, all right.' He backed away defensively. 'You've made your point. See you later.'

Killian carefully picked his way through the clusters of pirates intently gambling and made his way to the ladder at the far end of the room. As he wandered past Finn's hiding place he glanced down at her. She caught his eye and curled her lip, and Killian responded with a sympathetic head shake. He clambered down the ladder to the lower deck. This level, for the most part, was the sleeping quarters, though it wasn't filled with rows and rows of hammocks like standard vessels. Crewmates were in rooms of four to six, which offered more privacy and comfort. Lily must have redesigned it at some point. He was impressed by her ingenuity.

He tiptoed down a long corridor – notched doors leading to the crew cabins on either side – one hand running along the rail to keep his balance amid the constant lurching of the ship. Snores drifted through the closed doors, but the majority of the rooms were empty. When he reached the other end, he took another ladder down to the next level. The acidic smell of gunpowder easily overpowered the briny aroma of the waves down here. Killian ambled along. The air was surprisingly dry considering how close to the water he was. He walked past a large wooden door held closed by a thick bar of timber tinted green from dried-on algae.

He heard a noise from farther along the corridor, followed by a string of curses so tightly packed that they merged into one. Curious, he proceeded along the ship to investigate. The noise had come from behind a small door. He knocked.

'Yes,' shouted a flustered voice. 'Come in!'

'All right?' he said as he walked in.

'Pissin' rat!' the cook hissed. He was standing in the middle of the room holding a pan above his head.

Killian scanned the floor for a sign of the offending creature. It's long worm-like tail poked out from behind a deflated sack of flour in the corner of the room. He put his finger to his lips to silence the cook. He bent his knees and slowly crept towards the unsuspecting rodent, angling his body to hide his shadow. Carefully, he removed one of his swords as he approached his prey. He stood poised, his blade glinting in the warm glow of the kitchen. Quick as a cobra, he struck, impaling the creature with one smooth, precise movement. It let out a squeak of alarm before falling limp on the end of his sword.

'Oh, well done, well done, very impressive,' said the cook, clapping.

'No problem,' Killian replied and went to deposit the corpse in the bin.

'Oi! What you doin'? I need that!'

'Really?'

'Yeah! To go with weevils on toast!'

'Ah.' Killian glanced to his left.

The cook roared with laughter. 'Your face! Don't worry, I'm just tuggin' your mams.' Killian joined in, although not entirely sure what had just been said. The cook blinked away his tears of jollity and wiped his eye with the back of his hand. 'You're even better than Rangi.'

'Rangi?' Killian asked as he shook the dead animal from his sword.

'My cat. She's out in the bilge, many more rats in there,' he explained. 'Seth,' he added, holding out his hand and grinning broadly, 'the cook, but you probably guessed that.'

Killian shook Seth's hand; he had a firm grip, which was somewhat at odds with his slender frame. Seth's skin was a deep golden brown, and his hair – a great wiry black mess – stuck out a good distance from his head and was held in place by a bright green bandana. Clusters of painted wooden beads were threaded through clumps of his hair.

'So, you're the reason we're off on this . . . endeavour?' asked Seth.

'Sort of. Sorry about that.'

'Don't be. It's good to get out and about. We been on dry land for so long I was beginnin' to wonder if these pirates still 'ad their sea legs, you know?' Seth joked, his mouth cutting a huge grin across his face.

He handed Killian a small shot of something. 'For killing that damn rat for me. Were pissin' me right off,' he said, thoughtfully scratching the scar on the left side of his face.

Killian downed the fiery liquid and coughed as soon as he drew breath.

'Good?' Seth beamed as he filled one for himself. 'Warms you right up. You drink too much, you lose half your sight.' He burst out laughing and tapped the red-and-orange patch that covered his left eye.

'Yeah,' Killian managed to choke out between fumy coughs. 'Caught me off guard.'

'S'from old Seth's special store – don't you be telling no one about it.'

'Got it. So are you the cook, or are you third mate? Lily's left-hand man or something?' Killian asked, eyeing Seth with slight suspicion.

'What d'you mean?' asked Seth, frowning.

'Nothing,' said Killian. 'It's just Raven told me he was the lookout, so I thought maybe you were something else too.'

Seth chuckled. 'That's the funniest thing. Raven, he's a funny one. Him and the cap'n are like that.' He held his hand up and crossed his fingers, his bracelets clashing together. 'But I know what you're gettin' at,' he added, narrowing his eye.

Killian shrugged.

'You think just because I cook I can't fight. Well, I tell you this for free: I fight just as good – better – than any of those up there, 'cept Raven. He's one mean fighter. I don't know how he does it. I seen him running along buildings, up the mast, jumpin' so high he makes the birds shit themselves. Some say it's dark magic at work. I don't care myself, no. Just glad he fights with us, know what I'm sayin'? The way he soars in the air, it's like watching an artist at work.' Seth's singular eye glazed over as he wistfully digressed over the many impossible feats of Raven.

'What about you?' asked Killian, interrupting his musings in an attempt to veer the subject away from the miracle man.

'Expert with them.' He pointed over his shoulder. Hanging behind him, crossed over, was a pair of hooked swords. Their long narrow blades were dulled with age, but the sharp edges still gleamed. They curved back on themselves, the ends pointed rather than the usual rounded style. The hilts were wrapped in a yellow material, and each pommel consisted of a collection of feathers, beads, coins and strips of brightly dyed fabric. 'I've taken down men twice my size with both eyes intact without even breaking a sweat. How's that for you?'

'Not bad,' said Killian, unsure if he was being rhetorical.

'I'm more of a pacifist these days, but one day you might be lucky enough to catch Seth in action,' he said proudly. 'What about you anyway? The way you got the rat was beautiful. Also heard you beat on Morton Roberts. Tut, tut, he won't 'ave liked that.'

Killian waved off the compliment. 'I could probably take him down with my hands tied.'

Seth bawled with laughter once again. 'I'd like to see that!'

Killian smiled to himself and glanced at the door. 'I'd better leave you to it.'

'And I'd best get in the bilge and round up some tasty vermin!' He gave him a wink, or was it a blink? Killian couldn't decide. He was about to leave the mess when an idea popped into his head.

He paused in the doorway and turned around. 'You wouldn't know where I could get hold of some paper and ink, would you?'

'I deal in food. Paper and ink is hard to come by on a ship. Reckon the cap'n is your best bet.'

Killian winced. 'Got any salt-laden spikes hanging around?'

'What are you talkin' about?' asked Seth, confused.

'Nothing,' Killian muttered.

'You're a crazy man.' Seth chortled.

CHAPTER
SEVENTEEN

HAVING SPENT THE MORNING BARKING ORDERS at her crew, Lily retired to her cabin for the duration of the afternoon, surrendering control to Raven and Morton. She removed her coat and hat – complete with feather – and hung them on a curvy wooden hat stand. She unbuttoned her doublet, stretched her arms and yawned deeply, appreciating the quiet and solitude. With a flick of her wrist, she tossed the doublet in the direction of her bed as she walked by; it fell short, but she didn't care.

She sat down at the dressing table and stared at her face in the mirror. Dark circles had formed around her eyes, and her hair was a wild windswept mess. She uncorked a slender glass bottle of herb-and-citrus-scented oil and poured two drops into a small bowl of clean water. She swirled it around with her hand, her mind elsewhere as the oil separated into beads and flitted about the surface. Without looking she scooped up some of the liquid in cupped hands and poured it over her face.

She slowly massaged the oils into her skin. For the past two days she'd found it difficult to sleep, lying alone at night in the dark, a deep sense of foreboding keeping her awake. She ran her damp fingers down her neck. It wasn't because she was worried about him; she was definitely *not* worried about him. She didn't care about him. She couldn't and wouldn't – the man was an idiot. She only cared for herself and her crew, nobody else. It must have been the thought of the loot keeping her awake. The mission had to be successful, and in order for that to happen, he had to stay alive. She reached for a towel and patted her skin dry. The reflection staring back at her smiled; the natural glow was returning to her skin.

She picked up a brush and raked it through her dishevelled hair. If he didn't make it, there would be no loot, and he'd be gone. Her stomach clenched at the thought. The whole journey would be for nothing. The only change would be he'd be gone. But would that really be such a bad thing? As she finished removing the last stubborn knot, a knock sounded at her cabin door, and she jumped slightly. The brush stuck on the knot. She tried to force it through, but it wouldn't budge. Invulnerability came at a price – difficult hair. Hissing curses, she removed her ring, a thick silver band in the shape of a crescent moon coloured with myriad shades of green swirling beneath a layer of glass. The colours had dulled since her encounter with the statue, but they'd be back and as bright as ever with the new moon. They always were.

'Come in,' she called out, wincing as she drove the brush through the afflicted area, snapping and plucking hairs as it went.

The door opened and Raven swooped in, closing it behind him.

'You know,' she said, 'it's a good job I don't have many enemies. If anyone wanted to assassinate me, they'd just have to wait for me to get a haircut.' She put the brush down, smiled and turned to face him, replacing the ring. 'To what do I owe this pleasure?'

'I wanted to make sure you were all right. You seemed depressed.'

'I'm fine, just a little tired.' She yawned, rubbing her eyes for added effect.

'You're worried,' he stated bluntly, taking a step forwards.

She chuckled innocently. 'Me? No, I've nothing to worry about.' She tried to keep her voice light but knew it had come out as instantly defensive.

'I didn't say you were worried about yourself, Lily. I've known you long enough to know when you're brooding.'

She curled her lip and folded her arms tightly across her chest.

'It's all right,' he said comfortingly.

'Maybe I'm a little concerned,' she admitted.

'He could die.'

'I know, and if that happens, there'll be no booty for us. I wish he'd come to his senses and let you or me go instead.'

'Why won't he?'

'Because he's stubborn,' she snapped. 'A stubborn, foolish idiot.'

Raven crossed the room to sit down on the corner of her bed.

'For some reason he has this stupid belief in his own importance in all this. He reckons he has to be the one because Ren was sent to him. He refuses to let you or me do it even though we all know that would be the sensible option.' She noticed Raven's gaze had become lost in the pastel-coloured houses of his own painting and felt a pang of guilt; sometimes his expression could be so sad. 'Have you ever heard of anything so ridiculous?' she added to try to lighten the mood.

Raven's attention turned to her. 'Perhaps he has a point,' he said gently.

'You think?'

'Why else would Ren's father have told him to find Killian? There must be some kind of reasoning behind it.' Raven slowly got to his feet and took a step towards her. 'He was sent to Killian, not you, and not me.'

'Ren's father. Ren's bloody cretin of a father!' Lily stood and paced towards the window. The wind blew back and forth, lashing the panes with icy drizzle. She slammed her warm palms against the cold glass and sneered. 'I can't believe he's going to his death because of the words of someone he's never even met. For all we know he's a raving lunatic, babbling nonsense about magical artefacts and ancient temples.'

'Calm down, Lily. I think it unlikely,' Raven said softly, coming up behind her and placing his hands on her shoulders for reassurance. 'Ren's a sensible boy, and in any case, what he's told us so far has turned out to be true. The temple is there, and it's certainly well protected. There must be something of great significance held within for someone to go to such lengths to contain it.'

She shook her head in irritation. 'The whole thing is absurd,' she growled, turning around, shrugging him off and clomping past him.

'It's all right to be upset, Lily,' he said after her.

'I'm not upset – I'm angry. There's a difference.'

She slumped on the edge of her bed, and her shoulders drooped. Even Raven seemed to be convinced of Killian's role in all of this. Raven was her oldest and most trusted friend; if he believed in Killian, she could too. But what if he was only saying all this to make her feel better? She glanced at him and instantly disregarded that wayward thought. He'd never do anything like that. He wouldn't knowingly allow someone, especially someone he now knew, to throw themselves to their own death; it wasn't in his nature. He'd always been the kind side to her cruel streak, the voice of calm amid her rages.

'Hearing it from you makes it seem more plausible, I suppose,' she said. 'But I still don't like it.'

Raven knelt down and rested his hands on her knees. 'You need to stay calm and think rationally. I honestly believe he's going to be fine, so stop worrying.'

'Thanks.' She smiled genuinely. She placed her hands on top of his and squeezed them tight. 'I don't know what I'd do without you.'

'That's something you needn't worry about. As long as you need me, I'll always be here.' His voice was hushed, belying the passion in his statement. He slowly rose to his feet, gently kissing her cheek on the way up. 'I should get back to my post.'

Lily nodded. 'Thank you.'

'It's okay,' he replied, then turned and walked away.

KILLIAN jumped back as the door to Lily's cabin swung open and Raven emerged. He was cold, and his clothes and hair were wet from the rain; the last thing he needed was to see Raven strutting out of the captain's quarters.

'Raven,' said Killian, trying as hard as he could to not sound irritable. He couldn't stack up next to Raven's godlike appearance on his best days, but in his soaking-wet state he felt all the more inferior. He folded his arms, using subtle animosity to make up for what he lacked in confidence.

'Killian.' Raven smiled pleasantly and gave him an acknowledging nod. 'I was just leaving.'

Killian's gaze followed him as he left. He purposefully made sure that he didn't watch him run up the mast – as Seth had claimed he did. He didn't want to be forcibly impressed by his athletics. Instead, he stepped into the cabin and focused on Lily, who glanced up at him awkwardly. A ripple of paranoia ran through his body. Why had Raven been here? Why did Lily look so guilty? She wasn't wearing her hat, coat or even her doublet. He felt as if he'd been punched in the stomach. He berated himself internally for feeling anything. Why did he even care about what she got up to? He didn't. He didn't care. She could sleep with every man on this damn ship if she wanted – every man except for him. He didn't want her touching him. He pushed his wet hair back, ran his hand along his stubbly jaw and regained his composure.

'Afternoon, Lil. I just wanted to ask a favour,' he said quickly and with forced politeness.

'Okay,' she replied, straightening up.

'Sorry if I interrupted anything important,' he muttered out of the side of his mouth.

'I'm sorry, what was that?'

'Oh nothing, nothing.'

Lily stood up, thrusting her chest out to assert her authority. 'Out with it. What d'you want?'

'No need to be so snippy.' He held his hands up in mock defence. 'I want some paper and ink. I thought you might have some lying around.' He bent one knee slightly and leant back, trying to look like his usual laid-back self.

'I do,' she said, then went to rummage through one of the drawers in her dresser. 'What do you want it for? Trying your hand at drawing now, eh?' she asked playfully over her shoulder.

'No,' Killian replied, short and sharp. She'd hit him directly in his Raven inferiority nerve. He cursed inwardly for allowing her to wound him.

'Sorry.' Her tone was lined with a healthy layer of sarcasm.

Killian grunted a response and remained silent. She was such a dick; she knew exactly what she was doing. How dare she try to belittle him like that. He couldn't believe he was spending the last of his days in the company of such a caustic person. In a few weeks he might very well be dead. Did she not even care about that? His gaze roamed the room, settling on her unmade bed. Evidently not.

His tongue curled as the metallic taste of blood filled his mouth. Subconsciously, he'd chewed the inside of his cheek. He felt like slapping himself; what was wrong with him? He didn't normally let things get on top of him. It must've been the feeling of impending doom; counting down the days to your own death would make anyone irrational. He put his shoulders back and hooked his fingers through his belt loops; he couldn't let it show. He wouldn't break in front of anyone, especially not her.

'Here you go,' said Lily, handing him ink and paper.

'Thanks,' he muttered, snapping back into reality as he snatched the items from her.

'You're welcome.'

He managed to force out half a smile and turned to leave.

'Killian,' she called out to him, 'bye.'

'Yep,' he said blankly. Then he left without looking at her.

Killian stalked along the deck, a scowl set on his face. Up ahead, he spied Ren, who was hanging his head over the side of the boat, facing in the direction of the wind. His fine indigo jacket was held tight to his chest with one arm, and his woolly scarf billowed out behind him. Killian sidled up next to his friend. The rain had cleared, leaving a fresh, crisp breeze in its wake. They stood in silence, breathing in the clear, clean air blowing in from the ocean. The cold buffeting wind helped to chase away Killian's feelings of frustration and anger. He gripped the rail and leant forwards, feeling the speed of the ship as it cut through the waves. His hair rippled as it was blown dry, and his shirt flapped as refreshing air blew between his buttons.

'How're you feeling, Thorny?' he asked.

'Not very bad, not very good,' Ren murmured.

'Don't worry, it'll pass. I know,' said Killian with a smile. 'Keep drinking water and try to eat something.'

'The thought of eating anything makes me feel sick.'

'Just try a few dry biscuits. Believe me, it'll help. I'm an expert in hangovers.' He turned his back to the ocean and leant casually against the bulwark.

'I suppose,' Ren muttered. 'You have a solution to everything, don't you?' He gave him a sad faded smile.

'Most things,' Killian replied with a cocky grin.

'Yeah, most things,' Ren repeated, his voice low and forlorn. 'You can fight, you've found a way to save my father, and you know how to cure my hangover.'

'That's three things,' said Killian, laughing.

'Three more than me. I'm so useless. I can't even save my father without help.'

'Don't be so down on yourself, and you're not that useless. Come on, remember it was my fault you got stabbed.'

'But you saved me. Without you I'd be dead. And it wasn't really your fault. I stormed out. I was a brat.' He rested his elbows on the rail and dropped his chin into his hands. 'I never did thank you for that.'

'No, you didn't.'

'Thank you.'

'No problem.' Killian paused, deep in thought. 'The fish guts – you got us out of that one. I mean you got us into the guts, but the situation, you got us out of that.'

'It was nothing.'

'It got me out of a ruckus with Sullivan. It was some quick thinking.'

'Yeah, yeah, it was, wasn't it?' said Ren.

'See?' Killian nudged him in the ribs. 'Two more uses and you'll be my equal.'

'Yeah, kind of.' Ren chuckled. 'You know, you're right, I should eat something.'

'See Seth. I'm sure he'll sort you out.'

'Yeah, I will. Thanks, Killian, thanks for . . . well, you know, thanks.'

'It's okay.'

Ren turned and walked shakily below deck. Left alone, Killian gripped the edge of the ship again and frowned.

CHAPTER
EIGHTEEN

THE NEXT FEW DAYS PASSED WITHOUT incident. Killian did his best to stay out of Lily's way, but this course of action often led him straight into the path of Ren. As soon as Ren's hangover was cured, his enthusiasm for the mission grew at an exponential rate; it was all he talked about. Killian tried to be patient, but the young man's constant excitement and awe were beginning to grate on him, especially as he was feeling the polar opposite. Whereas Ren seemed to relish the time he was spending on the ship, Killian felt trapped. Ren was ecstatic that they were so close to saving his father, whereas Killian's mind was preoccupied with thoughts of his own death. One thing that bothered him was he couldn't get away from anyone. Not that he was the type of person to sit and brood, but he did like to spend a little bit of time alone. He was used to it – he'd lived by himself for years.

One calm day a week and a half into their voyage, he was standing on the deck enjoying the feeling of the wind in his hair and the calming sound of the waves as they broke against the hull. The ship was gliding through the water, its movement swift and even. He'd managed to slip away from Tom, Blake and Finn with minimum fuss. He'd skilfully dodged Morton and smoothly changed his direction when he'd seen Lily on the deck. He rested his arms on the rail and emptied his lungs in one breath. He felt as close to peace as he could. He'd even managed to forget about drowning, bleeding to death or getting crushed. Everything was going fine until Ren appeared unexpectedly.

Killian let out a discreet groan of disappointment.

'What are you doing?' Ren asked.

'Nothing.'

'Did you see those fish?' Ren garbled, excitedly pointing to the sea.

'Nope,' Killian replied, turning away from the ocean and clasping his hands behind his head.

'Oh, they were amazing! I've never seen anything like them.'

'Oh, now there's a surprise.' Killian raised an eyebrow.

'They were so brightly coloured – I'm surprised you missed them. They were jumping right out of the sea. They looked like they had wings!'

'Great.'

'I suppose we don't get fish like that near Vermor,' Ren said, carrying on, ignorant to Killian's disinterest.

'No.'

Ren moved closer to Killian and turned his back to the ocean. 'Isn't this great?' He beamed.

Killian glanced at Ren and was horrified by what he saw. Ren's arms were wrapped around the back of his head, and he was leaning against the railing, his legs slightly bent. He was mimicking his pose! If Killian had been feeling more like himself he would have ordered Ren to stop standing like that, but he didn't have the energy to expend on such trivialities. He dropped his arms and swivelled around. 'What?' he asked.

'This, you know, being on a ship, the adventure, the excitement.'

'No, actually, I don't find it great at all. This ship is a shithole, and the adventure is dull, therefore the excitement is non-existent,' Killian said.

'Oh, come on, Killian, it's exciting!'

'No, Thorncliffe, I think that you'll find it's shit, bland and monotonous,' Killian replied flatly. *I wonder how excited you'd be if you were sailing to your doom too.*

Killian's shoulders tensed involuntarily; he was letting it get to him, and he knew he shouldn't. He had to stay positive – he might live. There was definitely a chance he would live. Ren had been sent to him; he was the one who was meant to help him. He would help him. Everything would be fine. He breathed out and relaxed his muscles. In a couple of months' time he'd be back in Bracky, playing cards, drinking ale with Barrington, with a fortune to his name and his past sins wiped clean. All of this would be a distant memory.

'But just look out there.' Ren gasped and waved his hand at the ocean. 'You can't say that's . . . not very good. It's amazing.'

'No, it's not. It's shit. It's just the big wet flat thing that keeps us trapped on this ship.'

'But the ship's amazing,' Ren protested.

'No.' Killian held up his index finger to emphasise his point. 'It's not.'

Ren shook his head. 'Why don't you come for a walk with me and I'll show you how amazing it is?' he suggested zealously.

'No.'

'Why not?'

'Because it isn't amazing and there's nothing I'd like to do less than walk around and take in the sights with you.'

'What else are you going to do today?' Ren asked, his arms crossed, refusing to take no for an answer.

Killian was at a loss. He let out a string of curses and begrudgingly followed Ren, dragging his feet. They walked past a group of pirates fishing amid clouds of smoke, encircled with dice and uneven piles of coins. They grunted to one another in rough voices punctuated with throaty coughs, pausing in their incoherent conversations only to drink, roll up cigarettes or stuff pipes. Killian glanced down into their bucket to see a colourful heap of dead fish and was temporarily mesmerised by their flashing rainbow scales. He opened his mouth to say something to Ren but quickly remembered he didn't care about fish, and they were definitely not interesting.

'Calm down, Thorny, they're only fish,' muttered Killian as Ren gawped into the bucket, completely transfixed.

The group of fishermen chuckled harshly at Ren's naive fixation.

'Oh, sorry,' said Ren, sounding a little flustered, his cheeks colouring. 'Let's move on.' He angled them away from the edge and towards the middle of the main deck.

Every few steps Ren would stop and point something out, insisting on telling Killian all about it. During these tedious mini-lectures, Killian occupied himself by moving the buckle on his goggles to keep himself vaguely amused by something. He didn't want to be here; he didn't care. His mood was plummeting to new depths as each second ticked by with all the predictable uniformity of a metronome. A light feeling filled his body, like it didn't even belong to him anymore; he was becoming increasingly detached. He was losing himself. He had to stay strong, had to remain positive, or what hope would he have for survival? He was a good swimmer, which was one point in his favour. Why was he even worried? He smirked at the absurdity of the situation and had to catch himself before he burst into insane laughter.

Ren's droning voice filtered into Killian's disjointed, beleaguered mind with alarming regularity. To keep up his carefree, tough pretence, Killian had the same opinion on everything Ren pointed out.

'It's bollocks.' Killian sighed as he put the goggles on top of his head, pushing his hair back.

'Doesn't the sheer size of the mainmast impress you?' Ren held his arms aloft dramatically, his eyes glistening with wonder.

'Not really,' said Killian, pulling the goggles down so they hung around his neck.

'You do know that without the mast and the sails the ship would be useless,' Ren insisted.

'I'm no seafarer, but I'm sure I could have worked that one out,' Killian grumbled, moving his goggles back to his head. 'I think I'm done. Don't you want to annoy – I mean hang out – with Finn, Tom and Blake now?'

'They're busy.'

'Busy!' exclaimed Killian, genuinely shocked. 'Doing what? Sitting around drinking and dicing?'

'No.' Ren sounded irritatingly pleased that he'd finally

garnered a shred of Killian's waning attention. 'Finn's below deck sifting the gunpowder to keep it from separating. Tom and Blake are up there.' He leant back and pointed upwards.

Killian squinted into the sunlight. There were at least fifteen men and women scurrying back and forth across the rigging, but it was impossible to tell one person from the next against the white glare.

'Ay! Oi!' Tom shouted down, waving his hand.

Killian waved back slowly.

'Gainsborough! Stop messin' about,' yelled Morton from below the sails.

'And I thought they just sat around,' muttered Killian.

'No, they don't. They do have duties besides shooting. I was going to ask if I could help on the rigging, but I don't think I'm quite ready to go up there yet.'

'That's probably the best decision you've ever made. With you on the sails we'd probably end up back in Bracky.'

'Thanks,' said Ren glumly. He glanced up and down the ship before hitting Killian with another fascinating fact. 'Did you know there are twenty-eight gunners on this ship and Finn trained every single one of them?'

'Wow, Ren! That really is amazing.' Killian clamped his hands firmly on Ren's shoulders, stared into his eyes and smiled. 'I'll die a happy man knowing that.'

Ren's shoulders drooped, and he shrugged Killian off. 'Are you not bothered about any of this at all?'

'Not really. To be honest, I'd rather be polishing my swords and drinking myself into a coma.'

'Well.' Ren sighed sadly and took a step back. 'Don't let me stop you.'

'Are you admitting defeat?'

'Yes, I am,' Ren murmured.

'Good.' Killian smiled, slapping his hands together. 'I'm going below deck, by myself.'

'Bye.'

Killian waved. 'I think I liked you better when you were depressed,' he muttered to himself as he stalked away.

CHAPTER
NINETEEN

FTER THREE WEEKS AT SEA, EVEN REN WAS starting to feel a hint of boredom creep over him. There were only so many rainbow fish one man could see before it felt like he'd seen them all. He listlessly wandered the deck as the tropical sun beat down on him. It was only recently that he'd decided to forgo his jacket. Having felt ashamed of his waif-like stature, he'd tried to stay covered, but in this heat it was impossible. Today he'd even gone so far as to roll up his shirtsleeves, revealing his breadstick forearms to everyone.

The gunners were once again up the rigging, and Finn claimed to be busy, though she bluntly refused to tell him what that entailed. As much as he thought it would never happen, he'd actually come to enjoy the company of these freebooting lawbreakers, so it was always a bit of a disappointment when he found himself alone. He could try to make friends with some of the others on the ship, but that was far too intimidating a task. Knowing a few by name for the occasional wave was enough for him. Descending the stairs to the mess was always an option. He'd found comfort in Seth's company.

As he was contemplating visiting the cook to see if he could use his help, he noticed Killian sitting hunched over in the distance. He put his hand up to shield his eyes from the sun. He looked like he was writing something. Ren picked up his pace; perhaps he'd be grateful for some company.

'What are you doing?' Ren asked when he was within talking distance.

Killian stopped writing and shoved the piece of paper and pen into his trouser pocket. 'Nothing.' He moved to fold his arms but seemed to change his mind and casually wrapped them about his head instead.

'It looked like you were writing something.' Ren looked straight into Killian's eyes.

'It's a list,' said Killian, easily holding Ren's gaze.

'What kind of list?'

'A shopping list . . . for Seth.'

'Why would he need a shopping list when we're in the middle of the sea?' Ren frowned. He was unconvinced. There was something shifty about his friend's behaviour.

'For when we stop for supplies.'

'Right, but why would he get you to write it? How do you know what to put on it?'

'He told me.'

'And you remembered it?'

'Yes.'

'And then came up here to write it down?'

'Yes, Ren. Yes!' Killian snapped. 'Are you a bookkeeper or a prosecutor?'

Ren jumped back at Killian's abrasive tone. He'd been acting strange for the past few weeks now; every day he was a little worse, often skulking off by himself and seeming to consciously avoid everyone. He'd started keeping conversations to the bare minimum – one-word answers were becoming something of a speciality. His general manner was distant. The person Ren had met over a month ago was fading away.

Ren knew what was wrong, of course – he wasn't a complete idiot – but he didn't want to talk about it; he was riddled with guilt as it was. Talking about it would only make it worse. So his conversation tactic was to be as upbeat and enthusiastic as possible to try to cheer him up. There was nothing else he could do; he couldn't tell Killian not to go. If he did, his father would certainly die, and he'd be lost. The mere thought of it brought tears to his eyes. He swiftly brushed them away. At least Killian had a slim chance of survival, and it was that Ren clung to.

The wind picked up Killian's hair and blew it over his sulky face. 'Did you want something?' he asked.

'Not really,' Ren replied. Killian's piercing azure glare twisted his train of thought. Fervent and optimistic clearly weren't working anymore, if they ever had at all. Ren swallowed; it was time to face the truth. 'Well . . .'

Killian raised his eyebrows and brushed his hair out of his face. 'Now there's a surprise,' he muttered icily.

'It's just—' Ren stopped mid-sentence, took a deep breath and started again. 'I'm a bit concerned.'

'About?'

'You. You've not been yourself since we set sail. Is anything wrong?' He crouched down to Killian's level.

'Nope.'

'Sure?'

'Yes, of course I am. I think I know how I feel.'

'Of course,' said Ren hurriedly, 'of course you do.'

'You're worried I'm not up to the job, aren't you?' Killian asked, his tone laced with subtle venom.

'No, no, not at all. I'm worried about *you*.'

Killian shrugged.

'I am. We're friends, aren't we?' said Ren, and a tiny hollowness opened up inside him. 'That's what they do.'

Killian grunted in response.

The empty feeling collapsed into a painful stab of loneliness. Was that all their friendship warranted, a grunt, and a lacklustre one at that? Was that all he was worth? He truly believed he'd found a friend in Killian, one of the only people in his life he could call a friend. The hurt was almost too much, but he managed to keep it together. 'If you want to sit here and sulk by yourself, then that's fine by me. You'll find me with Seth if you want to talk.' He got up and walked away before the threatening tears could fall.

'Wait!'

Ren turned around to see Killian had hung his head, hiding his face from view. He walked back and sat down next to him. Killian didn't move or make a sound to acknowledge his presence, not even a grunt.

'Killian?' Ren ventured softly.

'I'm scared.' Killian's voice was barely audible.

Ren turned towards him, but his head was still down. A sickening feeling was building in his stomach, and he didn't know what to do, what to say. His cocky, tenacious friend was falling apart in front of him. He shouldn't have asked him what was wrong. He should have stuck to his original plan to stay optimistic and upbeat. Now all he'd done was create a mess. How was he supposed to keep him from breaking? He tried to think back to how he'd helped his father after his mother had left them, but there was nothing. His mind was blank.

'It's all right,' he said quietly; it was all he could think of to say.

'It's not,' said Killian. 'I'm . . .' His voice became choked by tears and emotions.

'Don't be scared.'

'I am scared,' Killian replied.

'Don't be scared,' Ren repeated, hoping he'd struck the correct balance of comfort and enthusiasm in his tone.

'I am.'

'You can't be.'

'I am.'

'Please, Killian, you—'

'I know.'

There was a moment's silence, and it was obvious Killian had no more to add. Ren felt awash with nerves; despite the heat, his skin prickled with goose bumps. Killian was the strong one, not him. He couldn't say anything to make it right. He was useless, and besides, it was all his fault. He was the one sending Killian off to face impossible odds. If not for him, Killian would be his usual self. A stab of guilt pressed into his gut, but it was not enough to outweigh his personal desires. Without Killian's help his father would die, and he'd be more alone than ever. He needed him.

He cleared his throat. 'Are you sure the captain or Raven can't go instead of you?' he asked, even though he already knew the answer. He just felt like he had to say something.

'No, it has to be me,' Killian murmured.

'But—'

'No. We both know you were sent to me, not them. I'm your man.' He lifted his head, rubbing away all traces of tears from his eyes and cheeks. 'I'm gonna fall down that hole, I'm gonna come back up, and I'm gonna save your dad,' he said, some of his old strength creeping back into his voice. 'And then you're gonna damn well pay me what you owe me.'

All Ren could do was nod numbly.

'I let it get on top of me,' said Killian. He pulled out one of his swords, its blade glinting in the sun, and polished it with the corner of his shirt. 'Honestly, Thorny, I lost it for a bit. It's this ship, the boredom and frustration. I've been letting it build up. My mind's been wandering where it shouldn't, but now I've spoken to you I feel fine.'

'Really?' Ren gasped, unable to mask the astonishment in his voice. He'd helped Killian? He couldn't quite believe it.

'I'm a strong swimmer,' he joked. 'I've got nothing to worry about.'

Ren slowly got to his feet and dusted himself down. 'Want to come for a walk?' he offered feebly.

Killian chuckled. 'I'm fine here.'

'Okay.' Ren shuffled awkwardly; he was emotionally drained and just wanted to leave.

'You don't have to stay with me. Go and soak up the wonder of the ship.' Killian grinned. 'You'll regret it if you don't.'

'Only if you're sure.'

'Go.'

'All right. I'll see you later.' Ren smiled and turned to leave.

'Thorny,' Killian called after him, 'sorry I've been such a miserable bastard.'

'It's all right,' said Ren cheerfully, brushing it off, 'you've a lot on your mind.'

'Yeah,' he muttered.

CHAPTER
TWENTY

KILLIAN LEANT FORWARDS AND STARED UP AT the clear night sky in wonder. It was a deep blue, nearly black, and covered with thousands of shining silver stars. The larger more prominent stars shone out a brilliant white light, while others – which looked as if they'd been sprayed arbitrarily onto the sky by an artist's giant brush – were content to softly glow. Some were as fine as grains of sand, and together they formed beautiful swirling patterns across the sky. Waves of subtle purple and green occasionally rippled within the dark. Out in the middle of the ocean, the night sky came alive in a way he'd never seen before. He found his mind wandering to Lily's painting and how perfectly Raven had encapsulated the glittering spectacle. He bit down on his lip in frustration.

He hung his arms over the side of the ship, watching the stars prance upon the sea as he tapped a bottle against the bulwark. The air had cooled down enough to warrant a coat, though he left it undone. He brought the bottle of watered-down sweetened rum to his lips. It didn't have the kick of Seth's secret stash, but it helped him to forget his problems, and right now that was all he wanted to do. The gentle chatter of the three pirates and Ren stirred the air behind him, along with the familiar smell of Finn's smokes.

A slight breeze ruffled his hair, and he glanced to his right to see Raven. His sudden appearance didn't startle him; it was the sort of thing he expected of the enigmatic man.

'Nice night,' Raven said.

'Uh-huh.' Killian took a swig from the bottle.

Raven leapt onto the rail without a sound, crouched down and cast his gaze out to sea. 'How are you feeling?' he asked.

Killian emptied his lungs and looked up at Raven, the small smirk on his lips highlighted by the starlight. 'I'm fine.'

'Glad to hear that,' said Raven.

Killian said nothing. He turned his attention back to the reflection of the stars, staring as they twirled and shimmered on the gently lapping waves.

'We're almost there.'

Killian's chest tightened. 'We are?'

'Another week at the most. I hope you're ready.'

'Yeah,' Killian replied, trying to sound as indifferent as possible.

'That's good,' said Raven, though his tone suggested he'd detected his pretence. 'You will be able to do it,' he added with reassuring credence. 'I have faith in you.'

Killian wrapped his arms about the rail and glanced at Raven, whose strange eyes were glowing faintly as he watched the dark horizon. There was something odd about him – he had no doubt about that – and he was far too perfect looking for his own good, but maybe some of Killian's initial animosity towards him had been unwarranted. Raven's faith in him gave him a shred more confidence.

'Thanks,' Killian murmured. 'That means a lot.'

Raven smiled softly and nodded.

Killian took another swig from his bottle and straightened up. 'Why don't you join us?'

'Thank you, but I think I'll just stargaze tonight,' he said softly. Raven leapt down to the deck, his feet barely making a sound. 'It's not often I'm blessed with such a view.'

'Well, you know where we are.'

'Thank you.'

With that, Raven back-flipped neatly up to the quarterdeck above the five friends, disappearing from view as soon as he lay down. Killian scolded himself internally for the jealous feelings he had towards Raven, but it couldn't be helped. Anyone would be jealous.

'Killian! You gonna get your skinny arse over 'ere or what?' Finn barked.

Killian sauntered over, made a few insincere apologies and sat down. The small group had gathered beneath two sunstones; the soft pink-and-peach glow from the unusual crystalline rocks bathed the deck in a warm mellow light.

Tom lay sprawled on his front. He chucked a pair of dice along the deck, accidentally rolling them just out of his line of sight. He shuffled and pushed himself up, then collapsed back down, not caring enough to check what he'd rolled, and nobody else was playing anyway.

'Don't you wanna know what you threw?' Killian asked when Tom didn't move.

'Nope,' he replied. 'It wouldn't matter anyway. The result is random.'

Killian smirked and took a drink.

'Say, Killian,' he said tentatively, 'if you die . . . can I have your gun?'

Killian yanked the bottle from his mouth and almost choked. 'That's nice, Tom. Cheers, mate.'

'Well, you won't need it if you're dead, will you?' said Tom, relentlessly pursuing the matter.

'I don't suppose I will,' said Killian, leaning back on his elbows, his legs at full stretch.

'How will you get it, Tom?' Ren asked. 'He'll be taking it down with him.'

'No he won't. It'll get ruined,' Tom replied.

'He's right,' said Finn. 'The salt water'll ruin it.'

'I'm right here you know,' said Killian sharply. 'You make it sound like I'm not coming back. Thanks for the vote of confidence, guys. I may as well go drown myself now.'

An uncomfortable guilty silence settled on the group. Tom picked at the stitching on his trousers, Finn occupied herself by constructing a roll-up, and Ren looked to Blake for help. His only response was to curl his lip in disgust. Killian smiled to himself, enjoying it.

Tom eventually left his clothes alone and looked at Killian. 'I'm sorry,' he said meekly.

Killian turned to face him and gave him a lopsided grin. 'It's all right, Tom.'

It took a second for him to realise that he'd been duped, but when he did, Tom laughed. 'You cock! I honestly thought I'd upset you. For the first time in my life I genuinely felt bad, ashamed even.'

'Well, maybe I've done you some good,' said Killian.

'Yeah, Tom,' Blake said. 'He's helped you discover a new emotion.'

Tom grimaced at them both and folded his arms sulkily across his chest.

Killian reached under his coat and pulled out his gun, looked at it briefly, then tossed it to Tom.

'Look after it,' he said.

'What? Really? I can have it?' Tom gasped with surprise.

'Yeah, why not? But I want it back if I live, all right?'

'Fingers crossed then,' said Tom with an evil chuckle.

The five of them sat listening to the calming lull of the waves and watching the endless number of stars drift across the sky. As Killian looked up, he couldn't help but wonder whether this would be one of the last times he would see them; at least they were putting on a good performance for him.

'Tom,' said Ren, 'can I ask you something?'

'You're asking if you can ask?' replied Tom as he shoved Killian's gun in his belt. 'Your politeness can be sickening at times.'

'Well . . . I don't want to cause any offence.'

'Go ahead. It takes a lot to offend me.'

'Where are you from?' Ren asked hesitantly.

'Vermor,' Tom replied simply.

'No, I didn't mean—'

'Ridley, if you wanna get all precise and that,' Tom added.

'Okay.' Ren's skin flushed scarlet.

'Oh.' Tom chuckled. 'Sorry, you're asking because of my eyes?'

'Those peridot peepers,' Blake muttered.

'No, not your eyes. I-I didn't mean—'

'I know!' Tom cut Ren off with a laugh. 'I'm trying to make you feel rotten, like he just did to me, though I'm just not quite at his level of cock yet.' He flashed his eyes in Killian's direction. 'Of course I wasn't born in Vermor; I think that's pretty obvious, though that sweet country is all I know. But I tell you what, Ren, the tale of Thomas Gainsborough is dark, so dark, darker than a moonless night, darker than the sweetest rum, darker than . . . my skin.'

'I'm so sorry!' said Ren, aghast. 'I shouldn't have asked.'

'I'm just kidding. Nothing is darker than my skin, eh?' He winked at Ren. 'Blake, do you wanna tell my tale? You are the dream weaver.'

'Ah, no,' grumbled Blake, shaking his head.

'Why not?' Tom moaned. 'You're so much better at it than me, and you can use your smoke. It'll be great!'

'I'm not spending the evening telling your life story.'

'Why not? Is it because I'm the hero?'

'No, it's because it's messed up and depressing.'

'Fair enough.' Tom shrugged. 'But you're all missing out.'

'Blake,' said Finn, steering the conversation elsewhere. 'Tell us somethin' else then.'

'Yeah, go on,' said Tom eagerly. 'It won't be as good, but y'know.'

Blake frowned.

'Go on, call it a final request,' said Killian, sitting up and leaning forwards. 'It might take my mind off my inevitable death.'

'Well now you've put it like that . . .' said Blake.

Killian lay back and grinned triumphantly.

'Please don't tell another scary one,' said Ren.

'I think you should tell a scary one.' Tom leered.

'I'll tell what I want to tell,' said Blake firmly. 'You guys are forcing me to do this, like I'm a sideshow. You can at least let me pick.'

'You love it, Blake,' said Finn. 'Don't grumble like a bitch.'

Blake scratched his head. He pushed his floppy dark hair out of his eyes and lay back on the deck. 'Okay, maybe I enjoy it a little,' he said. 'I shall tell you the story of the Demons' Maw, which I believe was found on one of the islands of Venario.'

Blake had one last swig of his drink, an awkward manoeuvre since he was lying down. He sat up and reached inside his cloak to pull out his bronze pipe and some tobacco, which was wrapped in a discoloured piece of parchment. He placed a meagre amount of tobacco into the pipe and lit it, creating the now familiar sweet smell. Putting his lips to the pipe, he inhaled the smoke and shut his eyes, holding it in his mouth briefly before blowing it out. He reached his hand out and ran it slowly and gracefully through the drifting curls of smoke. His eyes opened wide, and they glowed with dazzling white light. Slowly, the luminosity within them dimmed, but they remained completely white as an image formed in the smoke.

A shimmering translucent cliffside scene was left suspended in the air as the smoke evaporated into the night. Blake moved his hands through the picture with swift precise motions. Drawing his hand upwards, he created craggy cliff faces with soft green-blue waves lapping at their feet. He clicked his fingers, and a flock of nimble birds darted across his intangible landscape. He cleared his throat and sent another wave of birds flitting across the scene before launching into his story.

'No one suspected what they would find. It was so well hidden, it was perfect. Until nature decided to play a part.'

Blake clicked his fingers, and the scene was replaced with an underwater landscape. He swiftly drew in the air as he spoke.

'There is no name for them, though *fish-demons* is the term most commonly used. No one knows where they came from, but it is widely accepted that an earthquake split the ocean bed, and as a result, these beings seeped from some demonic dimension into ours. They were human in shape, but that is where their humanity ended.'

Blake crafted a series of monstrous creatures within the smoke, which drifted up from a dramatic fissure in the seabed. Lithe humanoid bodies glistened with blue and green scales and danced amid masses of purple tentacles. Golden shells shone like the sun, while silver fins glowed like a winter's moon. Barnacles, limpets and muscles attached themselves to webbed feet and hands, amid layers of seaweed and sludge. Soulful blue eyes were countered by rows and rows of tiny sharp teeth.

'The fish-demons floated from the cold ocean depths to the surface. They coasted on the currents, which eventually drew them to warmer climates. They settled happily in the warm oceans, enjoying the soft feel of the temperate salty waters on their scales. Yet they knew they couldn't live by frolicking in the sea. They started to move closer to the shore. They desired somewhere secluded and private, somewhere they could grow the coral that supported their very existence without being interrupted.'

Blake recreated his original scene.

'After some searching, they found such a place within the cliffside of one of Venario's islands. A narrow tunnel hidden beneath the surface of the water led to a grand cavern with a circular lake at its centre. What made it all the more enticing was the fishing town nearby. The fish-demons, you see, had grown fascinated by humans. They'd watched them in their boats, paddling in the sea and strolling along the beach. They felt a fierce desire to be near to them. It was almost like they needed them.

'After the demons had set up their new home, they sent out scouting parties. These parties were tasked with enticing humans into their lair. They would float to the shore and capture the gaze of a human, luring them back to the cavern. They possessed a powerful glamour in their eyes, which made it impossible for anyone to refuse their requests once eye contact had been made.'

Blake swirled his hand in the smoke and painted the image of the hapless humans being led into the fish-demon lair.

'Over time, people were reported missing. Men and women of all ages and races were simply disappearing from the town without any explanation. Search parties were sent looking, but nothing ever came of them.

'Then one day, an earthquake struck the area. The ground split and shook, some houses toppled and . . .' Blake paused for dramatic effect. 'The roof of the cavern caved in, creating a jagged circular hole.'

Blake painted in the sky as he spoke.

'Once the dust had settled, locals from the village marched up and peered down into the hole. As the town clock struck noon, the midday sun poured into the cavern through its circular skylight. Shafts of golden light beamed into the turquoise waters below. All around the edge of the pool grew bizarre coral structures in various soft pastel shades, each one about the size of a sapling. Curiosity got the better of the villagers, and they constructed a pulley system to winch a resident down for a closer look at this strange new place.

'They winched down a local woman whose husband was one of the many missing. She wandered about the coral trees, in awe of such a wonderful, tranquil place. She took a closer look at one of the trees, and what she saw froze her blood. Staring back at her from within the mauve coral was a face, twisted and bent in distortion, its mouth open, screaming a horrific sound that nobody would ever hear.'

Blake paused, took another drag on his pipe, and blew out a plume of smoke. He ran his finger through it, and it changed into various pastel shades. With a gesture he sent the coloured smoke all around his audience, and behind each of them he grew twisted and bent pieces of coral with tortured-looking faces at their centre.

'The woman ran around the coral frantically until she found that which she knew she would: her husband's face, locked in agony, staring pitifully out of a rose-coloured lump of coral, begging for help that would never come.

'The faces were all eventually identified as the missing townsfolk, but the fish-demons were nowhere to be found. Some say the earthquake opened up the way back to their home dimension and they were summoned back. Others say they simply grew bored of their lair and moved on up the coast to start again.'

Blake clicked his fingers, and the haunting coral formations exploded in wisps of multicoloured smoke. He blinked, and his eyes reverted to their usual hazel.

'The end,' he quickly added.

He was then treated to a small round of applause and cries for another story.

'Another time, my friends. You'll get sick of it if I keep telling them.' He picked up his bottle and took a long swig.

'So,' Tom said. 'Is that all true?'

'It might be. I can't say one way or the other.'

'It might be!' Ren gasped. 'But it was so horrible . . . it can't be.'

'Tell you what, Ren,' said Tom, through a grin. 'How about once this is all over, me and you take a trip to Venario and find the island? We can become true adventurers. We can hunt down the fish-demons and make them pay. What d'you reckon?'

'I don't think so,' said Ren.

'Ah, c'mon, they've got some good wine and women in Venario.'

'I don't care.'

'Are you scared?'

'Yes, yes I am,' said Ren. 'I don't want to be turned into coral. I don't care how good the women and wine are.'

Tom chuckled, but Ren remained mute.

Killian frowned. Ren was terrible at hiding his emotions, at least from him anyway. There was fear and confusion in his shimmering brown eyes. His skin was ghostly white, and his mouth was drawn into a tight line. It was the same expression he'd worn when they were planning the great feather heist. Blake was a mage. It had come as a surprise to Killian, but Ren looked close to tears.

'Come on, Blake,' said Tom cheerily, 'giz another.'

'I don't think so,' said Blake, and he took a long gulp from his bottle. 'I plan on spending the rest of the night getting battered.'

'Ugh, you only ever tell the one.'

'And you always moan, so we can't break tradition, now, can we?' Blake responded with a wink.

'Excuses, excuses,' Tom murmured. 'You're just bloody lazy.'

'Says you!' Blake laughed, spinning around to deal him a punch to the shoulder. 'I don't want to run out of ideas, and, more importantly, I want to get steaming.'

'Don't worry about running out of ideas,' said Killian. 'I reckon you'll get some inspiration from this trip.'

'As if you're coming back to tell him anything. You'll be lucky if you get turned into coral,' said Tom slyly.

The pirates and Ren fell about laughing. Killian screwed his face up into a furious expression and glared at Tom. Holding the expression proved impossible, however, and he was soon on his back laughing too. He was heading into the unknown with only the ramblings of an old drunk to guide him.

CHAPTER
TWENTY-ONE

A LOUD EXPLOSION RIPPED THROUGH THE AIR. Killian didn't move; it was right on cue. For the past four days the frequent roars of the geyser had gradually got louder.

At first everyone was startled and talk of turning back was rife, but once word of the geyser had infiltrated every ear on board, the crew calmed down, all except Killian. The first night he'd heard it he couldn't sleep. Every time he came close to drifting off, a moan from the geyser would awaken him, each distant blast driving a fresh spike of fear through his mind. He was going to die. The louder it got, the closer he was to death. By the second day he'd become accustomed to it, but that was when the plumes of steam started drifting in, creating dense clouds. These clouds intermittently burst, spewing a deluge of rain onto the ship.

Killian lifted his head and wrapped his arms about the bulwark. He could feel the atmosphere changing. The air was becoming warmer – if that was possible – and increasingly damp. The moisture mingled with his sweat, resulting in a permanently drenched look. He'd never been so hot and uncomfortable before. He shifted his weight from one leg to the other as his trousers hugged his thighs like long-lost friends.

'Well, well, look who we have 'ere,' a voice growled behind him. 'It's the dead man.'

Killian turned around. The last thing he wanted was a run-in with Morton. It was too hot.

'Haven't you got things to do?' he asked wearily.

'Aye, plenty. Just thought I'd let you know, I'm takin' a few wagers,' Morton wheezed at him. 'If you ain't coming back, this whole trip is a bust. I ain't coming down to this foul hot stink just ta make no cash. Care to bet on ya life?'

'I . . .' Killian was unable to answer. People were actually betting on his life? The thought of it drained the self-worth from his body. He tried to search for some sort of witty retort, but nothing would come.

'The Drop is in sight!' Raven's voice boomed from the crow's nest, interrupting Killian's hopeless thoughts.

'I'll take that as a no,' grunted Morton. 'Be seein' ya,' he added as he walked away, a spring of arrogance in his step.

Killian's chest tightened, and he felt sick. His body was light and his limbs unsteady. He gripped the rail and turned around, leaning back against the bulwark for support. The crew scrambled around him in a wave of organised chaos to lower the sails and the anchor. There was a lot of fiddling with ropes – some tightened, others made slack, all held firmly in place with a complicated system of knots – and he was glad he didn't have to get involved with it all, though he might have taken rope tying over leaping to certain death.

He took a deep breath and slowly peeled himself off the rail. As he ambled towards the middle of the main deck, the clouds finally broke and doused the ship with warm rain. He didn't care. He was already wet, and the rain was so warm it was almost like having a bath. A group was already gathering, awaiting the captain.

'Found yer hole then?' said Finn, sidling up next to him.

'Uh-huh.'

'Nervous?'

'Nah.'

Tom appeared over Finn's shoulder, water trickling down his face and dripping off his nose. 'Liar! Even I'd—' A loud bang drowned out the end of his sentence.

Lily was part way up the rigging of the mainmast, holding a smoking gun. Her long black hair dangled limply around her face, and her soaking-wet clothes clung to every inch of her body, showing off all her feminine curves. She said nothing, staring at her crew with a stony look that demanded respect. She brought her flintlock up to her lips, the white light of the cloud-smothered sun dashing off its gold plating, and blew away the twisting plumes of smoke. It sent a shiver coursing through Killian's body; he quickly straightened himself and hoped nobody had noticed.

'I'm sure all of you with working eyes and ears will notice we've arrived. The ship will move no further and will remain here for six days.' Her voice was loud and crisp, and it easily carried through the crowd. 'Treat these days like a holiday, a sodden but warm holiday.' She returned her gun to its holster. 'Right, everyone, rest up, and good job on some excellent sailing. Killian, my cabin please.'

'Ey up, looks like you're in luck.' Tom grinned, giving Killian an elbow to the ribs.

Killian didn't indulge him with a response. He turned and squeezed his way through the pirates who were still staring in awe at the ocean, some muttering about their previous disbelief that the Drop existed, others weighing up his chances of survival, Morton taking bets. When he reached the captain's quarters and saw the door had been left open, he still knocked, just to be polite.

'Come in and shut the door behind you,' Lily said from somewhere inside.

Killian did as he was told and stepped in. He had a quick scan of the room to make sure Raven wasn't lurking in some dark corner. Once he'd satisfied his paranoia and was confident they were alone, he spoke. 'You wanted to see me?'

Lily was facing the window and showed no sign of turning. Her jacket and doublet were hanging up, dripping water onto the floor, her long wet hair slowly turning the back of her shirt translucent. Killian moved from one foot to the other and scratched his arm. Why did she do this to him? He was as cool as ice normally, so why was she making him so nervous? It must've been the Drop doing it to him, not her. He was an emotional mess over it. She had absolutely nothing to do with his racing pulse, trembling hands and the hot rush that coursed through his body. The spacious captain's cabin was cramping him; he needed to leave and sort himself out. He glanced around the room. This time he spied the table and chairs hidden away in a corner, and he briefly examined the various objects on show in her cabin. Once he was satisfied that they were indeed identical to the ones that had been here last time, he opened his mouth and was about to prompt her when she finally spoke.

'I wanted to say sorry for mocking you . . . about the paper and ink.'

'Is that it?' he asked, breathing a tiny sigh. 'Don't worry about it. I'd already forgotten.'

'And I think what you're doing is ridiculous, foolish and idiotic. You do realise, if you're this hard up, I can chuck you some cash. You don't have to sling yourself into the abyss. I could go, or Raven. We'd be fine.'

'I know,' said Killian, his voice heavy. 'But it wouldn't be right. It has to be me.'

'I know, I know, Ren was sent to you, not us. You can't blame me for trying one last time though.' She turned to face him, her olive skin glistening, her damp shirt plastered to her body. Killian's eyes remained on her face, her beautiful, conflicted face. She held his gaze and then lowered her eyes as she spoke. 'I'm worried about you.'

'I'll be fine,' he said, taken aback.

'I feel like you're part of my crew now,' she said, taking a step towards him. 'And as much as your very existence is like a poisonous thorn in my side . . .' She paused and drew a deep breath. 'I'd like it if you didn't die.'

Neither of them spoke. The only sound in the room was the soft splash of water as it dripped from Lily's hair. Killian's wet shirt was sticking to his skin like glue and made him feel a little self-conscious.

'Tomorrow you may take one of my small lifeboats to the Drop. I'd recommend that you bail out before you go over. You wouldn't want to end up impaled when it breaks up.' She let out a husky laugh. 'I'm giving you five days down there.' Her voice became serious again, businesslike, as if she'd been practising this speech for a long time and was now tired of saying it. 'If after that time you don't return, then I'm sorry, but we'll have to leave. I'll see you have a flare so you can signal us from wherever it is you resurface.'

'All right,' Killian replied, trying his best to sound breezy. 'Sounds fair enough to me. I can't expect you to wait around forever.'

'Nope.' After a small delay, she spoke again. 'I'll see you early tomorrow morning then.'

'Eleven o'clock sharp it is,' he replied.

'If you want.' She sounded deflated. 'You deserve a lie-in.'

'You need to be careful with throwing compliments like that about, Lil.' He smirked.

She smiled softly and nodded, yet her eyes were full of sadness. 'In that case you'd better get out before I take it back.'

'I'm gone,' he said, walking away with a slight swagger in his step.

'And, Killian, I meant what I said. You have five days, no more.'

'I understand.'

'Okay. Now go and rest. You'll need it.' She raised a hand in goodbye.

'I'll be fine,' said Killian as he left her cabin.

He lay silently in his hammock for some time. Thankfully, the cabin was empty, so he could be alone with his thoughts. He stuck his leg out and pushed it against the wall, idly swinging himself. He put his arms around the back of his head and stared at the wooden ceiling. The woodgrain and knots welcomed his gaze, and when he became bored of them he searched out the splinters and tried to count them. But these monotonous distractions couldn't block out the intense fear building in his stomach. The ceiling became a blurred mess. He blinked, and two great tears rolled down his face. Turning onto his side, he gave in and sobbed, his body convulsing with every shuddering breath he took.

WITH Killian gone, Lily could let her mask of pretence drop. She walked over to her bed, put one hand on the bed-post to keep steady and stared out of the window at the vast ocean. It all seemed grey to her – grey waves, grey sky, grey light. She looked at her dripping hat and damp feather. Even they were tinged with grey. She rubbed her eyes and turned to her bed, then flopped down gracelessly. A lump was building in her throat. With her head propped on her hands, she gazed out towards the mercilessly dull ocean. She trembled and tried to take a calming breath to fill her body with control, but she couldn't, and her charade broke down. For the first time in her adult life, tears flowed down her face. They dripped from her chin, splashing over the bed-sheets like gentle summer rain.

CHAPTER
TWENTY-TWO

KILLIAN WOKE LATE THE NEXT MORNING FROM a disjointed, dreamless sleep. Slipping out of his hammock, he dressed, buttoning his shirt with a distinct lack of enthusiasm. Today could be his last day; by the time the sun set he could be merely a memory. There was a stab in his gut. He tensed and tried to ignore it.

He yanked his coat from the back of the door, then took his goggles from the pocket and hung them around his neck. He chucked the coat over his shoulder and into the hammock. There was no point in taking it, as it would only slow him down. After one last look around the room, he left. Instead of going up on deck straight away, he went down a level.

He walked along the lower deck, dragging his feet as he went. He felt fragile; his skin tingled, and his heart hammered so hard he worried it might dislodge itself. He shouldn't have been doing this. It wasn't him. It wasn't too late to back out. He crouched down and put his head in his hands. He was nothing, insignificant. The ship creaked in answer to his thoughts. The money would help, but that wasn't all he was doing it for, and he knew that as much as he tried to pretend he didn't. Why was he doing this? Why did he have this ridiculous urge to prove something? Who was he trying to prove it to? He lifted his head and rocked it back against the wood, then closed his eyes and allowed himself to drift with the sway of the ship. Sometimes he'd hear her scream his name; other times it would be him, and he'd feel the warmth of their blood on his face. He always fought hard to bury those thoughts and feelings, but they found a way in when his defences were down.

He wasn't trying to prove anything to them; he'd already failed them, and nothing could change that. He had to prove it to himself, to know he was more than that coward who'd let them die. It was his fault they were gone, but saving someone else could redeem him. Pressing his palms into the floor, he pushed himself to his feet and started walking again. He had to relax; his emotions were threatening to take over.

Seth's distinct mutterings grew louder the farther he went. He stopped outside the mess, squared up to the door and knocked on it sharply.

'Oo's there?' Seth demanded harshly.

'The rat killer,' Killian said to the door.

'Ah! Come in, come in! Door's always open to you, you know!' said Seth cheerily, the initial animosity melting away as soon as he recognised Killian's voice.

Killian walked in to find Seth hunched over a chopping-board covered with sweet-smelling dried herbs. Next to him lay a small heap of salted, gutted fish, the smell of their flesh mercifully masked by the scent of the herbs. Seth stabbed his knife into the board with gusto and wiped his green hands on his stained apron.

'Good to see you,' he said, turning to Killian and beaming. 'You good?'

'Fine,' said Killian with a casual shrug.

'Ain't you goin' down that big sea hole today?'

'Yep,' Killian replied, trying to sound brave.

'Must be scared out your wits.'

'Nah, I'm fine.'

'You not just a little scared, no?'

'Of course not.'

'I'd be out of my mind!' roared Seth. 'Couldn't do it. You're one brave guy, you know that?'

'It's nothing,' said Killian. 'Anyone could do it.'

'Oh!' Seth chuckled, giving him a friendly slap on the back. 'When I first met you, I thought you were a crazy guy. Now I know you are!'

'Yeah.' Killian nodded. 'I'm completely insane.'

He looked around the kitchen. A large pan was bubbling away on the stove, its lid rattling every few seconds, and slumped next to it was a sack of oats. Another door led out of the back of the room, and the muffled clucking of chickens could be heard from behind it. He found his gaze drawn to the weathered cupboards that lined the room. 'Seth, look, do you think I could have a little something to warm me up?'

'Ah, you want somethin' from Seth's secret stores?' Seth gave him a knowing look. 'No problem, my friend!'

Seth crouched down and pulled a half-empty bottle of rum from the back of a cupboard, knocking a small bag of flour onto the floor in the process and swearing. He set a mug down on the square notched table in the middle of the room and poured in a generous slug of the fiery liquid. Killian picked it up and inhaled the intoxicating vapours, and in one swallow it was gone. He silently set it down and blew out a long hot breath.

'So you are a little scared,' said Seth as he poured again. 'Nah.'

Once again Killian drank the shot in one. The burning liquid warmed his insides with a soothing glow. He held out his hand and watched as it gradually stopped shaking. Seth filled the mug again, and he emptied it again.

'How about we finish it?' said Seth, and he divided the remains of the bottle between Killian and himself.

They clinked mugs. Seth gave him a slow wink, and they drained the vessels in one, slamming them on the table in unison. For the first time in days, Killian cracked a smile without having to force it.

Killian was on his way up to the main deck when he ran into Ren, who looked perilously flustered.

'Where have you been?' Ren asked fiercely. 'You weren't in the cabin, you weren't on the deck—'

'Good morning to you too,' said Killian with a mild slur.

'You've been drinking, haven't you?'

'And? What's it to you?' Killian snapped, rapidly losing his cool with the flapping person before him.

'How are you supposed to do anything if you're drunk? You stupid fool!'

'Firstly, I'm not drunk,' growled Killian furiously, holding up his fingers. 'And B, I don't remember the wedding, and if there was no wedding, then don't talk to me like you're my fucking wife! The Drop, the Demon's Drop, the

Hole in the . . . whatever you wanna call it, isn't going anywhere. There's no rush.'

'I don't believe this,' said Ren, rubbing his face with despair.

'Oh, shut up, Thorny. Stop being a dick. You're blowing this out of proportion,' said Killian, trying to defuse the situation.

'I'm being a dick? *I'm* being a dick? Speak for yourself!'

'I am not a dick!' Killian snapped through gritted teeth.

'Yes you are, just look at yourself! You've ruined everything, you drunken, idiotic—'

'Fine.' Killian swept his hand out in front of him. 'If that's how you feel, you can front this little expedition yourself. I'm going to bed.'

'Killian, I—'

'Shut it, Thorny. I don't care anymore. I'm sick of solving your problems. Sort your life out yourself.' He turned his back.

'Killian, please . . .'

Killian kept his back to Ren, enraged that he should insult him after all he'd done for him. He was risking his life to help him. Granted, he was paying him, but that didn't lessen the risk, the ungrateful little cretin. He'd got him in with the pirates, saved his life and cured his hangover. Demanding he was sober was just too much.

'Killian, please, I'm sorry.'

Killian remained silent. A feeling of inadequacy pressed hard against his chest, and he looked at the deck. He knew Ren was right – he was definitely the dick here – but he couldn't admit that to him.

'Please, I really am sorry. I let my emotions get the better of me. Please, Killian, please. I need you,' Ren grovelled.

Killian ignored him, his hands in tight fists at his sides. He had to better himself, had to save a life for the two he'd lost. A great wave of clarity washed over him, and he lifted his head.

'Please, Killian, please. I'm begging you.'

'All right, all right. Just shut up. I'll do it.' Killian moaned. 'Come on.'

He turned round to find Ren on his knees, his eyes shimmering with tears. The sight was too much for Killian, who slowly shook his head and sniggered. Ren appeared hurt, but then he glanced down at himself and giggled. Killian offered him a hand and pulled him to his feet. He put an arm around his shoulders and gave him a friendly squeeze, and they made their way up to the deck.

There were surprisingly few people milling around, and Killian was thankful for this small mercy. He sauntered over to the group of people who awaited him. Lily was there, with Raven standing beside her, looking every inch the chiselled hero. The three gunners hung back.

'Afternoon, Killian,' said the captain.

'Morning, Lil,' he replied impishly.

'Ready to go?'

'Yep,' he said, flashing what he hoped was a confident smile. He glanced at the party of people around him. 'It's quiet,' he remarked.

'I didn't think you'd want the whole bloody ship waving at you,' she explained, nodding towards the group.

There was a tense pause before he spoke. 'I'd better be off then.'

He moseyed over to the bulwark and looked down to the sea, where a small boat bobbed in the surf, awaiting him. As he prepared to descend, Finn, Tom and Blake grabbed him, pulling him back onto the deck.

'Careful down there,' said Tom, his voice slightly higher than normal. 'I'd rather you came back for this gun. I'd only break it anyway.'

'Take care,' said Blake sincerely. 'And keep your eyes open. I want all the details when you get back.'

'I'd best see you again, you great pretty-boy shithead,' said Finn in her usual gravelly tones. 'If I have to come down and get you, I'll kick you so hard that you won't need a lift home 'cos you'll fuckin' fly back.'

'Touching, Finn, really, but it won't be necessary. I'm coming back,' said Killian, flattered they cared that much. 'Take care of Thorny while I'm away. Don't let him do anything stupider than normal.'

Finn gave him a parting punch on the arm. Raven was the next person to delay Killian's departure.

'I will watch the ocean day and night awaiting your return.'

'Thank you,' said Killian. Maybe Raven wasn't that bad.

'Take care, my friend,' he added, giving Killian's shoulder a firm squeeze before stepping back.

'Killian,' mumbled Ren, 'I-I don't know—'

'It's all right,' he said. 'I do this sort of thing all the time.'

Ren nodded and stepped back to join the gunners. Killian turned around to climb down, but just as he put his leg over the side of the ship, a hand grabbed his arm and pulled him back. Turning back, he was surprised to see it was Lily.

'I almost forgot to give you this.' She delved into her coat, pulling out the flare she'd promised. 'Send it up when you come back.'

'Thanks.' He felt a slight resistance on her side as he took it.

'Take care of yourself.'

'I will.'

Killian found rowing towards the hole disturbingly easy. As soon as he'd untied the little boat from the ship he'd felt the pull of the water. The hard part was keeping it straight, although he wasn't sure if it mattered which way he was facing anyway. A cool breeze blew across the surface. It was as if the Drop were devouring the warmth as well as the water. It was unnaturally cool down here. He regretted not asking Seth for some more rum to take with him; the fear was rapidly sobering him up. The sound of the rushing water grew louder with every second. He pulled his goggles up over his eyes. Then he saw it, and he stopped breathing.

It looked like the edge of the world. The seawater was falling away into oblivion right in front of him. His boat hit a small wave, which provided him with a better view. The hole was huge, so wide that he couldn't fit it all in his vision, and for a few terrifying seconds he saw the other side – a gigantic wall of cascading torrents. Witnessing the ocean falling away in front of his very eyes was simultaneously the most terrifying and amazing thing he'd ever seen. Now he saw how much water was tumbling over the edge, he felt certain he'd drown.

He stood up in the boat and took one last look at the *Tempest*, which by now was nothing more than a tiny dark patch on the horizon. He blew a sad kiss in its direction and plunged into the ocean, diving under the surface and swimming towards the hole. Looking straight ahead, he could just make out the edge, a bizarre frosted window where the sea should've been. The sea bed rose up like a huge underwater volcano, with the water pouring ferociously into the crater. He came up to the surface for some air and trod water. There was no point in swimming; he was already moving at an exponential rate, and he wasn't in a hurry anyway.

He was pulled swiftly towards the edge, and then he was falling, along with thousands of gallons of salty water. A surge of adrenaline ripped through his body, and with a bit of twisting he managed to manoeuvre into a graceful diving position. He looked around as he plummeted; it was truly colossal. Violent white water cascaded over the edge in an endless torrent. He was enclosed within a ring of white. Below, a vast indigo pool circled with an exploding white halo churned as it eagerly awaited him, its choppy surface desperate to pull someone down into its uncharted depths. The noise was immense, a deep, powerful roar. It was never-ending; he felt like his ears would burst. The pool was getting closer, filling his vision with a bottomless icy blue.

His body broke the surface with tremendous force. The immense power of the pouring ocean pushed him down, giving him no choice other than to go with the direction of the raging water. He twisted and dodged the remains of countless ships that had been battered into submission by the power of the ocean. Looking down, he saw he was being pulled towards the sharp end of a mast. With great effort he managed to fight the current and move himself, escaping with cuts to his arm and back.

The plunge pool was lit by an eerie green light that drifted up from beneath the dilapidated wrecks, making the sight of them all the more unnerving. The light poured through the cracks in the ships, blasting through their torn hulls and leaking from the empty windows. They were piled on top of one another, layer after layer of fallen ships, devastated titans that had valiantly fought a losing battle against the Drop. Now all that remained were battered, cracked husks, deformed ghosts of past glories. Countless lives swallowed up, leaving nothing but a graveyard and the waterfall a guardian for lost souls.

He was pushed down to the middle, and then a different undercurrent seized him, dragging him off to the right and towards another shipwreck. There was a huge hole ripped in its side, and he was headed straight for it. He leant his body to the right so that he was on course, and to his relief he was pushed through the gaping maw.

The interior of the ship was a flooded mausoleum crammed with grinning skeletons. Their bones glowed with a sickly jade light, and they stared jealously at him as he swept through. He wished he could close his eyes to shut them out, but he had to see where he was going. Collapsed masts split the decks in two, creating fractured ramps for the cannons to careen down. Below him, forty or more cannons slumped on top of one another, trapped forever in a crevasse forged by the fallen masts, a seething mass of brittle rusted edges and slimy green algae. He followed the current the length of the ship and shot through a splintered hole into a vast expanse of water. It seemed like he was back in the sea; all around him was endless blue.

He was carried a good distance forwards until he slowed and was liberated from the violent grip of the current. His body fell limp, and he was too numb to move. As he drifted, he felt the pull of the surface. With a fresh surge of strength, he turned his body around and kicked towards it. A faint glimmer of light shone through the water, encouraging him to kick harder. His lungs burned, black spots invaded his vision, and his limbs felt heavy. It was like swimming through syrup. Every movement became more of an effort than the last, but he refused to give up. The light above the water was getting brighter, forcing itself between the flashing black spots. With a final thrust, he burst through the surface, gasping and panting for breath as he rushed to fill his burning lungs.

He yanked his goggles around his neck and fever-ishly looked about his surroundings. He was inside a giant under-sea cave, the ceiling so high it was lost within a strange multicoloured haze that swirled above him. He couldn't see how far it extended, but the water seemed to go on forever. Behind him, a craggy rock face stretched up and disappeared into the haze. Languidly, he moved around in the water until he saw a beach a few hundred metres to his left. His skin was without sensation, his body unresponsive, and there was a hum in the back of his head that was grad-ually getting louder. He had to make it to land before the oncoming delirium drowned him.

Forcing his drained body into action, he pushed for-wards in the direction of the beach, moving automatically. It was the only way to keep himself going; if he allowed his mind to wander away from the task of swimming, he'd never make it. As he neared the beach, he found the seabed had risen sufficiently for him to stand. He planted his feet in the soft sand and heaved his body up. Standing, once so simple and natural, now felt like one of his greatest achievements. Waist deep in water, he trudged towards the land, his wet hair flopping in his face, his lungs aching from their torture. He was so tired, every footstep was an effort. As he reached the shore, his knees gave way, and he fell onto the sand. He lay still, listening to the soft sounds of the tiny waves break-ing, then rolled onto his back and stared up, mystified by the whirling colours that shrouded the apex of the cave. He listened to his breath – slow, even, another achievement – and put his hand on his chest. His heartbeat was strong. He was alive, and that was all he cared about.

He shivered; he was soaked, his wet clothes plastered to his body. An icy cold fused to his bones even though the air was temperate in the cave. He sat up, wrapped his arms around his knees and rubbed himself to try to warm up. It wasn't working. He lay down and scrunched his body into a tight tremulous ball. It didn't take long for the exhaustion to get the better of him. His eyes closed, and he lost consciousness on the strange under-sea beach.

CHAPTER
TWENTY-THREE

RAVEN STOOD STARING AT THE SEA, ALONE. The others had left the deck as soon as Killian had gone, no doubt seeking a way to blot out the creeping feeling of loss. Lily retired to her cabin almost immediately, and from the look in her eyes, he knew better than to disturb her.

He rested his hands on the rail and gazed at the spot where he'd last seen him. With his sharp vision he'd been able to watch Killian stand in the boat and bid the *Tempest* farewell before leaping overboard to become lost amid the churning waters. Raven's fingers pressed into the wood, and he blew out a slow breath. It had been a long time since he'd felt like this – hollow, helpless and redundant. If he could have taken his place, he would have done so in a heartbeat, but he knew he couldn't have. This was something Killian had to do.

Bright white sunlight flashed upon the surface of the ocean, and Raven squinted. A hot sweat broke out on his back, luring his shirt towards his skin. He rolled his shoulders, and his scars itched. Waves broke against the hull, and he stepped back from the bulwark. He should have left the crew long ago, should have disappeared and become somebody else, but he'd made a foolish promise to Lily and now felt himself growing attached to Killian. In the past he'd kept his distance with most of the crew, not wanting to forge deep friendships with anyone. Yet since Killian had appeared, he'd found himself more at ease with socialising, and it didn't sit well with him. No good would come of it.

He peeled off his wet shirt and threaded the sleeves through his belt loops. His dark olive skin gleamed with a layer of moisture. Against his better judgement, he reached his hand over his shoulder and traced one of the blackened scars that ran along the blade. It was wide and rough. The scars and his facial brand were the only parts of his body that refused to heal, even after all this time. For a split second he felt the pain of being torn apart again. He'd never screamed like that before; it had been so intense he'd wanted to die. When they were done torturing him, they'd cradled his head in their hands softly, gently, brotherly, before permanently branding his face. As his beautiful rich skin burned, pain finally granted him the mercy of unconsciousness.

It was only a lingering memory, but every time he recalled it, it felt worse. He stretched his back, and every inch of his body crackled with a vestige of pain. A breathless sensation descended upon him. He needed to clear his mind and regain his composure.

The mainmast beckoned him and he raced towards it, not caring if his prominent scars once again caused talk of a demon amongst the crew. He leapt from the deck to the thick wooden post, not slowing in his movement, and raced up its full length vertically. His hair blew back in the cooling breeze, and his shirt flapped at his side; neither did anything to hinder his concentration. Reaching the top, he pushed off, vaulting high into the air. The wind lashed at his eyes, and they streamed. For one absurd moment he wanted to surrender to the itch in his back and escape, disappear from the ship, from everyone, and start again.

He forced the errant thought away and landed neatly in the crow's nest, then straightened up and turned towards the Drop. He put a hand to his face to wipe away the tears, only to find they were still falling.

KILLIAN peeled his heavy eyelids open. Colours twirled and danced above him. Purple, green, orange, pink and blue all spiralled and swirled together in a nebulous intangible mist. He blinked and rubbed his eyes, but the colours remained. Was he dreaming? There was a beach to his left and a row of trees, their leafy tops swaying. It all looked real enough. Before him lay a vast lake; it was so familiar. He blinked again and breathed deep. It wasn't a dream. The lake was where he'd emerged from. This was the other side of the hole. He grunted and lay back, gingerly moving his limbs, which felt like lead weights.

He shuffled his hands behind his lower back and pushed himself up to a seated position, drawing his legs up and bending his knees. Something was vibrating rapidly. Was it the ground? Did the roar of the Drop cause such oscillations? It took him a moment to realise he was shivering.

Hunching his shoulders, he leant forwards and wrapped his arms around his knees. He was so cold. His body was completely soaked, to the point where it was painful.

There was a tear in his shirt surrounded by a patch of red. With trembling hands he half unbuttoned it and shrugged it off his shoulder. A wide cut ran along the back of his upper arm and onto his back. It shimmered with wet blood and throbbed with a dull pain, but there was nothing he could do about it now. He dragged his shirt back on and rocked his head back to gaze at the colours stretching out above him, their perplexing presence a welcome distraction from his current predicament. He took a deep breath, inhaling the smell of salt and wet ageing rock.

Reluctantly, he tore his eyes away from the confusing spectacle above and hauled himself up from the soft sand with a groan. He rubbed the stray grains from his face and body and surveyed his alien surroundings.

He stood facing the water and looked to his right. A massive blackened cliff face covered that side of the cave, its edges glistening white as if it were outlined with thousands of crystals. The water below the cliff rushed with bubbles and currents, indicating the passage he'd entered by. There was no chance he'd get back that way.

He turned around to see a gigantic temple carved into a wall of rock. It was colossal, too vast for his gaze to take in. Two huge pillars tangled with thick green vines soared up towards the coloured mists, melding back into the cliff and becoming lost. Four smaller pillars stood proudly in line before the entrance, a ball of coloured light resting on top of each one, showing the way. The temple doors were cut from two single pieces of what looked like marble; they glistened blue and sea-green, and a strange silvery light shimmered across their surface. Still shaking with fatigue, he staggered towards it. There was nowhere else for him to go. The dull throb of his cut rapidly morphed into a sharp acidic pain; he clamped his hand over the wound in an attempt to placate it.

He looked to the trees and plants thriving beyond the beach, turning his head as he followed them. The beach extended farther than he could see into the distance, the vegetation with it. He had no idea how it grew down here, beneath the sea, and he was too tired to dwell on it. Upon reaching the temple, he climbed two steps and then leant against a small pillar atop which pulsed a ball of green-and-pink light. He looked at the doors before him. They were huge; he would never be able to open them. It was futile to even try.

'Hello?' he called throatily. The sound echoed around the pillars, but there was no response.

Never had he felt so alone, his only companion the soft lapping of the waves on the beach. He trudged away from the doors, dragging his weary feet as he went.

'Hello?'

He walked towards a soft patch of ground near the temple where fresh grassy shoots stood proud amid the sandy earth. The bright green plants blurred, and he sank to his knees in desperation.

'Hello?' he said again, but still his cries were unanswered.

He stooped forwards, and a black wave of despair washed over him. What if he couldn't get out? What if he was trapped down here forever? This was where he was going to live out the rest of his days, alone, under the sea. He released his arm – it still ached, but he didn't care – and pulled his knees into his chest, pressing his cheek against them. He shouldn't have done it. What had he been thinking? He looked out towards the lake and the imposing black cliffs. There was no way back, and even if he could swim against the current, it wasn't as if he could climb up the sides of the hole.

His vision momentarily dimmed, and he felt an odd sensation at the top of his spine. Something warm pressed against the back of his neck, but almost as soon as he registered the feeling, it was gone. He shivered with cold again and put his hand on his neck. There was nothing there. Was this what drifting into insanity felt like? He flopped forwards again.

'Hello,' said a voice as soft as crushed velvet.

Killian lifted his head and lost the ability to breathe. At first glance, the man before him appeared to be nothing out of the ordinary. His face was human and accompanied by a short thick golden beard. His hair was a shoulder-length tangle and his skin a warm brown. Curly black tattoos ran along his collarbone and disappeared under his shirt. It was his eyes that sent shivers down Killian's spine – two expressionless globes of amber split by horizontal pupils. A pair of thick ridged horns grew from his head, curling back and downwards, framing his face. A furry golden tail finished off his demonic appearance.

Killian was gripped by unimaginable fear. He fell onto his elbows and kicked at the ground ferociously to get away.

'Stay away from me! Get away!'

He trembled uncontrollably, but somehow, despite his weakened state, he managed to get to his feet. Unable to take his eyes off the strange creature, he backed away.

'Stay away! Stay back!' he cried as he shakily removed his swords.

The creature remained motionless.

Killian's legs were unsteady with panic, and he staggered to the side as they gave way beneath him. He feebly held his swords up in front of him in defence. Then his body betrayed him, and he collapsed forwards onto his hands. His breathing became turbulent as a dreadful realisation dawned.

'I'm dead,' he said in disbelief. 'I didn't make it . . .' His voice descended into a hoarse whisper.

The creature spoke again. 'It is fine.'

'No, it's not!' Killian shouted. 'I can't die – not yet.'

'You are not dead,' it said.

Killian didn't respond, he just continued to stare at the ground in front of him. He felt like such a failure. What a fool he was to believe he'd made it through the Drop with nothing but a graze to show for it. He'd thrown his life away, all because he wanted to prove something to himself. His body shook with despair, and his eyes welled up with bitter tears. It wasn't worth it. It wasn't worth this.

'You are not dead,' it said again, and this time its voice was firm. It softly placed a hand on his shoulder.

'I'm such an idiot,' Killian mumbled unsteadily. 'Why did I think I could do this? One of the others should have come – Lily, Raven – not me. I'm such a cock. A stubborn, useless, dead one at that.'

He became fully aware of the being's hand on his shoulder and swiped it away.

'I told you to get away from me, you monster!' he seethed as he shakily got to his feet once more. 'Don't come anywhere near me.' He pointed his swords at the horned beast. 'I'm not going with you, so leave me alone.'

'I am not going to take you anywhere you do not want to go,' the creature replied softly. 'And I am not going to hurt you,' it added, holding its palms out to Killian as evidence.

Killian looked at the creature's hands suspiciously as he took a wobbly step backwards. Then he cried out in frustration and threw his swords to the ground. He sank to his knees again and buried his head in his hands.

'What's the point?' he whispered to himself. He lifted his head and held out his arms, defeated. 'Go on, take me away.'

The creature walked over to Killian and squatted down next to him.

'You are not dead,' it said again.

'I feel dead,' Killian mumbled back. He shoved his hands into his armpits to try to get some warmth back into his body.

'I would not be able to talk to you if you were dead, would I?' said the creature, its voice light again.

'No,' Killian murmured to the sand, digging his nails into his numb skin to test the theory. 'But if you were a demon, you—'

'Do I look like a demon?' the being said, its tone friendly and reassuring.

Killian's eyes met the creature's, then flicked to its horns. 'Yes.'

'Ah.' Its brow furrowed. 'I can assure you I am not.' It frowned.

Killian managed a trembling nod; he was so cold and so tired, he barely knew what he was nodding for.

The creature got to its feet. 'I am sorry I startled you,' it said as it held out a hand. Killian eyed it warily, then reached out and took it. It was warm and dry; it felt real and solid.

The blood rushed from Killian's head to his toes as the creature pulled him up. His hearing became muffled, and a sickening wave of dizziness smothered him. He staggered forwards, his legs threatening to give way. A hand clamped him firmly on the shoulder, and he closed his eyes, leaning into it, waiting for enough of his strength to return so he might be able to stand unaided. The creature was holding him. It was saying something, but its words drifted through him like the whispers of a spectre. He shuddered as a sharp spike of cold pierced his body, bringing with it an infinitesimal flicker of energy. Slowly, he opened his eyes and stepped away from the horned creature, determined to prove that he could stand.

The being stood before him, looking at him.

'I'm fine,' Killian croaked, rubbing his arms.

The creature nodded, turned around and picked up his discarded swords. A ripple of horror coursed through Killian's body. Maybe the demon was going to finish him off now. His muscles twitched; he didn't know if he'd be strong enough to fight it off unarmed. Tensing, he prepared himself; he wasn't going to die without a fight.

'The swords,' the creature said, handing them to him hilt first.

'Thanks,' Killian said, trying to ignore his feelings of guilt as he sheathed them.

'Come, I will take you to the others. We have been waiting for someone like you,' it said.

Killian nodded, too numb to question.

'Cassius,' the horned being said, holding out his hand again. 'A cornelian, not a demon.'

'Killian,' he replied, shaking the offered hand, its warmth making his cold skin throb. 'A . . . human?'

Cassius smiled. 'Follow me, Killian.'

Cassius led him through the dense undergrowth that surrounded the temple, his long tail swishing behind him.

He moved with the grace of a cat and seemed to know the exact position of every branch and root, dodging them expertly.

Killian staggered behind, carefully keeping to the path Cassius followed. He was exhausted. His limbs were so heavy he was having trouble controlling them, and his arm seemed to sting more with every passing second. His cold damp clothes clung to his body, and his wet hair stuck to his face.

The air was clear and fresh, the lush undergrowth easily masking the briny scent of the lake.

Cassius glanced over his shoulder. 'So, what is it like above the hole?' he asked enthusiastically, his eyes glittering.

'Different,' said Killian, surprised that he'd managed to form words from his frozen lips.

'In what way?' he asked, skipping over a root without giving the ground so much as a glance.

'Depends where you go,' replied Killian, wanting nothing more than for the conversation to end. He was beyond fatigued, so cold that every movement hurt. The last thing he wanted to discuss was the world he'd left behind.

'Ah ha!' Cassius laughed triumphantly. 'So there is more than one land up there?'

'Yes.'

'Just as I thought.' He clapped his hands. 'Once you are rested you can tell me all about it.'

Killian forced out a smile to humour the cornelian, inwardly wincing at the prospect of that task.

A faint murmur filtered through the trees, growing louder with every step they took. Killian's stomach coiled with apprehension as he realised it was rapidly unfolding into the clamour of voices. Cassius slowed his pace and came to walk beside him.

'Killian,' he said in a low voice. 'We are almost at the village. The others will stare at you, but do not take offence.'

'I won't,' he replied as they stepped out from the undergrowth.

Killian's hands instinctively came to rest on his hilts at the sight before him.

The flat ground was covered in large tents crafted from what looked like animal skins that had been dyed with natural earthy colours. They were spread out on the grass, but their positions were far from arbitrary. Sandy pathways lined with coloured glass globes dangling from bent sticks acted as walkways between tents. Cornelians wandered up and down paths, some sat outside their tents crafting jewellery, and others appeared to be preparing what looked like vegetables.

'Come on,' said Cassius softly, taking Killian by the arm.

Killian had no choice but to step into the daunting village. All the twinkling jewel eyes seemed to turn to him, and the voices dropped to whispers as he walked by. Demonic horns flooded his vision. His chest tightened, and his body felt heavy, but he kept his head up to appear strong. Maybe that would deter them from attacking him. A large cornelian with glistening purple horns and a long black tail fell into step with Cassius. He was tall, and his shoulders were broad. He had to bend to whisper in Cassius's ear, his amethyst eyes flicking towards Killian as his mouth moved. Killian tensed, his exhausted muscles bunching together. He had no idea what was being said. Was this it? Was he going to die now? Were they plotting how best to rush him? He wouldn't be able to fight them all off. His arms dropped to his sides. There wasn't any point in trying to defend himself, as it would only prolong the inevitable. Cassius smiled, nodded and whispered back. The large cornelian looked at

Killian again, lowered his head respectfully, and turned in the opposite direction.

The centre of the village opened out into a clearing. The ground was covered with soft mossy grass and dotted with colourful wildflowers that filled the air with a delicate sweet scent. Insects akin to bees, but with wings of deep shimmering cerise, flitted about the flowers, gently humming to one another. In the middle of the clearing was a huge pile of sticks. Killian's beleaguered mind raced again, and a lump formed in his throat. Was that his funeral pyre? His fists bunched up; he had to get a grip. To his left was a large semicircle of low wooden tables, behind which ran a row of tree trunks covered with multicoloured dyed rugs carefully arranged as seating. To the right was a tent twice as big as any of the others Killian had seen in the village. It was dyed black and painted with white markings similar to the tattooed glyphs he'd noticed running along Cassius's collarbone.

'Wait here please,' said Cassius.

Killian did as he was told and watched Cassius disappear inside the ominously dark tent. Alone again, he pondered his fate. What were these odd creatures going to do with him? Eat him? Murder him? Let him go? Would he ever see his friends again? Would he ever see Lily again? Gritting his teeth, he inwardly scolded himself for his last thought.

His gaze darted around, looking for a means of escape if it did turn out that the cornelians enjoyed a good human steak. His palms pressed against his hilts. All he could do was run and slash, but where would he go? He couldn't swim back; he'd already established that. Perhaps he could climb up the blackened cliffs and disappear within all the colours. His thoughts were interrupted as the flap of the tent lifted and Cassius appeared again.

'I have spoken with the Tia—'

'Tia?' Killian said.

'Nesta, the Tia, our leader, our . . . queen. I have told her of your arrival, and she has requested your presence at the evening meal tonight.'

'The evening meal?' Killian's shoulders stiffened.

'Yes, we all sit together and eat. Do you not have such customs? I was sure you did.' Cassius rubbed his beard thoughtfully.

'Eat what?' Killian asked quickly, ignoring Cassius's question.

'You will see.'

Killian's stomach curled into a tight ball.

'Come,' the cornelian said, putting his arm around Killian's shoulders, which only added to his sense of doom. 'I shall get you some dry clothes. You can worry about Nesta later.'

Killian allowed Cassius to lead him through the clearing and back into the village. Once again, he felt the eyes and horns turn towards him, but he was getting beyond caring. He was too exhausted, too cold and too bedraggled. His arm no longer stung and seemed to have finally ceased bleeding, his blood having dyed most of his sleeve a watery crimson. All he wanted to do was collapse, pass out, and hopefully wake up somewhere else. The whispers of the cornelians gradually rose to a normal speaking level, though Killian couldn't catch any of what they were saying. Their words mashed together into a nauseating audio pulp.

Cassius took Killian to the edge of the village, stopping outside a brown tent set back against the edge of the forest.

'This is where I live,' he said proudly, clasping his hands together. 'Wait until you see inside.'

From out of the gloom of the forest appeared another cornelian. She moved with the elegance of a prancing deer as she loped towards them, her deep red dress fanning open to reveal a split at her thigh. Her snow-white skin bore the same black tattoos as Cassius's. She came to a halt in front of Killian and stared at him. A pair of horns curled about her pretty face and glowed with a silvery sheen.

'Cassius,' she said, mock disappointment lacing her airy tone and a stony glare in her silver eyes. 'Are you not going to introduce me to your friend?'

Cassius cleared his throat. 'Killian, this is Freya. Freya, Killian.'

'Hello,' said Killian, shaking her hand. The bangles which adorned her wrists softly jingled.

'Hello, Killian.' Freya fixed her attention back to him. 'I presume you are from above?'

'I am.'

'Very impressive. You must be quite the swimmer,' she added with a sweet smile. There was an air of normality about her that relaxed him.

'I'm all right.'

'Modest, or . . .' She wrapped her tail, ruby furred and adorned with beads and bangles, around her body and held it in her hands. 'Blasé?'

He encircled his arms about his head, and for the first time since he'd arrived he felt a little like himself. 'Definitely the latter,' he replied.

She looked him up and down. 'I disagree.'

'Funny, that. So do I,' he said.

She huffed and looked towards Cassius. 'I think there has been a mistake. We should send him back.'

Cassius laughed. 'We cannot do that.'

Freya groaned and ran a hand over one of her horns.

'I'm not that bad, am I?' asked Killian, feigning hurt.

'First impressions, yes.' She grinned. 'But if Cassius likes you, I am willing to give you a chance.'

Killian went to respond, but a yawn took him unawares. He stretched in an attempt to cover it up. 'I'm honoured,' he said wryly.

'You are tired,' she stated, looking at him with one crimson eyebrow arched. 'Make sure you get some rest, and tell Cassius to shut up if he keeps hounding you about your world.' She gave him a wink.

'I will.' He smiled back.

Cassius rolled his bizarre eyes at Freya. She grinned at him and stretched up to plant a kiss on his lips. He put his arms round her and kissed her back.

Freya twisted herself from his grip and smiled. 'I will see *you* later,' she said softly, placing a finger on his lips. 'Bye, Killian,' she added politely, and then she bounded away.

'Sorry about that,' said Cassius as he regained his composure.

'It's fine. Is she your—'

'My life, my light, my star, the breath I breathe, the owner of my heart,' he replied earnestly, clasping his hands to his chest.

'I was just gonna say wife,' said Killian.

'Oh, yes, of course, that is the term.' The cornelian looked down at the grass, seeming embarrassed by his passionate outburst.

After a lengthy pause, Killian spoke again. 'Right, dry clothes.'

'Ah ha, of course, of course.' Cassius nodded, ducking inside the tent.

Killian stood outside, listening to him fumble about inside. When the noise ceased, the flap lifted to reveal Cassius's smiling face. He stepped out and held the flap open for Killian, motioning for him to go in.

As soon as Killian walked in, Cassius dropped the flap for privacy. A glowing globe of purple set within the central support beam cast light about the inside. Killian froze and looked around.

The tent was filled with all sorts of items from the surface. There were stacks of artwork – mostly of nautical scenes – and a wooden stand containing countless swords, many of them dull and blunted with age and rust. Another stand was covered with clothes, tired-looking jackets and decaying trousers, the sight of which made Killian feel oddly light-headed. There were three carved wooden chests. He walked over to the first. It was green with old mould and encrusted with dried barnacles. He gingerly opened it to reveal a plethora of different items: rusted old guns, shattered pottery, shabby hats, small carvings, blackened coins, weathered books and an unfathomable amount of jewellery. He carefully closed the chest, took a step back and breathed out.

A space in the middle of the tent had been cleared for sleeping; it was covered with furry skins and dyed fabrics. Killian took a deep breath, inhaling the scent of fresh herbs and flowers. He detected something akin to the soothing aroma of lavender; the familiar smell crawled over his weary body and massaged his muscles.

Yawning, he peeled off his heavy wet clothes and grabbed the baggy trousers and dull green tunic Cassius had left out for him. The trousers were much too big for him. He unbuckled his sword-belt and fastened it round his waist to keep the trousers from falling down. He threw the tunic on, pulling it beneath the belt to further secure the trousers. The fabric made his skin itch, but at least they were dry. He scooped up his wet clothes and went out to join Cassius.

Cassius beamed when he saw him. 'Ah ha! You look good,' he said, taking the wet clothes from him and hanging them on a wooden post. 'Just like a man from the surface.'

'I didn't before?'

'No, no, you did,' said Cassius, nodding hurriedly, almost as if he was afraid he'd caused offence. 'But now you look more like how *I* envisioned a man from the surface. So, did you like my treasures?' He grinned and strode over to Killian.

'All the stuff in your tent?'

'Yes,' said the cornelian ardently. He gripped Killian by both shoulders and squeezed. 'I have always been fascinated by your world, hence my collection. To have you here and to be the one who found you is more than I could have ever wished for.'

Killian felt slightly unnerved by Cassius's attitude and wondered whether he'd end up part of the collection.

'Killian,' Cassius said, releasing his shoulders and taking his hand. 'Please tell me about your world. I want to know everything. How you live, what the land is like, everything.'

Killian nodded slowly and failed to suppress a yawn.

Cassius's enthusiastic smile morphed into a frown, and his golden eyebrows knitted together. 'Freya was right,' he said softly. 'I am sorry. I got carried away. You should rest.'

'I'm all right,' Killian lied, his second yawn betraying him.

'No, you should rest before tonight. There will be plenty of time for you to satisfy my curiosity later.'

'I'm all right,' Killian murmured.

'No. You have been through a lot.' He held the tent flap open. 'Sleep. I will come for you later. Rest well. You will need your strength.'

Killian didn't know what was meant by that, but he was too exhausted to talk anymore; it could wait. He ambled back into the welcoming purple glow of the tent, took off his clothes and flopped onto the floor. The skins were soft and snug, and the lavender-like scent helped to ease his worries. He fleetingly wondered whether he'd been drugged, but he was so comfortable that he didn't care either way. His eyelids closed without him noticing, and he drifted off into a dreamless sleep.

CHAPTER
TWENTY-FOUR

'COME ON.' AN ANXIOUS WHISPER FOUGHT its way through Killian's heavy slumber. 'Wake up, my friend. It is time.'

Killian grumbled something incoherent as he sat up and rubbed his eyes with his palms.

'I shall wait outside,' said Cassius, getting to his feet.

Killian reached over to grab the tunic and shrugged it on. He threw the soft cover back and pulled on the trousers, tightening his belt. As he got to his feet, his head rushed, and his vision blurred. He took a step back and steadied himself by bending his right knee and resting his palms on his thighs. The dizzying fog in his mind eventually cleared, and his stomach growled with despair.

He stepped through the awning and followed Cassius back across the village. The earlier bustle had dissipated, leaving it quiet and peaceful. As they walked, his gaze wandered towards the sky and the mystifying scene above. The colours had become deeper and more vivid, losing the washy, hazy appearance they'd had earlier. The light was fading, but the cornelian settlement basked in the warm, comforting glow provided by the red and orange orbs lining the walkways.

The fire was already lit in the clearing. Its heat wafted over Killian's skin, demanding his attention. Long orange tendrils of flame reached towards him, and he looked to the fire's burning white heart. The pure warmth soaked into his body, and he willingly received it. Cassius grabbed him by the arm, breaking the crackling spell of the flames.

'Come,' he said, pulling him towards a semicircle of low tables. 'You can sit with me.'

Killian saw the mountains of food, and he moved without hesitation. Clusters of cornelians sat around the tables, their heads down, deep in conversation. Their eyes occasionally flicked up and in his direction. He responded with a series of shaky smiles.

'Is here all right?' said Cassius, stopping where the tables overlooked the fire.

'Sure,' said Killian as he sat down.

'Ah, good,' said Cassius, joining him. 'And do not worry about tonight. Everything will be fine.'

'Yeah, I know,' said Killian with a grin that he hoped masked his creeping nerves.

Cassius smiled back, his eyes glowing like amber lamps.

Killian's attention quickly fell on the piles of food before him. He presumed it was all fruit and vegetables, although they were alien to him. Some of them were covered in prickles, and he wondered how exactly one was supposed to eat them. Others were strange colours, colours he didn't really want to put in his mouth. Delicious smells radiated from them, some savoury, some spicy and some sweet. They all mingled together in the air around him. It was almost like walking through Brackmouth on market day. His hollow stomach moaned once again, reminding him of its neglect.

'Where do you get all this from?' he asked.

'We grow it.'

'How?'

'Much the same as you would on the surface, I suppose,' Cassius replied. It was obvious from the twinkle in his eyes that he was keen to ask Killian about the surface, but he managed to restrain himself.

Killian shrugged and tried to make himself comfortable, which turned out to be no easy task. The table was too low for him to stretch his legs under, so he was forced to put them to the side and adopt a lopsided position, which he supported with his right hand. It wasn't ideal, but it'd do. He looked at Cassius, who was sitting straight-backed and cross-legged, and considered altering the arrangement of his legs. He shuffled once, gave up and slouched back down.

It wasn't long before more cornelians filed into the clearing, a mass of tails, horns and large horizontally slit eyes glittering like brightly coloured jewels. They each glanced at Killian with some interest, which made him feel a little uncomfortable. Freya appeared with them and skipped over to Cassius, settling down next to him and taking his hand in hers. The rest of the cornelians sat down and waited. Killian drummed his fingers impatiently on his thigh; it was maddening to have all this food set in front of him and not be able to eat it. He didn't care how strange it looked; he was forgetting his manners as the hunger made him increasingly irrational. He'd missed breakfast – Seth's rum didn't exactly count.

Cassius seized Killian by the shoulder and yanked him up as the other cornelians rose to their feet. He glanced around to see the cause of the rapid change in mood. A tall statuesque cornelian stepped out from behind the fire, her deep umber skin soaking up the colours of the flames. A massive pair of ridged golden horns curled back and culminated in sharp points. White make-up ran over her gold eyes in a stripe, giving the appearance of a mask. Long thick hair glistened with a silver hue as she moved, twinkling like a river of stardust. She wore a deep-purple cloak over a black dress, its sleeves and skirt split and tattered, rolling down her body like octopus tentacles. She walked towards the table with a powerful stride. Everyone stood in respectful silence, waiting for her to speak. There was no doubt in Killian's mind that this impressive woman was the Tia, Nesta.

'My friends, please sit,' she said, her voice strong and clear. She waited patiently for them to sit before she continued. 'I am sure you are all aware that a surface dweller has made it down to our domain, alive.'

All the sparkling jewel eyes turned to focus on Killian. He shrank as far into the ground as he could and lowered his gaze to avoid eye contact.

'Do not be startled by him,' she continued, addressing the cornelians. 'I am certain he is not here to cause harm.' She shifted her attention to Killian. 'Please, surface dweller, tell us all your name.'

'Killian,' he replied, wincing at the sound of his own voice as it echoed about the table.

'Welcome, Killian,' said the Tia. 'Please, everyone, eat. Killian, I will speak to you after the meal.'

Killian nodded. He clenched his fists under the table to stop them from shaking and then filled his plate with food. It was tempting to try one of the spiky things, but he was too nervous to ask how to eat them. He picked up what looked like potatoes instead and ate his way through them. For once he ate slowly, glancing around the table every so often to observe his strange hosts. Thankfully the focus was now on the meal rather than on him, although he still couldn't ignore the notion that he could be for dessert. He risked a sly glance in Nesta's direction but averted his eyes when he found her golden gaze firmly upon him.

'Are you enjoying the food?' Cassius asked.

Killian swallowed before he answered. 'Yes, thanks.' He was so hungry he could've been eating anything and enjoying it, not that he was about to voice that to the eager cornelian.

'Ah, good, good,' said Cassius, a satisfied smile breaking out across his face. 'I helped to grow most of it.'

'Do not let him bore you, Killian,' said Freya, reaching over Cassius for some of the potato-like things. The five chunky crystals adorning her necklace cast out rainbows and chimed softly as she moved.

'Freya,' said Cassius, looking a little hurt.

'Come on, my dear,' she said. 'Sometimes I worry as to what you love the most: me, your surface treasures or your plants.'

'I think you know the answer to that.'

'Do I?' she said. 'A girl could get jealous.' She looked at Killian and gave him a slow wink.

Cassius turned to Killian with an anxious look on his face.

'It is her,' he whispered.

'What?' Killian asked.

'I love her more than any of those things.'

'I know you do.'

'Does she?'

Killian shrugged.

Cassius turned to Freya. Snatches of their conversation, often punctuated with lilting laughter from Freya, drifted over to Killian. He smiled to himself; they were an odd couple.

He picked up another of the potato things and chewed it slowly as he glanced around. A little to his right was a dainty female. She was laughing and flashing her rose-quartz eyes at a purple-horned female, who smiled back with obvious fondness and stroked her cheek. The purple-horned cornelian picked up one of the spiky things Killian had been contemplating. She split it in half with her thumb and turned each half inside out. She offered half to her rose-eyed companion, who took it with a coy smile. Killian looked away; he was surrounded by all these beings, but he couldn't seem to shift that empty feeling of loneliness. He looked back at the spiky things. His hand hovered over them for a few seconds, but he decided against it. After all, he had no one to share it with.

After what seemed like hours of picking at his food, Killian noticed the cornelians were leaving. Cassius stood and walked over to where the Tia was seated. He spoke a few words and motioned towards Killian. The Tia nodded, and Cassius returned to his seat.

'She will see you now,' Cassius whispered to him.

Without a word, Killian got up and moved towards the majestic cornelian. He tried to formulate a speech as he walked, but words escaped him. It was an odd feeling to be wordless; it never really happened to him, well, except when he was alone with Lily, and only then when he feared for his life. She could never render him speechless by herself. His chest tightened, and his shoulders stiffened. He didn't miss her.

Killian stood to the right of the Tia and waited to be addressed. Nesta turned her great golden eyes towards him. It felt as if she were looking straight through him and into his innermost secrets. He instinctively placed a hand over his heart; perhaps he was trying to protect his deepest thoughts from the penetrating gaze.

'You wanted to see me, Your Majesty,' said Killian, inwardly recoiling at the formality.

'Please sit.' She indicated the cushion on her left. 'No need to stand on ceremony, and please address me as Nesta. I am not your Tia.'

Killian nodded and sat down.

'Now, isn't this a privilege.' The cornelian's eyes shone with delight as she focused on Killian. 'It is not often we are blessed by the presence of beings such as yourself. The remote nature of this place is not at all conducive to outside visitors. Most are washed up on the beach dead, sometimes in pieces, but not you, and with just a mere scratch, I hear.' She nodded towards Killian's arm. 'Most impressive.' Nesta's voice was as strong and powerful as it was reassuring.

'I was lucky,' Killian admitted.

'Luck had nothing to do with it,' said the cornelian, shaking her head. The myriad crystal charms that adorned her horns chimed softly as she moved. 'You need skill to navigate our gateway.'

'Thank you.'

There was a long silence between them. Nesta narrowed her eyes, their golden flare momentarily lost amid her white mask. Killian fell back beneath the gaze; he felt as if he was being judged. Her face was expressionless, giving him no indication of what his score was. *She'd be good around the card table.*

'May I see your swords?' Nesta asked.

Killian removed his sword-belt and passed it to the queen, stunned by the sudden request. He was thankful to be sitting, or his trousers would have fallen down – not a good look for his first encounter with royalty.

Nesta examined the hilts, drawing her finger across their patterns. She turned them carefully in her hands in a way that reminded him of Geoffrey. To his surprise, she drew one from its scabbard and examined the blade.

'I see you have had the blades reforged,' she said without raising her eyes.

'They were only hilts when I got them.'

'Yes, it is the hilts that hold the power,' Nesta mused. 'They have the contact with the wielder; the blades are inconsequential. I must say they have been marvellously restored. The new blades do them justice.'

Killian was about to enquire how Nesta knew about the swords when he was swiftly cut off by a question.

'Now, Killian, what is it that brings you down to our domain? What has driven you to risk your life in coming here? Or did you just fall overboard?' she added with a soft chuckle.

Nesta's soothing voice had an almost hypnotic effect, and he forgot what he was going to ask.

'I have a friend whose father is dying,' he said after a short pause. He frowned – had he really just called Thorncliffe a friend? 'There's this thing on the surface that can save him.' He moved his hands to help describe the Gramarye, but he stopped after realising he had no idea what it looked like, dropping his arms to his sides. 'It's sealed in a temple by some powerful magic. Someone I know told me about the Demon's Drop – your gateway – and what was beneath it. He reckoned you could help me break the magic and get the . . . thing . . .'

'Why is it that you have come and not the one with the ailing father?' Nesta asked.

'Thorny?' Killian stifled a snigger.

'Yes.'

'He's not exactly equipped for such endeavours himself. He was sent to find me by his father to ask for my help. Coming down here is my way of helping him.'

'Noble,' Nesta muttered.

'Not completely,' said Killian. Somehow he knew if he didn't say something now, it'd come back and haunt him.

'This Thorny, he is rewarding you for your efforts?'

'Yeah,' said Killian, feeling a pang of shame, 'with money.'

'Understood.'

She regarded Killian, her eyes once again dimmed by the white mask; it was as if she were boring into his soul. It was a disconcerting experience. He felt naked under her gaze. The cornelian pursed her lips, and her brow furrowed. Now Killian knew how Ren had felt when he first met him. All his hopes were pinned on what the Tia would say next. He bit down on the end of his tongue. Returning a failure was not an option.

'Well, Killian,' she said at last. 'You seem acceptable, and the nature of your plea is just.'

'Thank you,' Killian replied. A weight lifted from his heart, and a drunken euphoria surged through his head.

'You are worthy of performing the tasks,' she announced.

'Thank you. What?' Killian asked, confused, momentarily forgetting his manners.

'The tasks. Did your knowledgeable someone not inform you?'

'No, his great knowledge extended only to your existence,' said Killian, trying his best to bite back the sarcasm in his tone. The weight returned ten times heavier than before, and the euphoria was replaced by burning apprehension. Why was nothing ever simple? Couldn't diving down the Drop be task enough?

'Well, let me explain as best I can,' said Nesta, her voice like honey. 'You must run the gauntlet and navigate the labyrinth to get to the darkest truth. You must undertake these three tasks to prove yourself. Only those who have completed the tasks will be granted the reward.'

'Gauntlet, labyrinth, darkest truth?' Killian muttered. 'Can you tell me any more about them?'

'It is forbidden. All I can say on the matter is this: They will push your physical and emotional strength to the limit. They will show you what kind of man you truly are and what you are capable of. In order to survive, you must believe in yourself. Your own strength of body and heart is the only thing that will get you through.'

Killian took a deep breath and said nothing, his nerves silencing him. His stomach flipped, his skin went numb, and his bottom lip trembled of its own volition. He encircled his head with his hands and leant back into them, casting his gaze up to the pirouetting colours to disguise his expression.

'You have nothing to worry about. I have a good feeling about you.'

'Has anyone ever—' Killian began.

'No,' she said flatly. 'But do not let that discourage you. You are the first I have deemed worthy to undertake them. Now if I were you, I would get some rest. You will need it.'

'When do I begin?' Killian asked, moving his head back to look at Nesta.

'Whenever you feel that you are ready. You are welcome to stay here and train for as long as you deem necessary.'

'How long will they take?'

'I cannot say.' Nesta shook her head, the crystals on her horns casting tiny dancing rainbows on her skin. 'Hours, days – no one has ever attempted them.'

'I'll start tomorrow then.' Killian's jaw set hard with determination.

'So soon?' said Nesta, sounding concerned.

'There's a ship waiting for me on the surface. They'll leave in four days,' said Killian, his voice edged with melancholy.

'In that case, I wish you luck.'

Nesta gave him a nod and got to her feet. She handed the sword-belt and swords back to him, and he fastened them around his waist. He felt much better when they were at his sides.

'Meet me by the temple in the morning, and then you may begin.'

Killian watched Nesta disappear beyond the fire. Once she'd gone, Cassius came over. He'd kept at a respectful distance during their conversation.

'Are you all right?' he asked in his usual buoyant tone. 'You have gone pale.'

'I have to do three tasks to prove my worth,' said Killian monotonously.

'You did not know?'

'No.' He shook his head and got to his feet. 'Oh well, if I can jump down the Drop, I can do your tasks, can't I?' he said, the confident grin back in place.

'Of course you can,' said Cassius, giving Killian a reassuring pat on the back. 'Come, you should rest now.'

Killian followed Cassius back through the cornelians' village. Most of them had retired to their tents, but small clusters remained, gathered together around the light of the globes. As Killian and Cassius walked by, they looked up and nodded respectfully. Some even went so far as to greet Killian vocally.

'What's with them?' he whispered to Cassius.

'They honour you due to your bravery in the gateway: the Drop.'

'I've had scarier baths.'

Cassius chuckled and clapped him on the shoulder.

A group of cornelians were clustered around a fire a few feet from Cassius's tent, Freya amongst them. Killian watched their faces flickering with the flames. They were passing a giant smoking pipe between them. A long colourful tube extended from a dark base. It had a glass ball fixed in the centre, which flashed through all the colours of the spectrum whenever anyone took a drag. The air was heavy with the sweet scent of the violet smoke that gathered around them. A bottle was also working its way around the group in the opposite direction to the pipe. He smiled to himself when he saw them; they reminded him of his shipmates. A sudden pang of sadness descended upon him. He'd only known them for a short while, yet they'd all become close.

'I am going to sit with my friends awhile,' said Cassius,

bringing Killian's thoughts back to the present. 'You are welcome to join us.'

'I would, but I should sleep. I've got those life-threatening tasks in the morning.'

'Of course, of course, you should sleep,' said Cassius. 'Freya shares my tent, but do not worry. We will be quiet.'

'You won't wake me. I'm a heavy sleeper,' said Killian. He winced at the prospect of sharing a tent with a couple so deeply in love as Freya and Cassius.

'Good, good.' With that, he went to join his friends.

Before going inside, Killian glanced up again. The swirling colours had changed. They were still moving, and he could still pick out individual hues, but they were much darker now. Deep purples, dark midnight blues and pine-forest greens swirled together to create the night sky. If not for all the pressure he was under, he would've happily lain outside and enjoyed the aerial display – and whatever was in the cornelians' bottle and pipe.

He pushed back the cloth of the tent and collapsed onto the soft floor. He rolled onto his back and lay with his arms around his head, breathing slowly and calmly. After a few minutes, he sat up and removed his top. He held his arm out and examined the damage he'd suffered from the mast. It was just a graze really. He flexed his back; that didn't feel too bad either. He'd had worse before, and worse was no doubt yet to come. Slumping back down, he pulled a thick blanket over his body.

As he lay awake in the darkness, his mind drifted to his friends. Would he ever see them again? Would he ever see Lily again? As much as he tried to repel them, thoughts of her always found their way into his mind. His eyelids drooped. She still had his necklace. His body tensed as the night they met replayed in his mind. He'd get it back – by rights it was his. As Lily reached towards him to take the necklace from his open hand, sleep descended and whipped him away from her.

CHAPTER
TWENTY FIVE

FTER A NIGHT OF SCATTERED DREAMS, Killian awoke. He sat up straight, blinked several times and looked around the tent. He was alone. At the foot of his blanket were clothes that had been neatly arranged for him. He flopped back down onto the soft bedding and watched the tent move against the breeze. Today was yet another day where he'd have to risk his life. Perfect. Why was he compelled to do these ridiculous things? If he were Morton, he'd have bet against himself too.

He grabbed the warm covers and threw them over his head, groaning contentedly as he closed his eyes. All he wanted to do was drift back to sleep – lovely, safe, comfortable sleep. He wasn't ready for what lay ahead of him today. He had trouble admitting it to himself, but travelling through the Demon's Drop had left him weary, both physically and mentally. Frowning, he tossed the covers back and sat up. But he had no choice. He had to do the tasks today or risk missing his lift home.

He stood up and put his arms behind his back. He grabbed his elbows and arched his body, stretching out his chest, his tired joints popping and cracking in a deeply satisfying manner. After a few more deep stretches, he threw his own clothes on, glad to feel the familiar fit. Next, he attached his sword-belt and placed his goggles on his forehead; he'd become so used to their presence he almost felt underdressed without them.

He stepped out of the tent and almost walked straight into Cassius. The cornelian nimbly sidestepped out of the way, which was lucky, as he was carrying a flat wooden tray full of fruits.

'Sorry,' Killian exclaimed, holding his hands up.

'Ah ha, that is quite all right. I brought you some breakfast.' He set the tray of fruit down and sat next to it. 'I picked it fresh for you this morning. I hope you like it,' he added anxiously.

'Thanks,' said Killian, joining him on the ground. He picked up something plump and yellow. It smelt divine, both sweet and fresh. He put it in his mouth, and when he bit down it exploded with delicious syrupy juice.

'Do you mind if I join you?' Cassius asked.

'Not at all,' said Killian, reaching for another of the succulent yellow fruits. 'I've never eaten anything like this before.'

'It probably does not grow where you are from.'

'You mean it only grows down here?' said Killian, frowning at the sticky fruit.

Cassius nodded.

'How do you grow it? I always thought plants needed sunlight.' He wasn't interested in the slightest, but he hoped a little mundane conversation would help to ease his worries.

Before he could answer, Freya appeared from out of nowhere. She gracefully sat down behind Cassius and wrapped her long legs around his body. She reached around him to scoop up a piece of fruit, her wavy ruby-red hair tumbling over her shoulders and glistening in the morning light.

'Good morning, Killian,' she said politely, her large silver eyes fixed on him.

'Morning, Freya.' Killian smiled back, already feeling at ease.

'So, what were you two deep in conversation about?' she asked breezily.

'Killian was asking me about how we grow our plants,' Cassius explained.

'Oh, very interesting,' she said, wrinkling her face.

Cassius tutted at Freya and rubbed her leg, then turned his attention back to Killian. 'I am sure you have noticed our polychromatic sky.' His face lit up with enthusiasm as he spoke.

Killian nodded.

'Well, that is how we grow it. We create night and day artificially – sunlight and moonlight, dusk and dawn.'

'But how do you do that?' Killian asked.

'Arkani,' said Cassius simply.

Killian frowned and puckered his lips at the answer.

'Magic,' said Freya. She bit into a chunk of yellow stuff.

Killian shook his head at the vague answer. Freya grinned and winked at his frustration.

'Yes, apologies, Killian. You would probably call it magic or something to that effect. To us it is arkani. It is raw, and it is powerful,' said Cassius. 'With it we can easily recreate night and day to help us live. Our daily cycle mirrors your own on the surface. We have lived this way for centuries.'

'You are so dramatic,' Freya mocked, sucking the sticky juice from her slender fingers.

'I am just trying to make it interesting,' he said.

'If you don't mind me asking, how old are you?'

'I am about 1,200 of your years. You lose count after the first few centuries,' said Freya airily. 'Cassius is around a hundred years older than me though,' she added with a sly grin.

'Do not exaggerate,' Cassius scolded. 'I am barely fifty older.'

'What?' exclaimed Killian. 'You can't be.'

'I know,' said Freya, her eyes twinkling mischievously. 'The way he waffles on about fields and fruit, I would put him at least two hundred older.'

'No, not that. Your age – I thought you were my age.'

'What are you then? Five hundred, six hundred?' asked Freya.

'Twenty-seven, pushing twenty-eight,' said Killian flatly.

'Why thank you,' said Freya, laughing and flicking her hair.

'That's a long life,' Killian muttered as he picked a piece of fruit. He popped it in his mouth and slowly chewed it as he looked at his two horned companions. Freya's hand had wound itself around Cassius's waist, and he pressed his head back against her chest.

'Don't you ever get bored?' Killian asked.

'Never. We lead contented lives,' said Cassius. 'I want for nothing.'

'Me either,' said Freya as she ran her fingers affectionately through Cassius's messy golden hair.

'I wish I were like that,' Killian murmured, his eyes focused intently on the thick emerald grass.

'What is it that you want, my friend?' Cassius asked.

Killian opened his mouth to say something but couldn't find the right words. What did he want? Redemption? Purpose? Value? Love? He winced. What the hell was wrong with him? He was becoming far too sentimental. 'I don't know,' he said, shaking his head.

Cassius watched him curiously but didn't pursue the matter. 'So, you are really going to begin the tasks today?' he said.

'Yeah,' said Killian, glad of Cassius's tactical diversion, 'after breakfast.'

'So soon,' said Freya, all her playful mirth absent in her expression.

'Are you sure you do not want to train up first?' Cassius asked. 'I could help you – it is no trouble.'

'I don't have time, otherwise I would. I'm rested, I'm in pretty good shape anyway, and I think if I stayed any longer I'd eat all your food,' said Killian as he picked up another piece.

'I can grow more,' said Cassius, although his voice sounded defeated.

They continued to eat their breakfast without speaking. When they'd cleared the tray, Killian got to his feet, Freya unfurled her legs from around Cassius and they joined him.

'I suppose I should get going,' said Killian. 'She's probably waiting for me.'

'I will come with you,' said Cassius.

'Me too,' added Freya.

They walked in silence, Cassius leading Killian back towards the shore. Killian focused unsteadily on the beach.

Not long ago it had seemed like such a sanctuary. He'd welcomed the soft sand on his face, he'd thought he'd been through the worst and survived, but from the quiet concern of his cornelian companions, it was clear the worst was yet to come. He tried not to dwell on it, but it was impossible not to. Death was calling him once again.

Gauntlet, labyrinth, darkest truth. He didn't like the sound of any of them, but his mind kept coming back to the darkest truth. What could it mean? What would it do to him? He shuddered as each individual vertebra iced over, and his shoulders became as rigid and hard as a frozen oak. He had to relax. If only he'd got some of Seth's rum, that'd sort him out, defrost his muscles. A day hadn't even gone by, and he was already doing something ridiculously dangerous. He bit his lip to keep from laughing about it; there was something undeniably amusing about the situation he was in. If it were anyone else, he'd probably feel sorry for them, but all this was his own doing. He curled his fingers; he would make amends or die trying.

Their pace slowed as they approached the temple, the pillars before it casting beautiful soft light into the still air. Cassius spun around and grabbed Killian by the top of his arm. There was a desperate urgency in his firm grip.

'You do not have to do this yet. I cannot . . . I cannot bear the thought of you throwing your life away. You are my friend.' His hold tightened as he spoke. 'You are not ready yet. You need rest, training. Killian, please. I do not want you to die.'

Killian looked at the pleading cornelian, and his heart swelled with emotion. 'I'm sorry. I have to, or I'll be left behind.'

'Cassius,' said Freya with a weak smile, 'we have to let him.'

'I know.' Cassius released him.

'I'll be fine,' said Killian, though he wasn't quite sure who he was trying to convince – Cassius, Freya, or himself. 'Don't worry.'

Standing before the great temple doors, her back to them, was Nesta, her long silver hair shimmering with patches of pink and green as it absorbed the light from the glowing orbs atop the pillars. Cassius and Freya stood back as Killian slowly ascended the steps to approach the queen of the cornelians. His nerves screamed, making his whole body throb. His footsteps were heavy. They felt so final. He stood a respectful distance away from the Tia and waited to be addressed.

'So, you are determined to enter today?' Nesta asked.

'I am,' said Killian, his confident tone belying his true feelings.

Nesta turned to Killian, her eyes a dazzling gold against her dark skin and white mask. 'Remember all that I told you last night. Should your will falter, your body in turn will falter. Once you go in, there is no turning back. You finish, or you die. Do you understand?'

'Yes.'

'Then I can be of no further assistance,' said Nesta. She placed both hands on Killian's shoulders and looked him in the eyes. 'Good luck.'

Nesta turned to the temple and took a step forwards, tilted her head back and held both her arms out, spreading her fingers. Her body glowed with bright silver light. Then the giant doors glowed, the green and blue effects on the marble seeming to flow into each other like tributaries into a river. Long strands of silver light drifted from Nesta's body and glided towards the doors, snaking up their surface upon making contact. They settled into the same shape as the glyphs that adorned Cassius's collarbone, Freya's body, Nesta's tent and countless other places and bodies around the cornelian settlement. The doors shone with a brilliant white, forcing Killian to shield his eyes from the glare. Then they opened with the breath of a summer breeze.

Nesta turned to Killian, her eyes gleaming like the sun itself. 'Ahead lies the pathway. Do not forget what I have told you.'

Killian nodded.

'Good luck, Killian,' said Freya, her face grave.

'Good luck, my friend,' said Cassius solemnly.

'Thanks,' Killian replied. He turned to face the temple, and without hesitation he walked inside.

The doors shut behind him with a thunderous crash. The sound echoed down the long tunnel stretching out before him. He stood in darkness, his body tense. There was a tingle in his feet. Looking down, he saw a pulsing blue light beneath him. He took a step backwards, and the stone floor erupted with light, two bright beams of blue pouring from it, flowing up the walls on either side. With a crack, the beams raced down the length of the corridor, illuminating the walls with the now familiar yet endlessly strange twisted glyphs. They shimmered with a shifting turquoise colour, bathing the tunnel in an eerie light. Killian squinted into the distance. A shadowy gateway loomed at the end of the corridor.

He sucked in a deep breath and took a few tentative steps forwards. With a harsh snap, three vicious spikes sprang out of the wall. He leapt forwards and rolled across the stone ground, clumsily smashing his shoulder as he went. He looked back, his heart pounding. The spikes were stuck in the opposing wall. One wrong move and he would have been dead. They were as black as ebony but glinted like glass in the light of the glowing symbols. He reached forwards to touch one. It was cool and hard, and its surface was jagged and uneven.

He took a guarded step forwards, but his following leg sank backwards. A dizzying rush of blood flooded his body. There was no time to think, so he pushed on, his foot sinking once again, throwing him off balance and causing him to stumble into the wall, which flashed with a full spectrum of colour. The air grew thick, and he glanced down. The floor beneath his feet was turning to dust. An almost intangible feeling gripped him; he couldn't quite take in what was happening. It took him a frozen second to gather himself before he could lunge forwards, feverishly battling his way through the dust to solid ground. There was a roar from behind as the stone slabs that had supported him fell away completely. He had to move quickly. Another set of black spikes ripped out of the wall just behind him. He darted ahead and broke into a run.

Long strands of violet and turquoise whipped out from the centre of the glyphs as Killian ran by. He ducked and dodged away from their coils, fully conscious of the collapsing floor behind him. He darted to the right, avoiding the reach of a purple strand. With his attention taken, he didn't notice the blue one until it had tightened about his wrist. It brought him to his knees with a jarring snap. He unsheathed a sword with a clammy hand and tried to hack through the bond. It flashed with a bright silver light and sent a numbing pulse of energy down his blade, causing him to drop it. The tunnel rumbled, the collapsing floor drawing closer. He grabbed his sword and got to his feet. Gritting his teeth and swearing, he pulled against the rope of light and, feeling a slight give, tensed his shoulders. With one swift powerful movement, he yanked his arm back. The light broke with a flash of blue and the shatter of broken glass. Killian stumbled backwards, quickly regained his composure and ran, the glittering dust of the disintegrating floor in hot pursuit. The blue bond on his wrist faded away in a curl of smoke.

Before he could fully register it, a hole appeared in front of him. He misjudged his footing, slipped and staggered forwards. Instinctively, he flung his arms out and managed to grab the ledge in front of him. His chest ached, his legs ached, his right arm had been noticeably weakened, and his lungs felt as if they were being crushed with a white-hot anvil, but he managed to hold on. His breath was short and his hope waned as he dangled helplessly, waiting for the moment the ledge would fade to dust and he'd plummet into the darkness below.

His thumping heart and laboured breath were all he could hear. Relief rippled through his body as he realised the roar of the collapsing floor was no longer present, and he just hung. His right arm sent him a warning pain; it was going to betray him if he wasn't careful. With a strained groan, he hauled himself up onto the ledge. He glanced back at what his fate might have been. The distant depths of the pit sparkled with uneven black crystal spikes.

As he straightened up, a flash of red light shot from the wall at ankle height. He leapt over it only to find himself in the path of another. He jumped over this one too and quickly developed a swift rhythm for running and leaping over the bolts of light. Searing heat radiated from them, filling the corridor with stifling warmth. Just as he got into the flow, an orange flare exploded from the wall at head height.

He ducked under and kept going, keeping low. Sweat poured into his eyes, making them sting and his vision blur. Then, as quickly as it had begun, it was over, and he was in front of the dark gateway. Before him was an arch a little over six feet at its zenith with swirling blue symbols throbbing on each individual stone. A layer of moss clung to its edges, weaving itself into the crumbling ancient brickwork. He cautiously walked through and followed a tunnel around to see what awaited him.

He stepped into darkness but could tell from the way his footsteps echoed that he was in a spacious high-ceilinged room. The air inside was cool and fresh, a dramatic change from the heat and dust of the corridor. He wrapped his arms around his chest, shuddering from the wintry chill that inhabited this pitch-black space.

An iridescent light erupted in the gloom, illuminating the walls. Killian blinked, his breath catching in his throat. The room was gigantic, the walls rippling with waves of colour – red, blue, purple, yellow, green. Before him lay a great chasm, its floor lined with more razor-sharp black crystals casting cruel shadows up the walls. Across the sea of spikes, another archway shone with blue light. He looked to his left and right; there didn't seem to be any way around the room. He wiped the sweat from his forehead with the back of his hand and grunted.

As he squinted across the abyss, a blinding white light burst in front of him. He stumbled backwards, putting his hands up to protect his eyes. When the light dimmed, he dared to look. A pillar of glittering marble lay in front of him, its surface pitted with deep dents providing easy hand-holds. With no other options, he stepped forwards, grabbed on and hauled himself halfway up. He shimmied around and looked out over the pit. A blast of iridescent light burst from the pillar and shot through his chest. All the breath rushed from his body. The light ricocheted about the room, creating a pathway of glowing white objects.

Behind him hung a thin white walkway. He climbed a little higher and grabbed hold of it. With a groan of exertion, he hauled himself up and crouched down on the end. The harsh sound of cracking glass came from behind him, and he glanced back to see the pillar crumble into wisps of dust. Thankful he was no longer on it, he turned his attention to the walkway that stretched out before him, ending abruptly at another pillar. Keeping low, he scurried along its length, jumping off to grab the pillar. As soon as he touched the cool marble, the floating path dissolved. There was no way back now.

He spied a pathway of white stones suspended in mid-air above him and began climbing towards it. There was a muffled blast. A bolt of red light was heading directly for him. He swung around the sparkling column, using it as a shield. The red light exploded on impact, sending shocks through his arms and weakening his grip. He tensed, regained his composure and hurried upwards, his progress hindered by blasts of red energy.

He twisted behind the pillar, using it for protection with increasing frequency. It was hard work, and his movements became sluggish as they took their toll on his body. Sweat was making his hands slippery, and his muscles trembled with the strain.

Letting go would be so much easier than climbing . . .

Thoughts like that wouldn't help. As soon as he reached the top and stepped out onto a glowing stone, the pillar disappeared.

The room flashed, and all four walls faded to violet. Long threads of coloured light reached out of them, trying to grab hold of any part of him they could. Killian gritted his teeth, leaping from stone to stone, the path behind him vanishing as he moved forwards. The ropes of purple and blue light grasped for him with increasing aggression.

The room pulsed with red light, and he had to dodge the hot blasts as well as the coils. He darted from stone to stone, the blue archway below lodged firmly in his vision. He was so close now. The room had heated up intensely; sweat trickled down his back and fell upon the black crystals in the pit, teasing them. Then the path of white stones abruptly ended, and all that lay beneath him was the dark chasm. There was nowhere for him to go; the stones behind had dissolved to nothing.

He crouched down to keep clear of the blasts of red light. His body stiffened as he looked at his stone. Its surface was shifting, and it was already crumbling at the edges. Killian's heart raced, and his muscles tightened. Jumping down wasn't an option, and he wasn't close enough to jump for the arch, but he couldn't stay where he was either. Colours danced in his peripheral vision, making his head swim. His sight was filled with purple as one of the coils whipped towards him. He sprang to his feet to avoid it, and as it lashed back, he lunged for it and grabbed on, using his momentum to force it in the direction of the arch.

The stream of light pulsated with power, sending shocks down his arms. He grimaced, ignoring the tremors reverberating through his muscles, focusing everything on the gleaming blue archway. The shocks grew more violent as the glowing rope fought to dislodge him. Killian felt his strength fade as the potent flashes of purple leaked over his body. He knew he couldn't hold on for much longer. When he was as close to the arch as he would get, he let go, the thrust of his initial jump carrying him forwards.

There was a sharp crack as his bond with the coil was broken. He tumbled through the air, his gaze fixed firmly on the arch and his arms outstretched. All his breath was smashed from his body as he hit the ground roughly. He lay before the archway on the cold hard stones, his body cast in blue light, his chest heaving. Staring up, he watched the colours as they faded back into the walls, cloaking the room in darkness once again. Slowly, he dragged himself to his feet.

He leant heavily on the glowing arch. His right arm was aching – it had taken the brunt of the magic's abuse – but his whole body was noticeably drained. The tunnel beyond was shrouded in darkness. He took a cautious step forwards, keeping one hand on the arch for support. Once again, the ground beneath his feet glowed bright, sending out rivers of light and filling the tunnel with shimmering turquoise symbols. At the end was another gleaming arch.

He rocked his head from side to side and blew out a long breath. He pushed his hair back and shifted his goggles slightly. There wasn't any point in waiting. He could see the end, and what if the ground decided to fall away while he was gawping at it? Keeping low, he darted down the full length of the corridor – and nothing happened. He rounded the corner to see another long corridor with a black gateway at the end.

He took a step forwards, and there was a loud boom immediately followed by another. The path behind him was closing up. Blinding flashes of light cracked as the walls collided with each other. Drenched in panic and fuelled by fear, he ran, breaking into a sprint within seconds.

The walls flashed purple and turquoise as he dashed by, the strange coils reaching out for him. The smashing of the walls grew louder. He put his head down and ran faster than he'd ever run before, forcing the pain of his burning exhausted limbs to the back of his mind, focusing instead on the looming doorway. The coils tried to grab him, but they merely brushed his clothing, unable to get a grip. The faster he ran, the faster the walls closed, and they got closer with every sickening crunch. Sweat poured down his face in rivulets; his skin was on fire, and it was increasingly difficult to breathe as dust and dirt rushed through the passageway. He was so close to the gap now that he could almost put his hand through it. Just as he reached it, he felt the wall behind him close, trapping a piece of his flailing shirt. With nowhere else to go, he launched himself forwards into the blackness of the hole.

The material ripped and sent him sprawling head first into the unknown. *Well, that's that then.* His thoughts were ended abruptly as his fall was broken by the welcoming cool of water. He allowed his body to sink under the surface before coming up for air. Torches embedded in the walls ignited, illuminating the new area in a warm orange glow. He was in a cold deep lake within a large shadowy cave. Dark stalactites glowing with green algae hung from the ceiling, reaching towards him like vicious claws.

He swam over to the side to see if there was any way he could climb out, his splashes resonating around the massive space. He reached the cave wall and used a protruding rock to pull himself out. It was slimy and slippery to the touch, making climbing out all the more taxing. He hauled himself onto an uneven ledge and sat, soaked through, in his torn shirt. *No use feeling sorry for myself.*

He looked around the cave, searching for an exit, but there didn't seem to be any clear way out. With a grunt, he slumped forwards and dangled his feet in the water as he gradually regained control over his breath. His arms hung limply at his sides, slowly regenerating their lost strength. As he sat there pondering which way to go, something beneath the surface caught his eye. A green light was flickering within the lake. Another appeared, and another, then the whole lake was glowing green with the light of the bizarre underwater torches.

Killian understood. He rested for a few more peaceful minutes and then stood up and set his goggles over his eyes. The lamps led towards a crevice in one of the underwater walls. He poised, took a deep breath and dived into the labyrinth.

CHAPTER
TWENTY-SIX

KILLIAN SURGED THROUGH THE WATER towards a fissure in the side of the cave, the strange underwater emerald flames leading the way. He gripped onto either side and pulled himself through. The gap led into a long tunnel. The sides were encrusted with sharp rocky outcrops that he clung to as he powered his body along. All too soon he was aware of a lack of breath. His lungs were burning, but there was no turning back; this was the only way. He scrambled to pull himself along the wall, hand over hand. Fortunately, there were no currents to battle against. The water was still and calm.

He reached the end, and it opened into a cramped underwater cave; a solitary green torch dimly illuminated the hollow. The walls were jagged, a jumble of sharp dark rocks presenting no clear exit. Killian's body numbed, and his thoughts grew meaningless. He had to breathe. A faint orange glow drew his gaze upwards. His tired legs kicked for it.

He burst out of the water and took a deep breath, filling his aching lungs with brackish air. His heart raced, thundering in his ears like a whipped horse, making it difficult to think. Robotically, he paddled to the side and gripped on to a slimy outcrop. He shuddered; he'd almost died again, and so soon into the second task. With a shaky hand, he pushed his goggles onto his head.

The small air pocket was illuminated by a smooth orange-and-yellow orb embedded in a wall. The ceiling was low and even, continuing down to the water on all sides except for the ledge he clung to.

He allowed himself to rest, savouring every breath as if it were his last, knowing in the back of his mind that it could be. Right now he had two options – drown or live – and he knew which he preferred. His legs recharged as they hung listlessly beneath him. He fixed his goggles back over his eyes and looked into the water to find the next path. A faint green light wavered in the blackness below.

Straight down. Fantastic.

He lifted his face from the water and took several deep breaths, then filled his lungs to capacity and dived under. The gap was right in the centre of the floor. The last thing he wanted was to go deeper into this underwater labyrinth, but he had no choice.

The hole was a lot smaller than he had anticipated. He put his hands in and pulled himself through. As soon as he was in he wanted to get out. The sides of the tunnel were frighteningly close and constantly snagged on his clothes and body. He winced as the sharp edge of a spiteful rock sliced into his arm. Salt water rushed in where the blood flowed out, making his arm sting. He tried to ignore the searing pain by dragging himself down the tunnel as quickly as he could.

The pressure was immense and getting higher by the second; he had to pause now and again to equalise his ears. There was no light down here – it was too narrow for torches – so all he could do was pull himself down and hope it would soon be over. He felt the walls all over his body, caressing him like an overbearing lover. At any moment they were going to crush him, he was sure of it. The life would be squeezed from his body. The pain in his arm was relentless, like it was burning, but that couldn't happen, not under water. He struggled on, pulling himself down using the sides.

He reached forwards, and his fingers grazed the bottom. Frantically, he groped around the walls looking for an exit, keeping a tight grip to stop himself floating back up. To his right he found another tunnel, which felt just as narrow as the first. A faint green light twitched within the darkness in the distance, and his heart soared. He put his hands down the narrow gap and twisted his body around so he could fit.

The green light beckoned him forwards. It softly illuminated the space, revealing just how confined it was – barely wider than his shoulders and covered with sharp ravenous rocks. The vicious points raked his skin with every movement. Tiny salty flames licked him all over, yet the pain served to spur him on.

The light hung just outside the exit. He stretched his hands out and placed them on the rocky walls either side of the aperture. He emerged into a large under-sea cavern. By now he was so desperate for air that black spots swam in his vision, unconsciousness rapidly closing in. An orange light glowed from above. He kicked as hard as he could in its direction.

He burst through the surface and took a deep, hoarse breath. The salty air cut through his lungs like a rusty saw, and he coughed violently with each gasp. He yanked his goggles onto his head again and scanned the air pocket. There was no way out, but there was a ledge running around the edge just above the surface.

With shaking arms he hauled himself out of the water, his muscles straining in protest. He slumped against the side of the cave and looked down at his shredded clothing and skin. He was a wreck. The deep gash on his arm throbbed; he held it up and watched, momentarily mesmerised by the blood dripping from the wound. It softly splattered on the rocks, creating miniature red pools in their rutted surfaces. His chest was covered with tiny scratches that bubbled with blood. He ran his finger over them, streaking crimson over his wet skin.

His breath caught in his throat, and he started to shiver uncontrollably, his lips trembling. The tunnel, the claustrophobia, the pain. He pulled his legs up, wrapped his arms around them and rested his head against his knees as despair settled over him like gently falling snow. He couldn't do it, couldn't go on; he was going to die. This was his lonely, bleak tomb. Warm tears streaked down his icy skin. Why was he doing this? Why was he even here? Because he wanted to feel better about himself? Because he longed for a sense of self-worth? Because he was the only one who could? Because he had to make up for what he'd done? Because of money?

He rubbed his face on his knees. It didn't matter why. He was here now, and there was no way back; he had to keep going. He had to get it together, had to focus. He couldn't lose it, not now. If his resolve faltered, so would his body. He rocked his head back and released his legs, letting his feet dangle in the water. All he had to do was stay strong.

He slipped back into the water. After sitting on the ledge, it felt warm, comfortable even. He gritted his teeth as the salt water greedily chewed at his wounds. Just like he'd done in the last pool, he put his goggles on and dipped his face into the water. To the far right was a dark shadow that could only be another tunnel, but it was a long way off. Doubt wrapped itself around his shoulders like a siren, whispering his fears, ordering him to stay in the cavern. He lifted his head and shirked her off.

He swam to the right, heading for the tunnel. He had been too fixated on not drowning to notice how immense the cavern was. The uneven ground below glowed faintly in the green of the torches. Shadowy crevasses and fissures between the rocks fell away into the unending darkness while proud stalagmites jutted upwards, their jagged ends twinkling in the eerie light. The craggy rocks that enclosed him glistened with a silver-blue sheen, highlighted by the emerald radiance. Gigantic onyx stalactites hung from the ceiling, their ends sharpened to glimmering points.

Despite the hazards, the loneliness and the suffocation, there was something terribly beautiful about the cavern. It was as if he were swimming through a landscape impression of an alien world. Killian had never seen anything like it before, but that was becoming something of a running theme of late. Nothing seemed real.

The flickering green flames cast dancing shadows about the cave, and they dashed like a shoal of fish as he swam by. Flecks of silvery light drifted in streams of stardust on the slow-moving currents that flowed through the submerged cave. Recounting it when – if – he returned and doing it justice was going to be difficult.

Killian's limbs tingled and grew heavy. He needed air. The cavern instantly lost all its beauty and became his bleak tomb once again.

He reached out and grabbed a stalagmite, not caring whether he cut his hand or not; injuries were now the least of his worries. He pulled his legs up onto the black rock and pushed off, launching himself through the water, then seized the next and did the same. He lost the need to think as he pushed himself mechanically from one rocky pillar to the next. Then he was at the mouth of the next tunnel. It was much wider than the last, but he didn't have time to be observant. His life was draining from his body; delirium was lurking, threatening to overcome him. Above was another air pocket. He swam for it.

He broke the surface, pulling in a glorious lungful of air. The ceiling was low and streaked with black shadows and orange light. A glass orb glowed dimly, looking as if every weak pulse of light would be its last. Killian could empathise with it. There was nowhere for him to climb out and rest, so he lay back in the water and let his limbs sink; it was the only way to relax his aching muscles. He floated in the small air pocket, listening to the soft lapping of the water. He wasn't dead yet. A smile formed on his lips, and he burst into fits of hysterical laughter. He was alive. Tears streaked down his cheeks. He sniffed, he laughed, he cried. He wasn't going to sit back and watch himself die.

His heart raced with the sudden burst of adrenaline brought on by his bout of hysteria. Closing his eyes, he waited for his pulse to return to normal. He rolled over and dipped his face in the water, washing away the tears and hardening his resolve.

He drew in a deep breath and dived under, making for the tunnel. It was long and circular, and like the previous one, it was dark, but at least it was wide enough to swim down. He half swam and half boosted himself along by pushing against the walls. It was hard going. Thoughts of his next breath drifted into his mind when his outstretched hand touched a solid wall. He swam up to it in disbelief and groped it, anxiously feeling for an exit. His fingers slipped on the sludgy layer of algae smothering it; it was definitely solid. There was no way out. He turned himself round and pushed off the wall, swimming as fast as he could towards the air pocket just outside the tunnel.

Dizziness washed over him, and black spots seeped into his vision, threatening to block everything out. With a last burst of power, he made it out of the tunnel and raced up to the air pocket.

As soon as his breath had returned, he let flow a string of obscenities. He knew it was his own fault for not checking the area completely. He dipped his face into the water and checked for a different route. A small green light flickered directly beneath him, catching his attention, and he allowed himself a faint glimmer of a smile. He felt he could trust the green torches. Taking a deep breath, he dived towards it.

As he swam down, his environment changed. The walls were no longer just natural caves; they were interspersed with what looked like the foundations of an ancient building. It was almost as if this part of the labyrinth had been purpose-built rather than hewn directly out of nature itself. The tunnel wasn't as long as the others. As soon as he reached the end, it turned off to the right and into another submerged pool. He swam up to the top and located an air pocket.

He floated on the surface with his goggles round his neck, enjoying the feeling of being able to breathe again. After all the misery and torment of the previous two tunnels, this one seemed suspiciously easy to navigate. He looked below the surface and saw his next destination. This tunnel was wider than all the others put together and clearly lit with torches. Surely he was at the end of his underwater ordeal.

He set his goggles, took a deep breath and swam towards the opening. As he reached it, he heard a loud mechanical noise from behind. Cogs whirred, something heavy thumped, and there was a splintering crunch. Before he had time to think, he was pushed forwards by an almighty current. There was no way he could swim against it, so he had to let it drive him down.

The tunnel was crammed with obstacles; he was right to have been suspicious. Sometimes he really hated being right. In front of him loomed a rocky column; he reached for it and grabbed on. It took all his strength to hold on against the battling water. He glanced over his shoulder and saw the wall directly behind him was covered with rock formations sharpened to merciless points. He shimmied along his outcrop so the murderous rocks were no longer behind him. When he was clear, he let go, and the current swept him safely past.

He kept his eyes wide open as he hurtled uncontrollably down the tunnel. Another rocky formation jutted out in front of him. He grabbed it, holding on fiercely as the wild current battered him relentlessly. This time, directly behind him was a solid wall. He dragged himself across the rocky protrusion until the wall was no longer a threat and let go. This pattern was repeated several times, and it wasn't long before his arms felt the strain of battling the rushing water. His muscles were burning with the pain of exertion as his strength ebbed away.

The tunnel changed the more he was forced down it. The current was inexorable. The walls became smoother, and there were fewer hazards to avoid, but it was now undulating. To avoid smearing his body over the walls, he curved himself up to follow it, but as soon as he did this, he had to arc downwards to keep to the trend of the tunnel.

Shooting towards him at a frightening speed was a wall. A long, narrow gap lit by a green light was cut through its centre. It was only just big enough to fit his body through. He knew he'd have to judge his trajectory just right or he'd be crushed to death against the sides. He managed to swim into the middle to line himself up with the exit. As he drew closer, he put his arms out in front of his head to make himself as streamlined as he could. He shut his eyes and allowed the water to do the rest.

There was a massive surge of acceleration as the current was forced through the narrow gap, but as suddenly as they'd started, the tumultuous waters became calm. He opened his eyes. The bottom of a deep and expansive pool swamped his vision. He gathered his fragmented thoughts and swam upward as fast as his aching limbs would allow. Gigantic marble pillars wrapped with leafy seaweed rose from the floor of the pool, supporting something enormous. He had no time to ponder over it; he was running out of air, fast. The salvation of the surface seemed so far away. Light patterns played across it, smugly taunting him. Black spots slithered into the edge of his vision. Everything burned.

With a final effort, he thrust upwards, shutting his eyes to block out the spots. Just as he felt hope slip away, he burst through the surface and inhaled the sweetest breath he'd ever taken. His lungs rejoiced as they filled, and he flopped into the water, floating on his back. The daunting shadow of a massive building cast itself over him.

When he felt strong enough, he swam to the edge of the pool. With trembling blood-streaked arms, he pulled himself out of the water and onto the grey stone platform that ran in front of the great building. He rolled onto his back and lay in a sodden heap, his legs hanging over the side into the water.

Lazily, he reached a hand up and pulled his goggles down around his neck. He shut his eyes and rested, letting the peaceful tranquillity of the under-sea cave relax him. All his worries – of suffocation, of the searing pain in his arms, of his aching limbs, of his death – left him, and he just breathed.

CHAPTER
TWENTY-SEVEN

REN LET OUT A DEEP MOROSE SIGH. IT FELT like it had been weeks since Killian left, though in truth it had only been a day or two. Guilt hung heavy on him. If that charlatan didn't return, it would be his fault. He would have died because of him. The thought of being responsible for someone else's death was too much for him to bear. He missed him too. Ren had grown fond of his easy-going attitude, and he was even getting used to his sarcastic comments. With Killian around he felt safe.

He looked out over the sea in the direction of the Drop and rested his hands on the rail. The air was heavy, warm and moist. Oppressive and foreboding. Thick grey clouds clogged the sun and sky from view. Ren's clothes were stuck to his back – what he wouldn't give for a bath right now. He hadn't felt properly clean in weeks. He groaned again.

'Come on, Ren!' said Tom, slapping him hard on his sweaty back. 'Stop moping. It's driving me mad!'

'I'm sorry,' Ren said feebly. 'I can't help it. What if he's . . . if he's dead?'

'There ain't nothin' you can do about it now,' said Finn sternly. She was sitting on the bulwark, her back to the others, a fishing rod in one hand and a smouldering roll-up in the other. She took a long drag on the cigarette and blew a curl of smoke out over the sea. 'Shithead's tougher than he looks.'

'Yeah,' said Tom. 'He can handle himself.'

'There's no point worrying until we know something,' said Blake.

Ren nodded sadly. 'But if he's dead, it'll be my fault. I'll have killed him.'

'Ren, if you don't shut your moaning, I'll punch you, and we all know I'm more of a lover than a fighter.' Tom clenched his fists. 'You're making me miserable. I don't like being miserable.'

'I'm sorry,' Ren muttered.

'And stop apologising. It's pissing me clean off!' shouted Finn.

'Sorry. I mean . . .'

Finn growled in response.

A loud cheer erupted from the entire crew, as it had done every other time the geyser blew. The captain had released them from their duties. They were mostly milling around on deck, drinking, dicing, smoking – all things Ren couldn't do well or didn't want to do anyway. It was far too hot to be below. The pirates were in good spirits, especially now the drizzle had subsided, though the overloaded clouds were threatening to dampen everyone.

Staring at the sea wasn't helping Ren's feelings – quite the opposite in fact. He walked over to where Blake was and sat down next to him. Of the three gunners, he still found Blake the most comfortable to be around, despite his strange performance with the smoke that indicated he was an illegal mage. Mage or not, he didn't seem a bad chap, and drawing pictures in the air wasn't exactly hurting anyone. Maybe the laws of Vermor really weren't fair after all.

Blake idly unbuttoned his shirt. He twisted the thin strap of plaited black leather he wore around his neck between his thumb and forefinger.

'Did you make that?' Ren asked in an attempt to start some sort of conversation.

'Nah.'

Well, that ended that.

'My sister made it for me,' said Blake.

'Oh, that's nice. I don't have any siblings. I always felt like I missed out on that. Has it been long since you saw her?'

'Too long. I can't see her or my brother anymore. It's too dangerous.'

'I'm sorry.'

Blake turned to Ren, his eyes growing serious. 'You've got nothing to be sorry for. Well, unless Killian dies, because that'll be your fault.'

Ren was utterly mortified. Was that how everyone thought of him? As Killian's murderer? He wasn't. He hadn't killed him. He hadn't forced him to go. But he hadn't stopped him. He knew the dangers, and he'd let him go. How selfish of him. His eyes burned with salty tears.

Blake's face cracked, and he chuckled. 'I'm only joking, Ren. Don't take it to heart.' He jabbed him in the ribs with his elbow.

'But if he is, it will be.'

Blake groaned. He reached into his trouser pocket, produced two biscuits and handed one to Ren. 'I mean this in the nicest way possible – please eat that and shut up.'

Ren took the offered treat and did as he was told. He looked over to Finn, who still sat on the bulwark fishing. In all the time she'd been sitting there, she hadn't had a single bite. She sucked on the pitiful remains of a roll-up and tossed it in the sea. At least her fruitless search for fish kept her occupied. She ran a free hand over her head, pausing to release her hair from its tight ponytail. It fell lank around her shoulders, and she growled.

Tom was quietly leaning against the quarterdeck, one golden-ring-covered hand resting on his thigh, the other supporting his neck. His eyes were closed, and there was a seedy smirk on his face. Ren didn't even want to know what he was thinking about. Tom could be vocally lewd and crass without a shred of shame, so what he mused on privately must have truly scraped at the barrel of depravity.

Ren brushed the sweat from his eyebrows and glanced down the deck. Three blurry figures emerged from the haze. White light dashed off a circular reflective surface, and he instantly knew who it was: Morton, with two others trailing behind him. Ren's pulse quickened; his nose grew warm and seemed to fizz. His throat dried up. He'd not seen Morton up close since the time Killian fought with him. He'd always managed to stay out of his way. The man reeked of bad news and violence, and he already felt like he was on his bad side just for existing, let alone being the reason for this mission.

'He ain't back then?' Morton grunted as he marched into the group, coming to halt at their centre. He was oozing with sweat. His brown leather cap clung to his head like a flap of rotten skin, and thin tentacles of hair had grafted themselves to his cheeks. The two pirates with him walked to the side of the ship and lit up cigarettes.

'Nope,' said Tom without opening his eyes.

'Probably dead,' Morton said abruptly.

Ren somehow found the courage to murmur to the deck, 'He's not dead.'

'Well, lemme tell ya something, boy. I got a lot of gold pieces,' said Morton, shaking his pocket so they could all hear the sound of clinking metal, 'that say he's a dead man. The guy was an idiot to go down there in the first place, wasting our time sailing round this backwater.'

Blake glanced towards Morton but said nothing.

'He's not an idiot,' said Tom. 'And we don't know he's dead.'

'You can keep your stinkin' opinions, Gainsborough!' Morton ran a peeling sunburnt hand over his leather cap. 'We all know this is a waste of time. We may as well have stayed in Bracky for all the good this is doing.'

'You don't know that—' Tom began.

'I told ya to shut it,' Morton snarled.

'Morton, you're such a—'

'If you don't shut it, Gainsborough, I'll shut it for you.'

'Why don't you keep your stinking opinions, Morton?' snapped Blake, his face full of rage. 'It's clear you're still bitter he beat the shit out of you.' He calmly pulled out his pipe, lit it and took a long drag. A thick cloud of dark purple smoke wrapped around him, and his eyes changed from soft hazel to gleaming white. 'That's pathetic.'

All attention snapped towards the normally placid crew member. Finn's rod clattered to the deck, and Tom opened his eyes. Ren's breath caught in his throat. This didn't sound like Blake talking. Blake, with the gentle voice and the handmade necklace. Blake, who missed his sister and brother. Ren edged away from him. What if he got caught up in that purple cloud? What would happen to him?

'That man down there,' seethed Blake, standing and taking a step towards Morton, 'has more decency in one of his hairs than you have in your whole body, you withered spleen.'

'Mage!' Morton spat on the deck. 'You ought to be shot. I should turn ya in, get some cash for your death too.'

'Go on then,' snarled Blake. 'I dare you.' His shining white eyes cut through the dark mists. 'I'll make you pay,' he muttered, taking a step closer, 'for everything.'

Ren got to his feet and tried to put some distance between himself and Blake. The gunner was usually so quiet and calm, and this sudden change frightened him. He felt trapped. Blake wasn't himself, and Morton was terrifying. Why wasn't Killian here? He'd know what to do.

Finn slid off the bulwark and edged towards Blake, holding her hand out. 'Come on, Blake,' she said. 'You need to back off.'

Blake's white eyes flashed malevolently. 'What do you know? You don't understand – the humiliation, the running, the insults. He disrespected our friend and wants to turn me in! No, never.'

Ren's hands balled up, and he dug his nails into his palms. Blake didn't seem in control. Surely he wouldn't hurt Finn? Perhaps the law was right after all. Mages were dangerous.

'Let it go,' Finn said, her voice unusually soft. 'And come back to us. You know this will only cause trouble if you carry on.'

'Come on, Blake, mate.' Tom was now slowly walking towards him too.

The dark mists were growing around Blake like a rampant fungus, hungry and evil. Ren wanted to say something, something to help the situation. What would Killian say? Ren racked his brain, but all he could think of was *Don't be a dick*, and that would not be helpful in the slightest.

'Blake, the cap'n won't like this. You know the rules.' Finn was close to him now, her outstretched hand almost touching him.

'She . . . won't.' Blake's voice trembled.

'A-aye,' said Tom. 'You don't wanna piss her off, believe me.'

Blake silently shook his head and staggered against the quarterdeck. With a listless click of his fingers, he banished the purple cloud. After a few blinks, the hazel returned to his eyes.

Morton took a step backwards. 'You really are a freak, ain't you?' His voice wavered, and he rubbed his monocle, keeping his head down. 'He's still dead though. The sooner you and the cap'n realise that, the sooner we get outta this stinkin' dead sea. I'll be back soon to pick up me winnings,' he added, shooting a glare in Finn's direction.

Once Morton and his smoking companions had gone, everyone turned to Blake. Ren couldn't stop shaking; his breath was ragged, and his teeth chattered. He'd never seen anything like that before. The dark cloud that had drifted around Blake hinted at a power beyond the smoky stories he told them, something wild and untamed. That kind of power was frightening, especially coupled with explosive tendencies. The shift from gentle man joking with him to wild magical beast was terrifying.

'Blake,' said Tom, shattering the uneasy silence, 'what was that bollocks?'

'I don't know. He vexed me,' said Blake, shrugging, his voice calm and flat after the raging storm.

'Don't think he'll be doin' it again any time soon,' said Finn.

'Y-you're a mage,' stammered Ren, finding his voice. 'You really are a mage.'

'Whatever gave you that idea?' murmured Blake, slumping down to the deck.

'Nothin' gets past you, eh, Ren?' said Finn, grinning. She turned around, scooped up her fallen rod and positioned herself back on the bulwark.

UP in the crow's nest, Raven stared out to sea, his keen eyes searching for a sign. He didn't expect one so early on, but he'd told Killian he'd look every day, and he was a man of his word. The high breeze buffeting his body was most welcome and refreshing. Glancing down at the deck, he saw Killian's friends lounging in the heat. He scanned around the ship. It seemed that most of the crew had the same idea, and when he looked at the bow, he had to do a double take. At the front of the ship stood Lily. This was the first time Raven had seen her out of her room since Killian had gone.

He had one last look over the waves before gracefully leaping from his vantage point. He flipped his body over in the air and landed neatly on his feet next to Lily. She turned, gave him an acknowledging smile and looked out to sea again.

'Good to see you out,' said Raven.

'It's so stuffy inside,' she said, not taking her eyes off the water. 'Not that it's any better out here.'

'It's cool and breezy up there.' He nodded towards the crow's nest.

'I bet it is,' she said. 'This climate's vile. He'd better hurry up and get back.'

'I'm sure he's going as fast as he can.'

'He better be.'

They stood together in silence, both looking hopefully at the waves. The air grew warmer, more oppressive. Raven looked from the grey skies to his captain; they seemed to reflect her mood. A low rumble growled overhead, and the overloaded clouds gave in, unleashing a deluge of rain. Fat droplets hammered the deck unrepentantly in an uneven rhythm.

Lily laughed mirthlessly. 'It doesn't get any better than this,' she said, water dripping from her hat.

'I'm sure it will.' He gave her a reassuring smile and shrugged. 'I'd better get back to my post. Maybe he'll be early.'

'He's never early,' murmured Lily, keeping her head down to avoid the rain – and perhaps eye contact too.

'Maybe he'll surprise you,' said Raven.

Lily stretched up and planted a kiss on his cheek. 'Thank you,' she whispered.

Raven held her hand and kissed it. He turned and half flipped, half ran to the top of the mast. Once he was back in position, he scanned the dull waters, the already choppy surface now littered with thousands of tiny splashes. The surges of the Drop provided a constant background drone. He watched Lily pull her hat down and head back to her cabin.

CHAPTER
TWENTY-EIGHT

KILLIAN SLOWLY EASED HIS EYES OPEN TO THE gentle sound of lapping water and the smell of damp rock. He ran his tongue along his salty bottom lip; his mouth was uncomfortably dry. He couldn't tell how long he'd been asleep, but judging by his soaking clothes and throbbing skin, it hadn't been long. Grunting softly, he pulled his feet out of the water and reluctantly stood up.

His shirt was shredded beyond recognition; now there were more gaps in it than material. Why was he still wearing it? The unnecessary drag must have cost him valuable time in the last task. He pulled off the tattered remains, tore them into strips and assembled a rough bandage around his bleeding right arm. Even flexing his hands hurt; his palms were covered with tiny hairline nicks that flared with a burning sting whenever they moved. He pushed his wet hair out of his face and turned towards what undoubtedly housed the final task.

With a roll of his shoulders, he walked towards the huge building, leaving a wet trail on the stone platform behind him. It filled his vision with ancient degrading masonry stretching up to the roof of the cavern, a seething mass of angular blocks and supporting pillars. Bright green foliage speckled with star-shaped cerulean flowers draped over the structure, dangling from overhangs and easing into the dilapidated stonework. The closer it got to the ground, the browner and more withered it became, as if the proximity to whatever lay inside had killed it.

There wasn't a door, as such, just an opening flanked by two gigantic marble pillars swathed with interweaving coils of blue and green light. Beyond was ominous darkness. He straightened up. This was his only way out, and whatever lay within would either kill him or free him. He shrugged, stepped over the fallen blackened flowers without a second glance and proceeded into the shadows.

As he set foot inside, the lingering gloom was banished when several torches crackled to life in shadowy niches in the walls. He blinked a few times, allowing his eyes to adjust to the flickering orange light. The interior consisted of one enormous room with a solitary pillar in the centre. There were no doors, stairways or passages leading off anywhere. At first glance there didn't seem to be anything inside except the damp smell of long-settled dust. All that immediately stood out was the pillar, and he crossed the room to examine it further. He paced around it but saw nothing exceptional about it. He ran his hand over its surface. It was smooth, no hidden indentations, nothing; it was merely a support for the structure. He leant against it and looked up, hoping to find a clue. The walls stretched up a few hundred feet and disappeared into the darkness. He narrowed his eyes, willing a torch to burst into life somewhere up in the hidden rafters, but no encouraging light came.

A harsh pain lanced through his body, and he gripped his injured arm. He shut his eyes, sucked in a breath and waited for it to pass, wondering whether he should have lain outside and rested a while longer. He lifted his grazed hand from the wet blood-soaked bandage. It had to be properly dressed, and the only way to get that done was to carry on. He let his gaze wander about the room. Every wall was the same: large flat buff stones interspersed with flaming torches. He ground his teeth in frustration, looking for something that could help him.

This is it. This has to be the way out.

All that stood out, besides the pillar, was the far left corner. Unlike everywhere else, it was still shrouded in darkness. Feeling desperate and more than a little hopeless, he cautiously made his way towards it, keeping alert for any hidden trapdoors or booby traps; he'd had just about enough of dodging deadly objects. But to his surprise, nothing tried to kill him, which was novel.

Something on the wall glinted amid the murk; he put his hand out to touch it. The surface was cool and flat. He walked to the closest torch and pulled it from its alcove. Back in the corner, he held it up to reveal a sheet of glass mounted in a frame of twisted black metal. It showed an exact copy of the temple on the other side. Perhaps it was the way out. He squeezed his bottom lip thoughtfully. Something was odd about it, but he couldn't put his finger on what it was. He peered into it. A light shone in the room beyond. Moving his torch, he saw the light dutifully followed it. With a frown, he realised it wasn't glass at all; it was a mirror, and all it was revealing was the dimly lit room behind him. *But if that's a mirror, where am I?* His torch reflected back at him, but disturbingly, there was no reflection of him. It was as if it were floating in mid-air. He continued to study it, waving his hands in front of it to no effect.

He gazed into it, searching for a way out, for a clue, for something, anything. His fist bunched up in frustration. A pale figure appeared at the back of the mirror. He spun around to face it, but there was nothing there. *Now I'm seeing things.* He turned back to the mirror only to find it was still there, closer now. It was moving towards the foreground with heavy, trudging steps. An icy dread ran down his spine as the figure drew closer.

Its head was down, its face hidden, but he only needed to see its clothes: tattered trousers, no shirt, a pathetic bandage fastened about its right arm. They were his clothes; it was his body. From its belt swung a pair of swords – his swords – but with blood-red hilts and black scabbards.

His heart tremored, and he took a step back as it approached, dropping the torch and reaching for his blades. The figure stopped walking. Its skin was deathly pale and adorned with a tangle of black veins that twisted over its bare chest like unruly vines. It raised its head slowly, cocking it to the left. Its limp dark hair shifted, exposing its features: stubble and a tilted roguish smile. Killian's mouth fell open as a sickening feeling built in his gut. Dark veins scrawled spidery patterns over its pallid face, creeping down its forehead and over its defined cheekbones. As it drew its head level with his, two black hollows opened up before him, and blinding white pupils formed at their centres, gleaming with malice.

For what seemed like an eternity, this other version of him stared from the mirror, its face gradually contorting, the lopsided smile twisting into a leer of pure hatred. Killian's chest tightened. It wasn't him; it couldn't be him. As he took another step backwards, the hideous spectre moved forwards. He froze, but the creature kept moving. It was touching the glass, pressing its body against the smooth surface, its chilling glare fixed on him. With an icy crack, it freed itself from the mirror, the glass shattering behind it as it paced towards him.

Killian shuddered, backing off slowly as it advanced. He fleetingly wished he were still being shot at by the hot red stuff or getting dragged about by purple coils. He'd have even taken the suffocation of the labyrinth over facing this. What was it, anyway? It looked like him, but surely it wasn't.

The creature snarled, snapping him out of his trance, and reached for its swords. It rested its waxen hands upon the hilts and glowered at him. In one fluid movement, it drew its blackened blades and lunged for him.

The room burst into life. Curling glyphs hissed and scorched their way into the yellow stones, sending out bright ripples of blue, green and silver light. The white skin of the monster reflected the light with a dazzling effect. Killian quickly dived out of the way, drawing his own weapons as he moved. He glanced at the hilts; they were dull, the silver tarnished. They didn't work. Gone was the familiar feedback and energy he had come to take for granted whenever he wielded them. They felt heavy and weighed his arms down rather than lifting them; every movement seemed an effort. He pulled them up just in time to defend himself from the creature's next attack. Metal clanged, and he sent it staggering back. It nimbly regained its balance.

Killian took a clumsy step backwards, and his shoulders drooped. It took all his will just to remain standing. The other tasks had sapped his strength; the swords had been his only hope. Now they were betraying him. Never before had they let him down. Whenever he grabbed them in a fight, he knew what to do – it was almost as if they whispered advice to him – but now there was nothing.

The monster growled, a horrible guttural sound, breaking the silence. Killian went to move, but it was too late; it was already mid-lunge. Raw burning pain blossomed in his shoulder and arm.

He staggered back, putting his hand to the pouring wound, the blood warm against his cold skin. He needed time to collect his thoughts. This thing, whatever it was, was the final task, the darkest truth, and the only way to get past it was to kill it. He moved his hand, smearing the blood across his chest. Without the strength, clarity and coordination of the swords, surely he couldn't win. The creature attacked again, swinging for the kill. He brought his swords up and somehow managed to hold it at bay. It hissed and snarled at him through the cross of their blades, its terrifying eyes glowing with malevolence. It reeked of death and decay; his eyes watered as he fought the urge not to gag.

His biceps trembled as he kept it back; streams of pain ripped through his arms, his nerves set alight. He lifted his head and stared back at it. It was foul. It wasn't him. It couldn't be him. The dancing glyphs settled down to a deep blue. Killian's swords glowed in the light, giving them the illusion of power. With great effort he knocked it back and sliced at its arm. Thick black blood seeped from its wound.

'What are you?' Killian rasped.

It peeled back its lips to reveal sharpened teeth and leered at him.

'Good answer.'

It seemed unfazed by the injury and sprang at him again, moving with uncanny liquid fluidity and shattering Killian's tenuous morale instantaneously. A vile sound oozed from its mouth, and the room flared red as it swung. He dodged neatly aside. It grinned and beckoned him, goading him. He tensed and dashed forwards, determined, but every blow he brought down was effortlessly deflected or parried.

It laughed at him, a haunting sound that reverberated off the walls, mocking him. His confidence slipped away as easily as a greased eel. He drew back and stood facing the monster, panting with exertion, his heart hammering in his ears. The creature stared, a sinister grin torn into its face, black blood flowing down its arm, its body glimmering with scarlet light. It glanced at the wound, then back at him, and made a ferocious gurgling sound deep in its throat. Its grin grew wider, and it threw itself into another attack.

It swung at Killian with such speed, bringing one arm down after the other in an endless cycle of clashing metal, that its arms became a blur. Each time their blades met, the room responded by flashing a different colour. It was as if the glyphs were trying to confuse him. His weary arms shielded him against the torrent of blows, but he didn't know how much longer he could keep pace. Every blow he defended left him weaker. Sweat poured down his face as his body was forced backwards. Its crazed eyes glared at him, searching for a crack in his defence as it wore him down.

A grin split its face, and it changed tactics, thrusting its sword hilts towards him. It took him by surprise, and he suffered a tremendous blow to the jaw. His teeth sank into his tongue, filling his mouth with a sharp metallic taste. He stumbled back, blood pouring from his lip, his vision blurred. Flashes of bright colour swam in his head. It drew its arms back and buried the hilts into his stomach. Time stopped. He was weightless, and then he crashed to the floor. It glided over to him, a look of intense abhorrence on its twisted face. Killian filled his lungs with rotten air. The creature brought its swords down for the killer blow, and he rolled out of the way. He wasn't quite swift enough to avoid the blades completely. They ripped through his skin and tore a deep slash diagonally across his back.

Somehow he was on his feet, wincing as white-hot pain ignited his back. Blood poured down his body at an alarming rate. He stooped forwards in a feeble attempt to rest, but it only widened the slash. He looked through his hair to see the creature striding towards him, its swords sheathed at its sides.

It grabbed him roughly by his shoulders and pulled him straight. Despite the torment, he refused to cry out. It yanked him close, its face inches from his. The vile reek of its mouldering flesh forced itself down Killian's throat, choking him. It whirled him around and threw him against the central pillar. Pain exploded in his back, racing in agonising shocks down his arms, and he dropped his weapons. They clattered against the stone floor, taking with them his last drop of hope.

Exhausted, he slumped to one knee, listening to its footsteps as it approached. He'd feel another sharp pain, then everything would be over, and it would probably go dark – or light; he'd never given it much thought. Whatever shade his vision went, it wouldn't make a difference. He was going to fail. Fail Ren, fail himself, fail them . . . and never see Lily again. Would she care if he didn't come back? Would she come down looking for him? If she did, would she weep over the broken heap of his corpse, lamenting over all their arguments, all the times they should have and could have done things differently? Or would she not even care? She was so complicated that it was hard to read her. Maybe that was the appeal.

What was he thinking? He was about to die, his life quite literally dripping away, and the only thing he could think of was her. That salty narcissistic pirate. *And* she still had that bloody necklace, *his* bloody necklace! His arms tensed. He'd be damned if he was going to let her keep it. A surge of energy flooded his body, and he rolled to the side, scooping up his swords on the way. The harsh din of metal striking stone followed in his wake.

The creature spun to face him, a look of irritation and rage burnt into its sinister eyes. Killian straightened his aching body, casually brushed down his ragged trousers and glared defiantly back at it. He ran his tongue around the inside of his mouth and spat out a lump of grit-infused blood. He slowly wiped his lips with the back of his hand, not breaking eye contact with his other self.

'You really are a dick,' said Killian.

The symbols on the walls dimmed, and everything stopped. Killian felt an odd sense of calm descend upon him. His breath was even and controlled, his body had cooled, and he no longer felt the pain of his injuries. The rotten stench of his opponent lingered in the stale air, but he could ignore it. There was a crackling sound as the glyphs resurrected themselves. Bright white light flowed from them, filling the room with an otherworldly glow. Killian rolled his shoulders back and basked in the light, drawing strength from it.

'And I think I might have to kill you now,' he said softly. He offered the abomination a smirk.

It snapped with fury and raced towards him, shards of light glancing off its black blades. They became locked in ferocious combat, Killian defending every strike his other self sent at him before attacking back, but his blows were skilfully parried, and he was soon on the defensive again. It snarled at him as it swung and lashed out. It was relentless. Their blades jarred together. Killian had to keep strong and ignore the dizzying effect of blood loss; he could deal with that later. Would he bleed to death? *Focus, Killian, focus.*

Killian ducked under a swing, coming up to crack his enemy in the stomach with his hilt, followed by a swift kick to its chest. It wheezed and backed away slightly. For the first time, it seemed to be running out of energy, so he moved in to take advantage. Then it sprang, knocking him to the hard stone floor, jumping on top of him and pinning him down. He coughed up a clot of blood as he put his swords up to hold it back. It crowed manically at his struggle and prised his hands apart, making an opening. Killian stopped fighting, and it lurched forwards, slightly off balance. During this second of respite, he summoned everything he had and threw the monster over his head with a double kick to its stomach.

The creature went sprawling across the floor, giving Killian time to get to his feet. He gripped his swords with renewed vigour and charged at his other self. The apparition managed to get up to defend against one of his blows, but it wasn't prepared for his second swing, which caught it on the upper thigh. Blood poured out of the wound. He swung again, slicing deep into the sinew and muscle of its arm, and it dropped one of its swords. It looked at him, its face filled with rage, and thrust maliciously with its remaining sword, stabbing the top of his leg. Killian let out a short breath, and a frozen shock clawed through him. Cold metal slid into his flesh. He sucked in a trembling lungful of air and pushed forwards, which forced the weapon deeper into his own leg.

With one sword on the floor and the other stuck through Killian's thigh, the creature had no further means of attack or defence. Killian raised his eyebrows and slowly shook his head. Then he buried his sword in its heart. They froze, locked together with their weapons, staring intensely into each other's eyes, breathing heavily. The light shifted to blue, and the colour was absorbed into the monster's eyes. For a heartbeat it looked exactly like him.

Its lips pulled back over its teeth, and it spoke. '... have ... to ... live ... with ... this ...'

That voice, it was so familiar, and it hurt more than any physical wound. It grinned at him. He had to end this. He readjusted his grip on the hilt and, with his last ounce of strength, wrenched the sword from its heart, leaving a bloody void in the creature's chest.

Killian staggered back, and his opponent's sword slid out of his leg. He wanted to collapse, to fall to that comforting rocky floor, but he couldn't – not yet. He placed an ineffective hand over his bleeding thigh and stooped forwards. There was an eerie silence, as if everything in existence had stopped moving, breathing, living, except for Killian and his monster. Nothing else mattered but them. It reeled backwards with a look of revulsion scored onto its grotesque face. Its blood-covered sword dropped to the floor with a clang, fracturing the fragile peace. Showers of black blood exploded from its chest, and it crumpled to the ground, screaming. He stumbled over to it. It looked up at him with hatred and disgust brimming in its eyes and then dissolved into a puddle of black liquid soaking into the ground. The glyphs promptly faded from the walls, leaving the torches to ignite and take over as they disappeared.

A harsh splintering noise caught his attention. Glancing over his shoulder, he saw the mirror rebuilding itself, its shattered fragments being drawn from the floor and back into the frame. It glowed with a brilliant white light and dissolved back into the shadows.

Unable to stand, he dropped to his knees; his trembling blood-soaked hands were still clutching his swords. He released his grip, and his weapons slid smoothly onto the cold stone floor. He fell forwards, supporting his weary body on his hands and knees. His breathing was hoarse, laboured and uneven. Blood oozed from his wounds, and he listened attentively to the soft splats as it dripped onto the floor. A rapidly expanding puddle of blood formed beneath him. *It's a good job they didn't go for carpet,* he thought, smiling thinly.

CHAPTER TWENTY-NINE

REN STOOD OUTSIDE THE MESS LISTENING to Seth's nonsensical whistling. He'd decided it would be best to take his anxiety away from the gunners; he didn't want to annoy them with his state of mind anymore. They seemed to deal with loss and stress in a very different way to him. Sucking in a deep briny breath, he knocked on the door, hoping Seth would have some work to occupy him.

'Come in,' Seth responded.

Ren walked in. Seth gave him a nod and went back to peeling a pile of slightly sprouting potatoes.

'Hello, Seth,' he said with his usual politeness.

'Oh, you been bad again, boy? Cap'n sent you to work for me, eh?' he asked, shaking the knife in his direction.

'No, I came down of my own volition,' said Ren.

'Oh?'

'Do you have anything for me to do?' he asked, eyeing the potatoes.

'Wha?' Seth frowned like he couldn't believe what he was hearing. 'You wanna work down 'ere?'

'Yes, I need something to do.'

'Something?'

'To take my mind off things.'

'Things.'

'Yes, there's nothing for me to do up there. I'm clueless about everything nautical, and if they're not fiddling with ropes, guns or fishing lines, they're gambling, and I'm rubbish at that too.'

'Rubbish.' Seth tutted and shook his head, his wiry hair bouncing in time.

'Correct,' said Ren. 'So can I help you?'

Seth nodded vigorously. 'Sure you can. Plenty o' spuds to peel!'

'Take me to them,' said Ren a little too enthusiastically. He was peeling potatoes, not diving into the unknown. He felt a stab of shame.

'You sure? It's dull work.'

'I honestly don't care.'

Seth tossed Ren a slightly blunt knife, and they set to work emptying the sack. The job was monotonous, but Ren didn't mind. He'd got potato peeling down to a fine art. He was also quite the expert at carrots. In fact, he could cook and prepare most vegetables and meats – caring for his sick father had increased his culinary skills tenfold. At last there was something he could do to help. He gritted his teeth as he worked with the knife. The blade had definitely seen better days, but that meant he had to concentrate harder, which kept his mind from straying too far. *Maybe I can become a chef when all this is over.* After about an hour of silent peeling, Seth threw his knife into the table with a solid thunk.

'Break,' he announced.

Ren gratefully laid down his knife and sat on a rickety wooden stool. He put his dirty, starchy hands in his lap. Seth turned and put the kettle on for some tea.

'Sorry, rum's gettin' low, gotta ration,' he said as he tossed a handful of leaves into the pot.

'That's all right. I'm not much of a drinker anyway.'

'Not much of an eater neither, by the looks of you,' Seth remarked.

'No, not really. Well, I was, but after Father got sick, I found every meal became more of an effort. The smallest bites of food turned to rocks in my stomach. If you know what I mean?'

'Aye, the worry, it clamps you up.'

'Yeah, that's it, but since I've been here I've found it easier to eat,' said Ren.

'Hope'll do that for you. She's a good healer.'

While the tea was brewing, Seth rummaged in the cupboards, muttering to himself as his hands groped about in the dark. As Ren sat waiting, he felt something brush up against his bare legs. He jumped, freezing to his stool. *Rat*, he thought, and he regretted rolling his trousers up. It brushed by him again, and his skin crawled. It paused and rubbed its face against the back of his calf, and he realised no rat would be so bold. Looking under the table, he saw a lithe one-eared tabby cat. He tapped his lap, and the cat instantly leapt onto him. It pushed its face against his hand, purring loudly. He responded by tickling it under its chin.

'Here you go,' said Seth, setting the tea and some biscuits down in front of Ren. 'You made a friend for life there.'

He smiled and patted the cat's head fondly. 'She don't sit on just anyone, you know.'

Ren picked up his drink and took a sip. The tea was bitter and tasted vaguely of rum; Seth had no doubt used the teacups for shot-glasses.

'That's Rangi,' he said, plonking himself down on a wooden chair. 'She's my second-in-command rat catcher.'

'Really,' said Ren, smiling at the cat's affection. 'Who's the first?'

'Your crazy friend, of course.'

'Killian?' Just saying his name sent a bolt of pain through Ren's gut.

'Aye.' Seth grinned.

Ren's smile descended into a frown as he was brought roughly back to reality. He felt nauseous, and his forehead tightened. He hadn't thought himself capable of those sorts of feelings; after all, what was Killian to him? That charlatan who stole from him, who mocked him, mocked his town, made him feel so inferior, so pathetic. He lowered his eyes. He was the man who'd saved his life, taken him in, looked after him and was risking his life to save his father. Granted, he wasn't doing it for free, yet somehow that didn't seem to matter anymore. His chest ached. Killian was worth more than him. He may have been from Charrington and training for an honest job, but what was all that compared to what that swaggering shirker was doing? Was his father's life and his happiness worth Killian's own life? Tears clouded his vision; he nibbled the biscuit to try and disguise them, but he couldn't fool Seth.

'You all right?'

'Yes,' Ren lied.

Seth raised his eyebrows.

'No.'

'Wanna talk?' Seth asked.

Ren chewed the dry biscuit and took a long draught of tea to wash it away before he spoke. 'I feel guilty,' he said in a meek voice.

'What for?' asked Seth.

'Because he went down there. If he doesn't come back, it's my fault.'

'No, no, it's not, lad,' said Seth, staring sympathetically at Ren.

'I will have killed him,' he murmured.

'No, he will have killed himself. He knew the risks.'

'But if not for me—'

'But nothin', lad,' Seth said, shaking his head. The multicoloured beads in his hair clattered together. 'He went down of his own . . . volition. He knew what he was gettin' himself into, and if he don't come back, he's to blame, not you.'

'But—'

'Ah, ah.' Seth held up his hand to silence Ren. 'No buts. What's done is done, you know. You can't change a thing. Not now, not ever.'

'I know,' Ren mumbled as he stroked the cat, which had now curled up contentedly on his lap.

'So there be no point beatin' yourself up over it.'

Ren blew into his tea and took a small sip; he wasn't convinced.

'He'll be back in a day or two without a scratch on him,' said Seth with a grin. 'Just you wait and see.'

'I guess you're right,' said Ren. He put his mug down, gazed into the tea and let out a deep sigh.

'You're a difficult one today, ain't ya?' Seth ran a hand through his hair, pausing to thoughtfully twirl a green bead.

'I'm sorry,' said Ren, unable to meet Seth's eye. 'I'm just so worried ...'

'He'll be back, I told you that.' Seth grabbed his mug and had a deep drink.

'It's not just Killian.'

'Go on,' said Seth, an encouraging lilt to his tone.

'My father.' Two great tears rolled down Ren's cheeks, and his breath caught in his throat. His hand sank to the table, and he shook. The emotion was drowning him; he sniffed and sobbed while he tried to gain control. 'My father is ...' The tears choked off his words, and his shoulders heaved as he allowed everything to flow out.

'It's okay, lad,' said Seth softly.

Ren felt something warm press on the back of his hand. He opened his eyes and saw Seth's hand on top of his. He looked towards the one-eyed pirate, and Seth smiled at him.

'It's okay.' Seth nodded.

'He's all I have.' Ren spoke in a juddering whisper. 'He's the only person I have in the world, and ... and I'm worried we'll be too late.' He blinked, and a torrent of tears cascaded down his face. Seth gave his hand a gentle squeeze, which, though comforting, made him cry even harder.

'Take your time, lad.'

Ren took a deep breath and tried to steady himself. He took his free hand and wiped the wetness from his face. 'He got worse over time. Some days he didn't even make sense, didn't even seem like my father. It was almost like the sickness was eating his mind as well as his body.' He blinked. His eyes were sore, and his throat felt raw. He took a swig from his mug of tea. 'I'm worried that if we don't get back in time, there won't be anyone left to save. Some days he'd babble nonsense, and some days he wouldn't even remember my name. I'd tell him who I was, and he would ... he'd seem confused.' Ren sank forwards and sobbed as the painful memories lanced through him. 'I don't want him to be like that. I want to save him. I don't want to be alone ... not yet.'

There was a creak as Seth stood up.

The pirate's strong arms wrapped around Ren from behind. It felt warm and safe, like a genuine gesture of friendship.

'You ain't alone, lad,' said Seth, 'but I understand what you mean.'

'Thank you, Seth,' Ren whimpered.

'I know you said you ain't much of a drinker, but I reckon you need somethin' a little stronger than tea, eh?' he said, firmly clasping Ren's shoulder.

'That would be ... nice.'

CHAPTER
THIRTY

K ILLIAN OPENED HIS HEAVY EYELIDS. AT FIRST his vision was blurred; he blinked several times and waited for everything to come into focus. He lay on his back, taking slow deep breaths. His chest ached. It felt bruised and broken. *Where am I?* The ceiling looked familiar; he'd been here before, he was sure of it. But where was here? His mind felt foggy, like his thoughts were being held together by dusty spiderwebs. Was he conscious? As he sat up, a fierce shot of pain arced through his body. He gasped and lay back down again. He was definitely conscious.

He decided to concentrate on breathing before he tried to move again. He turned his head and observed his surroundings: soft animal-skin floor, colourful blankets, a dim but cosy feel, scent of lavender, cluttered piles of useless crap from the surface. It was Cassius's tent. He let out a soft moan of relief. The tasks were over; he was safe and, most importantly, alive.

Tentatively, he sat up again. Pain rippled through his body, though not quite as violently as before. He was hurt, badly, but he'd heal. The injuries were the least of his problems. He blotted out the nagging pains and focused on the next quandary: How was he going to get out of here? He was beneath the sea. Getting back to the surface was not going to be easy.

His thoughts drifted to his friends in the world above; he missed them – even Lily. He frowned as he thought of her. He couldn't believe that she was the only thing he could think about as he lay dying. She'd given him the strength to get back up and fight. He pursed his lips. It wasn't her; it was that necklace, the necklace she'd stolen.

Slowly and painfully, he got to his feet. His arms were covered with scrapes and grazes from dragging himself through the underwater tunnels. The deep cut in the top of his right arm had been bandaged, as had his left shoulder and arm. His thigh was bound tightly, and his chest was littered with thin spidery scratches and ugly bruises. As he moved his arms, he grunted in pain; he'd forgotten about the huge gash across his back. He checked and found it had been tended. His whole body was crawling with pain.

He looked straight ahead. Sandwiched between a pile of tattered paintings and a hat stand draped in moth-eaten coats was a slightly mottled full-length mirror. Feeling a little apprehensive, he approached it and checked his reflection, careful to stay back from the glass. He was relieved to see that his mirror image corresponded to his actions and didn't have veiny white skin, although he was quite pale. His bottom lip was swollen and split, and his body was a battered mess. He felt ill at the thought of that creature.

What was it? It was supposed to be an evil version of him. What did it mean? What was its purpose? Was this something he could turn into? Some sort of prophecy? How had it known what to say to him? He wasn't sure he wanted answers to any of those questions.

He scanned the room for the tunic he'd worn earlier; it'd have to do now his shirt was shredded. The coarse material snagged his ravaged arms as he pulled it on. *This is definitely gonna scar.* He threw on his trousers. Neat stitches had repaired most of the damage they'd suffered. He was grateful for this; at least he had some clothes remaining that fit him. He picked up his swords and hung his goggles around his neck.

He stepped out of the tent and was startled to find Cassius sitting directly outside.

'You're awake!' he exclaimed, beaming at him and leaping to his feet.

'Looks like I am.' Killian shrugged, trying to appear unperturbed. 'How long was I out?'

'About a day. I think you slept through most of the pain,' said Cassius, eyeing him with obvious concern.

'A day!'

'Yep, a whole day,' Freya confirmed, appearing from between the tents, the soft jingle of her bangles accompanying her voice. 'And you talk in your sleep,' she added. 'Who is Lily?'

Killian shook his head and apologised.

'It is fine,' said Freya with a grin. 'It was entertaining.'

'Glad someone enjoyed it.' Killian smiled back sarcastically.

'Please, sit down and eat,' said Cassius.

'Thanks,' said Killian, slumping down on the ground. Cassius and Freya swiftly joined him. He reached for a piece of soft, sweet fruit and chewed it over. It was exactly what he desired; his mouth was as dry as a barrel of salt. The food soon aroused the latent fires of hunger, but he continued to eat slowly in an attempt to be polite.

'How do you feel?' Cassius asked. His hand hovered over the tray, but he didn't take his eyes off Killian.

'A bit sore,' said Killian. 'I get a little twinge of pain when I move, nothing too serious.'

The cornelian bit into something green and crunchy. 'I wish there was more we could do.'

'Don't worry about me. I'm fine,' he lied. 'I'll heal.'

'All this damned arkani down here, and we cannot heal one simple human,' Freya grumbled, drawing her knees to her chest. 'It is pathetic.'

'Simple? Steady on,' Killian said sharply.

'You know what I mean,' said Freya, pouting at him.

'No.'

Cassius interjected before Freya could speak. 'Then allow me to explain. We cannot heal you despite having the power to do so. The rules of the tasks forbid it.'

'Tasks be damned,' muttered Freya. 'You know as well as I do that he is in pain—'

'I'm fine.' Killian jumped in to try to prevent a domestic dispute.

Freya fixed him with a silver glare. 'Do not lie,' she said slowly. She swept her hair over her shoulders and turned her attention back to Cassius. 'We have the power to stop it. We can make all the pain go away. We can remove his scars. Cassius, we should.'

'Freya,' said Cassius soothingly, 'you know it is forbidden.'

'It is stupid,' she hissed. 'Why should he have to suffer?'

'Really, I'm all right. It doesn't hurt that much,' said Killian, desperately trying to keep the peace. 'I'll be fine.'

'I have already told you, Killian,' said Freya, her voice cold and flat, 'do not lie.'

'Freya, you know the rules.'

'Yes, I do. But that does not mean I have to like them or keep them,' she said brusquely.

'Freya,' said Cassius, a hint of exasperated anger colouring his tone.

'I know, I know, do not interfere,' she replied defensively. She picked up a piece of fruit and aggressively crammed it into her downturned mouth.

'Killian,' said Cassius, turning his soft amber eyes towards him. 'The rules of the tasks state that we must not help you in any way. Saving your leg and giving you bandages is already overstepping the mark, but you were bleeding everywhere.'

'It was making a mess,' Freya said through clenched teeth, her mouth full of fruit.

Cassius smiled at her and continued. 'Nesta sanctioned the use of arkani to heal the hole in your leg, which was very generous of her, and I was allowed to rinse your wounds and patch you up, but no more.'

'Was it that bad?' asked Killian, looking at his leg.

'I could see through it.'

'It was disgusting. There was so much blood and stringy flesh,' Freya said, her tone blunt. 'If Nesta had not allowed Cassius to heal it, you would not have walked again. You would never have made it back to the surface.'

Killian's heart became a plummeting stone, tearing up his vital organs as it fell. The mere thought of never returning to the surface was almost enough to break him. He didn't know how close he'd come to spending the rest of his days beneath the sea. 'Sorry for causing you so much hassle,' he murmured. He looked at the plate of food, and eating didn't appeal to him anymore.

'You are not a hassle,' said Freya quietly, giving him a weak smile.

Killian pulled his knee up and rested his arm on top of it. He wasn't too fond of talking about his bloody, beaten body. He was still having a hard time believing he was alive. 'How did I get out of there anyway? I vaguely remember thinking something ridiculous about carpet and nothing more.'

'Carpet? I carried you out, my friend,' said Cassius.

'You didn't have to go through the other tasks, did you?'

'No, thankfully,' replied Cassius with a chuckle. 'I jumped straight to the finish.'

'Good,' said Killian, trying to smile. He ventured to pick up another piece of fruit. He squeezed it between his fingers and watched the juice flow out before he ate it. Glancing at Freya, he saw that her eyes still wore a cold stormy look. 'Cheer up, Freya. It's all right,' he said, giving her a nudge with his elbow.

'If you say so.' She sighed and uncrossed her arms.

'I do,' he said. 'Now, it's my last day here before I've gotta leave, so why don't you two show me around?'

'Fine,' said Freya. 'But we are going where I want to go. No orchards,' she added with a wink.

'I'm good with that.'

'You should spend the day resting,' said Cassius. 'Getting out of here will not be easy.'

'I've spent a whole day sleeping. The last thing I need is more rest.'

'I cannot tell you anything, can I?' said Cassius.

'Nope.' Killian grinned.

'I suppose you made it through the tasks, more or less in one piece.'

'Exactly.'

Cassius rubbed one of his twinkling amber horns and smiled softly at Killian. 'Come on then,' he said, getting to his feet and dusting down his chest.

Freya stood up. Instead of her red dress, she wore a short brown animal-skin skirt with a matching cropped vest and a long sparkling red cloak. Her exposed white skin shimmered in the morning light. She gathered the cloak around her shoulders.

'Ready for the orchards, Freya?' said Cassius playfully.

Freya held up her palm, curled her fingertips and jerked her hand in Cassius's direction in response. Killian put his hands on the ground and pushed himself up quickly. A searing pain ripped through his shoulder and back, and he winced. Cassius shot him an anxious glance.

'Stiff knees,' Killian explained, 'from all the sitting.'

'Come on then,' said Freya as she skipped off through the undergrowth, her ruby-red tail swishing behind her.

Killian walked behind as they led him through the thick vegetation that grew around the campsite. It was so gloomy inside the forest that he had to focus intently on Freya's flowing red cloak so that he didn't lose them. The tall slender trees grew extremely close together and were covered with dark green leaves. As the wind rushed through their tops, they whispered messages to one another in their secret woodland tongue. The ground was carpeted with a thick layer of soft, damp moss, which flourished in the moist conditions. The air was rich with the smell of fresh plant life and thriving earth. A pair of silver squirrels with tails twice the size of any Killian had seen on the surface circled each other about a vine-covered tree trunk. A nervous black deer with horns of tarnished gold and eyes of ruby took one look at him before vanishing into the undergrowth. From somewhere above, a chorus of birds trilled a complicated high-pitched tune, and the crawling plants of the forest floor complemented it with the hum of insects.

Killian struggled to keep up with Cassius and Freya, but he didn't want them to see he was having difficulty, so he ignored the pain as best he could and persevered. His back, his shoulders, his arms, his chest – there wasn't anywhere that didn't hurt him.

During his trip through the woods, he noted at least five different cornelians foraging, or perhaps just messing about; being an outsider, he wasn't entirely sure what they were doing. They shook his hand as he passed by and lowered their heads so their glittering horns were beneath him. Though it wasn't unpleasant, it was a slightly unnerving experience. They were treating him with respect, almost awe, something he wasn't used to.

'Do not worry about them,' said Cassius. 'They are excited to see you again.'

'Me? But I'm—'

'No one has ever survived the tasks before,' Freya said. 'In fact, no one has ever been allowed to undertake them. You are the first.'

Killian felt humbled by their reverence but secretly revelled in it. He was worthy of something, but it didn't seem right somehow. A mistake must have been made. What could be significant about a gambling, drinking slacker? He was at a loss for an answer but decided to enjoy his moment of glory, however bizarre and fleeting it might be.

'Here we are,' Freya announced as she bounded out of the woodland with Cassius in hot pursuit.

Killian pushed through the thick foliage, wrestling overgrown shrubs out of the way to join the two cornelians in the clearing. As he staggered out of the scrub, something caught his eye. He looked up, and his mouth dropped open.

In front of him, surrounded by more trees, was an immense indigo lake. Its gentle waters softly lapped at the white sands around it. All about the edge, gigantic crystals protruded from the shallows and shoreline. They were anywhere from three to nine feet tall, obelisk shaped and culminated with pointed tops. Some stood alone, others were in clusters. As the water splashed against the foot of the crystals, they chimed, filling the air with ghostly music. The light was split into hundreds of rainbows as it fell upon the gargantuan gemstones. Killian held out his arm and watched his skin change colour as it was cast with tiny rainbows.

'This is amazing,' he whispered, turning his hand back and forth.

'Yes, it is pretty,' said Freya airily. She meandered towards the shore, her long red hair flecked with multiple colours as it reflected the light.

Cassius smiled and motioned for Killian to follow them to the edge of the lake. Freya was already sitting with her feet in the water by the time he approached her. Killian followed her example. He was relieved to sit down; his wounds were screaming at him, and he was finding it difficult to mask the pain. Cassius hunkered down behind Freya. They sat in silence, listening to the ethereal sound of the crystals and watching the rainbows dance on the surface of the lake.

'What is this?' Killian asked quietly.

'A small piece of home,' Cassius replied.

'We did not always live here,' said Freya in an unusually solemn tone.

'We lived far away, in another realm over the hidden paths,' said Cassius.

'We had our own land. We did not hurt anyone,' Freya added bitterly. 'But some in our world were not content. They wanted more; they wanted everything. A war broke out amongst mages, north, south, east and west. Everyone fought, and the world was destroyed. It became an empty husk. We managed to flee before we too became husks. Nesta opened a portal to another world, this world, using the veins that connect everything. She was young, and it almost killed her, but she did it. She saved us all.

'These crystals,' Freya continued, swirling her toes in the water as she spoke, creating a myriad of rainbow eddies, 'grew all around the water in our part of the realm, in our home, our true home. I snapped off a piece as a reminder of our world before I left. After we created this under-sea sanctuary and this pool, I buried the shard in the mud beneath the water. When I returned to the lake days later, it had taken root. Within weeks they had spread all around the shore, chiming and casting rainbows like they did back home.' She smiled sadly as she stared out across the lake.

Killian turned to ask Cassius, 'How long have you lived down here?'

'About nine centuries,' Cassius responded. He laid a gentle hand on his lover's shoulder. Freya shuffled back and pressed herself against him.

'A long time.'

'It is.'

'Enough about us and our tragic past,' said Freya. It was obvious from her tone she was keen to change the subject. 'Tell us about you and your world.'

'My world, well, there's not much to say really.'

'Oh ho!' Cassius beamed, seeming more like his usual self. 'I am sure there is plenty to tell.' He moved from behind Freya and edged closer to Killian. 'Oceans, mountains, rivers, your way of life, there is so much! How your people look. Do you all have blue eyes?'

Killian laughed. 'No, we don't.' He scratched the back of his head. 'There's not much to say. Mountains, oceans – we've got all those things. To be honest, this is the first time I've left my own country.'

'Which is?' Cassius asked eagerly.

'Vermor.'

'Ver-mor, Ver . . . mor . . . Vermor,' murmured Cassius, trying out the taste of the new word. 'Killian of Vermor.'

Freya huffed and shook her head. She put one hand in the sand and swivelled around to face Killian. 'Why do you not tell us about Lily?' she asked with a wily grin.

'Nothing to tell.'

She narrowed her eyes suspiciously.

'All right,' said Killian. He put his elbows behind him and leant backwards, hoping to create the perfect picture of casual serenity. 'She's the captain of the ship that brought me here.'

'Oh really.' Freya raised her eyebrows playfully. 'Is that all?'

'She's also an incredibly nasty pirate, and we don't get on,' he added.

'Just as I thought.' She smiled, placed her chin on her hands and stared at him, her metallic eyes sparkling.

Killian shuffled, feeling a little uncomfortable under her gaze. 'Why are you looking at me like that?'

She slowly traced one of her horns with her finger. 'No reason,' she said innocently.

'Listen.' Killian's shoulders stiffened defensively as he spoke. 'There's nothing between me and her other than loathing, all right?'

'I did not say there was,' she said slyly. 'You did.'

'I don't...'

Freya's smile grew. 'In your sleep, it was "Lily this, Lily that." Sometimes you called her "Lil," and sometimes you even made—'

Cassius leapt to his defence. 'He was asleep.'

'I have never heard you do that in your sleep, my love.'

'He has been through a lot.'

'So have we all,' she said. Her expression softened, and she moved to sit behind Cassius. She pulled him onto her lap and tousled his messy golden hair affectionately. She glanced at Killian. 'Fine, nothing but loathing.'

Smiling to himself, Killian wrapped his arms around his head and lay back on the sand. He stared up at the sky and watched the swirling colours, letting out a long contented breath. It was amazing here. He shut his eyes, the fresh cool water lapping at his feet, and listened to the soothing melody of the crystals. All his thoughts drifted away with the chimes, and for the first time in months he felt completely at peace. His body was heavy yet relaxed.

Killian opened his eyes and shifted back onto his elbows. A long thin dragonfly-like insect hovered by his feet, its body a deep red and its wings daubed with bright yellows, rusty oranges and fresh greens. He wriggled his toes, and it flitted away. He watched it, but it became lost within the light of the crystals. As he gazed pensively across the lake, a memory returned to him. Cassius had said something to him when they'd first met, something that had bothered him at the time, but he'd been too terrified and delirious to ask about it. He'd been distracted by the tasks until now.

'Cassius.'

'Yes?' The cornelian blinked and sat up.

'Can I ask you something?'

'Of course.'

'When I first met you, you said something to me.' He paused, remembering.

'Go on,' Cassius urged.

'You said, "We have been waiting for someone like you." What did you mean?'

Cassius looked at Killian, his demonic eyes unflinching. 'You are a bearer,' he said simply.

'A what?'

'A bearer,' said Cassius, 'of the blades.' He reached over and tapped Killian's swords.

'I don't understand,' said Killian.

'Tell him, Cassius,' said Freya, wrapping her arms around his shoulders, her fingers stroking his tattooed collarbone.

'I do not know if it is my place to say,' said Cassius with a frown.

'I doubt anyone will mind,' said Freya. She rested her cheek on his shoulder and leant forwards, her ruby hair cascading over his chest like a flaming waterfall. Her eyes were fixed intently on Killian.

'This is true,' Cassius mused. 'Years ago, Nesta forged the hilts to the very blades you carry. She wove an arkani enchantment into them and sent them to the surface. She told us to wait for a sword bearer because only they would be able to complete the tasks and be granted the reward. They would be the one who stood between life and death.'

Killian couldn't believe what he was hearing. He felt numb and cringed when Cassius paused to look at him.

'We saw so much horror in the destruction of our world – civilisations crumbled in days, lives were destroyed, and the land was torn apart. Death and misery, devastation and blood. Nesta swore she would never let it happen again. So she created the swords. They were sent to seek out a person who could prevent such atrocities happening again and to bring them down here to us.'

Killian was stunned. It was more than he could take in. He couldn't prevent the destruction of worlds – he could barely prevent the destruction of himself. There had to be some mistake. He wasn't anything.

'But I chose to come down here,' said Killian, his voice low and a little shaky. 'Nothing made me do it. I chose of my own free will . . . didn't I?'

'Nothing made you do it?' Freya arched a doubtful eyebrow at him.

'Yeah, well . . . maybe there were a few outside influences that inspired my choice.'

'Unless I am mistaken,' said Cassius, 'you have done all this for someone else.'

Killian nodded slowly. 'In a way, sort of, but it's a little more complicated than—'

'So that is why you are here, with the swords,' Cassius said. His blind faith in Killian's good nature was admirable – mistaken, but admirable.

Killian twisted his lip as he thought. This was wrong, all wrong. He winced and quickly released the lip, having momentarily forgotten about the swelling. It had to be wrong. He was being paid for his services, after all; surely that wasn't the behaviour of some world-saving hero?

'But what about the guy who had them before me? I won them from him in a card game.'

'They left him and came to you, and the person before him, and the person before her, and the person before them.'

'For how long?'

'Five centuries,' said Cassius.

'It took them that long to find someone?'

'Well, not exactly,' said Freya. 'Every person who owned them before you would have been worthy too – that is the nature of the enchantment. So any one of those hundreds, maybe thousands of people could have come down here and tried their hand at the tasks.'

'So, I'm not some special and unique guy?' he asked tentatively.

'No,' she replied with a chuckle that served to highlight how ludicrous his question was. 'You were just in the right place at the right time with the right mission and the right object. Such is the way of life at times.'

Killian ran his fingers over his goggles just to give himself something to do and pondered his situation. The crystals hummed their ghostly song as the vivid rainbows played on the waters. It was like a dream. He turned to pinch himself, but when shooting pain raced down his back and his shoulder locked, he knew he was awake. He couldn't absorb it all; it was impossible. The biggest mistake in the history of the world was happening right now, and that mistake was him. It was all wrong.

'So, what does all this mean?' he asked when he'd rediscovered his capacity for speech.

'In short, you will get what you came for,' said Cassius.

'What about standing between life and death? What does that even mean?'

Freya huffed and wrapped her tail about herself and Cassius. 'You are down here to help save a life, are you not?'

'Yeah, you're right. I suppose that explains that.'

'You do not say,' she said, a playful musical lilt to her tone.

'Maybe,' murmured Killian. 'But it all seems a little insignificant, don't you think?'

'Perhaps he is more significant than you realise,' said Cassius.

'Perhaps,' said Killian, slowly lowering himself back to the sand. Ren's father, of course. Killian was merely a conduit for something much greater. That at least made some sort of sense. He reached his arms overhead and, wincing discreetly, laid his head against them. This was too much for him to take in at once. His head was spinning, and his body seemed to ache the more he dwelled on it. 'So, where do you grow your food?' he asked, changing the subject entirely to one that was far more comprehensible – painfully dull, but comprehensible.

'I can take you to the orchards if you like,' said Cassius eagerly.

An audible groan escaped from Freya.

'How about you just tell me about them. I kinda like it here. It's peaceful.'

'I knew it! You are in pain, are you not?'

'No,' Killian lied.

Cassius frowned and glared at him, his eyes demanding the truth.

'All right, yes.' Killian sighed.

'I knew it,' said Cassius, throwing his hands up in the air. 'You should have stayed at the camp and rested.'

'I know, but I can do that on the surface,' Killian said defensively.

'Cassius, do not be angry,' said Freya, glancing at her lover's furrowed brow.

'I am not angry, just concerned.' He turned to look at Killian again. 'If something were to happen to you, I would never forgive myself.'

'Don't worry about me, Cassie. I'm not made of glass.'

'But the way out is treacherous. Something could happen, and then all this would be for nothing.'

'I'll be fine,' Killian said.

'But you have to—'

'No,' Killian cut in, holding up his hand for Cassius to stop talking. 'You can tell me all about the dangers and the treacherous pathway tomorrow. Today we all relax and enjoy one another's company for the last time.'

'I agree with Killian,' said Freya, wrapping her legs about Cassius's waist.

'All right,' grumbled Cassius, defeated. 'You win.'

'Good.' Killian grinned triumphantly. 'Now tell me about your orchards.'

Cassius's solemn face melted into a picture of serene happiness, and he launched into the tale of the cornelian agricultural methods through the ages with great enthusiasm.

CHAPTER
THIRTY-ONE

ILLIAN AWOKE THE NEXT MORNING TO A searing pain coursing through his back. He sat up immediately to alleviate the pressure on his injuries, and his body jolted, sending another violent spasm of pain through him. His skin flushed, and his heart thundered; he chewed the inside of his mouth to keep from crying out. Today he felt even worse.

He tentatively touched his stiff shoulders; his muscles pulsed with a dull ache that seemed to have grown overnight. They were overbearingly heavy and weak, as if someone had removed the bone and muscle while he slept and replaced it with hardened lead. He swore and rubbed his sore, drowsy eyes with his rough palms. He'd had little sleep during the night. Every time he'd drifted off he'd been woken by the pain of whichever injury he happened to be lying on. He was ridiculously tired, and his body was a well of agony – not that he'd admit this to Cassius or Freya. They'd only get concerned and try to make him stay longer. Today was his last day; he had to leave or he'd be left behind.

Looking around in the dim purple glow of the tent, he saw that neither of the two cornelians were inside. *They always get up so early.* He slouched forwards and pressed his forehead against his knees. He was so hungry it felt like his stomach was trying to devour itself. Wistfully, he pondered Estelle's breakfasts. As tasty as the cornelians' food was, it didn't satisfy him like hers did. The more he thought about it, the more he ached. He took a deep breath and could almost smell that sizzling bacon, those frying eggs. His mouth watered, and nausea crept up on him. He just wanted something hot, greasy and unhealthy to eat, something that would make him feel human again. Surely that wasn't too much to ask. Worst of all, he knew he wouldn't get it when he returned to the ship. He'd be lucky if he got bland porridge made from water and weevils. Weevils. He hadn't even seen a weevil. Well, he didn't think he had. Truth be told, he didn't even know what one looked like. Weevils and ships were synonymous in his mind. They went together like cards and booze, a happy marriage.

He sat back and cursed himself for his overactive imagination. Still feeling dazed and weary from broken sleep, he got to his feet unsteadily. He blundered about the tent, searching for his clothes and equipment. Once he was sure he'd gathered everything together, he threw his clothes on. He felt a twinge of sadness as he dressed. Today he was going to leave the world of the cornelians forever. Everything was so calm and tranquil down here; no one seemed to have any worries or problems. Life just flowed in perfect harmony. He shook his head, and his bruised lips curled into a smile. It was too perfect – he could never cope with living here permanently. Lately he'd found himself yearning for a spiteful fight with Lily, for Ren to get his back up or for Tom to spin a tale of utter bullshit. He wanted breakfast with Stell, a friendly chat with Ruby and to drink with Barrington, then fleece him of his inheritance at the card table. He wanted a clifftop walk to feel the wind in his hair, to gaze out over the vast sea. He missed it all. He had one final glance around the tent, then stepped outside to find Cassius sitting on the ground alone.

'Oho! Good morning!'

'Morning,' said Killian, his voice gruff and croaky. He cleared his throat.

'How do you feel?'

'Fine, I'm fine,' Killian expertly lied.

'Food?' Cassius offered a plate to Killian.

'Thanks,' he said as he plucked a chunk of soft orange fruit from the plate. He chewed it slowly and thoughtfully; sharp tangy juices filled his mouth, making his eyes water. He wished it were bacon, hot salty bacon dripping with butter and oil, giving life to his weary body. His hollow, abused stomach moaned pitifully at him for fantasising again.

'You are leaving today,' Cassius said, his voice heavy.

Killian swallowed and wiped his sticky fingers on his trousers. 'I've got to.'

'I know,' said Cassius sadly. 'Freya and I will miss you.'

'I'll miss you too. This place is amazing. Part of me wants to stay, but . . .' He glanced at the swirling sky for inspiration.

Cassius finished his sentence for him. 'But you must leave. You have duties on the surface, and there are people up there who care about you.'

Killian nodded. 'Well, I don't know about the latter, but I do have something important to do up there.' He picked up something firm and purple. It crunched when he bit it. Though it tasted sweet, it had all the texture of dry bark. He quickly swallowed it and looked at Cassius. 'I should leave,' he said with a heavier heart than he'd anticipated.

'Now?' asked Cassius. He looked hurt.

'I'm sorry.'

'No. I am sorry. I am being selfish. You have to leave. You have a responsibility to fulfil.' He paused and rubbed his dense beard. 'I have enjoyed our time together, Killian of Vermor. Thank you for showing me what a man from the surface is truly like.' He clapped his hand firmly on Killian's shoulder. 'Come, I shall take you to Nesta.'

Killian followed Cassius through the cornelian camp and towards the largest tent.

'Wait here,' he told Killian before slipping inside the glyph-adorned tent.

Killian gazed around the camp. Two cornelians were stacking firewood in the centre, one male and one female. The female had long golden hair and dark horns; the male had a messy shock of red hair and silver horns. She mischievously poked the male while he adjusted the fire. He pretended to ignore her, a covert smile on his lips. He waited until she crept close enough, then spun around and caught her in his arms. She laughed and playfully punched him in the chest before giving in and kissing him. Killian smiled to himself and looked skyward. Life here was simple, easy, carefree.

'Nesta is inside,' said Cassius, reappearing. Killian snapped out of his trance. 'She has been waiting for you. Tell her what it is you desire, and it will be yours.'

'You mean I can have anything?'

'Within reason, yes.'

He could have anything, absolutely anything. This was everyone's dream, and he was giving it all to Ren. He'd almost died to give it to him. It didn't seem right. He ran his tongue along his puffy bottom lip; he could have *anything*, yet he didn't know what he'd ask for. He was sure resurrections weren't classed as 'within reason.' It was just as well Ren was going to be the beneficiary. He would only squander this opportunity on something utterly meaningless.

'I'm ready,' he said.

Cassius nodded and held the tent flap open for him, dropping it behind him as he walked through.

It was pitch black inside, except for a soft light flickering somewhere in front of him.

'Come to the light,' said Nesta's soothing, powerful voice.

Without hesitation, Killian did as he was asked. He squinted as he stumbled blindly ahead, mindful of any hidden objects that would trip him up. The tent had a warm, smoky scent to it, with just a hint of sweet spices, which re-awakened his senses. As he drew closer, he saw a pale flame dancing in Nesta's open palm. In the flickering light, Killian could just make out her majestic face, her sharp cheekbones and rich dark brown skin, her long flowing silvery hair shimmering like thousands of compressed stars. The flames brought out the dramatic gold of her eyes and made the tattooed mask they resided within shine bright. The whole thing had a ritualistic feel to it, and he wasn't sure what he was supposed to do, so he did the first thing that came into his head and dropped down on one knee in front of the Tia.

'Killian, please get up. I have no need for such formalities.'

Feeling slightly foolish and a little embarrassed, Killian got up.

'I should be kneeling before you,' Nesta said. 'After all, you have done what nobody else has, me included – completed the tasks. To be honest with you, I would be terrible.'

She lowered her voice to a whisper and gave Killian a slow wink, a golden eye briefly hidden in the mask. 'I cannot run fast, I despise getting wet, I do not like enclosed spaces, and as for that third task . . . well, the thought of it makes my skin crawl.'

'About that – the third one,' Killian ventured, keeping his gaze on the light.

'Yes,' replied Nesta.

'I don't know if I want to know, or if I should even ask, but what was that? Where did it come from?' He tried to keep his voice even despite his mounting fear. Did he really want to know if that thing was a true representation of him, or if it was somehow linked to his future? He gritted his teeth; he did. 'I've been trying to work it out, but I don't know.'

'Let me explain,' said Nesta. She lowered her head slightly, and as her horns caught the light, purest gold flashed upon their deep ridges. The crystals decorating them hummed as they cast hundreds of tiny rainbows about the tent. 'That thing was part of you. All the darkness that exists inside your soul was manifested into that being. Every malicious thought you have had, every sinister action you have committed, every evil you could possibly imagine, all contributed to that creature.'

'So it was me,' muttered Killian, putting his hand to his chest. His heart skipped, and his stomach lurched. It was as if he didn't even know himself anymore.

'In a manner of speaking, yes.'

'Is it gone now?'

'No. It will never be gone. It resides in you. We all have a demon within us. Yours merely became physical.'

'I won't turn into it, will I?' It was an absurd question, but he had to know; he needed some kind of reassurance.

'Of course not.' She smiled. 'In destroying it you proved you are strong enough in mind, body and soul to overcome any evils you might face, even if the evil is yourself. The final test is the most important. It proves you are worthy to wield any power we may bestow upon you. If your evil had been too great, it would have killed you, showing you had not the strength of spirit and responsibility to hold power without being corrupted.'

Killian was silent, thinking deeply on what had been said.

Nesta studied him closely before she spoke again. 'There is one thing I need to ask you, Killian.'

'Yes?'

'Why?' she said simply.

Killian frowned. He rolled his heavy shoulders and received a lance of pain to his back for his troubles. 'I don't know what you mean.'

'You have put yourself through so much torment and suffering. I do not need to tell you how close you came to death on several occasions. I wish to know why. Do not even think about saying it was for the money or that it was all for this Thorny. I will know you are lying. There is something more than that. I know it.'

Killian lowered his head. His left arm throbbed, and he clasped it to try and placate the pain. He swallowed. His throat was uncomfortably dry. 'I lost my mum . . . and my closest friend some time ago.' Despite his shaking voice, he managed to force out the name. 'His name was Clem.' He paused to regain his composure; he was determined not to choke up in front of the mighty Tia. 'It was my fault they died. With Mum, I was an idiot. I opened the front door when I shouldn't have. I let the cleansers into our house. She knew what would happen, she tried to protect me, but they overpowered her. She told me to run and not look back. So I did.' He moved his hand to his cheek, trying to wipe away a phantom spray of blood. 'Sometimes I can still hear her screaming my name.'

He paused again and focused on keeping his tears at bay. 'With Clem, it was different, but still my fault. He and I, we used to thieve together. Our dream was to leave Vermor and start again somewhere else. I had a hot tip. We were gonna get rich. I was confident, he was less so.' A rush of guilt, misery and loneliness surged through his body. Would he ever be free of it? He blinked, and tears rolled down his cheeks. 'The tip went sour, and he was shot, when it should have been me. It should have been me. It was my fault. He died in my arms, all for nothing.

'So the reason I'm doing all this is to prove to them, and to myself, that I'm not a waste of life. That I don't just ruin and end lives and fuck everything up.' His tears flowed in a steady stream, and he was powerless to stop them. 'That I can do something worthwhile, that there's a reason for why they're both gone and I'm not. Two people I love died because of me, and I'm still here.' He wiped his eyes with his sleeve. 'It's not right.'

Nesta took a step closer to Killian. 'If it counts for anything, you have proven your worth to me,' she said, her voice soft, belying her immense power.

Killian lifted his head and pushed his hair back. 'Thanks.' It was the only word he could bring himself to say. After all, he didn't believe her.

'You are not a waste of life, Killian,' she said, placing a hand on his shoulder.

He let out a joyless laugh. 'Maybe one day I'll see that.'

'You should.' She moved back and spread her arms. 'Now, you want help getting in and out of this sealed temple, correct?'

'Yes.'

'Are you sure that is what you need?'

'Truthfully, I don't think I can ever have what I need, but Thorncliffe has to have that thing.' He shrugged. 'And maybe it will sort me out, in some strange metaphysical way. I save his father, and it somehow . . .'

'Wipes your mistakes away?'

'Yeah, something like that. Stupid, isn't it?'

'That is not for me to judge.' Nesta fixed her eyes on Killian. She swept her hands together and held her palms out, the ball of flame hovering above them. 'I cannot promise by doing this you will heal your trauma, but I promise you entry to this temple.'

The flame spun, moving faster and faster, its colour growing brighter until it fluoresced like a star and Killian could no longer look at it. It hissed, and something leapt from its heart, leaving a trail of silver behind it. Nesta held out her left hand and caught the object as it fell. The flames gradually died down until they assumed their former pale glow. The Tia held the object out to Killian. A twisted metal pendant in the shape of a glyph hung from a silver chain. The warm glow of the flame gave the necklace a liquid effect.

Killian took it from her and examined it.

'It will disintegrate once it has been used to get you in and out of this temple. You may only use it once.'

'That's all right,' said Killian as he put it on. The metal felt cold against his skin despite having been spat from a flame moments ago. 'Thank you.'

'Come here,' said Nesta.

He took a step closer to the horned woman. Nesta held her palm out flat, and the ball of light melted into it. Her hand shimmered with a silvery radiance, and her eyes turned as golden as the morning sun, rivers of concentrated light pouring from them. She lifted her hand and placed it over the glyph on Killian's chest. It was warm and made his skin tingle. The cornelian pressed firmly, and with a thunderous crack a great flash of light burst from her. Killian took a swift breath as he felt a rush of raw, powerful energy pulse through his body. It was like nothing he'd ever experienced before. Every muscle snapped with vigour; he felt a strength he hadn't thought he was capable of. He felt invincible . . . until Nesta removed her hand. His body instantly reverted to normal, and he ached all the more after the intense shock of power.

'Now you will get past the seal,' said Nesta with a satisfied nod.

'Thanks,' Killian rasped. To have so much power, even for a fraction of a second, only to have it snatched away left him feeling stunned and enervated.

'One last thing. Hand me your swords.'

Killian unsheathed his dull blades and handed them over; he'd almost forgotten how they'd failed him. Nesta slowly ran her finger along each of the hilts and handed them back. They glowed softly as he took them.

'You had to do the tasks alone, without help,' she said.

'I understand,' said Killian, nodding. He eyed the blades, then loosened his grip and held them out before the cornelian. 'I suppose you should have them now. They are yours, after all.'

'And what would I do with them down here?' She chuckled. 'No, they have found an owner. Keep them. You have earned them. Now, I believe you must leave us. Cassius will show you the way back to your world. Good luck, Killian. It has been an honour.' Nesta smiled, lowering her great horned head respectfully.

'It has,' said Killian. He sheathed his weapons and bowed his head, then turned to leave.

LILY paced aggressively about her cabin; she'd asked Jarran to fetch Raven hours ago. Where was he? She glared at the idyllic picture on her wall. The pastel-coloured houses emanated warmth and tranquillity, and she wanted to destroy them all. It was meaningless; they were nothing. Her shoulders tensed, and her muscles trembled. *How dare that picture exist, how dare that place exist, how dare those people who live there exist when he's ...*

She spun around to stare at the chest of drawers. She wanted to smash it up, throw everything on the floor and pound it into the ground. The writing desk, her books, her maps, parchment, everything. It could all go. She whirled round and caught the emerald-green glint of her feather winking at her from the hat stand. *Rip it out of the bloody hat and toss it in the sea. Move on. Forget him.* It was a nice idea, poetic even, but she knew deep down she'd never be able to do it.

She turned back to the drawers and pulled the top one open. Inside lay the wooden box with the octopus carved on its lid. She popped it open and took out the shell. If ever there was a time to use it, surely it was now. The Big Blue, the ethereal spirit of the ocean, her saviour – they could help. They could save Killian. But was it worth summoning them? For his sake? She laid the shell back down on the soft green velvet. Her heart raced. It was a risk. She could lose them. She could lose him. She may have already lost him.

A knock sounded at the door, interrupting her thoughts. She snapped the box shut and dropped it back in the drawer. If he was already dead, calling them would be a waste. She could fall down and see for herself. Either way, she had to know.

'Come in!' she snapped testily.

Raven entered, closing the door behind him.

'Where the hell have you been?' she growled through clenched teeth.

'I came as soon as I was told.'

'That was hours ago.'

'No, it was a few minutes ago,' said Raven, remaining calm.

'Don't you ever talk back to me. Remember your place, Raven.'

'I'm sorry, Captain,' he replied, his soothing demeanour at odds with Lily's fury.

She grunted in response and stomped away from him. She wanted to hit him, hook him right in his lovely face. Her back bristled. She could do it; she could beat him down. Maybe then he'd know what her pain felt like. It would be like when they met – he fighting for the western district, she for the east – a good, cathartic, bare-fisted fight.

Tightness crept across her chest. What was she even thinking? Hurt Raven? The one person in her life who'd never let her down, the person she trusted implicitly? She was letting her frustration consume her. She stopped pacing and slumped onto her bed, hunching up on the end, her elbows on her knees and her face resting in her hands. The facade was too difficult to keep up.

The bed moved as Raven sat next to her, and she felt his warm arm around her. He pulled her into his muscular chest, and she cried against him. She wrapped her arms about him, her rigid fingers clawing for purchase on his back, and shut her eyes. For a precious few moments, she let go of her stony pirate queen persona. Her breath was ragged and her skin hot. She clung tight to Raven; she needed him, she needed to hold on to someone stronger than herself. Raven tightened his grip on her but remained silent throughout.

'Thank you,' she whispered, letting go of him and sitting back.

'Any time,' he said, and she knew he meant it.

She pushed her hair back, wiping her salty tears through it. 'I'm a mess. I didn't mean to shout at you. I'm . . .'

'It's all right,' he said, turning towards her, his soft purple eyes upon her.

'I let my emotions get the better of me,' she said, lowering her gaze. She hated to be seen like this. It wasn't her. She wasn't emotional; her heart was stone and iron. How dare *he* force her to feel like this?

'You don't have to explain yourself,' he said.

'If he's not back today . . .' Her trembling voice faded to nothing as fresh tears splashed down her cheeks.

'Think about that tomorrow.'

'I'm going down,' she said flatly, wiping her eyes. 'I'm going down right now.'

'Lily, please listen to yourself,' he implored. 'You're not thinking straight. You need to wait until tomorrow before you do anything. Remember, you need to think of your crew too. For all you know, he could be on his way up now.'

Lily fell into his arms once more and lay silently against his solid chest. She felt sick and dizzy, her body fragile. 'You're right. I'm sorry.'

'Don't apologise.'

'If he's not back by tomorrow, I'll go down,' she said, the stubborn determined streak present in her low voice.

'No, the crew need you. I'll go.'

'I can't lose you too,' she whispered. 'I can't.'

'You won't, I promise,' he said.

She peeled herself off him and nodded. 'You promise?'

'I'll always be around, as long as you need me. You can trust me on that.'

'I know,' she said with a feeble smile.

'I'll get back to my post,' he said, 'and keep an eye out for him.'

'Okay,' she said softly. 'Thank you.'

'But if you need me . . .'

'I know. Thanks.'

CHAPTER
THIRTY-TWO

ASSIUS PUT HIS HAND ON THE WALL OF smooth grey rock before them. He closed his eyes, and its surface came alive with bright blue symbols. It flashed with white light before fading away to reveal the gaping mouth of a dark cave. Twisted brown stalactites hung from its apex like a row of neglected teeth. Dense steam billowed out, and a deafening noise echoed around them. They'd hiked for close to two hours to get to it, and still the cornelians' lands rolled off into the distance; they were truly immense.

'This passage leads to the surface,' said Cassius to Killian once the noise had subsided enough for his voice to be heard. 'It is easy enough to follow. The only problem is that just beyond that corner' – he pointed into the cave mouth – 'it connects with the path of the geyser. The geyser erupts every hour and lasts for about twenty minutes, so you will have to be quick. You will have up to forty minutes to make it to the top, although I would advise you to try for thirty. It is fairly regular, but its timing is not perfect. You will come out on the island surrounding the geyser. As soon as you do, look for cover. You do not want to have come all this way just to get burnt to death.'

'No,' said Killian, curling his lip. 'You don't make things easy, do you?'

'Oho, no.' Cassius shook his head. 'There would be no fun if it were easy.'

'A leisurely stroll would be fun. I like walking.'

Cassius chuckled. 'You could always stay here.'

'Don't tempt me,' Killian muttered from the corner of his mouth.

'Aha! If only I could, my friend. One more thing you should know: the opening to the surface is sealed with arkani. It will clear moments before the geyser is ready to erupt. It looks like rock, it feels like rock, and for all intents and purposes, it is rock. But when the time approaches, it will become transparent and gradually disappear, so when you see sunlight poking through, you will know you do not have much time left.'

'So when I see sunlight, I hurry.'

'Hopefully you will already be beneath the opening. The window of opportunity is very small. It is dark in there, so take this.' Cassius unhooked a wooden baton from his belt and handed it to him. 'Hold it and will it to ignite. It will obey you.'

'Wait, wait!' shouted Freya. She came bounding over to them. She stopped in front of Killian, folded her arms across her chest and glared at him. He could tell from the look in her eyes he was in trouble. 'I cannot believe you were going to leave without saying goodbye,' she blurted out in one breath.

'Oh, er, sorry.' Killian ran his fingers through his hair and averted his gaze from hers.

'We tried to find you,' Cassius said. 'He does not have much time.'

Freya's face was stony and expressionless, her mouth set in a tight line. 'I just ran all the way from camp.'

Killian grovelled, wincing in anticipation of her reaction. 'I'm really sorry. Look, I am, I just couldn't wait around.'

Freya glowered at him through narrowed eyes, her eyebrows knitting together.

He felt awful. She should probably just slap him and get it over with; he deserved it. He stood before her, his arms limp at his sides, not even attempting to defend himself. Her angry expression melted away, and she pounced on him, kissed him on the cheek and wrapped her arms around him in a tight friendly embrace. She released her grip and took a step back, holding her forearm in front of her and studying her chiming bangles. After some brief deliberation, she plucked one from her wrist. It was a thin silver band encrusted with sparkling green and black jewels.

'Here,' she said, holding it out to Killian. 'Give this to her.'

'I'm sorry, what did you say?' he asked, a little taken aback.

'Give this to her,' she repeated as she placed the bangle in his hand and closed his fingers around it. 'A little souvenir.'

'All right,' he said as he slipped it into his trouser pocket, 'but her? Thank you,' he mouthed back furtively.

He turned to face Cassius. When he set eyes on his horned friend, he felt a wash of sadness; he was never going to see him again, and they both knew it.

'Thanks, Cassius, for everything,' he said stoically.

'It was the least I could do,' said Cassius, holding out his hand.

Killian ignored the hand and instead grabbed him in a tight hug. The cornelian squeezed him back fiercely.

'Thank you,' Killian murmured. He blinked back tears, and his throat tightened.

Behind them, the ferocious rumbling of the geyser and the sound of rushing water stopped.

'You should go,' said Cassius. He let go and gave Killian's shoulder one last squeeze of reassurance. 'And hurry.'

'Okay.' Killian nodded, edging towards the monstrous-looking cave.

'Bye, Killian,' said Freya, waving to him.

'Good luck, my friend,' said Cassius as Killian stepped into the mouth of the cave.

Killian ducked around the corner and onto the path that would lead him to the surface. It was still hot from the heat of the water, the slippery wet floor making running impossible. The last thing he wanted to do was fall over backwards and break something important, but boiling alive wasn't appealing either. He increased his pace to a swift manageable walk.

The light grew increasingly weak the farther he went. He looked at the torch and pondered it. Cassius had told him to will it to ignite. That sounded ridiculous, but so did fighting himself and horned people from another world. He smirked to himself. Compared to that, willing a stick to burst into flames sounded positively normal. He tightened his grip, and to his amazement, the end glowed for a second before sputtering dramatically into green flames reminiscent of those in the labyrinth. The light cut through the gloom, illuminating a pathway for him.

The tunnel was worn smooth from the scalding geyser water and glimmered green in the flames of the torch. The whole cavern was thick with the scent of hot damp rocks. The path spiralled around to the left at a slight incline like a giant corkscrew. It was dark, pitch black. If it weren't for the torch, Killian wouldn't have been able to see his hand in front of his face.

Steam from the raging geyser below slowly crept into the tunnel. At first Killian didn't notice it, but after a few minutes it was impossible not to. The ever-thickening fog made it difficult for him to see where he was going, so he pulled his goggles up to aid his vision and protect his eyes. The intense heat made him sweat copiously, and it seeped into his injuries, irritating them. He gritted his teeth as he resisted the maddening urge to claw away at his prickly skin; it felt as if ten thousand ants were crawling over him. The scorching mist rapidly soaked his hair and clothes. He sighed in annoyance; he was fed up with being wet all the time.

He moved as quickly as he could in the mounting humidity, his feet slipping on the smooth wet rock. A low rumbling sound came from behind, and he picked up his pace. He put his head down and powered forwards, ignoring the heat and the pain throbbing from his lacerations.

The geyser growled again, its foreboding snarls echoing off the glistening walls of the tunnel. They were becoming more frequent. Despite the sweltering climate, Killian kept an even pace. Another guttural sound tore from below and boomed around the tunnel, the intense oscillations making the hair on his body stand up and vibrate. He pushed his damp hair away from his face. He wasn't sure how long he'd been walking through the tunnel; he'd lost all concept of time. A great breath of hot air accompanied the geyser's next roar, making his skin tingle. In that instant, he forgot about his worry of slipping and put his head down and ran. Sweat poured from his brow, his wet clothes stuck to his body, and the twisted silver pendant slapped painfully against his chest with every step.

The curves of the spiral seemed to go on forever. They kept coming, looming towards him in the darkness but never getting any closer. The rising steam made it painfully difficult to breathe. Hot gulps of air clogged his throat as he desperately tried to get some oxygen down to placate his burning muscles. Every step became more of an effort; it felt more like he was wading through burning waist-high mud than running through air. His limbs grew heavy and his breath hoarse. His strength drained from his body as rapidly and freely as his sweat. The only thing keeping him on his feet and moving was his own sheer will, forcing his failing body to carry on. He bit the inside of his bottom lip and tried to focus on the sound of his footsteps. *One, two, three, four, one, two, three, four*, he counted rhythmically, the glyph smacking his chest in time. *One, two, three, four, one, two, three, f—*

The path stopped so abruptly that he almost ran straight into the rock at the end of the tunnel. He looked up and around for the exit but saw none. *Did I go the wrong way? No, that's not even possible . . .* Behind him, down the long dark tunnel, the geyser rumbled, sending a shiver up his spine. A soft natural glow caught his eye, and the ground gradually became dappled as sunlight filtered down through the rocks above him. The barrier was fading, losing its opacity.

He put his hand up to shield his eyes against the light as it beamed upon him. Fresh ocean air drifted down towards him, and he gratefully drew in a lungful. He reached up and touched the barrier. It was soft, yielding to his pressure, but it was still solid, and time was running out. He dropped the torch; it went out as soon as it left his grip. It was a shame to leave it, but he wasn't sure he could climb out while holding it. He bent over and tested the end of it with his finger; it was cold. He picked it up and stuffed it in the back of his trousers. Lily was getting a souvenir, so it was only fair he did too.

The opening was now almost transparent, and his hands passed through it with little resistance. The ground shook violently beneath his feet, and thunder roared up the passage. *This is it.* He leapt up to the opening and managed to grab the sides. They were damp and slimy, but he dug his fingers into the rock to anchor himself. He held on with all his remaining strength, took a breath and wrenched himself towards the light, his biceps trembling with the strain. The bandage on his left arm ripped off as he rubbed against an outcrop. He drew in a sharp breath as his skin was torn open and fresh blood flowed from the wound. He gritted his teeth and grunted; he couldn't let it hinder him. Once he'd got his shoulders fully into the hole, he let go with his right arm and clung on with his left. Straining, he managed to stretch his free arm up and get hold of the smooth and slippery outer edge. He blew all the breath from his lungs and followed with his left arm. With a final effort, he hauled himself out of the gap.

He fell over the edge. All he wanted to do was lie there and rest, but the next second he was on his feet, frantically searching for cover. He spied a collection of shallow caves towards the coast and ran towards them without another thought. As he got within a few feet of them, the geyser erupted with a ferocious roar, spewing out a huge fountain of boiling water. He leapt through the air and landed roughly inside a cave. He scrambled up onto a narrow ledge and pressed himself as close to the rock as he could, watching the scalding water burst from the geyser. The water splashed into the mouth of the cave as it rained down from above, but as long as he stayed pressed up against the wall, it couldn't reach him.

He was desperately tired, his legs shaking uncontrollably beneath him. He needed to rest, just for a minute. A minute would be enough. It wasn't much to ask for. The torrent was never-ending, and he kept catching himself nod as he drifted in and out of consciousness for fleeting moments. He knew if he gave in completely that nothing would wake him, not even a fatal shower of volcanic water. Eventually the waters began to recede, but the warm rain continued. Killian patiently waited for it to cease, then pulled his goggles onto his head and staggered from his hiding place.

The tiny island was nothing more than a collection of craggy rocks. It was steaming wildly from the rain. This cleared as he walked towards the shore and was replaced by a cool breeze. Squinting out to sea, he could just about spy the outline of the *Tempest*.

He put his hand in his trousers and groped around for the flare, but his pockets were empty. He swore in frustration. It must have fallen out while he was underground; he'd been too preoccupied to think about it until now. His knees gave up, and he slumped to the ground, defeated. Salvation was so close, but the ship may as well have been on the other side of the planet for all the good it would do him now. Swimming to it wasn't an option; he was so tired he'd sink after a few strokes. The torch prodded him in the back, reminding him of its presence.

With fresh hope, he pulled it from his trousers, grateful for not having left it in the geyser, and willed it to ignite. It crackled into life, but the green flames were almost invisible in the white glare of the sun. It was useless. He dropped it to the rocks, and it went out. He hung his head in misery and idly played with Nesta's necklace. As he rolled the glyph over the back of his hand, it fluoresced, catching a shaft of sunshine and sending a bright beam of dazzling light into his eyes. An idea formed in his head, and he shakily got to his feet.

He drew his swords, tilting them into the sun to catch the beams of light. He twisted and turned them, flashing them in the direction of the ship. After about a minute, he stopped and sheathed them, his heavy shoulders refusing to do any more work, but he was satisfied Raven's keen eyes would have picked up his signal.

He crouched down on the rocky beach and waited. Time crawled along like a three-legged insect. Every second seemed like a minute, every minute an hour. Maybe they hadn't seen his signal. He moved to get up, but his body stubbornly refused his request. Maybe they didn't want him back. *No, that's stupid. They would have left already. Unless they've been waiting for me to return so they can laugh as I'm steamed to death like a lobster. No, shut up, Killian, you're being ridiculous now.*

He laboriously removed his boots and dipped his feet into the refreshing seawater. With cupped hands, he scooped up some salty water and splashed it over his face. His gaze wandered to the sky above, and he let out a contented grunt; he felt slightly more alive. A dark speck appeared in his vision, growing larger by the second. Raven landed neatly and soundlessly beside him.

'Need a lift?' he asked, his silvery voice a welcome sound.

'Nah, I'm good thanks,' said Killian, narrowing his eyes as he looked up at him. 'I thought I'd stay here for a bit. Been weeks since I had a hot bath.'

'Nice tunic.' A puckish twinkle shone in his ethereal eyes.

'I thought so,' Killian said. 'It makes me look heroic.' He struck his chest with his fist.

Raven chuckled and held out his hand. 'That's one way to describe it.'

'The other way being *shit*.' Killian took the offered hand and allowed Raven to pull him up.

'I'm sure, however you look, the captain will be pleased you're alive.'

'Really?' Killian asked, knowing he sounded more hopeful than he'd have liked. Cursing internally, he crammed his feet into his boots.

'She'll be desperate to get her hands on all that treasure you told her about, won't she?'

'Yep,' said Killian shortly, but the damage to his facade had already been done. He scratched the side of his head and ran his fingers through his hair to avoid looking directly at Raven.

A tiny smirk formed on Raven's lips. 'Oh!' he exclaimed, raising his eyebrows. 'You thought that she'd be pleased because—'

'That's enough out of you!' Killian said. Raven must have been hanging around with Tom in his absence. 'Come on, let's get off this rock before the geyser blows again. I'm wet enough already.'

'All right, hold tight.'

Killian held on to Raven and shut his eyes as he effortlessly vaulted into the air. He was still confounded by the height and distance Raven could cover in a single leap. He briefly opened his eyes and once again thought he glimpsed black feathery wings coming from Raven's back. Immediately after he saw them, he felt the downward pull of gravity. Raven swung acrobatically around the mast before landing neatly on the deck. Deafening cheers exploded from the crew of the *Tempest*.

As soon as Killian let go, Raven fell to one knee, hung his head and breathed deep. In the tangled cacophony of the moment, Killian reached down and grabbed the first mate's shoulder, pulling him to his feet. He nodded his thanks and took a step backwards.

Killian's mouth opened in shock as he looked around. He was completely overwhelmed by the faces staring at him. Another cheer went up, and he couldn't help but smile. The whole bloody ship had turned up to welcome him back, but where was the most important person? He searched the mob of blurred features until he found her. She was at the back of the crowd, straddling a cannon. Her head was turned to the sea, but he could feel her looking at him from the corner of her eyes.

'Did you get it?' asked Ren eagerly, pushing his way to the front of the crowd.

'Get what?' Teasing Ren was never going to get old or any less enjoyable.

'You know, the power . . . or something.'

'What d'you think?' Killian shrugged.

Ren opened his mouth, then closed it again and shuffled his feet.

'Of course I got it,' said Killian, grinning, putting Ren out of his misery. He'd missed making him feel utterly uncomfortable; if it weren't so easy to do, he'd have called it a talent. 'Where's your faith, Thorny?'

Another roar of approval boomed from the treasure-hungry crew. Fists punched the air, swords were raised, drinks were taken, and guns were fired skyward in celebration. Towards the back of the crowd, Morton Roberts curled his lip and handed some coins over to Finn, who gave him her typical shark-toothed grin.

'In that case,' Lily shouted, leaping down from her vantage point. All eyes respectfully turned to her as silence descended upon the crew. 'We can get the hell out of here. Come on, you lazy scum, holiday's over. Move, move, move!' She clapped her hands three times, then walked away without a second glance in his direction.

CHAPTER
THIRTY-THREE

'So,' Blake began curiously, 'what was down there?'

'Planning a story around my heroics, eh?' asked Killian. He pushed his foot against the wall, and his hammock swung gently. His body felt as if it were going to slip through the netting, piece by piece, but he was so worn out he didn't even care.

'Maybe, but I'm also genuinely interested. Who wouldn't be?' said Blake.

They were both lying in their respective hammocks. Killian had gone below deck almost as soon as he'd boarded the ship. He was so tired, all he wanted to do was sleep for the next month and wake up at Ren's island. That would suit him fine. No more boring ship, and also an excellent way to avoid Lily. He couldn't believe she hadn't spoken to him yet. She hadn't even looked at him – not directly anyway. What was her problem? He ran his tongue over his bruised split lip; the puffiness was going down slowly. He wrapped his arms around the back of his head and gazed at the scattered knots that littered the ceiling. Even they seemed more pleased with his return than her.

Blake shifted onto his side and propped his head up with one hand, his dark hair falling to obscure his eyes. 'Whatever the others say, I can tell you now, we were all worried about you.'

'Really?' Killian asked, sitting back on his elbows and blinking with disbelief.

'Yeah, really. Well, maybe not Morton. I've the feeling he's lost some money,' said Blake slyly.

Killian was tempted to ask what Lily was up to while he was away. He opened his mouth to say something but couldn't bring himself to voice it. He knew what the answer would be anyway. She'd been fine, not a hint of worry or care; he didn't need his thoughts confirmed. He sat up in his hammock and swung his feet over the edge. Looking down, he realised he was still wearing his grimy tunic, now with added rips thanks to the path of the geyser.

He let his chin drop to his chest and blew out a beleaguered sigh. 'All right,' he said with a slight croak in his voice. 'I'll tell you what was down there, on one condition.'

'Yeah?'

'That you tell all the others. I can't be bothered to go through it again and again. You'll tell it better than me anyway.'

'Deal,' said Blake with a smile. He lay back, got himself comfortable and closed his eyes.

Killian told him everything; he left nothing out, which in truth was mostly due to Blake prompting him. The man wanted to know everything: the colours in the sky, the smell of Cassius's tent, the taste of their food. He sat up, his mouth gaping open as Killian described the three tasks. He couldn't help but notice the mage's eyes flicking to his bandages and obvious wounds. It made him feel uncomfortable and seemed to make them hurt again.

'Weren't you scared?' Blake asked as he told him about the labyrinth.

'Honestly, I was terrified.' He lowered his eyes, unable to look Blake in the face as he spoke. 'I thought I was gonna die in there.' He shook his head and huffed. 'I came close to it . . . but looking back, it was nothing compared to the final task.'

He went on to explain the apparition of himself in gross detail. The stench of its rotten flesh, the vile noises it made in its throat, the swiftness and fluidity of its movement. Blake winced when he told him of their battle, the oozing black blood, the disturbing resemblance to himself, its haunting eyes. He went over every injury it had dealt him and how he'd eventually prevailed by impaling himself. He told Blake everything, but he kept the dark significance of the creature to himself. That such an abhorrent being had come from him, that it was formed from the evil that lived within *his* body and soul, disgusted him.

Blake puckered his lips and blew out a rush of air. 'Quite a story.'

'Yep,' said Killian, yawning and stretching, 'and now it's yours for the telling.'

'Thanks, and don't worry. I'll do it justice,' said Blake. 'These cornelians sound like a fascinating race.'

'Yeah, they have everything sorted out: life, happiness, everything. They make up here seem crazy.'

Killian lay back in his hammock, arms around his head. He pushed against the side and rocked himself along to the sway of the ship once more. His brief comfort was interrupted by something digging into the back of his thigh. He slipped his hand in his back pocket and pulled out the bangle Freya had given him. Holding it between his thumb and forefinger, he rolled it backwards and forwards. The silver band shone dimly, and the green and black stones twinkled faintly in the dull light of the cabin. He eyed the piece of jewellery and pursed his lips. He wouldn't give it to her just yet; doing that would leave him vulnerable. No, he'd wait for the right moment, let her play some of her cards first. He leant over the edge of the hammock and stuffed the bracelet in his coat.

'Sorry to disturb you, Killian, but the captain wishes to see you now.'

Killian lifted his head to see Raven standing in the doorway. 'An order?' he asked huskily.

'You're not officially crew, so *request* is more appropriate.' Raven's tone was as soft and peaceful as ever.

'I can do requests,' Killian muttered as he swung his legs back around the hammock and slid out. Every movement he made was purposefully slow; he didn't want to appear too keen. He took an exaggerated stretch and looked down at his tattered, poorly fitting tunic. 'She can wait a minute.'

Raven nodded and left as silently as he'd come.

Killian pulled a bowl of water and a hard lump of soap from under the spare hammock. He would gladly have sacrificed a finger for a warm bath right now. He removed the tunic and his trousers, tossing them to one side, and cleaned himself. Gingerly, he rubbed his bruised body dry with a coarse towel, then rummaged under the hammock for a shirt and some slightly cleaner trousers. It wasn't that he was making an effort for her; he just wanted to feel human again, or so he kept telling himself.

'What're you looking for?' asked Blake.

'Something a little less shredded and sweaty,' said Killian from the floor.

He emerged holding a slightly crumpled white shirt and a pair of dull grey trousers. He readjusted his poor attempt at a bandage on his left arm before he put them on, casually brushing the creases away with his hands. Now he felt a little more like the person he'd been not so long ago.

'I won't be long,' Killian grumbled. 'I never get any peace, do I? It's always want, want, want with her.'

LILY curled the corners of her eyeliner with a dexterous flick of the wrist and stared at her reflection. Thankfully, the puffiness of the morning had left her eyes. She ran her fingers through her knotted hair and pushed it over her shoulders. Was she making too much of an effort? She certainly didn't want to look like she had. A swoop of eyeliner wasn't an effort, she told herself. She put a dab of perfume on each wrist and one on her chest; that wasn't an effort either.

She moved from her desk and sat down on the edge of her bed. She gripped her right shoulder with her left hand and squeezed as hard as she could, something she only did when nervous. There was pressure, but no pain. Gritting her teeth, she let go. She shouldn't have been nervous. She wasn't nervous. How could she even know what nervous felt like? It'd been years since she'd felt anything close to it. Anger, that was what she was feeling, certainly not nerves.

A brisk knock rattled the door. She moved her hands behind her and leant against them. She waited until he was forced to knock a second time before summoning him in. Straight away, she could tell he'd changed his clothes and spruced himself up a little. *Who are we trying to impress, Killian?* she mused, fighting to keep her friendly smile from turning into a knowing smirk.

'Nice to see you're back in one piece,' she said, raising an eyebrow playfully. Without breaking eye contact, she reached under the bed to grasp a bottle of strong, fiery rum. It was half-empty, but that didn't matter. She pulled out the cork and took a sip.

'Didn't I say I'd be fine?' he said, closing the door with his foot. He took a step back and leant against it.

'Come and sit down.' She patted the bed. 'You must be tired.'

'Thanks,' he said, crossing the room in a few strides. He sat next to her. His shoulders slumped slightly, and his whole body seemed to sigh.

She offered him the bottle, the liquid sloshing against the blue glass, and he took a swig. He blew out a long breath and downed another shot before handing it back to her. She knocked back a second shot. The fumes coalesced delightfully at the back of her throat, warming her body and soothing her mind. It was a strong brew, excellent at chasing away nerves . . . or anger.

'Tell me what happened then,' she said as she returned the bottle to the floor.

She listened attentively as Killian recounted his tale, finding herself both shocked and awed by his resilience. The tasks sounded horrifying; his voice hitched when he spoke of the nightmare version of himself. She found it hard to envisage this creature. She stared at Killian in an effort to see the baleful version of him, but she just couldn't. A soft pang of jealousy pulsed through her as he spoke of Nesta. It didn't seem fair that he'd met such a strong, commanding being as her and she hadn't. The cornelians' world sounded enchanting, idyllic. While he was down there frolicking with them, she'd been sitting on the ship waiting. It felt like a waste. Killian finished, and there was a beat of silence between them.

'Well, Killian,' she said, her eyes locked unwavering with his. 'You've done the impossible – you've impressed me.'

Killian's eyes widened, and his mouth dropped open. 'Can I have that in writing? Or maybe you could emboss it on one of those fancy medals of yours,' he gushed enthusiastically.

'Don't push it,' she said flatly. A patch of deep ruby red was expanding on his shirt. 'You're bleeding.'

'It's all right,' he said, brushing it off.

She tsked, got to her feet and walked to her dresser. She searched around in the drawers until she found a bandage, pausing as she held it. Was she really going to patch him up? She'd have to take his shirt off. Her tongue flicked against her teeth. The nervous anger surged through her again. She could summon Raven; he'd be able to fix him up, and he was more practised at it than she was. Her knuckles turned pale as she squeezed the bandages. She narrowed her eyes and released all the air from her lungs in one controlled breath, hardening her resolve. This was something she had to do. She stood in front of him and made a point of animatedly curling her top lip before reaching to unbutton his shirt.

'Lil, honestly, it's all right,' he protested.

'No, it isn't.' She deftly released his buttons as she spoke, the numerous shades of green within her chunky ring swirling with her movements. 'You might drip blood on my sheets, and that wouldn't be all right.'

'Can't have that, can we?' Killian cocked an eyebrow.

Lily peeled his sticky shirt back and tutted at his poor attempt at a bandage. It was hardly covering his wound; blood was seeping out, and it was full of grit.

'What? I thought I'd done it pretty good.'

Without a word, she unwound the bandage, discarded it on the floor and examined the bleeding wound. It was wide and stretched from his left shoulder down to his elbow. It glistened with fresh blood; a thin crimson tributary oozed and trickled slowly down the side of his body.

'A present from your lovely twin?' she asked, keeping her focus firmly on the horrible laceration.

'Yep,' said Killian, wincing as she moved the shirt farther away from his injury, 'amongst other things. He was a generous guy.'

She pressed her lips together in a tight line and went back to the dresser. *What the hell am I doing?* She opened a drawer and examined the colourful bottles of liquid within, then reached for the blue one. It would kill any lingering infections, but she'd been told that it hurt like the blazes. The last thing she wanted was to cause him more pain after everything he'd been through, but it had to be done. She poured some of the tart-smelling liquid into a wooden bowl and walked back to her patient, dragging a chair with her.

She sat down in front of him, but her knees got in the way, and she didn't want to ask him to move.

'This isn't working.' She frowned.

'I can move a little, and—'

'Nope.'

She got up and sat next to him on the bed, passing him the bowl to hold. Heat radiated off his body in intoxicating waves. Her pulse quickened as nervousness and excitement took hold. This procedure clearly needed more rum on her part. She moved closer and felt his free hand grab her hip. Part of her wanted to swipe him away, part delighted in his fingers on her, and another part told her she was deluded. He was clearly only grabbing her to keep steady. Excessive blood loss in a rocking ship coupled with a few shots of strong rum would make anyone grab the nearest thing. She dipped a piece of cloth into the liquid and dabbed it onto his bleeding wound.

He drew his breath back through gritted teeth and let out a string of tightly packed curses.

'It'll kill any infections,' said Lily in her best deadpan tone, desperate to give off the illusion that she didn't care for his pain.

'Cylus . . . gave me a better one. One that doesn't hurt . . . so much.'

'This is one of Cylus's. You're not his only customer.'

'Gah – man's useless!' He grimaced, and his eyes closed tight.

'If not for this it could get infected,' Lily said as she continued to feed the wound with the potion. 'Would you rather I was doing this or hacking your arm off?'

'This,' he managed to say through groans of pain.

'It's not that bad.'

'Easy for you to say.' He blenched, his back rigid, his fingers gripping her hip tightly. 'When did you last get injured?'

She gave him a wry smile and wiped the stream of blood from his ribs, but a hollow feeling fell into her stomach when she saw how beaten and bruised his body was. The temptation to remove the rest of his shirt to see the extent of the damage was strong, but she quickly told herself that she didn't care. He'd done all this himself and for himself. There was no one to blame but him. She mopped the wound once more and put the cloth down. His fingers pressed into her flesh and for a fleeting moment she thought she felt a pang of pain, but that was impossible.

'Cassius dressed it,' he said through gritted teeth as she started to bandage him. 'But it came off in the geyser.'

'You should be more careful.'

'Again, that's easy to say when you're not trying to out-run a jet of boiling water.'

'Nearly done,' she said, pulling the bandage taut. 'It's times like these when I wish I'd got an actual doctor on board.'

'You're doing all right.'

'I'm not bad. Raven taught me everything I know,' she said as she wrapped his arm, focusing intently on the bandages. 'I've not had to do this for a while though. Our reputation means injured crew members tend to be a thing of the past.'

'That and you've been sat on the island doing nothing for years.'

'Watch your lip, O'Shea, or I'll take this off and let you bleed out.'

She continued to wrap his arm in silence, picking up another bandage and binding his shoulder. It would probably restrict his movement somewhat, but she didn't want him losing it again. She pulled it as tightly as she could without causing him too much discomfort. When she was done, she sat back a little and admired her work.

'There, all done,' she said, rubbing her palms together. 'Your shirt's ruined though.'

'I'll add it to the pile,' he said. He looked from his arm to her. 'Nicely done. It looks like you're better than me at something. You've done the impossible – you've impressed me.'

The words of retort dried up in her throat when she realised he was still holding her. His grip was so feeble it barely registered with her and clearly didn't with him. He shouldn't have been touching her, and she shouldn't have been this close to him. It wasn't right, though she couldn't deny it felt good. What the hell was she thinking? It didn't feel good, did it? A rush of embarrassment ripped through her, and she quickly moved away from him, breaking contact.

'So, did you miss me?' he asked with a smirk, apparently oblivious to her discomfiture as he buttoned his shirt up again.

'No. Did you miss me?'

'No.'

Killian flopped back onto her soft, comfortable bed and let out a deep moan. He stretched his arms out either side of him, and his feet dangled just above the floor. The ship creaked and swayed, and the distant lull of the waves broke on the hull with a calming swash. Within seconds of lying down, his eyes closed.

Lily sat next to him and watched his chest rise and fall with slow, even breathing. She drew in a deep breath herself. She could smell him; he was like hot rocks after a rainstorm, a scent she'd always loved and enjoyed. The desire to reach over and touch him was strong, to unbutton his shirt, to run her fingers over his skin and take him in her arms, to kiss his bruised lips . . .

What was she thinking? This wasn't right. These thoughts weren't hers; they couldn't be. She cared for no one except herself and her crew, and he wasn't either. She sucked her tongue. It was the rum. It had to be.

'Sorry, Lil,' he said. 'I'm useless.' He slowly stood up. 'I should go.'

It was clear he was in no fit state for anything. He tried to walk, wavered a little and stumbled as his body gave up on him. Lily sprang up from the bed and caught him, holding him tight against her. His body was so warm; his full weight pressing against her felt soothing and real. Her heart thumped at a colossal rate. She needed to put him somewhere else before he felt it too and they both became confused.

'You should stay here,' she said, moving him towards her bed. 'It's more comfortable than your cabin, and this way I can keep an eye on you.'

'Worried about me?' He managed a cocky grin, but it quickly faded. He'd pushed himself too far and was paying the price for it.

'No,' she said. 'I'm worried about my treasure, and I need you to get it for me.'

'Of course.' He cleared his throat. 'Where will you sleep?'

She nodded towards the hammock.

'Lucky you got that.'

'Isn't it just,' she said briskly.

She helped him crawl up to the top of her bed and take off his boots and shirt. Both his arms and the sides of his body were covered with cuts and grazes, and his chest was littered with ugly purple-and-yellow bruises. When she caught a glimpse of his back, she saw a huge bandage across it and shuddered at the sight. As she threw his soggy blood-ridden shirt to the floor, her eyes misted over.

'You all right?' he asked, his voice throaty and faint.

'I'm fine,' she said, wiping her eyes. 'I just got something in my eye, that's all.'

He nodded, shut his eyes and sank into the bed; he seemed too tired to keep up the conversation. Lily brought a sheet up and covered his battered body. She straightened up and made for the door, in need of some fresh, clarifying sea air.

'Thanks, Lil,' he whispered.

'S'ok.' She smiled weakly and left the room.

CHAPTER
THIRTY-FOUR

K ILLIAN REACHED FORWARDS AND TOUCHED the black mirror. It felt frozen, yet its surface rippled, and everything in the reflection blurred and distorted. It took less than a second to settle down. Staring back was the horrific apparition of himself, its hollow black eyes and tiny white pupils blazing with malevolence. Blackened veins coursed through its pallid skin, and sharpened teeth sneered at him. Before he could move, a pair of ghostly white arms reached out from the glass and pulled him through.

A splintering crack echoed about the room as he landed face-first on the floor. Was that his bones? He pushed himself onto his hands and saw that the stone floor beneath him had shattered and split into shards. He scrambled to his feet only to face the monstrous version of himself. It grabbed him and twisted his arm around his back, forcing him to his knees. The foul stench of its foetid flesh forced its way up his nose. A sour taste filled his mouth, and he gagged. Its grip was strong as it wrenched his arm back. He cried out, and it kicked him to the floor.

The creature flipped gracefully through the air, landed on its hands and feet and crouched down. It glared at him, eyes blazing like a crazed beast, snarling, sharp teeth bared, black blood dripping down its chin. Killian forced himself to stand and unsheathed his swords. His arms were heavy and his grip slippery with sweat, but he had no choice other than to fight. It drew its own darkened blades. They scraped from their scabbards with a hideous high-pitched din. The sound shot through Killian's head and lodged in his brain like a rusty nail. He staggered, and with one neat swipe the blackened blades shattered his into thousands of pieces.

Killian backed away, clutching the useless dull hilts. Panicking, he looked around the bizarre room, searching for a way out, a way back through the mirror, but everything was distorted, bent out of shape. The stone walls were twisted and soft looking, and shards of rocky glass jutted up from the floor. There was no way out.

The monster looked at him with nothing but rage in its eyes. Saliva joined the blood that dripped from its gaping mouth. It charged him again, moving with an otherworldly swiftness, its body a blur of black and white. He was unprepared and suffered a kick to the stomach. He fell, breath crushed from his lungs. The cracked glass floor cut deep into his back, and hot sticky blood pooled about him. The creature leapt on top of him, pinning him down with its knees. It thrust its swords deep into his arm.

Killian screamed as the blades tore through him. The creature rasped a throaty chuckle. He looked at his arm, and to his horror, thick black blood seeped from the open wound. All he could do was watch as it oozed from his body.

Poisonous, tainted blood. The creature slashed at his other arm, and more darkness flowed out.

It leant down over Killian's helpless body and whispered, 'You're gonna have to live with this,' as it placed a cold hand over his heart.

'No! I can't! I can't!' Killian gasped.

It looked him straight in the eye and brought its blades crashing down. Killian felt them rip through his body and crack his bones before they plunged into his heart. The pain was intense; he could only scream as a fountain of black blood erupted from his shattered chest.

He cried out and jerked up, panting. His body was soaked with sweat and shaking violently, his heart drumming in his ears. Tentatively, he put a hand to his chest and was relieved, and a little surprised, to find that it was still whole.

'What was that?' Lily's gruff sleep-disturbed voice came to him from somewhere in the darkness.

'N-nothing.' His voice faltered as he tried to gather his scattered thoughts. He desperately wanted to light a lamp and prick his skin to check his blood was still red.

Lily's hammock creaked as she got out and made her way over to him. She sat next to him and glared as if trying to examine him by starlight.

'Are you all right?' she asked, her voice hushed.

'I'm fine,' he replied, examining the scrapes on his ribs by the dim light.

'Are you bleeding again?' She moved to touch his arm, but he pulled out of her reach.

'No, I don't think so.' Realising his sudden movement may have given away his ruse, he casually rubbed his shoulder in a cover-up attempt.

'Want me to light the lamp so you can check?'

'No,' he said a little too quickly. The fear of what he might find unnerved him. If his blood was black, what would she do? Strap a cannonball to him and chuck him overboard? His back twitched; he didn't want to dwell on it. 'I'll look in the morning.'

'Fine, I'm going back to sleep.' She yawned, rubbing her eyes.

She ambled back to her hammock, her body melting into the darkness of the cabin. A few minutes later, deep, even breathing signified she'd fallen asleep. Killian, however, couldn't sleep for hours, too terrified lest he never wake again. His eyes stung, his head pulsed, and his heavy body throbbed. As he lay awake, he watched the stars fade into the pale morning sky and the sun rise lazily over the horizon, scattering the wave crests with flecks of gold. He lost his futile battle and drifted off to sleep.

LILY awoke. She rose and wandered over to Killian. He was lying on his side, head resting on his right arm, his left hanging out of the sheet. He appeared to be in a deep sleep, so she decided against rousing him. After everything he'd been through, he needed all the rest he could get. His behaviour during the night had been concerning; he was too fragile and jumpy. She glanced at his tattered arms, and a stab of guilt penetrated her stomach. Her chest constricted; she had to get away from him. Tossing on her clothes and donning her hat, she strode out onto the deck.

The early morning heat beat down on the crew, who were hard at work after their brief sojourn. They leapt to attention as she passed, greeting and saluting her; she nodded back in acknowledgement. Creaking sails were pulled this way and that, and ropes were tightened. Morton bellowed orders up to the rigging, where blackened silhouettes scurried about in the glare of the sun.

'Omar, pull, pull! Throw to Gainsborough!' he shouted, angrily waving his arms. He paused as Lily approached. 'Mornin', Cap'n.' He saluted her.

'Working them hard, Morton,' she commented.

'Aye, Cap'n.'

'Keep at it.'

'Aye.' He nodded sharply.

She walked away to the sound of Morton barking aggressive orders and set her course for the wheel to find Jarran, the sailing master. A gust of fresh, crisp air blew in from the waves. She closed her eyes and breathed in deep. It awakened her senses and crushed her thoughts. She looked out over the sparkling turquoise waters. This was it; this was her place, right here. Too much time had been wasted living on that island, growing stale, lazy and bored. She had a ship; she could have sailed away at any time. It had taken the intervention of that scumbag thief to get her to do it. She balled her fists up, furious with herself for thinking about him. How dare he invade her thoughts again? This was her time with the sea, the wind in her hair, the sun on her face. He wasn't supposed to be here; he didn't fit in her life.

As she rounded the corner, she caught sight of Jarran standing proud at the wheel. He was a tall muscular man with dark skin and a shaved head, which he covered with a burnt-orange bandana.

'Mornin', Cap'n,' he said in a rich, deep voice. Eight

golden hoops shone from his left ear, basking in the glorious morning light.

'And what a fine morning it is.'

'Aye, true.' He turned back to the wheel, nudged it once and faced Lily again. He rubbed his hands together. 'What can I do for you, Cap'n?'

She folded her arms. 'You're assuming I want something?' she asked, tilting her head to the side.

'Aye,' he said. His earrings made a gentle tinkling noise as he ran a finger over them. 'S'usually why you come see me.'

She held her hands up. 'You got me.'

A deep rumbling laugh thundered from the sailing master.

'Can we make it to the Phantom without stopping in Bracky first?' she said. 'It seems pointless to return only to set sail again straight away.'

'You have a point,' said Jarran thoughtfully. 'Only problem is running outta food and water. Ocean's Bounty be more or less en route. I could change course, and we can stop off an' salvage, if you like?'

'How far off course?'

' 'Bout a day's sailing, should the wind stay with us.' A gentle gust flapped his murky orange waistcoat open, revealing the leather belt strapped across his chest.

'Do it,' she said without hesitation.

'Aye, Cap'n. Should be at the island in 'bout five, six days.'

'Very good,' she said. 'How long will it take us to get to the Phantom from there?'

Jarran rubbed his earrings again. ' 'Bout three weeks, I reckon.'

'Excellent.' She beamed. 'Thanks, Jarran. Keep up the good work.'

'Aye, Cap'n.' He turned back to the wheel.

Lily marched away with a slight spring in her step. She was satisfied with what she'd been told. The sooner this was all over, the sooner she could get Killian off her ship and out of her life. She gave the ship a quick patrol, sending acknowledging smiles and words of encouragement to any of the crew who looked her way. She didn't believe in shouting at her crew and undermining them to make them work; she believed in treating them with the respect they showed her, which was probably why they were some of the most successful pirates on the sea. The crew were more than willing to lay their lives down for her – not that they would ever need to, but it was good to be held in such high regard.

As she sauntered about the *Tempest*, the sun warm on her back and the air chill in her lungs, she found that she longed to return to her cabin. The deck was full of commotion and people, but she needed seclusion. She turned around, walking on the starboard side this time. On her way, she came across Ren, who was perched uncomfortably on the bulwark with Finn, fishing over the side of the ship.

Finn greeted Lily in her coarse, gravelly voice, a smoking roll-up lodged in the corner of her mouth. 'Mornin', Cap'n.'

'Good morning, Captain,' said Ren, leaping down from the rail to salute her.

'Morning, Finn, Ren,' she said, nodding at each of them. 'How're you getting on?'

'Very well, thank you, Captain,' said Ren, his voice sickeningly cheery.

'Good.' She managed a terse smile. 'Not long now, Ren,

and this nightmare will be over. We should be at the island in three to four weeks, weather permitting.'

'So soon,' Ren exclaimed. His mouth smiled, yet his eyes were dulled with sadness.

'That is what you want, isn't it?' she asked.

'Y-yes, that's great,' Ren blurted. 'I just . . .' He paused, then filled his cheeks with air and blew it out. 'I don't know. I think I'm actually going to miss it on here. Funny, eh?'

'Not at all,' she said, shaking her head, her mind elsewhere.

'And to think I was terrified of you all at the beginning. It turns out you're not that bad. With a few exceptions,' he added, indicating Finn.

'Ay! Get back in your shell,' Finn growled. 'There's time to keelhaul you yet!'

'Li—Captain, do you know where Killian is? I haven't seen him since he got back. I wanted to thank him, but he didn't come back to the cabin last night,' Ren said innocently.

A bolt of intense heat charged through Lily's body, but she quickly suppressed it and composed herself. Hoping that her skin wouldn't flush and betray her, she answered his question.

'He's resting in my cabin. He came to give me his report yesterday, but one of his wounds reopened. It needed cleaning and redressing, and after that he fell asleep.' *Why did I answer that? What right does he have to ask me such things? Nothing happened, and nothing's going to happen. This pathetic free-riding lickspittle shouldn't be interrogating me!* Once again, she composed herself. This time she hardened her face and made sure her voice was curt and stern. 'Is that all, Ren? Or do you wish to quiz your captain further?'

'Er, n-n-no, Captain,' said Ren meekly.

'It is not for me to keep track of your companions. I'll be kicking him out as soon as he's healed, which hopefully won't be too long now,' she added with a snarl. 'Now, if you'd both excuse me, I've things to do.'

She marched away with a swift, aggressive stomp.

CHAPTER
THIRTY-FIVE

LILY OPENED HER CABIN DOOR BIT BY BIT SO as not to wake Killian with a dramatic creak. He was still in bed, but he seemed to be speaking to someone. She walked over to his side. His eyes were tightly shut, lost to sleep, but he was thrashing around.

'Keep away! I'm not like you. I'm not like you,' he muttered over and over again. 'It's not mine. It's not mine. It doesn't come from me! Stay away. *Stay away!*'

He broke off into a throaty gasp and sat bolt upright, his eyes open. 'No, no, no,' he whispered, shaking his head, his hair hanging around his face. His arms dropped lamely to his sides. He was trembling, staring vacantly at the wall, seemingly unaware of her presence.

She sat down on the corner of the bed, put her arm around him and pulled him close. She said nothing; she just held him while he got his breath back. His body juddered and was damp with sweat. Part of her wanted to push him away, never to lay a hand on him again; the other part wanted to never let go. How she loathed the confused tangle of feelings she got whenever she was alone with him.

'I'm sorry,' he said through tremulous breaths, pushing himself free from her grip. 'Sorry.' He shook his head. 'I had a bad dream, that's all.'

'Want to tell me about it?' she asked, edging away from him.

'No,' he answered sharply. 'I can't remember it, anyway. All I know is it was bad.'

'You were talking in your sleep. It didn't make much sense—'

'I often talk in my sleep. It never means anything. It's fine,' he put in quickly before she could say any more.

'If you say so.' She was far from convinced by his excuses.

She stood up, feeling suffocated, her emotions threatening to rip from her. How was he doing this to her? He remained seated and pulled the sheet up to wrap it around his hunched shoulders.

'Do you want anything?' she asked. She had to get away from him; it didn't matter how.

'Something to eat would be good.'

'Fine,' she said, pacing briskly to the door.

'Lil,' he croaked, 'why are you doing this for me?'

'Because . . .' Why was she doing it? Because she cared about him? No. Because he could get at her treasure now? No. Because she had a kind heart? No. She didn't know. She kept her head low and her back to him as she spoke. 'Because while you're on my ship, you're part of my crew, and it's my duty to look after you, stop you bleeding to death, that sort of thing. Also, I need you to get my treasure. Let's not forget that.'

' 'Course. Thanks.'

She shrugged and left.

THE cabin door closed, and Killian was alone once again. All he wanted to do was sleep, but he was terrified at the thought of surrendering to his unconscious. He opened his eyes wide and splashed his face with a cup of water – anything to keep sleep at bay – and drew his knees up to his chest. He hated this, hated feeling so useless and terrified, held captive by his uncontrollable dreams.

He looked towards Raven's painting, the idyllic pastel town clinging to the cliff face. It was so peaceful and calm. He could almost hear the waves lapping at the harbour, smell the wafts of salt mingling with the warm rocks and herbs and feel the heat soaking into his bones. If only there were some way he could pull himself into it and exist in that never-ending sunset. One day he'd ask Raven if it was real and where it was.

Fatigue crept up on him, and he knew he couldn't keep fighting it off. His shoulders drooped, and his arms hung like dead weights; he would just rest – not sleep, just rest. Surely he wouldn't be able to fall asleep in this position.

That night the apparition came to Killian again. His own tainted black blood sprayed the walls as the creature destroyed his body, starting with his hands. He scraped at the floor with useless bleeding stumps in a futile attempt to escape the haunting version of himself. The cold black blade pierced his back, severing his spine. His head jerked back, and his mouth filled with foul-tasting blood. Everything around him faded to black as his life force ebbed away.

He was still crying with pain when his body jolted him awake. His eyes flashed open, and he sat up, drenched with icy sweat. Gripping his thighs tight, he slowed his breathing. He eventually managed to calm himself and sat silently in the pressing darkness of the room. The creaking wood of the ship and the soft break of the ocean waves came as some comfort, solid evidence he'd made it out of his nightmare alive. He ran his tongue along the inside of his lip; it didn't taste of anything.

He moved his brittle arms, gathering up the warm blanket to wrap it around his shivering body and hold it close. The fear of falling asleep again gripped him, so he turned to the window to watch the sky. He tossed the blanket over his head and rocked with the movement of the ship. All was silent except for the whispering moans of the *Tempest*, the hushed cries of the waves and Killian's breathing.

The dark night sky was punctuated with glowing silver stars, their soft light beaming through the window. As he gazed at the pinpricks of light, he was transported back to the night he ate with Lily, when she'd shown him the same stars from the same window. It seemed so long ago now. So much had happened to him since then. Would he ever feel the same again? Would he ever be free of his nightmares? If anything, he felt worse now than he had before. The feelings of guilt were as strong as ever, and now he had the vision of his dark side to contend with. He pulled the covers closer to his body.

'Are you going back to sleep or not?' Lily's stern voice sliced through the gloom like a freshly sharpened dagger.

Killian started; he hadn't realised she was awake. 'Probably.'

He cocked his head and listened as she swung down from her hammock and padded over to him barefoot. The bed creaked softly as she sat down. He turned his back to the glittering stars and blinked several times, waiting for her to come into focus. She was wearing her long green coat, its familiar hue apparent even in the low light.

'I don't think you are,' she said firmly.

'I will.' He yawned unconvincingly to back up the lie.

'Well, I won't. Not now,' she grumbled. 'You're ruining my sleep pattern, you know that?'

'Sorry,' he muttered, but he wasn't sorry at all. 'I had another bad dream, that's all. I'm fine. You can go back to bed.'

'I didn't come over here to check on you.'

'Oh, well, why did you?' he said briskly, pushing the blanket back from his head.

'To let you know that I'm going on deck for a walk,' she said. Killian looked up; her expressionless face was dashed with silver light. 'I was going to see if you wanted to come with me because it's quite obvious you're wide awake too,' she continued. 'A walk in the sea air might sort you out.'

He reached forwards and put his hand on her forehead. 'That almost sounded nice. Are you coming down with something, Lil?'

'You don't have to come,' she said airily, swiping his hand away. She stood up swiftly and made her way across the room to the door.

'Wait for me,' he said as he stumbled out of bed and grabbed his trousers.

Lily folded her arms, tapped her foot and sighed in mock impatience as she waited for him to find a shirt.

He cursed as he searched in the limited light for his elusive clothing. After some extended scrabbling, he gave up. Instead of a top, he pulled the blanket from the bed and wrapped it round himself like a cloak. He shuffled towards her and walked through the door as she held it open for him.

The air was cold and crisp. Killian breathed deeply, savouring its refreshing salty flavour and its cool caress on his skin. The crystalline sunstones cast out a subdued peach-and-rose light, bathing the deck with a warm soothing glow. At night, the ship took on an otherworldly tranquillity. Lily stepped in front of him, taking the lead; he was content to amble behind her at his own pace. There was no rush.

As they wandered around the silent deck, they passed by a handful of crew, their presence highlighted by the red glow of cigarettes and grey wisps of smoke. Much to Killian's relief, the shadowy faces he encountered were unfamiliar; he didn't want to be asked questions he didn't know the answers to himself.

Lily pressed on, walking up to the bow of the ship. She stopped, rested a hand on the rail and looked out over the shimmering obsidian sea. He paused a little way from her, leaning against the bulwark and gazing down into the water, watching the dark white-edged waves break against the hull.

The night air whistled through his hair, and he pulled his blanket up over his head. Despite the chill, he found the deck to be a serene place at night. The blackness wrapped itself around him like a comfortable old coat, and the stars beamed before him, lighting the way. Looking out over the vast black ocean eased his worries and helped him to distance himself from his nightmares, which even he found strange, considering most of his dream was comprised of swirling black liquid. Slightly amused by this thought, he let out a deep sigh of contentment and watched as the plume of steam expelled from his mouth was swept away on the breeze. He smiled to himself and hung his arms over the side of the ship.

'Killian?'

He turned around at Lily's soft voice.

'Come here,' she said, beckoning him. 'There's something I want to show you.'

He pulled his blanket close to his chest and shambled towards her. As he approached, he couldn't help but notice her bare legs extending from the bottom of her coat; she didn't seem to be wearing anything else. He averted his eyes from her legs and focused on her face. The pale starlight brought out all of her features, even the green in her eyes. It edged her body with a silvery glow. He glanced at her neckline; she was definitely only wearing the coat. A pleasurable warmth mounted in his groin and he stopped a few feet from her to loosen the blanket, hoping the cold air would calm him down.

'Come here and look,' she said.

He edged closer until they were side by side. *It's only Lil. It's only Lil.* He could smell her, fresh and light in the crisp air, comforting and familiar. Her long black hair glimmered with tiny stars and floated on the breeze like strips of silk. She'd left the top buttons of her coat undone, and it parted slightly, giving him a glimpse of her cleavage. Her smooth olive skin was beckoning him. Something had to be done to quash his unwanted physical reaction, something drastic. He gritted his teeth and sharply twisted his left shoulder, sending an icy spear of pain through his body. He grunted and put his hand on the rail to steady himself;

his arm bloomed with agony, but at least he'd forced the warmth from his body.

'You all right?' she asked. His strange movements hadn't gone unnoticed.

'Fine.' He let go of the rail. 'Just a twitch.'

She peered at him shrouded in the blanket and smiled, then focused on the sea. He looked too and could make out a faint glow deep beneath the waves. It seemed like a trick of sleep deprivation, so he rubbed his eyes, but it was still there when he looked again.

'Wait,' she said.

He nodded and kept his eyes locked on the sea. Strange-coloured lights emerged from somewhere under the water. The glow intensified as they slowly floated to the surface, vivid flecks of neon emerald and azure.

He'd never seen anything like it before. All across the ocean, the bright lights danced and twirled together, putting on an amazing display, just for them. Some of them fused with each other, creating clusters of brilliant phosphorescent light. Others joined together in long wavering lines that stretched out as far as he could see – shimmering ropes of intangible green and blue, flashes of silver, standing proud amid the black water.

'What is it?' he asked quietly, afraid the sound of his voice would cause the lights to fade and disintegrate.

'I don't know. Sea creatures, spirits, plants – your guess is as good as mine.'

'It's incredible,' he whispered. 'Have you seen it before?'

'A couple of times, and only in warmer seas.'

'I'm glad I came out for this walk.'

Even though he was transfixed by the astounding light display in the sea, he found his peripheral vision drifting towards her. She was a little hunched up.

'Are you cold?' he asked, turning his gaze back to the water.

'No.'

'Liar,' he said, shaking his head.

Before he could second-guess himself, he stepped close to her, opened his blanket and pulled her in. Lily entered its cosy warmth without any protest, pressing her cold body against his warm naked chest.

'Is that better?' He wrapped the blanket around them both.

'It'll do.'

'Good,' he replied as he impulsively put his arms around her. Much to his surprise, she didn't recoil in disgust; instead, she wrapped her arms tight about his waist.

Lily turned her head to the side, and her tumbling ebony hair tickled his skin, but he didn't find the feeling unpleasant. For over an hour they remained like this, in silence on the bow of the ship, while the lights pranced playfully across the ocean. Eventually, the luminous colours faded as the lights sank back into the depths. They left a trail of vibrant colour behind them as they fell, which slowly blended into the blackness of the water, leaving the sea darker than ever.

Yawning, Killian peeled the blanket away; he felt tired, so tired he no longer feared sleep. His legs ached, and his eyelids were heavy. He stooped to say something to Lily but she was already asleep, her head resting comfortably on his chest and her arms loosely framing his waist. He shifted so he could scoop her up without disturbing her too much and smoothly lifted her into his arms. Despite his best efforts, she stirred, but her eyes remained closed.

With Lily slumbering in his arms and the blanket half wrapped around them both, Killian began his slow, attentive walk back to her cabin. His body screamed at him to put her down and wake her up, but he couldn't bring himself to do it. The pain didn't seem to matter when she was so near, so close and warm. He passed the cluster of pirates from earlier; luckily, they were too busy half-heartedly playing cards and crafting roll-ups to pay any attention to him or their sleeping captain.

He had to crouch to open her cabin door. There was a click, and he straightened up and pushed it open with his foot. It was dark inside, the only light coming from the stars that peered through the window. He stood still, squinting into the blackness, waiting for his eyes to become accustomed to the hazy grey. The structure of the room eased into focus, and he crossed to Lily's hammock. He blinked until he could clearly see its nets in front of him; he didn't want to accidentally drop her on the floor. Despite the ache in his body, he managed to lift her up and place her in, easing her blanket out from underneath to cover her.

'Goodnight, Lil,' he whispered as he gave the hammock a gentle push.

He walked towards the bed and dropped onto it. He sat up, removed his trousers and threw them to the floor, then reached for his blanket and pulled it up over himself. Warm, comfortable and gloriously tired, he shut his eyes. Immediately, he opened them again. He couldn't sleep.

CHAPTER
THIRTY-SIX

LILY WAS JARRED AWAKE SEVERAL TIMES A NIGHT, every night, over the following days. Killian would gasp or even scream, and she'd find him covered in sweat, shaking. She always checked on him whenever he woke her, yet he insisted he was fine every time.

She didn't like leaving him alone in the dark, but there was not much else she could do. As his wounds healed, his eyes darkened with sleep deprivation. They were framed with an ugly purple border, giving the impression of grievous bruising, and the whites were permanently bloodshot. It didn't take her long to notice the difference in his face.

'How do you feel?' she asked as she stood above him, a subtle probing undertone in her voice.

'Fine,' he said, his winning smirk fixed perfectly in place.

Lily stared at him, her eyes unblinking.

'Look.' He sat up in bed and pulled down the sheets, showing her his faded bruising as evidence.

'You look a little better.' She nodded, but she wasn't entirely convinced. It was time to play a little game to weed out the truth. She tilted the corners of her mouth into a tiny smile. 'In that case, you'll be able to leave me in peace soon.'

Killian parted his lips, but no words came.

She sat down on the edge of the bed, her back to him, and buckled her boots. She pushed her hair back over her shoulders, tied a green bandana about her head and got to her feet with deliberate slowness. 'I'll get my cabin to myself again. You can go and sweat it up with the others in a hammock. You can spend some quality time with Ren. That'll be nice for you. I've missed my bed rather a lot. I'm sure it's missed me too. I'll have to—'

'I keep seeing it,' he said, sounding defeated.

'Seeing what?'

'My other side,' he whispered. She turned to look at him, but he was talking to his knees, not her. 'It kills me, every night.' He made a fist with his right hand, tensing his forearm. 'It cuts me up . . . and my blood is black.' He released one finger at a time as he spoke. 'It hurts so much. Every night, I'm ripped apart. Every dream has the same ending – I die.'

The iron in her heart cracked. She wanted to go to him, to tell him everything would be all right, to fix him, but she couldn't. She didn't care about him – she couldn't and she wouldn't. She didn't have the capacity to care, not like that. Feelings equalled weakness; she'd learnt that a long time ago. 'You should have said something.'

'No.' He lifted his head, his eyes black and blue. 'I'm just being stupid.'

'It's clearly hindering your recovery. You should have told me.'

'I'm worried that . . .'

'What?'

He closed his eyes and shook his head. 'I'm worried that I'll turn into it,' he murmured.

Her mouth dropped open. 'That's what's been bothering you?' she said with disbelief. Something that sounded so ridiculous to her was really doing a number on him. It sounded insane, but to him it must've felt incredibly real. 'Killian, don't you think it's—'

'There's something I didn't tell you.' He drew a deep breath before continuing. 'That thing . . . it came from me. It was part of me. Nesta – she said it was a physical manifestation of all my evil.'

Lily listened attentively as he recounted his conversation with Nesta.

'Killian,' she said softly once he'd finished, 'there's nothing to worry about. Nesta said so herself.' She sat on the table next to him, putting both her feet on the bed and leaning back on her hands.

'I can't stop. What if I wake up one morning and I'm that creature, that thing? The dreams, the nightmares, they must mean something. My blood, it's black! It wins every time. I die every night.'

'Think rationally,' she said, smiling to herself at her private hypocrisy. 'It's only a dream. You've already fought and defeated the real thing.'

Killian was still frowning, but he nodded.

'It's not gonna come and get you, and you're not gonna turn into it. It's all in your head.'

'And in my dreams,' he added.

'Same thing. You're impossible sometimes.' She reached forwards to flick the buckle on her boot. 'Look, you've done something no one else has done. You need to bask in it a little, embrace it. You don't know if something like this will ever come your way again.'

'Something no one else has done,' he repeated.

'Yes! It's . . . sort of impressive.' She spoke as if the words pained her, but only for his benefit. He had impressed her – not that she'd ever admit it without being sardonic about it.

'Whoa, careful there, Lil,' Killian said with a grin. 'You were dangerously close to paying me another compliment.'

'You heard what you wanted to hear, O'Shea,' she said sternly, slipping off the table to stand up. 'Now shut up and go to sleep. You look like someone poked you in the eyes with a hearth brush.'

With a lopsided smile on his face, Killian lay back down and closed his eyes. 'Make a note of this,' he drawled. 'This is the second time I've followed your orders.'

Lily snorted and shook her head. She watched over him for a while; his breathing soon became heavy as much-needed sleep came to claim him. She rolled her hands into tight frustrated fists. A tremor shot through her chest, and she felt as if she couldn't breathe. He was choking her, smothering the life from her. She spun around and walked out onto the deck.

Lily wandered the ship in a daze. Her mind was clouded by a foreign emotion, and she didn't like it. She grabbed the bulwark and looked out to sea. She felt weak. Her emotions were draining her. He was ruining her, and worst of all, she was letting him. Never in her life had she felt like this about anyone. It wasn't right, it wasn't natural, and it wasn't her.

Soon they'd be back in Vermor, soon the mission would be complete, and then she could jettison him from her life for good. But would that make her feel any better? Would that quash the revolting feelings that grew within her like a poisonous fungus? She shook her head and dug her nails into the wood, frustration and anger pouring out. Letting go, she marched off in a frantic search for Raven.

It didn't take her long to find him standing on the bow of the ship, his arms folded across his toned chest, his long dark hair shining with an inky purple hue in the morning light. His shirt was unbuttoned and flapped in the breeze as he gazed out to sea.

'Good morning, Lily,' he said without turning.

'Morning,' she replied as she joined him.

They stood together, shoulder to shoulder, their hair entwining as they stared at the gold-flecked ocean. Lily's pulse quickened; was she going to admit to him what she couldn't even admit to herself? She swallowed. Her throat was dry and raw. She had to say something. Raven was her first mate, the person she trusted unreservedly with her life, her secrets, everything. Her oldest friend. He'd help her. He had to.

'I need to talk to you,' she said with great effort.

'You know you can always talk to me. There's no need for apprehension,' said Raven.

'I think I'm getting too attached,' she said in one quick breath.

'Is that a bad thing?'

'Yes.'

'Why so?'

'I need to be strong, always. I need to be like iron, like rock. I'm not allowed feelings; they cloud my judgement. You saw how irrational I was when Killian was down the Drop. I don't want to be like that ever again, trapped in a net of disgusting anxiety and emotion.' She adjusted her bandana, not taking her eyes off the sea. 'As soon as people get feelings, they become weak and scared. They make mistakes . . . they die.' She gritted her teeth as a difficult memory tried to fight its way into her mind. 'As the captain of this ship, I owe it to all of you not to become like that.'

Raven shook his head sadly. 'You are allowed to feel, Lily. Are you sure you're not making excuses?'

'No,' she said bluntly. Her chest hurt, and her heart fell away. It crashed through the deck, plunging into the lonely watery depths where it belonged.

'I think you are. I think you're scared.'

'I am not!' He was wrong; she feared nothing.

'You are. You're scared of losing control of yourself and your crew. You're terrified of being someone other than the fierce pirate queen persona you've created.'

'I am not,' she spat. 'I'm not some weak simpering fool.' She slammed her fist into her palm. 'Or have you forgotten me?'

Raven stared back at the sea again. 'I'm sorry, Captain. I overstepped the mark.'

She dropped her arms limply to her sides, all her fire suddenly burnt out. 'No, I'm sorry. I didn't mean to speak like that,' she said, instantly feeling wretched for snapping at him. Tears fogged her vision. 'And don't bloody well call me Captain. I hate it when you call me that.'

'All right, Lily,' he said, turning his tattooed face back to her. She dropped her gaze, too ashamed to meet his eyes. 'Please, just think about what I said.'

'I will,' she mumbled.

He put his hands on either side of her arms and held her. 'Your feelings don't make you weak, Lily. On the contrary, they drive you. Emotion is what lets you know you're alive. You are a shell of a person without it. You won't become strong by shutting off a part of yourself and acting like it doesn't exist. It's weakness when you can't control the emotions that reside within you. If you can face that part of yourself and accept it, but not let it change who you are, you will be stronger than ever.' He let her go and turned back to the ocean. 'You can have feelings. Please don't waste your life.'

'Thank you, but—'

'I know. You have to make up your own mind. But please remember, sometimes you only get one chance.' His voice hitched as he spoke.

As she walked away, she knew, somewhere deep in her heart, he was right.

CHAPTER
THIRTY-SEVEN

L ILY'S BACK WAS STRAIGHT, HER SHOULDERS square. She'd neglected to wear her doublet, her boots weren't buckled, and she was without her hat or bandana. She'd left the cabin in such a flurry that morning she hadn't bothered to sculpt herself into her captain persona, but right now she really didn't care. All that bothered her was the ship moored at Ocean's Bounty.

Her lips twisted as her grip around the telescope tightened. She ground her teeth so aggressively she half expected a fine white power to explode from her mouth.

'Of all the shit-eating luck,' she grumbled, still glaring down the lens.

'Is it as I feared?' Raven asked. He was sitting on the bulwark, staring at the other ship too.

With a seething hiss, she took the telescope from her eye, the early morning light dashing off the gold-plated waves that encrusted it. 'I'd know that gaudy figurehead anywhere.' She shook her head. 'There's no doubt, it's the fucking *Libertine.*'

'Raphael d'Roué,' said Raven, more to the lapping waves than to her.

'I know,' she said impassively. 'Of all the places, of all the people, why that arrogant cock? Tell me, am I being punished for something? Actually, don't answer that.'

Raven chuckled. 'Do you think he's forgiven you yet?'

'He should be worried about whether I've forgiven him.' She folded up the telescope and went to clip it to her belt, but she'd neglected to put that on too. 'I really can't be bothered with this.'

A fiendishly handsome grin took over Raven's face. 'You know, he's probably got his eye on you right now.'

Lily huffed, but Raven had successfully managed to coax a smile from her. She leant forwards and pressed her hands into his back. 'I should shove you overboard.'

Raven neatly flipped off the rail, landing behind her. 'You wouldn't cope without me,' he said, pushing his hair back.

'Back to your post,' she snarled through gritted teeth, though she knew the playful smile tugging at the corners of her lips betrayed her. 'You're as bad as him!'

'Aye, Capt—Lily,' called Raven, laughing as he loped away.

KILLIAN left Lily's cabin while she was out on the deck. He'd been in there for far too long; he missed his friends, and he got the feeling she wanted him gone anyway. Every day she seemed to grow colder. She'd stopped coming over to check on him when he had a nightmare; instead, she'd sigh moodily from her hammock, audibly curse his name and go back to sleep. Lately, she barely even conversed with him. Sometimes she'd enter the room without even looking at him. He gathered his things and placed a note on the bed which simply read:

'Thanks Lil x'

As soon as he'd put the *x* on the note, he regretted it. The temptation to scribble it out or destroy the paper completely was there, but something made him leave it. He was still regretting it as he made his way back to his cabin. He slunk down the stairs and slowly pushed the door open to find everyone inside and asleep.

Nesta's glyph glinted at him from the pile of effects he'd stashed beneath his hammock. He picked it up and traced his finger over its intricate design. It was cool and smooth and shimmered with iridescence, even in the murk of the cabin. He fastened the chain about his neck and tucked the glyph under his shirt; he should probably keep it close.

Ren hadn't tried to invade his bed while he was away, which brought a smile to his face. All the fuss he'd made about being in the top one had clearly been forgotten – either that or maybe he actually respected Killian. The thought of that almost made him snigger; could the little uptight Chazzer respect the thief? Surely not.

He was too awake to sleep, but he didn't want to go up on deck in case he ran into her. He hauled himself into his hammock to ponder his options in comfort. Arrows of pain shot through his body, but he gritted his teeth and ignored them. He was fed up with feeling useless. He sat on the edge of the netting and allowed his feet to dangle in the air, swaying slightly with the soft tilting of the ship.

The familiar smell of stale smoke and salty wood, though welcoming, was a stark contrast to the fresh airy scent of the captain's quarters. A soft groan escaped his lips. He was already thinking about her again.

He closed his eyes and saw the lights drifting in the sea once more. She put her arms around him again, her smooth, cool hands on the small of his back, her head against his chest. Her soft hair tickled his bare skin, and he prickled with goose bumps. The smell of her skin chased away the odour of the cabin. That light fresh scent she wore was herbal, like sage and rosemary, with a hint of lemon. Not overpowering, not sweet, just enough to raise his pulse. A rush of warmth coursed through his body, and he wished he were alone in the cabin. A gruff voice snapped him out of his fantasies and brought him crashing back to reality drenched in icy water.

'Decided to come back then,' growled Finn.

She was lying on her side, staring at him through crusty bloodshot eyes while lighting her first roll-up of the day. Her hair, loose from its usual ponytail, fell about her shoulders in a limp tangle.

'Yeah,' said Killian, feeling a little uncomfortable.

'Good,' Finn replied.

Killian quickly explained his absence. 'Lily wanted to keep an eye on me because of my injuries. I'm fine now.'

'That's good,' said Finn, blowing out a cloud of smoke to accompany her words. 'We was startin' to miss you.'

'Really?'

'Yeah, you know me. My day ain't complete without gettin' angry about something, and your face never fails to annoy me,' she said with a dry laugh. 'Anyway, I'm glad you're feeling better. You'll be able to help out.'

'I will?'

'We're landing on Ocean's Bounty today.' She ran her finger thoughtfully along one of her scars. 'Means we'll 'ave some decent meals again.'

'Ocean's what?' Killian asked.

'Cap'n not tell you?'

Killian shrugged. 'Nope.'

Finn sat up and blew a jet of smoke from her nose. 'It's an uninhabited, unclaimed island.' She paused to crush her roll-up in her palm. 'It's more like a free shop than an island. People have been using it for years as a stock-up point. You take what you need, no more. There's a mutual respect for the place amongst seafaring folk, an unwritten law. Dunno how many it's saved from starvin' to death over the years. My guess would be shitloads.'

Finn launched herself out of her hammock. She kicked and punched the others to wake them as she tossed on her clothes.

'Look who's back with us!' She grinned, pointing in Killian's direction.

'All right,' said Killian, dreading the questions they were bound to ask.

'Hey, Killian,' Blake murmured groggily as he sat up.

'Killian, you're back!' exclaimed Ren excitedly.

'Wow,' gasped Tom. 'I didn't think we'd be seeing you again for quite some time.'

Tom looked like he was about to continue, but Finn shot him a steely glance, which instantly silenced him. A sharp knock sounded at the door, bringing a welcome, timely distraction from Killian's unexpected presence.

'Come in,' said Finn.

The door opened to reveal Raven. He stared at Killian with a look of confusion and disappointment. 'We'll be on the island within the hour,' he said.

'Sounds good to me,' said Finn as she tied her hair back. 'Can't wait to give me legs a stretch.'

'Also, I feel I should warn you, the *Libertine* is currently moored up on the Bounty.'

Finn groaned, whereas Tom mouthed a silent cheer of triumph.

'I thought that would be the reaction,' said Raven. He turned and swept out of the room in one even movement.

'The *Libertine*?' Ren asked tentatively, fear already building in his eyes.

Finn growled in her throat. 'It's a ship run by a complete—'

'Ah, Finn!' Tom said, an immovable grin plastered to his face. 'Let them meet him first.'

'KILLIAN!' Lily snapped as she burst into her cabin. 'We're docking for supplies. You can either stay here or come on land. It's your choice.'

When there was no response, Lily snarled to herself and stomped over to the bed. How dare he ignore her?

'Oi!'

Resting on top of the dishevelled bed sheets lay a note. She felt as if all the air had been punched from her body. She sat on the edge of the bed and picked it up, confusion mounting as she read it. Angry and frustrated, she screwed it up and paced over to the dresser, slumping down.

She let the paper drop between her fingers and buried her head in her hands. She cursed herself for letting him get to her. How was he doing this to her? No one had ever made her feel like this before – wretched, depressed, elated, relieved. She didn't know which emotion to cling to. She pushed her hair back and looked at her face in the mirror. Had she done the right thing? Did he now hate her? He'd chosen to leave of his own free will. He must've hated her, and who could blame him? She'd treated him with nothing less than contempt over the past few days. She'd nigh on forced him to leave.

She scowled. She shouldn't have been thinking like this; it was pathetic. She was a pirate queen, and he was a nothing. Snatching up her eyeliner, she pulled two black streaks across her eyes, then blinked. That was better. He would not get to her; she wouldn't forget herself because of him. She was the captain, and she would act like it. She didn't need him – not now, not ever. As she stood, she picked up his crumpled note and ripped it in two.

KILLIAN glared across the beach at the blond pirate in the red coat standing with Lily. So this was *the* Raphael d'Roué. The two captains had been talking for a long time, their heads and bodies extremely close. Killian strained to listen in, but the crash of the waves and the rustle of the palms drowned out any titbits of conversation. Raphael was devilishly handsome and had the swagger of someone who knew it. He wore his coat open with nothing underneath. Killian was sure he saw him flex into the sunlight to show off his toned physique. It made him cringe. What did this man have to prove to anyone?

He glanced around their small scavenging party. The gunners were there, as was Ren – looking as uneasy about being somewhere new as usual, his fearful eyes skipping between Lily, Raphael and the undergrowth behind them. Seth was straining his dark eye, staring up the beach with a look of concern. Morton stood with his arms folded; his face bore the sort of expression someone might have if they were chewing through a bag full of sour wasps. He glared at Killian, staring him up and down with an unnerving look of interest gleaming in his eyes. Raven was standing just behind Lily. There were about twenty other pirates in the gang. Killian recognised their faces but had no idea of their names.

'Right,' said Lily sharply, clapping her hands. 'Raven, you're on water detail. The rest of you, split into groups and, well, you know what to do. Make sure those two' – she jabbed her fingers in the directions of Killian and Ren – 'respect the island.'

'Aye,' Finn grunted.

Raven gave her a swift nod before racing off towards the undergrowth, performing a series of acrobatic flips as he went.

'Show-off,' Tom muttered to Killian.

'He's only cutting loose, Tom,' said Blake quietly. 'You know how cramped he gets on the ship.'

'S'pose.'

'C'mon, let's get started,' said Finn. 'We didn't come 'ere to chat shit on the beach.'

Killian shot a quick glance at Lily before they left. As their eyes met, she averted her gaze. He snapped his head back around and walked away. He didn't really want to leave her with that other pirate. The thought of her alone with him made his back tense painfully; he was so damn handsome, even with one eye and a scar. He wasn't jealous, surely? No, no, he wasn't. He just didn't trust him. There was a difference. He used to be jealous of Raven – if honest truth be told, he still was – but Raven didn't ever look at Lily in the way that crimson pirate did. He grabbed the glyph dangling from his neck and twisted it between his fingers. There was some kind of history between him and Lily, he was sure of it, but did he want to know? Of course he did.

'Who was that guy?' Killian asked casually when they were safely out of earshot.

'D'Roué?' said Tom in a condescending tone that suggested Killian should have known. 'Only the greatest sexual beast to sail the seas.'

'Ugh . . . here we go,' groaned Blake.

'Shut it, Blakey boy!' snapped Tom. He levelled his pace with Killian's. 'Raphael is *the* pirate to be. He even outranks me in the women-bedding area, a true master of the art of debauchery. He don't just have a woman in every port, he has every woman in every port!' He lowered his voice. 'He's even had our cap'n more than once.'

A dull pain throbbed in Killian's stomach, and his heart plummeted through his body. His knuckles whitened as he squeezed the glyph. Within seconds he rebuked himself; he'd slept with other women, so why couldn't she sleep with other men? He released the necklace, and it slapped against his chest. Why was he bothered? He didn't care about her, and she didn't care about him; it didn't even matter to him if she was riding that dashing pirate right now.

'Tom!' Finn barked, aiming a misjudged swing at the younger pirate's head. 'Don't talk shit about the cap'n.' She raised her fists.

Tom scampered out of the way. 'I'm only sayin' what everyone else does,' he retorted.

'And if she hears you sayin' that, she'll have your eye like she did his,' Finn snarled.

'She took his eye?' Ren piped up.

'Yeah,' said Finn, 'the bastard deserved it too.'

'ALONE at last,' said Raphael, a mischievous glint in his eye, 'Captain Rothbone.'

'We appear to be,' she said, folding her arms tightly across her chest, 'Captain d'Roué.'

'Ah, you don't have to call me that. It's so formal.' He dropped his hat to the beach and ran his fingers through his golden hair. 'I seem to recall you weren't calling me Captain d'Roué last time we met.'

'Of course, silly me.' Lily narrowed her eyes and took a step closer to him. 'I think,' she said slowly, as if trying to recollect the events in her head, 'I was calling you a *fucking cock* as I scarred up that lovely face of yours.'

Raphael laughed like her words had no effect on him. He pushed his coat farther back onto his shoulders, flexing his abdominal muscles as he did so. 'I didn't mean *that* time.' He grinned slyly, tapping his eye patch. 'I meant the time, or should I say times, you called me *Raffa*.'

'You need to get over that,' she said, trying to sound blasé.

'Come on,' he said. 'It was fun. Don't you say it wasn't.'

Lily glared at him.

He wrapped his arms around the back of his neck and puffed out his muscular chest. 'No one has ever quite called out *Raffa* the way you did.' He pouted his lips and blew a light puff of air between them. 'Sometimes I get hard just thinking about it.'

'I don't need to hear this.'

'You don't, but you want to. I know you do. I've had many women, Lily. You know, I didn't think it possible, but

I've had more since you restricted my vision. It seems the ladies love a scar.' He flicked the patch up, revealing his completely white sightless eye. 'I don't often take it off, but occasionally I do. Some women find the eye more of a turn-on.' He grinned at her as he replaced the patch and cleared his throat. 'It makes them truly believe I'm part demon.'

He took out his waterskin and had a deep swig, then offered it to Lily. She snatched it and took a sip. It tasted of him. Disgusting. She thrust it back into his hands. He flashed her a polite smile, poured the remains of the water pouch over his face and then stared off into the distance.

'Anyway, I digress.' He shook the water droplets from his shimmering hair and pushed the damp strands away from his eye. 'My point was, of all the thousands of women I've laid, you were definitely one of the best. Top three, easily. No one matches you for power, stamina and aggression.' He took a step towards her, shrugging his coat even farther back. 'How about showing me you've still got it?'

Lily teemed with anger; he was so smug, so arrogant. He hadn't changed at all. She hadn't thought it possible, but somehow relieving him of an eye had made him even more of a confident swaggering cock. She'd play his little games if he wanted and then show him just how far below her he was. Smiling, she pressed two fingers on her lips salaciously.

'Right here, on the beach?' she said.

'It's as good a place as any,' he murmured, his lips pouting slightly.

'You always were shameless.'

'And you always loved me for it,' he said, moving closer.

'Try not to get love and lust confused, d'Roué.'

'It doesn't matter what it's called when we're together.' His tone was soft and passionate. 'It always ends the same way – you on me, me in you, excitement, pleasure.'

'Want to know a secret, Raffa?' She popped a button on her shirt as she moved towards him. 'You were pretty good yourself. Sometimes when I'm alone in bed, I close my eyes and think of you.' She placed her fingertips on his chest, gliding them up and down his body as she spoke. 'Your strong arms.' Her nails teased his hard abdominal muscles. 'Your soft kisses.' She brushed her lips over his unscarred cheek. 'Your stiff cock.' She dragged her hand over the growing bulge in the front of his trousers, pausing to give him a tantalising squeeze. She gazed at him, her mouth inches from his. His breathing was heavy; he wanted her. 'And then' – fiery anger surged through her – 'I think about how you tried to screw me over!' She thumped him just hard enough to make him double over, gasping for breath. She didn't want to cause too much damage. Then she kicked his legs away, sending him tumbling to the beach in a puff of sand.

Coughing and spluttering, he got to his knees. 'Touché,' he said hoarsely. Despite the indignity he should have suffered, the look in his eye suggested he didn't care.

Lily's fists bunched up. 'What did you expect?' she seethed. 'You tried to steal my ship!'

He stood, casually brushing the sand from his coat. 'And you stole my eye. I'd say I came off worse in that respect.'

'If you hadn't tried to steal my ship, you'd still have both your eyes.'

'A minor indiscretion on my part. Can you not forgive me?'

Lily answered him with a petrifying glare.

'I've forgiven you for the eye.'

'That was your own doing, d'Roué.'

'So I cut up my own eye, did I? How stupid of me.' He

was pushing her to her limit. 'Come, Lily.' He stepped towards her, arms open. 'What's wrong?'

'Come any closer and I'll cut something else up.'

'Ah.' He nodded once. 'I see.'

'See what?'

'Tell me, Captain Lily Rothbone, when was the last time you had a man?'

She was so taken aback by the bluntness of his question that she couldn't form any words.

'Hmm.' He ran his hand along his jaw. 'So, it's been a while?'

'That's nothing to do with you,' she snapped back when she found her voice.

'Lily.' He motioned as if to put his hand on her shoulder but clearly thought better of it and ran it through his hair instead. 'You need a night with a man, a good man, one on par with me, whom I know will be difficult to find. I've never seen so much explosive tension in such a beautiful woman. You're wasting yourself. There must be someone for you, someone you desire in your bed.' The flecked ring of bronze in his irritatingly striking turquoise eye flared as he spoke.

I've already had him in my bed, and I messed that up. Lily's heart vibrated her ribs; what was she thinking? She didn't want him. Her shoulders turned to rock. She didn't. She despised him.

'That crew member of yours,' Raphael began, watching her intently.

'My crew member?' said Lily, her fire smothered.

'The handsome one,' Raphael pressed. 'Not the demon – Rook, or whatever it is you call him—'

'Raven,' she said bitterly. 'And he's not a demon.'

'Then I'm not the greatest sexual being ever to fuck his way across the world.' Raphael raised his eyebrows. 'I didn't mean him anyway. I meant the new fella – Mr Blue Eyes.'

Lily's insides squirmed, but she kept her body hard; she wouldn't show any emotion.

'I may have one eye, but that doesn't make me blind. I saw the look he gave you.' The pirate captain grinned, and she wanted to kick him to the beach again. 'And I saw the look you gave him – when his back was turned, obviously. We both know you're not one for giving too much away.'

'You saw nothing,' she growled through her teeth, 'and if you don't shut it, I swear I will blind you.'

D'Roué held his hands up and took a step away from her, but he was still grinning that infuriatingly beautiful grin. 'Your vicious protests give you away.' He scooped up his hat and knocked the sand from it before putting it on. 'I should get going.'

He walked towards Lily and paused to put a tentative hand on her hip. He leant down to whisper in her ear.

'My advice to you is just take him. It may be the best thing you ever do. And if it's not, I'm on my way to Venario now. I'll be at the usual spot for a few months if you want me.' He raised his eyebrows. 'We both know I can satisfy you.'

Before she could even think of the words to respond, he was already in the distance, his long red coat billowing out like a great column of blood. She shook with rage and frustration; she'd let him beat her.

'Y'KNOW,' Tom garbled, 'since she cut his eye up, his crew ain't allowed to say *aye*. It's banned.' Tom hadn't shut up about the amazing Raphael d'Roué since Killian had asked about him. He was beginning to regret it now. 'I heard—'

'Enough,' snapped Finn.

'No, no, this is a good un.' Tom beamed.

'Don't care,' said Finn.

'Ren does, don't you, Ren?' Tom spun to face Ren.

'I-I d—' Ren stammered. His trembling gaze darted from Tom to Finn and back again.

' 'Course you do!' Tom punched the air triumphantly. 'Well, I heard one of his crew slipped up once, said "Aye, Cap'n" rather than "Yes, Cap'n." Raphael was so furious he blew out his knees and lobbed him overboard. What a guy! And I bet he banged two or three hot women that night too.'

'Right, I've heard enough. Let's split,' said Finn. 'We can cover more ground, an' that way I don't have to listen to him go on and on.'

'Me?' said Tom incredulously.

'Split up?' asked Ren, his eyes growing wide.

'Scared?' Tom grinned at him.

'No . . . no, of course not.'

'You can help me,' said Seth, putting a protective arm around Ren and pulling him close. 'Need some sugar cane for me rum. You lot nearly drunk it all. I'll be needin' a lot more cane to boost the next batch. I got some brewin' back at the castle, but I don't think it'll be enough. You lot drink it like water, you know.'

'Sure, I'll help. Thanks, Seth.' Ren's face lit up at the prospect.

'Booze is the only thing that stops me from killin',' said

Finn, shooting a deadly glance in Tom's direction. 'So you best get a lot ... at least a lot.'

'No worries, Finn, I know the best spots for cane here, the ones no one finds.' With that, Seth led Ren away, his arm still around his shoulder.

The remaining four split up and fanned out into the tropical woodland. Killian grunted; he was hot, sweaty and aching, but he was glad to get away from everyone for a while. He idled along a well-trodden path and into the lush tropical forest. The air was clear, and it was refreshingly cool beneath the canopy of trees. A bird shrieked, and he looked up to see a rainbow of coloured feathers swoop through the treetops; another answered it with a low whirring drone. The second bird had the most impressive beak he'd ever seen. It was bright orange, marbled with deep red and hooked like a claw. It fanned its feathers, a rippling collection of blues and purples.

He wrapped his arms around the back of his head and trudged onwards. His mind was a mess of emotions and confusing thoughts. All this would be over soon, and he could get back to his normal, complication-free life. A feeling of contentment settled on him as he wistfully mulled over the many carefree nights he'd spend in the Laughing Swan. He'd drink, he'd play cards, he'd ...

His smile melted into a malcontent frown as the realisation that he could never go back to that lifestyle dawned on him. All he'd seen and experienced over the past few months had opened his eyes. His old monotonous, pointless existence wouldn't satisfy him anymore; he'd been ruined by adventure, and he already felt himself yearning for more.

The flourishing green woodland opened out onto a tiny white sandy beach lined with tall bent palms loaded with coconuts. The warm crystal-clear waters teased the shore with miniature waves. Killian glanced about; he was alone. He pushed his hair back as he approached a collection of freshly fallen coconuts. Two of them had shattered; he picked up a chunk and crunched it. It was deliciously sweet. There was just enough milk left in the flesh to keep it succulent. He glanced up to see more swaying seductively in the treetops. He placed a hand on the long slender trunk and jumped on.

Even though the curve of the trunk certainly helped, it was an arduous process, and his body didn't appreciate the strain one bit, but he was determined to prove he could do it, however much his arms, shoulders and back protested. He wasn't useless, and he was going to prove it to himself and – he glanced up through his damp hair – the sky, and all those trees that were watching him, their thick emerald palms trembling as he moved. They'd all see he wasn't useless.

As he pulled himself up, hand over hand, his legs shuffling behind him, his mind wandered to help him block out the pain. He'd escort Ren back to Chazza, see his dad right, then what? Back to Bracky, say his farewells and leave? But leave to go where? Travel the sea to Freischen? Cross the country to the allegedly beautiful Venario? Was he finally going to try to do what he and Clem had always planned? It didn't seem right without him, but he couldn't stay in Vermor any longer; he could already feel it suffocating him, and he wasn't even back.

He ran his tongue along his salty lips. He could find himself a nice Venarian woman, and they could thieve together across the sunlit coastal towns. Play cards until dawn, drinking fine wine. A certain sadness encroached on his chest. He already knew a fine part-Venarian woman. His right hand slipped, and his heart stopped. He desperately lurched forwards, locking himself in place with his left. After a few breathless moments, he carried on climbing. She didn't want him though; that was clear. He frowned as he hauled himself onwards. He didn't want her either. She was too difficult, too confusing, too stubborn. She wasn't for him.

Finally, he reached the top and glanced down. The beach seemed a long way off now. He turned around and leant his back against the trunk while he regained his breath. The wide, glossy palms provided him with shade against the glare of the sun while he enjoyed the view. He looked to his left to see a small rowing boat making its way towards the *Libertine*. He squinted; there appeared to be a man in red aboard. It seemed like Tom's idol and Lily's former lover was on the move. The ache in his chest lessened, and he immediately bristled at his involuntary reaction. He didn't care.

He turned his body about to look inland. To the north of the island lay a collection of rocky cliff faces decorated with a glistening spidery network of surging waterfalls. Tropical trees of all sizes and shapes grew all around them, their luminous green leaves quivering on the warm breeze. Vivid-coloured specks, which could only be birds, flew in and about the craggy cliffs. As he drank in the scenery, he caught sight of Raven's shirtless acrobatic body leaping effortlessly through the treetops.

RAVEN tore through the forest faster than he'd done in a long time. He leapt expertly from one tree to the next, enjoying the feeling of the tropical breeze in his hair. He took a deep breath and charged down a tree trunk to the soft woodland floor below. Back on the ground, he bounded through the trees, pushing himself to the limit. He leapt up, bouncing from one tree trunk to the next, challenging himself to stay off the ground for as long as possible. He couldn't remember the last time he'd been able to run this free. The feeling of liberation grew inside him and made him faster, helped him jump higher.

He burst out of the woodland and arrived at the sand-coloured inland cliffs. He sprinted up their vertical craggy faces, punctuating his run with acrobatic flips. It was such a rush. He did a handspring across an overhang and propelled himself off the hardy dark trees that grew from the rock face, teasing their slim branches with his gentle touch. He charged through waterfalls, their rainbows playing on his tanned skin, their cool refreshing spray giving him yet more energy. When he reached the top, he stood tall and pushed his wet hair out of his face.

He curled his toes around the edge of the cliff and looked down at the inviting pool the waterfalls tumbled into. He was completely still, his arms folded across his statuesque body. The air was fresh and his surroundings beautiful. Trees clung desperately to the cliffs, bunches of brightly coloured fruit weighing down their thinner branches. Thick vines wound about their trunks and draped over the rocks. The waterfalls sparkled like snaking silver ribbons as they cascaded towards the deep indigo pool, emitting dusty rainbows from their misty spray.

Raven scanned the island; he could see Killian in the distance lying on the top curve of a palm tree, but there was no one else in his line of vision. With the sun where it was and the distance between them, it would be impossible for Killian to have a clear view of him. Raven held his arms out, and with the breath of a rushing gale, two great black feathered wings appeared from his back. He stretched them out to their full span, the feathers glinting with a purple hue as they moved, and rocked his head back. It felt so good to release them that he wanted to cry with joy. He flapped them once and drifted a little way off the ground. Ever since he'd fleetingly used them on the Phantom Island and at the geyser, he'd been filled with an almost overwhelming desire to unleash them. Only when they were out did he feel truly whole. His body hummed with pleasure, and his muscles chorused with delight.

He flapped over the edge of the cliff, closed his eyes and listened intently to the sound of the rushing water; it roared and surged, full of power. Opening his eyes, he smiled to himself and dropped into a dive. He banished his wings in a cloud of purple and black to go into a free fall. He twisted gracefully through the air, arching his body into all sorts of acrobatic shapes as he hurtled towards the cool, hungry water.

LILY remained on the beach, scowling into the undergrowth as she waited for her foragers to return to the ship. She'd told herself it was to coordinate the operation, but really she just didn't want to risk bumping into Killian in the forest. She was already confused enough about her feelings for him, and Raphael hadn't helped the situation.

She glared out to sea, following the *Libertine* as it sailed away. *What an arrogant, pompous cock,* she mused as she watched its sails flapping in the wind. What did he know about the relationship between her and Killian? Not that there was any relationship, besides the mutual hatred. She didn't care about him. The sooner he was off her ship and away from her the better.

Over the next few hours, the scavenging pirates lumbered back and forth to the ship in twos and threes. Lily greeted them as pleasantly as she could despite the foul mood she was in. Raven bounded tirelessly to and from the *Tempest* several times, carrying great water barrels on his broad shoulders as if they weighed no more than a sack of air. He didn't even break a sweat; today his energy was limitless. When Killian eventually emerged from the trees, Lily lowered her head and counted the grains of sand at her feet. She couldn't help but look up when he walked past, and a hot rush coursed through her knotted stomach.

'Killian,' she said curtly as their eyes met.

'Lillian,' he replied pleasantly with a nod. He put his bag down on the sand with a thud, and they waited in silence for someone to share a boat to the ship with.

Lily glowered at his back, briefly considered some idle small talk, then dismissed it. Why do one of the things she hated the most with one of the people she hated the most? After what seemed like hours, they were joined by Finn.

'Most of the others are on board,' Lily said to Finn. 'You two can go. I'll board with Raven.'

'Aye, Cap'n,' said Finn. 'C'mon, shithead,' she added, reaching down to drag Killian to his feet.

As Lily watched them go, she felt a yearning desire to be in the boat with him, but she'd made her decision. He didn't fit into her life; he couldn't, and she wouldn't let him. Never again would she allow herself to be distracted by idealistic, romantic feelings. It only led to ruin.

CHAPTER
THIRTY-EIGHT

KILLIAN WATCHED THE ISLAND UNTIL IT disappeared from view over the horizon. He leant against the bulwark with his face to the wind. Though his body still ached and his wounds throbbed, he felt much better in himself for leaving Lily's cabin that morning. There were too many confusing feelings flying around in there for his liking.

He pushed his hair from his eyes and mused over what to do with the rest of his day: stare at the sea, walk around the ship, play cards or sleep. Sleeping wasn't such a bad idea; maybe he'd have a dream that was more exciting than being on the ship – which wouldn't be hard. He frowned. Or maybe he'd have a nightmare. He rested his elbows on the rail and cupped his chin in his hands.

Three weeks left, three weeks, then I'll be free of this place, of her, of any responsibility. Then I just have to work out what to do with the rest of my life.

He groaned and slumped forwards. He didn't want to have to make any big decisions, but in his heart he knew his old life was stale; he couldn't go back. Leaving Brackmouth, leaving Vermor, leaving everyone he knew – they were big decisions, some might say life-changing. Could he do it? Could he really start again? Ren's money would certainly help with that. Leaving had been his plan years ago, after all, so it stood to reason the urge would never fully abandon him. Back then, though, he'd had Clem; now he was alone. A deep sadness crept into his chest and rested atop his heart, and he blinked away the impending tears.

A vicious slap to the wound on his back dragged him out of his musings.

'Ah! Fuck!' Killian spun around. 'That was not funny,' he snapped, trying to regain his composure through the stinging pain.

Morton nodded once, and the man to his left, a tall and muscular man, seized Killian's injured left shoulder in a tight grip. His whole arm immediately bloomed with intense fiery agony, but he stubbornly kept his expression even so as not to betray any weakness.

'Sorry, I never congratulated ya for survivin',' hissed Morton, his eyes gleaming with delight.

'That's fine,' said Killian. 'I'll forgive you. How much money did you lose, by the way?' He offered a lopsided smirk with the question.

An aggressive snarl came from his left as his shoulder was squeezed even tighter. *A fair bit then.* Killian bit down on the inside of his lip to keep from crying out. The strength drained from his legs, and his knees trembled; he didn't know how much more he could take without showing the pain.

'Just thought I'd come over to see how you were doin''

and bring these fellas along,' Morton said through his teeth. 'I was a little worried that ya might have got injured or somethin'. Can't have my mate Killian not being well, now, can we?'

'No, Morton, that wouldn't do, would it?' said Killian.

Morton sneered, stepped forwards and punched Killian as hard as he could in the stomach. As he did, the other pirate released his grip, and Killian crumpled to the deck.

'That wasn't . . . very friendly,' Killian gasped as he got up on one knee.

'Wasn't meant to be!' Morton kicked him in the ribs.

Killian's body smacked against the side of the ship, and he fell to the deck once again.

'I've been waitin' so long for this,' said Morton.

Killian coughed. Everything hurt. He picked himself up onto all fours. If he could just get to his feet—

Morton's boot connected with his stomach, and he fell again. *This is becoming embarrassing.* He tried to move, to haul himself up, but he couldn't. His head swirled, and his body was alive with pain.

He tried to curl up defensively as the other two waded in. There was nothing else he could do, but the blows rained down. His hips, ribs, stomach, legs, arms, shoulders, anything they could get at, they punched, kicked or slapped. The rank taste of blood filled his mouth; he tried to spit it out, but he couldn't even do that. All the breath was pounded from his body. Then the beating stopped, and the air around him stilled. He wanted to sigh with relief, to make some kind of noise, but he refused. Despite his bloody mouth, he couldn't let them know they'd hurt him.

'Get 'im up,' Morton grunted with a low chuckle.

The two pirates grabbed him by his shoulders, their fingers digging into his flesh, and dragged him to his feet. Killian sagged forwards, all his weight resting on their arms.

'Is this the only way . . . you'll fight me?' he asked hoarsely, a warm dribble of blood running from his lip. 'Beaten down, restrained and injured?'

'I don't care, so long's I win.'

Killian spat a lump of blood on the deck, then raised his head to level his eyes with Morton's. He stared at the quartermaster while he waited for his ragged breath to come back under his control. Somehow, he managed a smile.

'You really are quite a bastard, aren't you?'

'Like I give a shit.'

'How about they let me go, and you and me can sort this out . . . one on one?'

'I ain't fallin' for that shit. I got you right where I want ya. I ain't about to give this up.'

'So what're you gonna do, run me through? Lob my body overboard?'

'Nah.' Morton leered, shaking his head. He ran a hand over his oozing leather cap and smiled unnervingly at his captive. 'I'm gonna beat you to within an inch of your life while they hold ya steady. Then I'll let ya recover, just so's I can beat ya down again. You're gonna wish you were dead. You'll be begging me to kill ya.'

'Not exactly what I'd call a balanced fight.' Killian shook his head to clear his hazy mind. He subtly tensed his muscles. He still had something left; hopefully it'd be enough. All he had to do was goad them a little more to buy himself some recovery time. 'What about that "no fighting on board" rule?'

'That applies to crew. You ain't crew.' Morton gloated, folding his arms.

Killian twitched his shoulders, and a fierce rush of energy pulsed through his body. He blew out a heavy breath; it was as if Nesta had her hand on his chest again. His body grew rigid as he waited for the moment the feeling would abandon him.

He lifted his head. Morton was moving towards him; he had to act now. Killian twisted both his arms quickly. His captors were taken completely unawares, and he easily slipped from their hands. As he moved, the glyph leapt from under his shirt to catch the sun and flashed with a brilliant iridescent light. He ducked under Morton's cumbersome swing to land an uppercut in his stomach, followed up with a swift kick to the face, knocking him to the deck. He pushed his hair back. He felt invigorated, strong even. All his pain had temporarily receded. The larger of the other two pirates lumbered forwards and launched his fist at him. Killian blocked and jabbed his elbow sharply into his ribs before bringing his knee up to drive it into his belly. He cried out and fell to the floor, whimpering with pain. Killian stepped back and rubbed his hands. He looked at the last man standing.

'Want a go?' he asked, stooping slightly and beckoning him forwards.

'You shouldn't have done that!' he snapped as he backed away in the direction of the fallen men.

'Probably not, but I doubt any of you will speak of this.'

The man curled his lip in response. Killian knew if any of this got out, Morton's reputation would take a severe knock.

'I won't tell if you don't,' said Killian.

'Deal,' the pirate grunted.

'Good. I need a drink,' Killian muttered as he walked away.

He ducked below deck and made a beeline for the kitchen, rapping on the door when he arrived.

'Who is it?' a voice called back.

'Killian.'

'Come in!'

Killian opened the door to find Seth surrounded by dead chickens. Blood was smeared all over the surfaces and sprayed on the wall, feathers and fluff sticking to it in sodden clumps. Seth was standing in a blood-splattered apron holding a cleaver in one hand and a head in the other. Killian wrinkled his nose in disgust; it was hard to hide it given the circumstances.

'Sorry 'bout these,' Seth said, indicating to the carcasses with the severed head. 'Thought I may as well. They given up layin', and we're on our way back now.'

'I guess so,' said Killian.

Seth frowned when he looked at Killian, his dark eye narrowing. 'S'up with your lip?'

Killian wiped away the blood with the back of his hand. 'Nothing.'

Seth continued to frown but nodded all the same, his beads clattering together in his wiry hair. 'Drink?' he offered.

'Please.' Killian smiled.

Seth reached in his cupboard, moved a bag of flour out of the way and pulled out an unopened bottle of rum and two cups. He poured a liberal shot in each, and they downed them together. He refilled them, and they drank again.

'You should have come seen me sooner,' said Seth, filling the cups again.

'I know. I'm sorry,' said Killian, picking up the cup and

tossing the shot down his throat. He set it down and swayed as an odd tiredness descended upon him.

'I heard 'bout what happened down there. That's some pretty heavy stuff. You okay now?'

'Yeah, I'm fine,' said Killian. 'I feel more like my old self – especially today, but maybe it's just the rum.'

'That's good,' said Seth. He kicked a wooden chair over to Killian. 'Here, reckon you need it.'

'Thanks,' said Killian as he sank into it.

He stretched his legs out, let his arms dangle limply at his sides and closed his eyes. All his aches and pains were slithering back up on him. He could feel bruises forming on his ribs and stomach, his arms and back were sore, and his lip throbbed. A soft grunt escaped his mouth; he was desperately tired. Where had that rush of energy come from? And why had it left only to be replaced by pain and exhaustion?

'You all right?' asked Seth softly.

'I'm fine,' Killian said in what was little more than a whisper.

'You do know you're bleeding, don't you?'

Killian's eyes peeled open, and he glanced at his shoulder to see fresh blood seeping through his shirt.

'Shit,' he grumbled, sitting up and hunching forwards. 'This is my last good shirt. Bastards.'

'Who did this to you?' asked Seth.

'No one here – well, not exactly. My other half did this. It just got opened up again.'

'You should tell the cap'n. There's rules 'bout that sort of thing, you know.'

'I know. I handled it though. I don't need her involved.'

'If you say so.' Seth grimaced as he sat on a creaky backless stool.

'I do,' said Killian, peeling his shirt away from the blood in a vain attempt to save it.

'Here,' said Seth, getting up and sticking his head in one of the cupboards. 'I got bandages. Always need 'em in the kitchen.'

'Thanks,' said Killian, giving up on adjusting his shirt and taking it off instead. He unwound Lily's neat bandages and dropped them in a heap on the floor.

'No problem.' Seth tossed the roll to Killian and sat back down. 'You need a hand with that?'

'Nah, I've got quite good at it.' As he set about dressing his own wound, his mind wandered back to the day Lily had done it for him. Her soft body near his, her delicate fingers working to ease his pain and discomfort. Warmth crept into him, and a lightness filled his chest. She was still doing it to him; she was controlling his thoughts. He tightened the bandage. Three weeks and he'd be off the ship and could forget about her once and for all. 'Done,' he said with a weak smile.

Seth poured them one more drink.

'Best leave it at this. Gotta sort out all the gear from the foraging and pluck an' cook the chicks.'

He and Killian drank together and set their vessels down.

'I'll leave you to it then,' said Killian, putting his blood-stained shirt back on and eyeing the dead chickens again.

'Aye. You should send li'l Ren down to help me.'

'Will do, though I can't promise he won't faint at the sight of blood.'

Killian turned and left the kitchen-cum-abattoir, accompanied by Seth's booming laughter.

CHAPTER
THIRTY-NINE

A FAMILIAR VOICE BROKE INTO KILLIAN'S unconscious mind. 'Ay! Fancy some fishin'?'

He felt a sharp punch to his side. 'Wh-what?' he mumbled, disorientated by the rude awakening.

'I said do you wanna come and fish?' asked Finn. 'All that chicken we had the other day has got me wantin' more flesh.'

'Erm, okay.' Killian sat up and rubbed his face.

'Just so you know, you ain't my first choice. Blake an' Tom are up the rigging, and Ren is helpin' Seth, so I'm scraping the bloody barrel askin' you.'

'You'd pick Thorny over me? That actually hurts.'

'Aye! He don't answer back, and he's got manners.' She grinned wickedly at him. 'I'll be on the starboard side setting up the rods. Get up, get dressed and meet me there in five minutes.'

'Starboard side?' Killian yawned, still picking the sleep from his eyes.

'The right-hand side.'

'Got it.'

'Good.'

Killian yawned again, stretched, flopped out of bed and set about washing himself with the bowl of cold water he'd left under his hammock the night before. He rubbed the hard chunk of soap over his body. *What I wouldn't do for a bath right now.* It wasn't like he was asking for a solid gold horse or even a warm juicy bacon sandwich. He just wanted to feel clean for a couple of hours. A decent bath should be everyone's right.

Feeling curious, he unwound the bandage on his right arm to survey the damage. There was a thick crusty scab where he'd been torn open on the rocks. He poked it; it was still sore and would definitely scar, but it had almost healed. He could see where the scab was beginning to flake away from the new skin underneath. That was more than could be said for his other arm. *Bloody Morton.* He hadn't touched that injury since he'd bound it in Seth's kitchen a few days ago. It would take twice as long to heal now they'd ruined the scab, and the scar was inevitable. Shaking his head, he wrapped his arm up again.

He tossed on his trousers, then peered under his hammock and reached for a slightly crusty shirt. Folded in a neat square next to it was his coat. He grabbed it and shook it open. Several pieces of paper fluttered out from within it. He grabbed one, smoothed it out and forced himself to read it. He winced. It read like the diary of a condemned man, which, he rationalised, at the time of writing he had been. It was embarrassing. Who had he been a few weeks ago? Why had he felt the need to write all this down? If he'd died down the Drop, this would have been his legacy: the ramblings of a terrified man musing on his own life, death and mistakes for pages and pages. He grabbed every piece that was tainted with his scrawl and shoved them in his trouser pocket. No one must read them, ever. Before meeting up with Finn he'd show his diary to its watery grave and never write anything again – just to be safe.

'Took your time,' Finn grumbled. She was sitting on the rail, a small pile of crushed roll-ups behind her on the deck.

'I went to the right.'

'Your other right, idiot,' she muttered, shaking her head.

'You didn't tell me which direction I had to be facing,' Killian protested. 'How the hell was I supposed to know? You lot and your bloody ridiculous nautical terms.'

'How long have you been on the ship?' Finn gripped a roll-up between her teeth and lit it.

Killian cracked a lame smile and pulled himself onto the bulwark, dangling his feet above the ocean. 'So what d' we do?' he asked, not bothering to put the faintest glimmer of enthusiasm in his tone. He stretched his arms above his head, wishing he were still asleep.

'You never fished before?' said Finn with a look of pained disbelief.

'Nope.'

'Well, I've baited the rod up for you,' she said, handing it to Killian. 'All you do is sit here and wait for something to bite. When it does, pull it in. Nothin' to it. Even a shithead like you can do it.'

Killian wiped away the layer of moisture already building on his forehead. 'Doesn't sound very interesting.'

'It is,' said Finn defensively.

'Whatever you say.'

For over half an hour they sat quietly, watching the clear blue sea churning below them. The sun was a disc of gold set within a cloudless sapphire sky. Killian rolled his trousers to his knees and undid his shirt slightly, the glyph glowing with a multitude of iridescent hues in the sunlight. He absently took the pendant in his hand and twisted it, wondering how it worked or indeed if it would work. He instantly dismissed that last thought; Nesta didn't seem the type who'd give him shoddy merchandise after he'd almost died for it. He gripped it tight in his fist. But how did it work? Perhaps he should have asked what to do with it before he left. It slapped against his chest as he released it. He couldn't go back and ask now.

'Won't last much longer,' said Finn, breaking the silence.

'What won't?'

'The heat. I feel the temperature droppin'.'

'I don't,' said Killian, licking his tangy lips.

'Wouldn't expect you to. You ain't exactly the seafaring type.'

'True.' He stared at the water. 'So, how long have you been at this, you know, whole piracy game?'

Finn rubbed her scar while she thought, her fingers gliding up and down the broken flesh. 'Over twenty years now, I reckon.'

Killian whistled softly. 'Long time.'

'Yeah, I started when I was 'bout twelve. 'Course, I weren't a pirate back then. I was a cabin girl on a merchant vessel.' Finn gazed out over the waves as she spoke, her harsh voice unusually low. 'My parents didn't have much coin. They thought sending me off on a merchant ship was the best chance I had at gettin' a better life. That's what they told me anyway. I think they just got sick of caring for me. It was sorta the done thing round my way, especially with girls. Nice little earner, selling your kid to some merchant.' She chuckled to herself. 'I was on that ship for a couple of years. I spent my time doin' bullshit tasks, you know, swabbin' the decks, clearing the bilges of filth, servin' the nob of a cap'n his food, all the crap jobs no one wants.

'One day we was attacked by pirates. Now, I ain't stupid. Soon as I saw 'em, I hacked my hair off. I looked like a proper little lad. They ransacked the ship, murdered most o' the crew and kidnapped those they thought would be useful. Luckily, that included me. When they were done killing and lootin', they blew the ship up. Loaded the shitheap with gunpowder an' blew it to bits. The smoke reached up to the clouds. Watchin' it blow and take my old life with it was a great feeling. That was when I promised myself I wouldn't end up another little bitch on this ship.

'As luck would have it, they were down on gunners. Must've been the gunpowder in the air or somethin', but I jumped at the chance to get trained. This salty old sea dog called Gilly took me under his wing and taught me everything about firearms. From blunderbuss to musket, and from cannons to swivel-guns, he even had a fancy thing a bit like yours. I worked my arse off until I was the best shot on the ship. I grew me hair. To be honest, pretending to be a boy by then was gettin' a pain in the arse. There's only so much you can hide, and the crew didn't care. They respected me. I stayed on there for 'bout four years before I moved on to another, the *Golden Kraken*, it were called. I'd heard their cap'n gave you a better cut o' the loot.

'One evening we pulled into port at Perranham and were told to go and enjoy the town. This was about six or seven years since I joined the lads on the *Kraken*. We all ran off to the first tavern we could find to squander our cut on booze an' women an' men. I would 'ave just been happy to find a guy who could keep up with me for one night; you wouldn't believe what a rare thing that is,' she added with a sly wink. 'I remember I was in this dingy little place, full of scum, cut-throats, mercenaries, ex-sentinels for hire and us, of course. It stank of stale beer and sweat, but I didn't care. I went to the bar and ordered. That's when I met them.' She paused, took a dry biscuit from her pocket and offered it to Killian.

'The cap'n and Raven were in that same bar, scouting for crew members. I ended up going over to 'em. Who wouldn't? A big hard-lookin' bloke and a pretty girl in her early twenties – I thought he was pimping her out. I was about to give him a stern talking to and a punch in the face when they told me they had a ship and needed more crew. It caught me off guard – a female cap'n. It seemed like a bad joke. They told me they were off down to the Causturs and they needed a decent gunner to train their slack-shot bunch of wasters. They were willing to line my pockets well if I joined. I took a moment to weigh my options. I was gettin' restless on the *Kraken* as it was, an' they didn't seem your average pirates – I mean, a girl as cap'n. I remember one of my fellow crewmates trying to flirt with her, trying to touch her and that. She was having none of it, almost put the guy through the wall. That was it. I was sold. That evening I left the port with her an' her crew, an' after 'bout ten years, I ain't looked back.'

'You enjoy this life then?'

'I enjoy it now,' said Finn. 'Cap'n Rothbone's the best thing that happened to me. We have riches, a place to live that ain't a ship an' a fair cap'n. It's great.' She dragged her hand along her ponytail.

'All those years under Lily. I don't know how you've managed to cope. I've known her a while, but this is the most time I've ever spent with her. I don't think I can handle much more.'

Finn barked a laugh. 'I think your issues with the cap'n are, how shall we say . . . special.'

'What's that supposed to mean?'

'You really want me to answer that?'

Killian shook his head. 'I met Lily in Perranham,' he said, neatly changing the subject.

'Oh, aye,' said Finn, smiling.

Killian nodded. He was about to say something when his line jerked. 'Hey, I've got one!'

'Pull it in then,' she said gruffly.

Killian pulled on his rod and hoisted the line out of the water. Squirming on the end was a silvery fish, its scales flashing in the sunlight. He yanked it up, and Finn grabbed hold of the slippery wriggling creature. She pulled the hook from its mouth and chucked it into a bucket on the deck behind her.

'Nice one,' she said. 'Looks like I'll get some meat after all. They should start coming in now; they don't swim on their own out here. We'll get some of his mates too.'

Killian turned and looked down into the bucket at his fish. He felt a pang of guilt as he watched it gasping, its fins twitching feebly in a useless attempt at escape. 'We don't have to leave it doing that, do we?'

'Nope.' Finn handed Killian her rod and dismounted the rail. Her dark shadow stretched over the unfortunate fish as she reached down and stabbed it in the head with her knife. 'Better?' she asked, pulling herself back up on the bulwark. She took both rods, baited Killian's and handed it back.

'Yeah, thanks,' said Killian, casting his line out again. As he moved, the sunlight glinted on his swords.

'Where'd you get those fancy things from anyway?' Finn asked, holding her rod in place with her knees while she adjusted her bandana and fringe.

'My swords?'

'Yeah.'

'Won them in a card game.'

'Oh,' Finn mused, moving on from her clothing and hair to construct a roll-up.

'The guy I beat hadn't any money left, and all he could give me were these hilts.' He patted them gently, and they flashed bright to his touch. 'The blades had rotted away, but the hilts looked pretty decent, and as soon as I held them, I felt sort of different. I don't know . . . like they were mine.' He paused and ran his fingers through his hair; it wasn't something he'd ever spoken about before. He glared at the waves, willing a fish to bite and interrupt their conversation, but he had no such luck. 'Anyway, I took them as my winnings, then I took them to Geoff.'

'Aye, I know Geoff,' said Finn, nodding.

'He was fascinated by them. He said they were ancient and it would be a huge undertaking to restore them. You know what he's like; he wanted them to be perfect. He offered to buy them off me for a small fortune, but I refused. I'd got quite attached to them, and after all his enthusiastic waffling, I thought they must be something pretty special. Still, looking back on it, I couldn't tell you why I didn't take the money. If it were anything else, I'd have bitten his hand off.

'I couldn't afford to pay him to restore them, so he did me a deal: I'd work for him for a year for free, and he'd work on the blades. I accepted – didn't really have a choice. So

I spent a year keeping his shop tidy, running his errands, meeting his buyers, doing all the stuff he couldn't be bothered with. During that time, he trained me up in combat whenever he could. He said if I was to own blades like this, I had to know how to use them properly. He was a rough teacher. I'd always hobble home covered in bruises. He's an ex–black sentinel, so he knows a few tricks, and more often than not he forgot to hold back. As soon as my year was up, to the day, he handed me back my swords. That feeling came back as soon as they were at my side.'

'Lucky swords, eh? So that's your secret.'

'Yeah, sort of. It's almost like I know what to do whenever I touch them,' said Killian. 'I don't really understand it myself.' He ran a finger along the leather strap of his goggles. He didn't want to tell Finn all his secrets; secrets had a way of getting out, especially if you didn't want them to. It wasn't that he didn't trust her, he just didn't want to put her in an awkward position. 'It's probably all just in my head.'

'Reckon you're right there,' said Finn, blowing a wisp of smoke from the corner of her mouth.

Killian hunched his shoulders and cocked his head to one side. 'When I was down the Drop,' he said slowly, carefully; even thinking about what had happened to him brought pain, and recalling it to someone else was even worse, 'I didn't feel it. I was completely alone. They felt heavy and lifeless.' He gritted his teeth, trying to fight off the melancholy that dwelling on the tasks always brought. 'Sometimes I can't believe I'm alive.'

After a long pause, Finn grabbed his shoulder. 'But you are!'

'I guess so.'

'Maybe you're tougher than you think.'

'Perhaps,' said Killian. He gazed out over the ocean for a couple of breaths, then turned to Finn and jabbed her softly in the ribs. 'So you'd better watch out!'

'Ay!' she grunted through a smoky grin.

THAT evening, Ren helped Seth carry his cooking pot up onto the deck. They had spent the morning chopping vegetables and drinking tea and all afternoon gutting fish. Seth was determined to make a fine stew with them, and Ren was eager to help. Working with Seth always put him at peace; he had such a calming presence. Learning about new techniques and flavours was always fascinating too.

Seth set his pot up over a fire and dropped in the generous hunks of fish, along with yam, plantain, breadfruit and sweet potatoes from the island. He cracked open some coconuts, poured in the water and handed the shells to Ren so he could extract the flesh. He topped it up with fresh water and tossed in a handful of dried red chillies, a few handfuls of flour, some salt, the juice of several limes and whatever herbs he had left. Ren pounded the coconut flesh until he had a paste and passed it back to Seth, who chucked it in the pot. Ren gazed in wonder as the one-eyed cook slowly stirred the stew. It smelt divine – sweet, spicy and tangy all at once. His mouth watered in anticipation; he couldn't wait to have a taste.

'That's how you make a good fish stew,' said Seth proudly.

'You're good,' said Ren.

'I know. My ma was top chef on the Causturs. Folks island-hopped just for a taste of her stew. She told me all her secrets.' Seth tapped his nose as he spoke. 'Maybe I'll pass 'em on to you one day.' He squinted into the pot, watching it bubble hungrily. 'It'll take 'bout two hours to cook. You don't have to stand with me the whole time if you don't want.'

'No, that's fine. I enjoy watching you cook,' said Ren, fixated on the pot.

'It'll be borin',' Seth warned as he dragged a huge blackened metal spoon through the mixture.

'I don't mind,' said Ren, smiling politely. 'It won't be boring anyway because I'll be with you.'

'Don't you go making me cry now!'

'Sorry.'

'I'm just tuggin' your mams. I don't cry – well, not often. You can take over the stirrin' when my arms start to ache if you want?'

Ren gasped. 'It would be an honour.'

Seth slapped him on the back and burst into a fit of hearty laughter. 'I'm gonna miss you when you're gone.'

'I'll miss you too, Seth.' He really would.

KILLIAN tapped his finger on his hip and leant against the quarterdeck. It was chilly. The creeping night was bringing in a cold breeze. He shuddered and looked down at Tom and Blake, who were sitting on the deck playing dice.

'Seth better be cooking us something decent tonight,' Tom moaned. 'I'm so hungry I could eat you.'

'I wouldn't recommend it,' murmured Blake. He was slouched across the deck, his chin propped on his hand. 'Come on, it's your turn.'

Tom picked up the dice and rolled them with an artless flick of his wrist. They rattled across the wood and wedged themselves in a crack in the deck. Blake stretched towards them, leaning down in an attempt to read the number, a difficult task in the fading light.

'What is it?' Tom asked, not making the slightest effort to move and check for himself.

'I think it's a four, but it could be a six. I don't know.'

'This is rubbish!' Tom grumbled. 'We may as well just sit here and wait for starvation to take us.'

'A little dramatic,' said Blake, sitting up. He ran his hand along the thin leather plait about his neck, twisting his finger through it to create a tiny loop.

Tom grunted and sagged forwards. 'My insides are eating themselves. I think I'm dying.'

'Can you do it more quietly?' Killian said, crouching down to join them.

'Are you coming to play dice with us?' Tom asked, smirking.

'What do you think?'

'It's too dark here anyway. We should have played closer to some sunstones,' Tom said. 'It's your fault, Blake, your fault. How am I supposed to improve my game in this light?'

'I did say we should move,' Blake muttered.

'Maybe you don't have to,' said Killian. He pulled the stick Cassius had given him from his belt. 'I've got this.'

'A stick,' Tom said. 'Great.'

'Yes, a stick,' said Killian, disregarding Tom's attempt at sarcasm. 'It's a special stick. I got it from the Drop.'

'Ooh,' Tom drawled. Hunger and boredom were drawing out his inner brat.

'Watch,' said Killian simply, blocking out Tom's retorts.

He held it out in front of him, hoping it still worked, and shut his eyes while willing it to ignite. The end crackled and burst into green flame.

'Shit!' Tom sat up straight, and his jaw dropped open. 'How'd you do that?'

'I just willed it to light,' said Killian, sweeping the flaming stick in front of him, the bright tongues of green fire licking the air.

Tom gasped. 'That's amazing.'

Killian stared at the green flames flickering on the end of the baton and willed them to stop; they obeyed immediately.

'Let's 'ave a go,' said Tom eagerly.

Killian tossed him the stick, and he dodged out of the way, going sprawling to the deck.

'Hey, you could have—'

'It's not hot.'

'Oh.' Tom picked it up and checked the end. 'What do I do then?'

'Like I said, will it to light.'

Tom gripped the stick and glared at the end, but nothing happened. He put both hands on it and scrunched up his eyes, but still nothing happened.

'Why's it not doin' it?'

Killian shrugged and held his hand out. Tom passed it back, and it burst into flames again.

'What? How come you can do it and I can't?'

'Maybe you're not doing it right,' said Blake, a hint of disdain in his tone.

'Easy for you to say. You try it.' Tom huffed.

'Okay.'

Killian extinguished the fire and gave it to Blake. He

held it for a few seconds, and it erupted into flames. He glanced at Tom and gave him a smug look.

'Ah, what?' Tom exclaimed, slamming his hands on the deck and wincing straight afterwards. 'How come he can do it but I can't?'

'I don't know,' said Killian, twirling the glyph in his fingers.

'Here, Blake, gimme another go,' said Tom, reaching towards him.

Blake snuffed out the flames and passed it to Tom. Tom held it and stared at it, but still it refused to work. He gritted his teeth, strained his neck, tensed his muscles and growled at it – nothing. He swore at it – still nothing. His cheeks grew sweaty with frustration, and the vein at the side of his head pulsed. After five minutes of staring at the stick and grinding his jaw, he threw it to the deck in exasperation.

'Useless piece of shit,' he mumbled. 'You should take it back, Killian. It's obviously broken.'

Killian picked it up and lit it. Tom folded his arms across his chest and muttered something vague and obscene.

'Hey,' said Blake, 'you rolled a six.'

'I'm not playing anymore,' Tom spat petulantly.

Blake rolled his eyes, picked up the dice and shoved them in his pocket.

Killian wrapped his coat around him. Finn had been right; it was getting colder. A week ago he could have sat out on the deck in the early evening wearing just a shirt with his trousers rolled to his knees. He looked at the green flames and smiled sadly. There were some aspects of the ship he was going to miss. Not the lack of baths or decent breakfasts, but he'd miss the life. He watched Blake trying to cheer up a disgruntled Tom. He'd miss them.

He looked up at the pale twilight stars pricking through the thin blanket of grey clouds. The *Tempest* rocked on the waters with a calming and restful sway. The ocean murmured, and the sails flapped in the wind, the comforting scent of warm timber combining with brine.

Killian closed his eyes and took a deep breath. He felt so close to peace it almost seemed tangible, as if he could wrap his hand around it and pull it close to his body like a blanket. Being here with these people was right; for the first time in his life, he almost felt like he belonged somewhere, but he knew he could never join the crew permanently. For one thing, he didn't like being told what to do, nor did he know or care to know anything about running a ship. Also, long voyages, he found, bored him to the brink of insanity, and he was certain living on the island would have a similar effect. And then there was Lily. She was too confusing. He couldn't work with her again. It was too difficult. He didn't understand his feelings whenever he was around her, and he certainly didn't understand hers.

Footsteps echoed along the deck. Killian held the torch up to reveal Ren's cheery face; he was carrying a deep wooden bowl, which was sending curls of steam out into the night.

'Hey, Killian, nice torch,' he said, crouching down, filling the air with a rich, spicy aroma.

'It's not bad,' he replied, swishing it through the air for effect.

Tom looked up, and his wide eyes fell on the bowl in Ren's hand.

'What you got there, Ren?' he asked slyly.

'Some of Seth's fish stew,' he said.

'Gimme some,' said Tom, edging towards him.

'Go and get some. Seth's made plenty. He's only up there.' Ren indicated up the deck with his spoon.

Tom collapsed to the deck, shaking violently and breathing heavily. 'Can't . . .' he whispered.

'What?' said Ren.

'Can't . . .' he gasped, holding out a trembling hand. 'Too hungry – can't make it, can't move. Please help me.'

Ren puckered his lips, and his brow furrowed with concern. He leant over to Tom and offered him his bowl. Tom's eyes gleamed as his prize hovered inches from him, but before he could take it, Killian yanked Ren back.

'But, Killian—' Ren began.

'He's having you on.'

'He's not. He's—'

'He is,' said Blake, shaking his head.

'Am not,' Tom groaned pathetically. 'Help me, Ren, please.'

'Bein' a lazy oik again, Tom?' said Finn, ambling towards them, also brandishing a bowl of delicious-smelling stew.

'Finn!' Tom wheezed, grasping for her legs. 'You'll save me . . . won't you?'

'No fuckin' way,' said Finn, sitting down.

'Scum,' hissed Tom, dragging himself to his feet. 'I'm going, but if I collapse and die on the way, you've only got yourselves to blame.'

'Get me some while you're there,' Killian called after him.

'Bollocks to you!'

CHAPTER
FORTY

I T WASN'T LONG BEFORE THE WINDS BECAME colder and the rain more frequent. Finn refused to sit out and fish, much to Killian's disappointment. He'd come to enjoy the peace and tranquillity fishing had offered over the last two weeks. It helped him to forget himself and his problems, and having Finn so close stopped his mind from wandering into difficult areas.

Now the days dragged, each blending into the next, an endless cycle of grey skies and damp air. Ren would disappear off to help Seth, and the three pirates went about their daily duties – with the seas now more turbulent, all able hands were required to help with sailing. Much to her disgust, that meant even Finn had to clamber up the rigging. Only Killian was left unoccupied.

He kept himself mainly below deck and out of the way. He certainly wasn't about to haul himself up the rigging and flap his arms about, not knowing what to do with himself.

In a moment of madness, he briefly considered learning something about sailing, but he rejected the thought almost as soon as it had formed in his head. He didn't need to know about sailing, rigging, ropes, starboard sides and sterns. Soon he'd be off this ship and gone for good.

For him, every day was the same. He'd sharpen his swords with a whetstone, polish the hilts until they dazzled him, roll the glyph about his knuckles and examine his wounds. Then he'd close the door, do push-ups and pull-ups until his shoulders could take no more and practise with his swords. It was difficult in such a confined area, but he learnt to bend his body to fit the room. He could have gone on deck, but there was always the possibility of running into *her*.

They'd not had a real conversation since he'd left her room; the grunts she'd huffed in his direction while on Ocean's Bounty certainly didn't count. He didn't want their friendship to end like this, but he didn't have the strength left to salvage it either.

When he was sure nobody was going to burst into the cabin, he'd take out Freya's bangle and roll it between his thumb and forefinger, and the unusual gemstones winked at him as it moved. It truly was a beautiful piece of jewellery and would no doubt fetch a good price. He slept a great deal, too, and had only once been jerked awake by a nightmare. Thankfully, that had happened in the daytime, so nobody had been about to see him trembling and terrified.

His mind often drifted to thoughts of his mother. Would she be proud of what he'd done? Was her sacrifice worth it? Could he have saved her if he'd not run? If he'd not opened the door, would she be alive now? The answers were always the same: no, no, yes and yes. Then he'd think about Clem lying in his arms, blood oozing everywhere as the light in his eyes went out. Nothing he'd done mattered – the Drop, the tasks, crawling out of the geyser. They were still dead, and it was still his fault. At times he couldn't believe how foolish he'd been; he'd honestly believed by helping Ren the hollow in his chest would close up. He knew now nothing would take that pain away. He could stuff it full to bursting with Ren's money, yet he'd still be empty. Nothing would lessen his guilt. He'd have to learn to live with it all over again.

He slumped in his hammock, dragged a blanket on top of him and closed his eyes.

It was late in the evening, and the weather had taken a turn for the worse, if that was possible. The ship was rocking more than it ever had before, groaning forlornly with every movement. Killian was thankful he was in a hammock and not in Lily's bed. He gazed at the ceiling; she'd probably be sleeping in the hammock now; choppy seas and flat beds didn't mix. It was just as well he'd left her room. He didn't fancy the idea of bunking up with her in such a small space.

The thought made his pulse quicken. He closed his eyes and could almost smell her over the odour of salt-encrusted wood. Her arm rubbed the back of his shoulder before coming down to rest on his chest. Her hair tickled his back. Her warm body pressed against him, and her lips brushed the nape of his neck. They curved into each other. His eyes flickered open, and he screwed his fists up, digging his nails into his palms to stop his body responding to his mind. Something had to be done about his errant thoughts. They weren't healthy, especially when everyone else was in the cabin.

Finn's loud snores droned in time with the ship's moaning. Elsewhere in the room, Tom was muttering away to

Ren, who was enthralled, while Blake lay on his side, reading a piece of paper and making the occasional adjustment to its contents.

The door swung open, and Raven breezed into the cabin, interrupting Tom's sordid tales. The warm glow of the oil lamp highlighted his rich skin, enhancing his painfully handsome features. Looking at Raven sometimes made Killian feel physically sick.

'We'll be at the island tomorrow morning,' he said, turning his entrancing eyes in Killian's direction. 'The captain has ordered you and Ren to accompany her to the temple. Once she knows how much treasure is in there, she'll send teams to retrieve it. Understandably, she doesn't want to risk too many crew members against those statues.'

'That's fine with me,' said Killian airily. He'd known it was coming; he'd be forced to spend time with her. After all, he was the only one who could get her precious treasure – which may or may not exist. He traced his finger over the glyph, feeling somewhat relieved it was one use only, but she didn't need to know that. He grinned slyly to himself and laced his fingers together behind his head. Part of him really hoped there was nothing in there except for Ren's thing. It wasn't lost on him that she'd only chosen to take him and Ren, the most dispensable people on her ship. It hurt a little.

'Me too?' Ren asked, his voice wavering.

'Captain's orders,' said Raven.

'But I'm ...'

'You'll be fine,' said Raven softly. 'The captain and Killian will be with you, so there's nothing to worry about.' Before Ren could protest further, Raven swept out of the room.

Killian frowned and bit the inside of his cheek. He couldn't work out whether Raven was being sarcastic or not.

He was another person who was difficult to read; he and Lily made a good pair.

'Killian,' said Ren. His voice sounded tentative.

'Yes?' Killian braced himself for Ren's inevitable pathetic whinging about going on the island.

'I don't think I've ever thanked you for . . . well, you know.'

Killian sat up. That was unexpected. 'No, you haven't, come to think of it.'

'Well, thank you . . . for everything.' His voice jerked with emotion as he spoke. 'I couldn't have asked for more. Sometimes I can't believe what you've done. Thank you.'

'You're welcome,' Killian replied politely. It was a strange sensation, to feel appreciated; he wasn't used to it. With nothing else to say, he lay back, put his arms around his head and pressed his toe against the wall to keep his hammock from swaying too much.

Ren dragged a blanket over his head and fell silent. Finn rolled over and, as a result, ceased her snoring. Blake yawned and put down his pen.

'How's it going?' Killian asked him. He rolled onto his side and propped his head up with his hand.

'Pretty good,' said Blake, smiling. 'Don't worry, I'll do you justice.'

'Just make sure you mention my chiselled features and godlike bravery,' said Killian with a smirk.

Blake grinned. 'Can I show you something?' he asked enthusiastically, his eyes brightening.

'Sure,' said Killian, intrigued by Blake's sudden excitement.

Blake hung upside down over his hammock and rummaged in his coat-pockets. He growled as his hair dangled in his eyes.

'Maybe you should cut it,' Tom murmured sleepily.

'Maybe you should shut it,' Blake replied. He pulled himself back up and sat down, his face red from the rush of blood to his head. 'Okay, Killian—'

Tom interrupted him with a dramatic hacking cough.

'And Tom,' said Blake through his teeth. 'Watch this.' He stuffed his pipe. 'Killian, you have to tell me honestly what you think.' He sounded a little nervous. 'If it doesn't look right, say and I'll change it.'

'All right,' said Killian, sitting up and forcing his sleepy eyes open a little wider.

Blake lit the pipe. He inhaled a deep puff of smoke and held it in his mouth, then slowly blew it out to form a sweet-smelling cloud. He moved his hand through the air, whirling his long fingers elegantly as if he were oil painting with the smoke. His eyes glowed with an eerie white light. The smoke vanished with a click of his fingers, and all that remained was a small ghostly image of Freya.

Blake stared at his image, and she walked through the air with long-legged strides. She stopped a few feet in front of Killian and twirled. As she moved, her ruby hair glistened like jewels and her red dress fanned open at the sides, revealing the tops of her thighs. She bowed her head, and her silvery horns twinkled. She wrapped her bangle-covered tail around her body and then flitted away, bounding through the air towards Tom, where she came to a halt. She danced sinuously and blew him a kiss before returning to Blake. He clicked his fingers again, and she disappeared in a puff of sparkling red smoke. The cabin was silent.

'So, what did you think?' Blake asked tentatively.

'I thought . . .' Killian stopped and ran his hand through his stubble. 'She's good. She's not exactly like her, but you're not gonna know what she looks like without seeing her. She's close enough.'

'Really?' said Blake.

'Really,' said Killian. 'You're a talented man.'

'She's got a cracking set of chebs on her,' Tom put in.

'You should have seen my first attempts. They were hideous,' replied Blake, blatantly ignoring Tom.

'Ah, is that why you kept sneaking off on your own?' asked Tom. 'I thought you were working on your rhythm.'

'No, Tom. My rhythm is just fine.'

'So I really was seeing little clouds of red smoke everywhere?'

'Yes, Tom.'

'Good, I'm not going insane then. I did start to wonder,' said Tom lethargically. He stretched his arms above his head and cracked his shoulders. 'Good work though, Blake. She's quite the stiffener.'

'Nice,' said Killian.

'All's I'm sayin' is she gets me horny,' said Tom. He glanced from Killian to Blake. 'Sharing a room can be such a pain in the arse at times.'

'You . . . I don't know.' Killian shook his head, smiling. 'You're like a walking, talking cock with a man glued to it.'

'Too bloody right,' said Tom. 'One hell of a mix.' He shuffled his body and smiled to himself. 'Oi, Killian, how come the cap'n kicked you out her cabin?'

'She didn't. I left,' Killian replied. He really didn't want to get into this.

'How come? Seemed like you had a pretty good deal going on there – decent bed, decent room, female company.'

'I don't know. She got really moody about something. Must have been something I did. I can't for the life of me think what.' Killian ran his fingers through his hair and scratched the back of his head. 'All I did was lie there.'

'Oh yeah?' Tom raised his eyebrows and winked. 'I reckon that would do it. I bet when she was with d'Roué he didn't just lie there.'

Killian remained silent; he'd left himself wide open for that one but was too tired to retort.

Blake returned his pipe to his coat. 'I'll work on the rest,' he said as he lay down. 'I'm just building up to it.'

'I can't wait to see me,' said Killian.

'You'll have your work cut out making that face look good,' said Tom. 'I don't envy you, Blakey boy.' He chuckled to himself devilishly.

'I don't know. All I do for everyone, and I still get abuse,' Killian muttered with an exaggerated sigh. 'How do you do it anyway?' he said, looking towards Blake.

'Do what?' he asked, sitting up again.

'You know, the smoke picture things,' said Killian. 'You're not a standard mage,' he added, rolling the glyph over his knuckles without breaking eye contact with Blake.

Blake grinned. 'No, I'm not a standard mage. It's a shame really. I reckon setting fire to certain people with a click of your fingers would come in handy.' He shot a friendly glance in Tom's direction. Tom puckered his lips in response. 'Or drown, suffocate, fry with lightning, drain the life from . . .'

'You love me,' said Tom, blowing a kiss in his shipmate's direction.

'Unconditionally,' said Blake, deadpan. He turned his attention back to Killian. 'When I lived at home, I was left to look after my little brother and sister almost every night while my parents went out to their swanky soirées to get steaming on imported wine and faun over the latest fashionably rich couple. I'd invent stories to keep them amused. We had a lot of books in our house, so I could always find an influence from somewhere.'

'Fnar, fnar, fnar,' said Tom in a low voice.

Blake opted to ignore the dig. 'I'd visualise the characters in my mind, and one day they just appeared from the smoke of the fire. I was pretty scared at first. It made me light-headed. To be honest, I threw up and passed out that first time. But with a bit of practice, I found I could control the images and keep myself from feeling dreadful. I read up on other people who could do it. They called themselves illusionists.' He shrugged. 'An elaborate name, but when it came down to it, they were a type of mage. I think a lot of illusionists like to think they're slightly . . .' He stuck out his bottom lip. 'Slightly above a standard elemental mage somehow.'

'Is that because you're all rich hoity-toity snobs?' Tom suggested, a playful glint in his half-open eyes.

'I think you're right there, Tom. Well, that and we pull our magic through from another world. Elementals channel their power from this one. Anyway, that's not important. I felt sick when I found that out,' he continued. 'I was a mage. I hadn't asked for it or even practised at it. It just sort of happened. A bullet through my head and my rotten corpse swinging in the breeze for the crows to peck at wasn't exactly how I wanted to go out. But I couldn't suppress the desire to call on the magic.

'My brother and sister loved it. It was a secret we kept between the three of us.' He paused, smiling softly to himself. Then his blissful expression swiftly dropped into one of distant turmoil.

'One day my parents came home early and caught me conjuring. I should have been more careful. It was bound to happen. They were steaming as usual. I still remember the stench of sweet wine on their breath as they beat me half to death with an iron hearth poker.' He stared at the floor. 'My brother and sister were begging them to stop. My sister, my silly sister . . . she tried to throw herself on me, to defend me. Daft girl was only seven. My father threw her aside like she was nothing and slapped her face. All the time he and my mother were screaming at me, telling me I was evil, my soul was dirty and tainted, all the usual crap.' He sighed and rolled his eyes. 'I'd brought shame into their respectable house, practising in the illegal arts was vile – in their eyes, it was worse than murder – I was no son of theirs, etcetera, etcetera.

'I was given a delightful choice: stay and wait for them to fetch the cleansers, or get out and run before they got there. So I ran, well, staggered really. I left town that night. I ended up living on the streets of Torran for a few years, though I spent that time productively, learning and teaching myself about the art and what I could do with it. I used it to distract shopkeepers and people in the street while I stole food and cut their purses. I found I could have quite a bit of fun with it.' His eyes sparkled mischievously. 'I was careful not to make any friends though. I couldn't trust anyone to not turn me over for a reward. Then one horrible night, I bumped into Tom.'

Tom snickered from his hammock. 'I remember that.' He sighed wistfully.

'Yeah.' Blake laughed. 'For some ridiculous reason, I'd decided to mope about the docks by myself at night. A stupid thing to do, but I had no home, no family, no friends, nothing to live for. I was on a low that night. I was deep in my own wonderfully miserable thoughts when that filthy pirate over there' – he motioned towards Tom, who was casually sprawled, swinging in time with the ship's movements – 'sidled up to me and demanded everything I owned, which was nothing. I backed away. He looked pretty menacing, leering at me with his knife in his hand. All I had was my pipe, so I pulled it out and conjured up some dancing smoky demons. I shocked him into a state of paralysis—'

'You couldn't do that now,' Tom said.

'Of course I couldn't,' said Blake with a grin. 'Nothing scares you, eh, Tom?'

'Shit yeah!'

'Anyway, after I dismissed the illusions and he could move again, we talked like civilised people. He persuaded me to meet Captain Rothbone and, well, here I am. Sorry, I didn't mean to get on to my life story. You didn't ask about that mess.'

'No, it was an interesting mess,' said Killian.

'Almost as interesting as my mess,' Tom butted in.

'In all honesty, nothing is as interesting as your mess, Tom,' said Blake.

Tom grinned to himself, looking like he'd won some kind of private competition.

'Sorry about your folks,' Killian continued.

'Pah, it's their loss,' said Blake with a nonchalant wave of his hand. 'Bastards probably did me a favour in a way,' he added as he pulled his blanket up.

Tom's drowsy voice drifted over. 'Oh, Killian. I think this is yours.'

He leant to Killian's hammock and dropped in his gun. Killian picked it up and held it tightly.

'I was beginning to wonder when you were gonna give it back,' he said, running his fingers over the familiar cold metal.

'I didn't even use it. I was tempted. A few birds flew over while you were gone, and I'd be lying if I said I didn't reach for it. But I didn't wanna waste it in case you came back. Besides, I already owe you at least a lot.'

'Thanks,' said Killian, examining his long-lost gun. He reached over his hammock and placed it in the one below.

Blake dangled an arm to the floor and turned out the oil lamp without looking, plunging the room into darkness.

CHAPTER
FORTY-ONE

K ILLIAN WOKE WITH THE RISING SUN, GRATEFUL for another night of peaceful sleep. It seemed as if the haunting nightmares had stopped; perhaps he was finally getting over his ordeal. Every night before he slept, he'd lie awake thinking about Nesta's words while tracing the smooth surface of the glyph with his fingers. This little routine helped him to relax and forced him to think rationally.

He wandered out of the cabin and up onto the deck. Glistening streaks of gold danced over the thin wispy clouds that gathered in the morning sky. For all the shimmering brightness beaming across the water, it was still bitterly cold on deck. He pulled his coat close to his body and wrapped his arms tight around his chest.

Everything is coming to an end, he thought, listlessly watching the golden wave crests. He didn't know whether to feel relieved or miserable. He couldn't wait to get off the ship, see Estelle, go to the Laughing Swan, thrash Barrington at the card table, drink ale for ale with Ruby. To sit around in his flat and relax, free of all restraints and responsibilities. Then he would leave town and go wherever he pleased; the world was his. Just the thought of it lifted some of the pressure from his tense shoulders.

He drew in a bracing salty breath. Soon he'd be away from Lily. He'd given up trying to understand her; the farther away from her he was the better. With distance and time, he was confident his confused feelings would eventually dissipate. He scrunched his fingers up, cracking his knuckles with a satisfying pop. However, he was going to miss his companions on the ship. Life on the *Tempest* had almost bored him to tears several times, but it was the crew that made it bearable. He'd miss Finn's gruff, cynical moans, taking the piss out of Tom and Ren, and Blake's dry wit, which somehow held them all together. Not Lily though – definitely not. His chest constricted painfully; well, perhaps he'd miss her a little.

He bit his lip, cursing his unnecessary masochism, and unravelled his arms from his body. He ambled below deck in search of some food.

He was finishing his breakfast of disgustingly bland porridge when he was sent for. Lily and Ren were already waiting for him by the time he got on deck; behind them, the island rose up out of the inky waters.

'You ready?' Lily asked him flatly, avoiding eye contact by staring out to sea and adjusting her belt.

'Yep,' he replied, mindful to keep his tone just as blunt.

'Let's go then,' she said.

Ren hung back, waiting for Killian as Lily marched towards the bulwark. 'Killian,' he whispered softly as they fell into step, 'I'm so scared.'

Killian moaned and looked at Ren. The fear in his big brown eyes was all too apparent. He could've easily ridiculed him, but what would that have achieved? A smirk from Killian and a yelp of fear from Ren, but he didn't much feel like smirking, and making Ren even more useless than he already was would do nothing to further their cause. He put his arm protectively around his shoulders and pulled him close. 'Do you remember what I said to you when we first set out?'

A thoughtful expression crossed Ren's otherwise troubled face. 'Th-that you'd get me out of this alive, that whatever happened, you'd make sure I survived.'

'Exactly.'

'You're at my side, so I've got nothing to worry about.'

'I gave you my word,' said Killian. 'I promised you I'd get you out of this. Do you think I'd go back on that?'

'No, you wouldn't,' said Ren. 'I know that now. I trust you.'

The choppy sea was doing its best to keep them away from the island. Killian begrudgingly rowed while Ren sat hunched up at the back of the boat and Lily did nothing. They were silent throughout the duration of the trip. With each pull of the oars, Killian wished for less and less treasure within the temple. His back was aching and his arms sweating. The pirate queen could have helped him. She could have easily rowed them by herself; he'd seen what she could do. She was clearly using her power over him one last time. *That's it, no treasure.* He hoped there was no treasure.

When it became too shallow to row anymore, they jumped into the cold surf. Killian grabbed the edge of the boat and gave Lily a pointed glare. To his surprise, she actually helped him – even Ren did too. They dragged it a little way up the beach, leaving it as close to the shore as possible should they need to make a quick getaway. Once more they began the journey up the rough track through the forest and towards the temple. The fresh scent of damp pine needles mixed with the sharp saline tang of the waves. The way was littered with uprooted trees and tattered dried-up vegetation. The statues had ploughed headlong through the forest and in their fierce pursuit had ruthlessly destroyed whatever had happened to be in their way. Giant pines, which had no doubt lived for centuries, had folded beneath their might. Mud-covered roots stuck up from the fallen trees like a tangle of desperately grasping fingers. Bedraggled ferns and yellowing mosses mixed together within heaps of moist disturbed ground. Occasionally Killian stepped down into the deep soggy ruts that had been created by the crushing feet of the statues, and thick mud oozed over his boots. As they walked, Lily outlined her plan of action.

'Right,' she said as she ducked under a thick splintered trunk lying diagonally across their path. 'The plan is to approach the temple from the north side, which will hopefully give us an advantage. There's no telling what those statues are gonna do. When the time comes, we need to stay focused, ignore them to the best of our ability, run for the temple and get inside for cover.'

'Oh, what a brilliant plan,' scoffed Killian, vaulting over the same trunk. 'It's taken you, what, three, four weeks to come up with that?' He puffed out his cheeks and wiped his brow. 'I'm glad we employed the services of such a master tactician.'

Lily shot him a steely sideways glance. 'Maybe I should have brought Raven along,' she muttered.

'Yep, maybe you should have,' said Killian breezily. He didn't want to sound affected by her obvious sniping.

'He'd be a lot more use than you,' Lily growled. She upped her pace and powered forwards. 'Quieter too. It's a good job those statues don't have ears or they'd be on top of us already.'

'Well, perhaps you should go back and get him,' said Killian, pushing forwards to match her pace.

'Yeah, perhaps I should.'

'Maybe you should.'

'Maybe I should.'

'You should,' Killian hissed through gritted teeth.

'I should.'

'Well, why don't you go then?'

'I would, but that would be wasting time, wouldn't it?' she said acerbically.

'Because moaning about me has been a very effective use of time, hasn't it?'

'Look, I'm in charge, and if I want to stand around here all day explaining your unsuitability for this mission, then I can. So shut up and keep moving.'

'Why even bring me then? You're so fucking difficult!' He groaned, slapping himself across the forehead in exasperation.

She stopped walking abruptly and spun to face him. 'Better to be fucking difficult than a waste of space,' she growled, her eyes narrowed into fierce slits.

'Oh! It's finally out!' he shouted, a triumphant tone to his voice. 'So I'm a waste of space, am I?'

'That's not all,' Lily snarled aggressively.

'Please continue,' said Killian, holding his arms out wide, a gesture that implied he was ready for her barrage of abuse.

'I don't think we have that long before nightfall.'

'For crying out loud!' Ren yelled. Killian jumped at the sudden outburst from Ren, of all people. 'Will you two please grow up and stop behaving like a couple of spoilt children for just a few minutes? W-we have a dangerous mission ahead of us. We n-need to stay together, focused. I don't know how you both feel, but I want to get off this island as soon as possible, and when I do, I'd like to be alive.'

Killian looked at Lily and then at Ren.

'Are we done?' Ren asked in a quiet, controlled tone.

'Yes,' they said simultaneously in low voices.

'Good,' said Ren. 'Let's go.'

They continued along the pathway in silence. Every now and then Killian would exchange a scathing glance with Lily, but he managed to press on without saying another word to her. Instead of taking the steps, they battled their way through the partially decimated woodland to come up on the other side of the temple. It was hard going, and Ren's feet constantly slipped, but Killian was always on hand to keep him from falling.

Keeping low, they crawled up the soft earth. Killian dug his fingers into the mud as he hauled himself up. By the time he reached the thick bushes surrounding the temple, he was covered in sweat. Lily and Ren crouched down amongst the foliage while he lay flat, propping his chin up with his hand. The pirate queen pushed the bushes apart to give them a view of their goal. The hideous statues stood ominously still.

'At least they're asleep,' Killian whispered.

'Asleep?' Lily jeered, rolling her eyes at him. 'And what would giant stone statues be doing sleeping?'

'Well, they're not moving.'

'Yes, they're not moving. Well done.'

'So they could be asleep.' He knew his argument was ludicrous, but he refused to give in to her.

'They are *not* asleep,' said Lily firmly through gritted teeth.

'Oh, not again.' Ren sighed, anxiously tugging at his scarf.

'Shut up, Ren!'

'Yeah, shut up, Thorncliffe!'

'Just you remember who brought you here,' said Lily.

'And who risked their life just so we could get in this place,' Killian added.

'He's paying you for it, though, isn't he?'

'Yeah, yeah, but that's not the point.'

'What is the point?' she asked.

'I could have died.'

'Fair enough,' Lily agreed.

Ren's pale skin flushed beetroot red.

'Hang on,' said Killian, holding up a finger. 'Why the hell is he here anyway?'

'What do you mean?' asked Lily over Ren's head.

'Well, no offence, Thorncliffe.' Killian gave him a comradely clap on the back as he spoke. 'But what possible use is he? I'd have brought Rangi the bilge cat before I brought him.'

'Hey, watch it. Rangi's good. She really comes through if you're in a tight spot,' Lily retorted.

'Which brings me to ask again, what's he doing here?'

'The whole expedition began because of him, so I thought it only fitting he play his part here, at its end.'

'That part being pummelled to death by giant living statues, I presume?' Killian stuck out his bottom lip and shrugged. 'I guess I can't argue with your logic there.'

'Thank you, I feel really useful now,' mumbled Ren sadly.

'I thought I told you not to take offence,' said Killian.

'You're right though.' Ren's shoulders drooped like they were bearing an immense invisible weight. 'I'm so useless.'

'I know, but don't you worry. If you get in trouble, Lil will save you by coincidence. She's good at that.'

Lily shot Killian a petrifying glare.

'Right,' said Killian, realising they'd probably exhausted the subject. 'The plan . . .' He purposefully left the sentence hanging.

She spoke with cool clarity. 'They're quiet now, but I don't know how long that will last. I suggest we get going and get in the temple before they know we're here.'

'That'll have to do,' said Killian mordantly.

'Do you have a better idea?' she asked. Her tone indicated that she already knew the answer.

'No, no, your idea's fine.'

'By the way, do you know how that thing works?' she said, jabbing her finger at the shimmering glyph around his neck.

'Of course I do,' he lied as he twirled the strange pendant through his fingers.

'How then?' she asked, arching an eyebrow.

'Well, I suppose we'll walk up to the temple, and I'll get us through the wall – I think. Maybe you two should hold on to me or something,' he said. His vague outline didn't seem to inspire much confidence within the party. Ren looked close to tears, and Lily looked as if she wanted to do nothing more than blacken his eyes. Killian flinched at her expression. To cover up his involuntary movement, he ran his fingers along the leather strap of his goggles.

'You think?' she snapped incredulously, her furious eyes boiling over. 'You didn't ask them how to use it?'

'I forgot,' he said defensively. 'I had a lot of stuff on my mind.'

'It was the sole reason you went down there!'

'We all make mistakes. Anyway, it doesn't matter because I've got a fantastic idea. You'll like this, Lil. It's almost as good as one of your plans. Why don't we sail back to the Drop, and you can go down and ask them how it works?'

Lily glared at him.

'We don't have time to do that,' Ren murmured hopelessly.

'Of course we don't, you cretin!' Lily seethed. 'He was trying to be sarcastic, but he can't even do that right.'

'Look, let's just go. We're wasting our time sitting here,' said Killian shortly. He got to his feet and dusted himself down. He held his hand out to help Lily up, but she ignored it. Ren, however, was grateful for the assistance.

Killian marched from their hiding place, exuding a meticulously crafted cocksure mettle. The wind moaned ominously as it wended through the statues' stony limbs, kissing the top of the temple before racing off over the rest of the island.

Despite the aura he gave off, Killian was anxious to get to the temple. His heart was hammering so hard against his breastbone he was surprised the glyph wasn't jumping in time. He knew Lily was right, not that he'd ever admit that to her; he should have asked Nesta how it worked, but back then he'd been so glad to be alive that nothing else seemed to matter. They soon reached the walls of the ancient building. The silence in the air was unbearably tense.

'Right,' said Killian softly, 'give me your hands.'

The words had barely left his lips when the sickening crumbling sound of the statues disturbed the quiet. Three of them were moving towards them in the same jerky motion as before, dust and debris tumbling from their limbs. Killian held out his hands urgently. Ren took one, Lily the other.

'Killian, if this doesn't work . . .' She didn't need to finish the sentence.

'You worry too much,' he replied, giving her a confident wink for good measure despite having no idea what he was doing.

He took a short sharp breath and walked forwards. He hit the magical seal with a jolt that reverberated through his body. Opening his eyes, he could see it now: a golden shield wrapped around the temple a few feet from the walls. Snaking tendrils reached out and coiled around the brickwork, anchoring it in place. Their intrusion sent ripples shooting through it, and the tendrils gripped fiercely to the building. The glyph glowed with iridescent light. It pressed so tightly to Killian's chest that it looked like it had fused with his skin. It flashed like a star, momentarily dazzling him, and then they passed into the solid rock. All light and sound were extinguished as they were cast into total darkness. Within a heartbeat, they stepped out into the inner chamber and were bathed in an eerie green light.

Lily couldn't let go of his hand quick enough, as if it pained her to simply touch him. Ren let go too, and Killian staggered backwards. He slumped heavily against the wall, his pulse racing and his body aching with fatigue. Grey clouds tried to clog up his vision, and for one horrible moment he thought he might faint. He blinked his sight back and tried to make a fist to test his strength, but he was too feeble to even do that. Complete exhaustion wrapped itself around his breathless body. What had happened to him?

'Are you all right?' asked Ren.

'Yeah, I'm fine,' he lied, pressing his palms into the wall to keep himself steady. A couple minutes of rest and he'd be all right, or so he managed to convince himself.

The temple's interior reeked of centuries-old mould steeped in a healthy layer of even older dust. The air was thick with damp and seemed to almost coagulate in the throat. The walls and floor were both made of the same smooth dark rock. Killian rubbed his eyes. Everything – even Ren's blond hair – looked dark in the soft green glow. A raised platform in the centre of the room housed the source of the light, but there was something smothering it.

'That's got to be it!' said Ren enthusiastically. He walked towards the muffled green light. 'Killian!' he called over his shoulder. 'You should get your stick out.'

'I beg your pardon?' said Killian. He straightened up, the strength returning to his body.

Lily stifled a snigger.

'The one you had the other week, you know, the one that glows.'

'Shit! I forgot it. Bollocks, it would have been useful.'

'Silly,' said Ren as he proceeded towards the light.

'Watch it,' said Killian. He stepped away from the wall and rolled his shoulders, twisting his upper body until it clicked. He let out a soft grunt. *That's better.*

REN edged towards the square raised platform. His courage came and left him like the changing tides. He bunched his fists up. He had to be brave; he had to be like Killian. All he had to do was reach the light and take the Gramarye. It wasn't life-threatening, and it certainly wasn't scary. His heart thumped. It was heavy, like a rock in his chest. The heat drained from his skin, and his body grew stiff. It was scary, and it could be life-threatening. He drew a hissing breath through his clenched teeth and forced his feet to shuffle forwards.

A collection of blankets obscured the glowing green light. They hung from the ceiling and formed a protective shroud around the precious artefact. Ren took another tentative step closer and put his hand out. A blanket brushed against his skin; it was coarse and made him itch. He steadied himself, took a deep breath and pushed it aside.

Something hard swung out and struck him on the shoulder. He wasn't alone. His breath burst from his lips in juddering gasps. It took everything he had to turn and face his assailant. His skin prickled, and he froze. Staring down at him was a robed skeleton hanging by its twisted neck. It was grinning at him, sniggering at him, mocking him. Its blank eye sockets glared with a never-ending darkness. He stumbled over his own feet, tripped on the edge the platform before him and tumbled past the cloaked skeleton. He landed on his hip with a heavy crunch. Dazed, he looked up, and his scream lodged in his throat.

All around him were skeletons. So many skeletons. They sneered at him. They roared with laughter. They hissed and they cursed. They dangled from the ceiling by their bent and broken necks. Their old bones soaked up the green light around them. A ripple of movement coursed through them, and their shadows danced over Ren's body. He put his hands up in defence and shut his eyes tight. He desperately wanted to call for help, but words had deserted him. He was alone and trapped with the ghastly dead. They were going to consume him, make him one of them and pull him into their world, rip out his soul and crush his heart.

Doomed, he was doomed, but they were dead. The sound of the swishing bodies stilled, and he slowly opened his eyes.

The skeletons scowled at him, but they were dead. Only the living could hurt him; his father had told him that countless times. Summoning all of his nerve, he pressed his hands into the icy stone floor and pushed himself up. He stared at a skeleton and locked his gaze with its dead one. It couldn't hurt him. Slowly, he turned back to the platform and his artefact.

Shining in front of him was the prize he'd been seeking: the Gramarye. He was momentarily lost in its beauty. It was a shimmering emerald pyramid. Its four sides gracefully curved, giving it the appearance of a green flame. It was about a foot tall, and strange twisted black lines outlined its base. The green light shifted within the artefact in waves, making it seem as if it had a motion of its own. Slender snakes of silver, gold and sapphire drifted within the green, and the whole thing throbbed rhythmically with a deep suffocated teal light, as if somewhere within the Gramarye its buried heart was beating.

He went down on one knee and leant over the precious artefact, his fingers shaking and his chest thumping. This was the thing that would save his father, he was right next to it, but he didn't quite believe it. He glanced over his shoulder and shuddered as he looked at the fifteen hanging bodies smiling down at him. They were urging him to take it. It was his; it belonged to him now. He put his hands on either side of it. It was cold and smooth as glass. At his touch, the snakes of shimmering coloured light retreated towards the teal heart. He picked it up carefully, holding it as if it were made out of gossamer. He rose to his feet, took a step back and moved away from the macabre circle.

AS soon as Ren emerged, the room was illuminated with an intense emerald light. Killian did a swift sweep of the building, and it was as he'd hoped and also slightly feared: no treasure, nothing. The temple was devoid of anything except for the three of them, the fifteen dusty skeletons and the glowing object in Ren's hands.

'Now, Lil,' he began as a look of hideous fury spread across her face.

'Don't you dare *Lil* me!' she roared, taking a swipe at him.

Killian neatly dodged out of the way. 'It's not what you think,' he pleaded, drawing his hands close to his body for defence. He'd witnessed first-hand what she'd done to a statue, and he didn't want to find out what would happen to him if she punched him that hard.

'How can *this* not be what I think?' Lily growled, flinging her arms back. 'Don't think you can trick me again, O'Shea. In fact, don't even dare to think!'

'Look, I'm sorry,' he said weakly, pathetically trying to appeal to her sensitive side.

'Sorry does not cover it!' she raged. 'This is an empty bloody room!' She ploughed on before he had time to cobble together a defence. 'Do you think *I'm* furious? Do you? Well just imagine how my crew will react when we go back with nothing but a mouldy green triangle!'

'It's not my fault there's no treasure.' He took a few more steps away from her. 'They must have gone on one last bender before they topped themselves,' he added, nodding towards the skeletons.

'You pathetic little maggot. Give me one good reason not to string you up with them over there, rip off that little charm of yours and leave you in here to rot!'

'One good reason . . . okay.' Killian folded his arms and pressed his thumb into his lips. 'If not for me, we wouldn't even be in here.' He winced. That was an abysmal defence.

'What kind of a reason is that?' she seethed. 'What exactly do I gain by being here? Absolutely nothing! You're a useless, lying, cheating scumbag. You're dirt.' Her lips curled into an ugly sneer as she spoke. 'In fact, you're lower than dirt. You're the dirt beneath the dirt the other dirt is ashamed to be seen with.'

'Oh, shut it, you miserable dick,' he said. 'Get out of my career.'

'Your career.' She laughed callously, taking a step closer to him. 'You call lounging around, lying, cheating and stealing a career?'

'And how is that different from yours?' he said. 'You lie, cheat and steal, and you supplement that with a bit of murder. You're a bloody pirate!'

'At least I'm good at it. What have you got to show for it? Oh, a little room above a shop. What have I got? Let's see.' She held out her hand and started counting on her fingers, taking a step towards him with each point she made. 'A faithful crew, my own ship, a castle, my own island, hoards of treasure. I have the freedom to go anywhere I choose anytime I want, and I didn't get it from traipsing around the world after cocky layabouts, searching for wobbly triangles!'

'You are such a bitch.' Killian sighed. He wasn't even going to attempt to match her fury.

'What did you say?' she spat, her eyes icy.

'You know what I said. I'm standing right in front of you,' he retorted. 'If you have all of that, why would you need anything else? Surely you have enough already, you materialistic, selfish bitch.'

'I am *not* a bitch!' she snapped back.

'Oh, I think . . . no, I know you are,' said Killian coldly, calmly looking her square in the face.

Snarling with rage, she grabbed him by the shoulders and pushed him hard against a wall. She buried her fist in his stomach, knocking all his breath from his body. He coughed and spluttered as she pinned him against the cold stones.

'Get your clawing hands off me,' he wheezed.

'Make me,' she snarled.

Killian glared at her. There was no use in fighting back; it would only end badly for him.

'Giving up, are we?' she said with a cruel smile. 'Now, what to do with you?'

'You are,' he said flatly.

'Excuse me?'

'You are a bitch.' He took a deep breath and kept his eyes locked with hers. 'You're materialistic, you think only of yourself and your own gain.' He winced as she dug her fingers into his shoulders. 'You're selfish, you're cruel, your mood changes like the weather. You're vindictive, malicious, you probably even bleed venom. You're one of the worst people I've ever met.' His voice was calm and controlled.

'Fuck you!' She pulled him back and slammed him roughly against the wall.

He drew his breath through his teeth. 'No, fuck you! If you weren't, then I wouldn't have had to trick you.'

'What do you mean?' she asked, her grip loosening slightly.

'I knew you wouldn't help Thorncliffe unless there was something in it for you. I had to appeal to your obsessive greed,' he said. 'So I lied about the treasure.'

Lily let go and took a step back. She looked wounded and lost. 'Is that what you really think of me?' Her voice wavered as she asked.

'Truth hurts.'

'Shut up!' She curled her fists, and he tensed, but the blow he expected didn't come.

'Sorry to state the obvious, but you're a pirate, Lil,' said Killian, rubbing his shoulder where she'd crushed him; he could already feel the bruising. 'It goes with the territory.'

'You could have just asked me,' she whispered sadly. 'You didn't have to lie.'

'You would have said no. You're a pirate, a notorious, nasty pirate.'

'You obviously don't know me very well then,' she said.

'Even if you had said yes, what would your crew think of trekking all over the place to help some guy's dad who they'd never met?'

'They do as I tell them,' she said firmly.

'It doesn't look good though, does it?' Killian peeled himself from the wall.

'You're right, it wouldn't look good,' she said, sitting down against the wall.

'It wasn't a total lie, anyway. I didn't know what was in here, and there could have been treasure,' he added, trying to lighten the mood.

He glanced at Lily. Pools of green light coalesced on her skin and clothes. She looked sad and smaller than before. It was his fault. Guilt prickled through him.

'I'm not all that bad, you know,' she said morosely, her eyes cast to the floor. 'Once you get to know me.' She drew her legs to her chest and slumped against them.

'Look, Lil, I'm sorry,' he said as he slid down to join her on the floor.

'You were only being honest for once,' she murmured without looking at him.

'No, I . . .' He shuffled his feet uncomfortably as he spoke. 'I may have elaborated slightly. I'm sure you don't bleed venom.'

'No,' she said, a distant hint of laughter in her voice. 'Not last time, anyway, but that was a while ago.'

'I'm sorry,' he said sincerely. 'I am, really. I just . . .' He idly played with the glyph. 'I don't know.'

'I'm sorry too, and you're not *that* useless. You did get us in here.'

'I did, didn't I?'

'Don't let it go to your head.'

'I reckon I'm the only person in the world with the skills to do it. You should feel privileged to be in here.'

Lily tutted and edged a little closer to him. Her shoulder pressed against his. She was warm. Just looking at her made his body ache. The bright green radiance of the Gramarye complemented her features, making her overwhelmingly beautiful. Her eyes shimmered like actual gemstones as they hungrily absorbed the glow. He stoically fought with his desire to touch her.

'What will you tell the crew?' he asked.

'The truth,' she said. 'This place was empty, the job was a bust. I'm not lying to my crew.' She turned her face towards his. 'Some of them might want your head on a stick, but you'll find a way to cope with that.'

'I will.' Killian frowned. He'd find a way, but would

Ren? He watched the young man anxiously pacing the chamber, the pulsing green artefact in his hands. He hadn't attempted to defuse their argument this time, which had probably been for the best.

'I'm sure Raven will defend you, so you've nothing to worry about. He seems to have grown quite attached for some reason,' she said.

'Is that jealousy in your tone, Lil?' said Killian playfully.

'Raven will save us both. I'm fine with that,' Ren said. 'Can we leave now?'

'All right, all right,' said Killian, getting to his feet, 'I just thought you might like to soak up the ambience of this charming building a little more.' He held his hand out and pulled Lily up. 'You got a plan of action?' he asked.

She raised her eyebrows but refused to take the intended bait. 'You get us out of here, and we run. Can't rely on me to protect us all.'

'That's good enough for me.' It was only then he realised he was still holding her hand, or was she holding his? He wanted to let go almost as much as he wanted to hold on. 'Come on, Thorny!' he shouted across the temple to Ren. 'What're you lingering for? I thought you wanted to go.'

'Sorry, yes,' said Ren as he scooted over to them. He put the Gramarye under his arm and took Killian's offered hand.

Killian sucked a deep breath through his teeth and walked forwards. First was the suffocating darkness of the temple walls, and then he pulled them into the golden barrier. The glyph sparkled with a myriad of colours, and he wished it weren't one use only; walking through walls could be quite handy. A shattering crack whipped through his head, and the shimmering barrier dissipated before them.

Then they were outside, and he was breathless once again. He let go of Lily and Ren to fall back against the temple wall. Sweat soaked his body, his heart was pounding, and blood rushed through his veins. He felt drained. Every muscle in his body throbbed with a dull pain. He desperately wanted to close his eyes, to fall to the ground, to rest.

'Killian.' Lily's voice fought its way to his teetering consciousness, and a rough shake snapped him to attention.

'Sorry,' he muttered.

'Are you . . . ?' Ren began tentatively, the glow of the Gramarye turning his left cheek green.

'I'm okay.' Killian looked down to see the glyph crumble into a fine silvery powder. A gentle breeze picked it up and carried it away. 'There it goes.'

'Never mind that,' said Lily grimly. 'We have more pressing matters at hand.'

They were surrounded by the statues; all that lay behind them was the impenetrable wall of the temple.

Killian winced. 'Ah. This isn't very good.'

'Killian,' Ren whimpered. 'They're going to kill me . . .'

All fifteen of them were intently focused on Ren. They were going to kill him. They were going to pound him into the ground until all that remained was a red smear. Lily was right; she couldn't save them, not from all fifteen. She'd be knocked back, and then he, Ren and the Gramarye would be crushed from existence.

Killian looked from the statues to Ren and realised they weren't looking at him; they were watching the Gramarye. A stupidly reckless plan formed in his head, but a promise was a promise. He'd given Ren his word. He'd get him out of this alive, and that was exactly what he intended to do.

'Give it to me,' he demanded, and a rush of adrenaline shot through his chest.

'Wh-what?' Ren stammered.

In answer, he snatched the Gramarye from Ren's slippery grip.

He ran straight ahead, the green artefact pulsing in his hands. It was oddly light for its size and startlingly cold to the touch. He glanced at the statues to see their expressions twist into a look of horror. Even the faceless ones seemed terrified of his advance, stumbling over one another as they tried to retreat. He slowed to a halt and held the artefact aloft. All at once, they screamed in unison, a horrendous cacophony that resounded around the clearing. They swiped at Killian, but they were slow, pained movements, which he easily avoided. They hissed, and one by one they crumbled into piles of rubble.

'Come on!' Lily shouted over the din. 'Now's our chance!'

Killian stood in the centre of the temple grounds, surrounded on all sides by the howling disintegrating statues. They clumsily swung at him, but their limbs were crumbling as swiftly as they moved them. He ducked and weaved out of the way, staying light on his feet. The air around him soon became thick with dust, irritating his eyes. He paused, flicked his hair from his face and pulled his goggles down. A giant fist hurtled in his direction; he hopped back, putting one hand on the ground to roll out of its way. He sprang to his feet and kept low.

The rocky monsters shrieked with despair, thrashing with frustration as they tried to get near him. The throbbing green light in his hands cut through the whirling clouds of grit, making it easier for him to locate Lily and Ren. He dashed over to them, a little unsure of his next move. Ren's head was down, and his hand was in front of his face.

'Finished playing hero yet?' Lily asked.

'Nah, I thought I'd bask in it a little longer.' Killian smirked.

Lily sneered. 'Let's go!' She ran, Ren following hard on her heels.

The statues continued to wail as they fell apart, some clawing at their own deformed faces, others still making vain lunges in Killian's direction. He tightened his grip on the Gramarye and chased after Lily and Ren. A quick glance over his shoulder showed the piles of rubble were degrading to dust and blowing away in the wind. There was a loud crunch as a statue fell to its knees and tore off its own screeching head. With a last flailing of limbs, it threw its great stone head in their direction. Killian darted forwards and pushed Ren out of the way just in time, gripping his arm tightly so he wouldn't fall.

'Thanks,' Ren panted, wobbling with shock.

'No problem. Keep going.' Killian gave him an encouraging nudge and released him.

Killian slowed his pace, whirling around to present the Gramarye to the tortured rocks. He grinned to himself, revelling in the power he wielded. It felt so good. He laughed maniacally as he was swept up in clouds of gravel and waves of green light. He felt amazing.

Everything fell silent. The screaming ceased, the explosive collision of rocky limbs stopped, and even the rumble of collapsing stone was absent. A deathly quiet settled over the hilltop as the air stilled. Killian pushed his goggles back onto his head and glanced around. All the statues were gone. The larger chunks of rubble were rapidly turning into dust before his eyes, their powdery remains drifting away on the wind. It was like they'd never existed.

A sharp pain lanced through his hand. He'd cut himself on the edge of the Gramarye, and a thin stream of blood flowed out. The wound stung from the grit and dirt already embedded in it. He swore and wiped it on his trouser leg.

'Wh-where's Killian?' Ren's shaking voice broke the silence from beyond the trees.

'I thought he was with you!' Lily's voice snapped back.

She sounded worried about him. Just hearing her speak in that tone sent heat through his body. He drew a deep breath, rolled his shoulders back and swaggered through the treeline. Lily and Ren were both crouched on the ground, seemingly unaware of his presence.

'That was unexpected,' Killian said to announce himself.

Lily started, which was incredibly satisfying for him to see. He nonchalantly sauntered into the undergrowth and placed the glowing green artefact in front of Ren, then casually leant against a tree, sucking at the heel of his right hand.

Lily got to her feet and stormed towards him. Her expression rippled with fury. 'You idiot!' she fumed. 'How dare you be so reckless. Putting yourself in danger like that.'

'What?' He took his bleeding hand from his mouth. He was confused; did she care about him or did she hate him?

She folded her arms aggressively across her chest, but her eyes turned glassy, all her fury extinguished. 'You could have been killed,' she said softly.

That answered the conundrum; she cared. He felt smug, powerful and a little in control for once. 'But I wasn't.'

All that power was instantly knocked away with a single face-stinging slap.

CHAPTER
FORTY-TWO

THE FIRST OF THE EVENING STARS SHONE through a deep turquoise sky and twinkled with silver light. Killian leant against the bulwark and watched the crimson sun sink into the depths of an indigo sea. It looked like a jewel being swallowed up by thick, murky oils. Waves broke against the hull of the ship with low mysterious murmurs. The air was fresh, crisp and cool. He pulled his coat closer to his body, shuddering at the chill.

'Gah!' grumbled Finn from behind him. 'So all that was for nothin'. The job was a total waste of time.'

'Not completely,' Killian replied. He turned around, casually spreading his arms along the rail. The deck was bathed in the glow of the sunstones, which highlighted the faces of his companions with subtle shades of pink and peach. 'Thorncliffe got something out of it.'

Killian watched Ren fidget and stare at the deck, his fear almost tangible. He jammed his fingernail between the planks to avoid facing Finn's stormy grey eyes. He really was a coward, but then again, Finn was pretty scary, so he couldn't blame him. A terrified pair of brown eyes looked towards him as if pleading for help. He could help, but that would be too easy, and Ren would learn nothing. Also, it wouldn't be as fun as making him sweat.

Ren winced as he pulled his hand back from the deck. A bubble of blood burst on this thumb.

'Aye, he did, didn't he?' She grunted and blew two great plumes of smoke from her nostrils. 'I've half a mind to take that thing from him and sell it myself.'

'Finn,' Ren croaked, 'I'm ... I'm sorry about the temple.'

'I bet you are,' she replied, 'especially now. So very sorry.'

'I-I really am. I thought that—'

As cruel as it was, teasing Ren still hadn't got old, though now there was an added risk to factor in. Would he be able to keep his mouth shut, or at the very least lie convincingly? Or would he spill out the ugly truth, revealing that the whole thing had been a lie all along? Well, sort of a lie. Killian wasn't sure. And if the truth got out, what would happen? It was possible the gunners would turn on them; they had been deceived, after all, and they were pirates at heart.

'Thought what?' said Finn.

'That ... I ...'

'Me too. I'm sorry,' Killian interjected; it wasn't worth the risk. 'It's pretty shit. You guys got dragged all over the place, and you've nothing to show for it.'

'Ah, it ain't your fault, mate!' said Finn. 'We just got some bad info is all. You didn't know there was nothin' in there.' She glanced at Ren. 'And neither did you. Ain't your fault.'

'Yeah, you must be gutted,' said Tom to Killian. 'All that stuff you did. I mean, we got the Gramaroo—'

'Gramarye,' Blake corrected him. He was sitting a little way from the group, his eyes freakishly white as he twirled and clicked his fingers through a cloud of smoke.

'Gram . . . whatever,' Tom responded with an insouciant shrug. 'Anyway, we got that, which is good, isn't it, Ren?' He poked Ren in the thigh with his toe. Ren managed a feeble smile. 'But it's not like you've got much out of this, Killian. I mean, I'm annoyed about the non-treasure, as is everyone, but you must be fuming. You got yourself well and truly messed up for nothing.'

'Well, yeah, of course I'm a bit disappointed,' Killian replied. There'd been a time when he'd considered telling them about his promised reward, but that conversation was definitely off the table now. 'But I don't know. Thorny got what he wanted, so maybe it's okay.'

'It's okay! A bit disappointed!' exclaimed Tom. 'If I were you, I'd be tempted to gut Ren!'

Ren shuddered and grasped at his heart; tears swam in his eyes.

Tom exploded into laughter. 'I'm only joking, Ren!' he gasped between chortles. 'You should see your face!'

Ren went back to studying the deck. Finn lit another cigarette while Tom continued to chuckle and Blake filled the air with sweet smoke and intangible pictures. The *Tempest* creaked and strained as the sails flapped in the breeze. Killian stooped a little. He'd be glad to get back on solid land. He was finished with ships and their lurching movements. He drew in a lungful of bracing sea air. It was delicious and invigorating. He'd miss that. The smell and taste of the open waves was different to the scents that wafted through coastal towns. His body grew tense. Soon he would be leaving that smell behind too. He had to move on, didn't he?

'So what are you going to do once this is all over, Ren?' A silky voice interrupted Killian's musings.

Raven was squat down next to Ren. Killian felt a gentle spike of annoyance. The strange enigmatic man must have detected Ren's discomfort and flown to his rescue. Was there anything he couldn't do? After all this time, Killian still hadn't figured him out. The mysterious demonic man had been sitting with them all evening, his bizarre eyes glowing more as the light faded. He hadn't said much; he'd exchanged a few nostalgic words with Finn and rolled dice with Tom when nobody else would, but otherwise he'd remained quiet.

'I-I think I might train to be a chef,' said Ren, a hitch in his voice.

'Well, I'm never eating again,' said Tom, lifting his head from the cannon.

'Who do you think has been cooking up your stews these past few weeks?' asked Ren.

'Seth.'

'And I.'

'I wondered why I'd been feeling like shit.' Tom smirked.

Ren's face drooped with despair.

'I'm only joshing you, Ren,' said Tom, reaching down to punch him lightly on the shoulder. 'Go, follow your dream.'

'Giving up the bookkeeping?' Killian said to Ren. 'Your honest job with your honest pay.'

A faint smile graced Ren's face. 'It's not as interesting. I don't want to spend my time looking at other people's accounts. I'm sure my father will know someone who can give me the correct training. I could move to Torran, cook in the fancy restaurants.' He sounded enthusiastic, almost passionate, as if he had a dream and was going to chase it.

'Whatever turns you on,' said Killian, rocking his head back.

'Killian,' Raven said, 'what will you do?'

'Be Ren's assistant!' Tom sniggered.

Even Finn laughed at this. 'Chief carrot chopper,' she added.

Killian looked to the group and frowned. 'Who knows,' he said with a blasé shrug. 'When we started I thought I'd want to go back to Bracky, but I don't know.' He cast his gaze towards the fluttering sails. 'My old life seems pretty dull now. You know, just hanging around, swindling card players, drinking. I fancy a change, maybe move on somewhere new.' He rubbed his stubble pensively; it was a strange thing for him to talk about. 'I don't know.'

'Why don't you join us?' Blake asked, his dazzling white eyes cutting through the blanket of smoke surrounding him.

'Yeah, be a pirate,' Tom agreed, pushing himself up. 'You're halfway there already.'

'Him! One of us!' Finn sneered. 'Pah!'

'Thanks, but no. I think I've overstayed my welcome as it is. Anyway, I said I wanted a change. You guys just sit on an island doing nothing.'

'I have a feeling the captain will want to keep on the move now,' said Raven.

'What do you mean?' Killian said.

'I've noticed a change in her. She seems much more focused. I think we might see a return of the old captain – ambitious and fearless.' Raven's tone was sombre. It almost sounded like he was delivering a warning. 'I wouldn't be surprised if she decided to take to the seas again.'

'Well, good for her, as long as she's happy,' said Killian with an unperturbed wave of his hand.

'You *can* come with us,' Raven suggested. There was a subtly veiled look in his eyes, like he was trying to tell Killian something, something important.

'No, no,' said Killian, shaking his head. 'Thanks all the same. I'll sort myself out.' He pushed himself off the rail and stretched with an exaggerated yawn. 'Right, that's me for the night.'

'It's well early,' Tom protested.

'Nothing wrong with an early night,' said Killian.

As he left, he caught Raven's glowing gaze again. He'd definitely been trying to say something, but it was as if he didn't know how to, or even if he should. Curiosity almost got the better of Killian, and he opened his mouth to ask what was wrong, but the only word that came out was, 'Night.' He swore at himself under his breath as he stalked back to his cabin, confused, frustrated and alone.

CHAPTER
FORTY-THREE

ALL KILLIAN WANTED TO DO WHEN HE SAW Brackmouth looming on the horizon was go home, have a hot bath and sleep undisturbed in his own bed for as long as he chose, but Ren had other ideas. Even though he didn't dare say it, his desperation to return to Charrington was obvious, and Killian didn't quite have it in him to deny him. His bath could wait, as could his sleep. He was surprised when Lily insisted on making the journey with them. She claimed it was for their own protection, should they come across any bandits with a penchant for mysterious magical artefacts. Ren wholeheartedly agreed with her; two bodyguards were better than one, after all.

It was a cold, dry day, and the sun was high, a pale disc of white that spitefully refused to provide any warmth. The three of them kept close as they made their way along the windswept coastal path that linked Brackmouth with

Charrington. The initial steep incline set Killian's pulse racing. A stairway had been crudely hewn from the rock face; most of the steps had been worn smooth in the middle from years of trudging boots, while others had crumbled into non-existence. As it levelled off, he crossed a small wooden bridge that sighed under his weight with a chorus of creaks. A bubbling stream ran beneath it, swollen with rainwater. To his right, craggy cliff faces tumbled down hundreds of feet to the sea below, where they were relentlessly battered by the tides. Rolling green hills lay to the left, covered with wild, untamed vegetation.

Ren was happier than Killian had ever seen him. There was a bounce in his step and a permanent grin plastered to his face. He scampered along the stones with all the youthful vigour of a spring lamb. 'You know, when I first came along here all those months ago,' he said, darting from one rock to the next, 'I found this path really hard going. I was out of breath most of the way. But look at me now.'

'It must be all that work you were doing on the ship,' said Lily.

'As if!' Killian chuckled. 'He's been slacking off with Seth most of the time.'

'You can't talk about slacking,' said Ren.

'Oi!' said Killian. He abruptly stopped and pushed his flapping hair from his eyes. 'I'd like to point out that I jumped down the Demon's Drop, completed three excruciating tasks, outran a jet of searing hot steam and waltzed with those bloody statues. I have been anything but a slacker. One day you guys will learn to appreciate me and my powers.'

'Your powers!' Lily exclaimed, sniggering. 'Now that *is* a good joke.'

The three of them started walking again. Ren's good spirits were infectious, and before long they'd spread within the group. Soon all three of them were laughing and joking with one another. The wind dropped, and at last the sunshine felt warm on Killian's back. He slid his coat off and hung it from his arm. Lily pulled a length of black material from her pocket and tied her hair back. She was wearing a simple pair of grey trousers, a rough-spun shirt and a black woollen coat, none of which did anything to show off her feminine curves. Today she wasn't Captain Lily Rothbone, the feared pirate queen; she was just Lily, an ordinary woman blending in. Killian glanced at her. Since the incident in the temple, their relationship had been a lot less strained. It was still confusing, but the sniping was less frequent, and he felt more at ease in her company. Maybe he really would miss her.

Snowdrops clustered together in the thick grasses, nodding their heads appreciatively in the breeze. Twiggy branches were shooting to life with tiny leaves. Seagulls chattered amongst themselves as they circled around the cliffs. Ren placed a hand on the bag containing the Gramarye, its green light radiating through the material. Killian watched him bound ahead and found himself envious of his simple dreams. Why couldn't he be content to settle down and become something like a chef? Or better yet, fall into the arms of an uncomplicated woman who loved him back? He always seemed to make his own life difficult.

Helping Ren had been a good distraction, yet now that it was all drawing to a close, he was facing who he really was. His life would have been infinitely easier these past few months if he'd left Ren dying on the cobbles that night. If he'd done that, though, he wouldn't be who he was now.

The pain of his past was still with him, but it didn't seem to haunt him at every turn. He knew now that nothing he did could ever make up for it or bring them back, but maybe he was at last learning to live with it. Perhaps what had happened to them wasn't his fault. He would never know.

'Can I say something?' asked Ren, interrupting his musings.

'Please don't,' said Killian with a playful smile.

'Go ahead,' said Lily.

'Well, I . . .' He paused, and his brow furrowed. 'I suppose I just want to thank you both. Killian, I know that you risked your life to help me,' he said. Killian raised his eyebrows. 'Several times,' Ren hastily added. 'For that, I don't think even our savings will be enough, but it's all we have – that and my thanks. Captain, you could have turned me away, but you didn't, and you've shown me parts of the world I didn't even know existed. I can only apologise about the contents of the temple, but that—' Killian shot him a fierce glare, and he abruptly stopped talking to clear his throat. 'You've given my father his life back, and you've saved mine. Thank you both so much. I wish we didn't have to say goodbye.'

'Ah, Thorny, you don't have to. I only live down the track, and she never leaves that island of hers,' said Killian.

'But the other night you said you might move on.'

Lily gave Killian a quizzical glance.

'The operative word in that sentence being *might*,' Killian swiftly replied.

'But you seemed so—'

'Might,' Killian said. For some reason he couldn't quite fathom, he didn't want Lily knowing about his plans for the future.

'I have the feeling Seth is gonna miss you,' said Lily.

'I'll miss him too. Please give him my thanks once more. He's taught me so much about food and flavour. The man is impossibly talented.' He swallowed hard before speaking again. 'Th-thank you both so much.' His voice wavered, and his eyes shone with tears.

'Please don't cry. You'll ruin that image you have as a big tough man,' Killian warned.

Lily laughed and turned round to grab Ren in a tight friendly hug. Ren's eyebrows shot up and his mouth dropped open. Killian offered him a shrug. The pirate queen seemed to be showing an emotion that wasn't anger or hatred. Was there something wrong with her?

'That was from Seth,' she said as she let him go. 'If you tell anyone it was from me, I'll gut you.'

Ren nodded and smiled, and they started walking again. 'So, Captain, what do you plan on doing next?'

'The crew and I will head out somewhere,' said Lily thoughtfully. 'Going away opened my eyes. We shouldn't be living on land all the time. We need to get out there, rule the waves again, discover new places. Places with treasure,' she added, giving Killian her best evil glare.

'Killian, you really should join the captain's crew,' said Ren.

Killian looked at Lily and grinned as she grimaced.

It was late in the afternoon when they descended into Charrington. Like Brackmouth, it was a seafront town, though slightly larger and much richer. The houses were constructed with rocks that had been smoothly plastered over and painted white, a fashionable look borrowed from the dramatic country of Freischen. Thick black wooden beams appeared to offer support to the uniform houses, but more likely than not they were only there for aesthetics.

There were no scrappy fishing huts blemishing the picturesque streets; even the harbour seemed to glow as if it were freshly washed and painted each day. The paths and roads were lined with dark cobbles specifically chosen to complement the houses and flanked by expensive iron-and-glass street lamps. The majority of the townsfolk were elegantly dressed; there were no drunken smoking loiterers here. Men bustled about in neat fitted suits while women flowed along the paths in graceful dresses complemented by dainty pointless hats and perfectly applied make-up. Killian shuffled uncomfortably, wishing he'd had that bath now.

'Thorny,' he whispered sharply, 'I knew Chazza was posh, but I don't remember it being this posh.'

'It's not called . . .' Ren let out a resigned sigh. 'It's not posh.'

'I suppose it was always dark when I used to come here,' Killian continued as though Ren hadn't spoken. He turned to Lily and grinned. 'Bring back any memories?'

'Only ones I'd rather forget,' she replied bluntly.

Ren shrugged and carried on walking. He led them down a few narrow twisting streets until they were near the centre of town. The square had a church at one end and was vaguely reminiscent of Brackmouth's, though it was noticeably more loved, looking like it was purpose-built and not a tragic composite of degrading buildings. Killian was willing to bet their seer didn't spend his days marinating himself in kegs of ale. A talented fiddle player in a black suit and hat entertained a group of pipe-smoking men while an exotic woman in a flowing red dress danced to his beat, occasionally thrusting her ring-covered hand out to collect payment from the gathering audience.

'Such a rich little town,' Lily murmured to Killian.

'A bit more up-market than Bracky,' he agreed.

'It makes me wonder how much cash the residents have lying around.'

He nodded and kept walking; she was getting at something. The sophisticated ladies of the town lounged on the benches in the square and clustered in huddled groups around the church.

Lily's voice was low so only Killian could hear. 'It also makes me wonder how much a dying man would offer to pay some charlatan to save his life.'

'I don't discuss my business deals with others,' he muttered back. 'It isn't professional.'

'Well, you'll discuss it with me, O'Shea. I am, in essence, your partner.'

Killian gritted his teeth and clenched his fists; he could feel his fortune slipping away. He kept his eye on Ren's blond head as it bobbed and weaved amongst the pockets of people around them.

'Look,' he said, 'I'm getting *some* cash.'

'You're getting a lot, aren't you?'

'I wasn't given an exact figure, but the term *life savings* was used.'

'I'm having half,' she said brusquely.

'Wh-what?'

'You heard me. I'm having half. It's the least you can do.'

'But . . . I nearly died,' said Killian. His defence sounded feeble even to him.

'And I provided you with transportation, food, drink and lodgings. It'll be payment for my hospitality, with some

left over to treat my crew. You're lucky I'm not taking it all.'
She flashed him a grin. 'I think I'm being quite reasonable,
don't you?'

It pained him – he was so close to getting it all – but he
couldn't deny she was right. 'Yes, you are,' he replied with a
beleaguered sigh.

'It's a deal then.' She discreetly offered him her hand.

'Deal,' he agreed, begrudgingly shaking on it. He
wouldn't breathe a word about the pocket watch though.
No, that was his secret.

They turned off the main square. Neither of them spoke
a word as Ren led them through more narrow streets, tall
white houses all around them, each one blending into the
next. He eventually stopped outside one. It was a terraced
building, whitewashed and with blackened beams like the
rest of Charrington. Its windows were framed with dark expensive mahogany, the only thing that made it appear mark-
edly different from the other houses.

'Why do you have to live on the other side of town,
Thorncliffe?' Killian asked with a roll of his eyes.

Ren dipped his hand in his coat for his key. After fumbling in every available pocket for some minutes, he called
off his search and looked from Lily to Killian.

'I think I've lost my key,' he mumbled, lowering his head
in embarrassment.

'I don't know,' said Killian, stepping forwards and slapping him on the shoulder. 'You're useless.'

Ren smiled feebly as Killian crouched down and se-
duced the lock. Within seconds it popped, and the door
creaked open.

'Ta-da!' Killian stood up and took a bow. 'Where would
you be without me?'

'My neighbour checks on my father. I could have asked for her key,' said Ren.

'Want me to lock it again?'

'Oh, no, I wasn't . . . I didn't mean it to sound sarcastic. I didn't, really.'

Killian grinned slyly to himself. He was going to miss making Ren feel uncomfortable.

'I meant to say thank you, Killian,' said Ren hurriedly. 'And welcome to my home,' he added humbly.

The three of them entered the hallway. It was long and narrow, with polished floorboards that matched the window frames. To the left of the hall ran a staircase with white-painted banisters.

'Father!' Ren called out.

'Who is it?' answered a frail croaking voice.

'It's Ren. I'm back!' he cried. 'Come on,' he squeaked excitely to Lily and Killian.

'Renwick,' the voice called back. There was a hint of hope in the grating tone.

'Renwick?' said Killian with a smirk.

Ren ignored him and launched onto the staircase. 'Come on!'

They followed Ren as he bounded up the creaking wooden stairs two at a time. He flung open the first door he came to and charged in.

'Father,' he gasped with joy as he came to a halt by his bed. 'You're alive. I was worried I'd been gone too long.'

'Worry not,' the man in the bed rasped.

With great effort, Ren's father sat up. He was an old man, but his sickness made him look even older. Cavern-ous wrinkles were etched into his face, and his sharp cheek-bones protruded beneath his skin as if they were about to tear their way out at any moment. His arms were like withered stalks, trembling with the effort of moving. Deep purple veins were visible through his sickly skin. His flesh had wasted away, leaving him a mere shadow of loose skin and jutting bones.

Killian locked eyes with the old man and forced out a smile.

'Don't loiter there in the doorway,' he wheezed. 'Come in.'

They shuffled into the room. Killian felt uncomfortable with the situation. This was Ren's moment; it wasn't right being here. It was personal, between Ren and his father. A charlatan and a pirate had no business cluttering up the family reunion.

The room was dark and stuffy; the curtains seemed like they were permanently drawn. Everything was covered with a layer of dust. The atmosphere was damp, fusty and dingy, and it smelt of sickness. Killian took shallow breaths so as not to inhale too much of the filthy air.

'Father,' said Ren softly. 'These are my friends. They've helped me more than I can say. This is Killian.' He indicated towards him.

'Hello,' said Killian, taking a few steps forwards to shake the offered hand. The skin was cold, and the twiggy fingers barely applied any pressure. It was like shaking hands with a frostbitten scarecrow. Looking down at the poor wasted old man who meant so much to Ren, it was impossible not to feel a gut-wrenching stab of pity.

'And this is Captain Rothbone,' said Ren.

Lily bent down and took the old man's hand.

'Killian, Captain, this is my father, Colm.'

'I see you keep very beautiful company,' said Colm as he laid his hand on top of Lily's.

'Thank you.' Lily placed her other hand on top of his. 'I was happy to help your son with his quest.'

'You wouldn't be the infamous Captain Lily Rothbone, would you?' Colm asked.

'I would,' replied Lily, smiling softly.

'Ah, who would have thought my son would go gallivanting around with pirates?' Colm laughed. 'Famous pirates too. It really is an honour to meet you, miss.'

'And you too, Colm.' She gave his hand a squeeze and let go.

'So, you're Killian O'Shea,' said Colm, turning his attention back to Killian.

'Yes,' said Killian warily. He leant back on one leg and rested his hands on his belt to try to appear casual, but all he wanted to do was get his money and leave. Then have a bath, some food, then sleep – so much sleep.

'It is an honour to meet you too. I had my doubts whether my son would be able to persuade you to help.'

'Why me?' Killian asked, intrigued. Maybe the bath could wait a little. 'How did you know?'

'Some things are written in the stars, my boy,' said Colm mysteriously.

Killian was about to question him further when Colm had a sudden and violent coughing fit. He pulled his bedcovers up to his mouth, much to Killian's relief. He didn't want anything from the old man to spray on him, if it could be helped.

'Sorry,' Colm whispered. 'I . . .'

'Father,' said Ren, sitting next to him on the bed and taking his shaking hands in his. 'I think it's time.'

With that, Ren pulled the precious artefact from his bag. Its powerful green light flickered around the room and danced in Colm's rheumy eyes. The teal heart throbbed to a steady beat as the shimmering colours floated through the emerald surface of the Gramarye.

'I'm sorry, but I have no idea what to do with it or how it works,' Ren confessed. 'It has all these strange markings on it, but I don't understand them at all.'

'Not to worry, Renwick,' said Colm, his voice quick and urgent. 'Just set it down on my lap and stand back.'

Ren did as he was told. Killian gave him a gentle pat on the shoulder, hoping it would offer a shred of comfort. Who knew if this would work? Would he still get paid if it didn't? Was he a bad person for thinking that?

Colm placed his hands on the sides of the Gramarye, and a smile spread across his face. It pulsed with energy, the heart beating faster, the gold, silver and sapphire flashing through the emerald green. Even the black symbols moved. As he drew his hands apart, it hovered, spinning rapidly between them. He shut his eyes tight, and his face became neutral, as if he was momentarily lost in deep concentration. When he opened his eyes again, they glowed with an unsettling oceanic blue and focused on the Gramarye.

Killian took a few steps backwards and instinctively grabbed Ren and Lily protectively by their arms.

'Something's not right,' Ren said frantically.

Colm lifted his head and glared at the three of them, his eyes gleaming and his mouth twisting into an approximation of a grin. His body slumped down like a rag doll, and a dark human shape soared from his broken frame, the Gramarye hovering in front. It lowered its head, covering where its face should be with its hands. In one swift sharp motion, it moved them to reveal what looked like a white porcelain mask. It twisted to form grotesque approximations of human expression.

'Father!' Ren cried in anguish and rushed forwards.

'No!' Killian lunged after him and grabbed him firmly about the chest. 'Stay back!'

'Your father's dead,' the dark form rasped. 'He's been dead for . . . such a long time.'

'H-how?' Ren stammered.

The mist didn't answer. It seemed it was an effort for it to talk.

'Why? Speak to me,' Ren demanded, struggling ferociously against Killian's grip.

'I do not need to . . . explain myself to anyone.' Its voice grated in its wispy throat.

'Yes, you do!' screamed Ren. 'You killed my father! You killed him.'

Before Killian could register what was happening, Ren had grabbed his gun from its holster and slipped out of his grip. With his face contorted in fury, Ren charged towards the floating apparition, brandishing the gun with both hands.

Fear splashed across the mask, the eyeholes widened, and the mouth dropped open. The dark shape behind it extended a hand, and Ren froze in his tracks, the gun clattering harmlessly to the floor. It moved its hand upwards, and with only the slightest flick of its wrist, Ren floated up into the air. He squirmed and wriggled against an invisible force, but all his efforts were in vain.

'Why did you have to attack me?' it said softly. 'I may have let you live. I hadn't decided. But it seems you have.' It shook its head slowly. 'Always so quick to destroy . . . that which is not understood.' Its voice was sad and tinged with regret. 'I fear your companions suffer the same traits.'

A blue mist seeped out of the Gramarye and towards Ren's helpless palsied body. The black shadow silently watched his desperate struggles, the white mask twisting into a distortion of sadness.

The mist wrapped around Ren's body. He twisted and turned as it enveloped him. Screaming in agony, he managed to rotate around to face Killian and Lily. He let out a piercing cry of pain and thrashed violently. His arms and legs twitched as his body slipped into painful convulsions. Blood ran down his chin, and the whites of his eyes turned red. The mist darkened, and his futile struggles ceased. His arms hung limp at his sides. He looked down at Killian with tears streaking down his face.

'Killian,' he whispered, 'help me, please...'

With that, his eyes closed, and his body fell lifeless to the floor.

'Ren,' Killian uttered in disbelief.

'Your turn,' the shape said calmly to Killian.

It raised its hand and threw him against a wall with another flick of the wrist, pounding all the breath from his lungs. Lily rushed to help, but she was thrown against the opposite wall and pinned to it by an invisible bond.

'Don't worry,' it said as she thrashed about, 'you'll get your turn.'

The dark shape glided smoothly towards Killian, stopping to hover above him.

Killian looked up, still dazed from the force of the blow. He tried to move, but his body was too heavy. He slumped against the wall, accepting his fate. Once again, the blue mist seeped out of the Gramarye, hungrily weaving its way towards him. As it got closer, his body prickled with pain; he shut his mouth and bit the inside of his lip to keep from crying out. He wasn't going to let this murderer have the satisfaction of hearing him scream.

He closed his eyes and focused; he had to get his mind away from here. Neon green and blue danced before his eyelids. Lily wrapped her arms around his waist and laid her head against his chest. He could smell her. Her hair tickled his skin, and he gripped her tight. She traced her fingers up and down his back. Suddenly, Ren was screaming again, begging for help, for *his* help, blood running down his chin in thick crimson tributaries.

Killian's eyes snapped open. Was that a dead body on the floor? Lily . . . he couldn't even see her. Was she dead? The pain rushed in, threatening to overwhelm him. It felt as if his very essence were being ripped out of his body through every pore. Rusted metal tore through his flesh, slicing and infecting. Glass shards grew beneath his skin, shredding and tearing their way out. Fire ignited on his back, scorching him to the bone. His eyes melted within their sockets, and his vision dimmed. The mist encircled him, trapping him in an inescapable torturous cloud of suffering.

'You must understand – I cannot let you live now,' the dark form said, its tone hauntingly guttural.

'That's a . . . shame,' Killian hissed, spitting out a lump of blood.

It nodded. 'It is.'

He dug his nails into the wooden floor as he prepared himself for his last moments. For a second, the mist hugged him, grew a darker shade of blue and then backed away. The ghostly figure narrowed its eyes, focusing on the Gramarye.

The mist moved in again, reaching for Killian with its deadly embrace. A bright light dazzled him. *I must be dying. Everything does go light after all.* But nothing happened. Squinting, he looked down and saw the light was emitting from his own body. A bizarre shimmering iridescence glowed on his chest, and it appeared to be diminishing the Gramarye's power. He tried to move his arms to touch it, but they refused to obey him.

'What . . . is this?' said the shadow, perplexed.

It tried again, but Killian's light glowed even brighter, forcing the blue mist to retreat into the artefact.

'Never mind.' It stretched out a ghostly arm and flexed its clawed fingers, but nothing happened.

'Having a little . . . problem?' said Killian faintly. Then darkness flooded his vision, and he was gone.

'Killian!' Lily's sharp urgent tone battled its way through the gloom. 'Killian!'

He tried to speak, but no words would come. Everything was dark. Everything was heavy.

'Killian!'

Someone grabbed his body and shook him roughly.

He took a deep gasping breath, and his eyes flashed open.

'Am I alive?' he whispered, his voice unsteady. 'Am I alive?' he asked again, clamping his hands onto her forearms.

'Yes,' she said, 'but we've got to get out of—'

'Ren!' said Killian urgently. He staggered to his feet and lunged towards Ren's body, which lay prone in the middle of the room.

'Ren, Ren!' he called desperately, falling to his knees next to the body. 'Wake up, wake up!'

He grabbed Ren's wrist and felt for a pulse. For over a minute he kept two fingers pressed firmly on his wrist, waiting hopefully for the slightest flicker of a heartbeat.

'Get up,' he said through gritted teeth.

There was nothing – no heartbeat, no breath. He was as silent and lifeless as the room. Even the blood had ceased to flow from his mouth. The dawning realisation his friend was dead settled heavily on Killian's shoulders, and he slumped forwards. It was too much. He looked at Lily, tears rolling down his cheeks.

'Nothing,' he choked out, his fingers still vainly pressed on the wrist. 'There's nothing. He's dead.'

'Killian, I'm so sorry,' she said, her eyes filling with tears. 'It's not your fault.'

'We have to go,' she said.

'It's mine.'

'We can't be found here.'

'He's dead. I should have—'

'Killian, we need to leave now.'

'I promised him he wouldn't die, that I'd look after him . . .'

'There was nothing you could do,' said Lily quietly.

'I'm sorry,' Killian whispered to Ren's lifeless body as he held his hand. 'I'm so sorry. This shouldn't have happened.'

'Come on. He's gone.'

'I know,' he said, letting go of Ren's hand and laying it at his side.

He pushed himself up, but his strength had left him. He tried to move, and his legs gave way. Lily dashed forwards and caught him. She put her hands under his arms and held him firmly against her chest. He felt so weak that he could barely stand, even with Lily as support.

'It'll be easier if I carry you.'

Killian nodded.

Lily scooped him up in her arms like he weighed nothing and carried him down the stairs. He glanced at her face, but her gaze was fixed ahead. He was so pathetic; she couldn't even look at him.

'Killian,' she said gently, putting him down and helping him lean against the wall. 'Wait here. There's something I need to do.'

Killian nodded and leant his head back against the wall as she raced upstairs. His whole body ached; everything was heavy. It felt like an effort to keep his limbs attached. The floorboards creaked above him as Lily's footsteps traversed the room. Killian's heavy eyes closed. The metronome of an old grandfather clock drifted down the hallway, the tick of the second hand sounding strangely aggressive, growing louder and more pronounced with each passing moment. He shuddered at the noise; it was as if the clock knew what had happened. It was angry with him. He couldn't blame it. Ren had died horribly, and it was his fault.

'Come on,' said Lily as she came down the stairs. 'We're done here.'

'There's blood on your hands.' He tried to move and stand up straight, but he couldn't. 'What'd you do?'

'I made it look like he did it to himself, so when his neigh—'

'Don't say it,' Killian murmured. An agonising pain coursed through his chest; he knew what she'd done. The thought of it was too horrific to bear.

'We're going,' she said, keeping her voice low.

Killian allowed her to prise him from the wall. She wrapped her arm around his waist and leant his body on her shoulder, helping him to walk. She stopped at the front door, put her ear to the wood and listened for voices.

'I won't be able to carry you out there,' she said. 'It'll look too strange. People will notice us.'

'I get it.'

'I can help you walk.' She opened the door and pulled Killian out into the street with her.

He leant on her for support, and they tried to put as much distance between Ren's house and themselves as possible, but every street looked the same. White walls, tall houses, black beams – it was like a maze. Killian's footsteps were heavy and weary. He was slowing them down.

He was so useless. He'd let his friend die. He couldn't walk properly. Even staying conscious was an effort. Lily should've cut her losses and dumped him in the street before he messed up again. He was a hindrance, a waste, a disaster. He was cursed, so cursed. His promises meant nothing. They were empty and hollow, just like him. Did she say something? He wasn't sure. She should've left him.

'Do you know which way to go?' she asked, her firm tone cutting through his thoughts.

'I don't. I ...'

'Killian, I need you. Snap out of it!'

She needed him? She was only saying that. Nobody needed him.

'Killian, which way?'

'I need ... a second.' He slipped his hand under his coat, gripped a sword hilt and closed his eyes. The familiar cold metal pressed into his warm skin. He pictured the windswept hills, the streets of Charrington and its people, the church, the dancer and the fine suits. Ren screamed, blood poured down his face, his eyes flooded with red. The jagged silver light ripped through Killian's mind, and then it was gone. An icy dread drenched his body, and his pulse quickened. He tried again. This time, however, the silver path lingered for a heartbeat before melting away into the blackness of his mind. He released the sword and grabbed Lily for support. 'I can't.'

'I'll work it out,' she said.

They walked down and around narrow cobbled streets flanked with terraces. Gulls congregated on the rooftops to jeer and screech at them. They knew what had happened; they knew about Ren. Lily kept them moving until they came back to the main square. People were rushing around everywhere, doing last-minute shopping, going home from work, lounging, smoking and watching. Killian spied a small dark alley in his peripheral vision; he motioned to Lily, and they headed for it. Once they were out of sight, he pulled his arm from around her shoulders and leant against the cold stone wall. It smelt of damp and dust, and it reminded him of the temple.

'Give me a few minutes,' he said. 'We can't keep going about like that. It'll attract attention.'

Lily nodded and leant against the opposite wall.

Killian took deep breaths and stared at his hands as if he could stop them from shaking by glaring at them. He used the sleeve of his shirt to wipe away the persistent tears.

'All right?' she asked.

'Fine,' he replied, looking towards her.

She tore her eyes away from him and glared at the cobbles. She was disgusted by him, and he couldn't blame her. She'd seen the extent of his weakness, had witnessed him let his friend die. Once again, he'd managed to not only ruin a life but end one too. Three out of three was pretty good going. Ren was dead, and it was all his fault. His mouth tasted of blood. His blood? Ren's blood? The blood of everyone he'd let down? He didn't know.

He glanced at Lily. She was still looking down. He wished she'd just get it over with; he wanted her to scream and shout at him, tell him how useless and worthless he was. It needed to be said, just so it was out there in the open.

Everything was his fault. That was all she had to say. Once the words were finally out, there was no taking them back.

His mind was a mess. He ran a finger over one of his sword hilts, but there was no comfort to be had there. They were cold and lifeless. Even they'd abandoned him. Even they knew he was worthless. He pushed his coat aside and looked at the hilts. They were tarnished, just like him. Nesta had made a mistake; she'd made such a huge mistake. He was a disaster, a living, breathing disaster.

These thoughts weren't helping. Lily was still with him. The least he could do was pull himself together for her. He turned his focus to his hands and commanded them to stop shaking. Eventually, he got them under control. His tears stopped, but his eyes were raw.

'We should go,' he said robotically, 'while I've got it together.'

They walked out of the alley and crossed the square, keeping their heads down so as not to make eye contact with the locals. Killian glanced out the corner of his eye and saw some of the townspeople peering at them with curious expressions on their faces. His skin tingled and tightened, burning heat broke out in his chest, and his heart lurched. They couldn't know what had happened; it wasn't possible. He looked to the faces again, and they skimmed past him, unbothered, unaware. They didn't know.

Lily led them over the square without too much hassle. All they had to do was keep heading in the same direction. She kept them on the main street. It would take longer, but it was far less confusing than using the side streets. Even though Killian wanted to go down the side streets, he felt like he and Lily both had big signs floating above them that read 'murderers.' Luckily, with the square being so busy, the main road was fairly quiet. Killian's gaze darted around to make sure no one was looking at them. At one point he caught his reflection in a window, and for the briefest of seconds he saw his doppelganger: white skin, black veins, glowing eyes. He shuddered.

The longer they were in the town, the more paranoid Killian became. Every shadow, every movement he saw sent an icy spear punching through his heart. He felt wretched, nauseous and depressed. Everything he'd done, everything he'd been through, had achieved nothing but the death of his friend. Ren, Clem, his own mother – he'd killed them. How long would it be before someone else died because of him? His foot caught on an uneven cobble, and he stumbled forwards. He quickly regained his balance and dropped his concentration to the road.

It wasn't long before the road came to an end and all that lay in front of them was the steep incline of the coastal path. A scattering of gulls drifted on the winds, calling mournfully to one another as they navigated the hillsides.

When they'd put enough distance between themselves and Charrington, Lily veered off the path and up the grassy hill. Killian followed. He was emotionally and physically drained. Whatever had happened between his body and the Gramarye had almost sucked the life from him, so climbing the hill was taxing. He was trembling again, but he kept it hidden from Lily. He had to focus his attention on walking, but his rapidly failing limbs weren't helping him, nor was his constant shaking. Every few steps he stopped for breath and tried to calm his shuddering body without success. Progress was slow, his movements heavy and laboured. He reached his hand up to touch the glyph, to try to draw some kind of fake energy from it, but it wasn't there. Of course it wasn't there; he'd watched it crumble and drift away on the breeze. His lungs burned, and his back ached. If only it were so simple for him to fall apart and blow away with the wind too.

When at last he pulled himself onto the crest, he found Lily sitting with her knees to her chest, staring out to sea. The view from the top was amazing. To the left, Charrington nestled snugly into its quiet rocky bay, while the right revealed parts of Brackmouth poking out from behind the hills, a few houses here and there illuminated with the soft glow of lamps. Everything was bathed in the pink light of the setting sun. A chilling breeze blew in from the sea, forcing Killian to pull his coat tight to his body. Lily glanced at him but said nothing. He slumped down next to her.

They sat in silence, looking out to sea, watching the beautiful sunset colouring the waves with purples, pinks and oranges. Lily released her long ebony hair from its restrictive ponytail and let it cascade about her shoulders. She pushed it out of her eyes and put her hands on either side of her body, palms flat on the ground.

The longer Killian sat, the less he shook. Deep breaths helped him get his body under control. He put his hands to his sides and allowed his weight to sink into them. Tears flooded his raw eyes again, and they streaked down his cheeks. He brought his hands to his face and quickly wiped them away with his coat sleeves, but they were relentless. The more he tried to stop them, the more they defied him. He turned his face so she wouldn't see.

'What now?' he asked, his unsteady voice betraying his emotions.

'Killian,' said Lily sympathetically.

'Don't say it.'

'It wasn't your fault.'

'It was,' he whispered, his voice so low he was barely audible. 'I promised him I'd look after him. I promised him he'd get out alive, and what did I do? I watched him die. I just stood there. I did nothing, and I watched him die.'

'It would have killed you too.'

'But it didn't, it couldn't,' he protested. 'I know something happened. Something stopped it, something saved me. If I'd tried to help Ren, whatever it was that saved me would have done something, and he'd still be alive.'

'You don't know that.'

'I do,' he muttered sadly.

'No, you don't,' she insisted, 'and you certainly didn't know anything at the time.'

Killian didn't respond.

'Look, I could easily be sitting up here by myself,' she continued, passionate anger in her voice, 'but I'm not, and you might not believe it, but I'm glad about it. I stood by and watched it happen too. I watched Ren die, and then I had to watch while you were tortured in front of me, and there was nothing I could do to help, nothing. I wanted to save you, I wanted to defend you, I wanted to stop your pain, but I couldn't.'

Killian kept his head down. There was nothing he could say to that. Something sinister loomed around them. Somehow, they'd unleashed something upon the world, and they'd have to set it right; nothing else mattered. Ren's murder felt like the start of something else, something much bigger than any of them. That mask – he would never forget that mask. Or the screams, the blood, the pain. He looked towards Lily. She was staring out to sea, running her fingers along the outside of her boots, pausing to flip one of their many buckles.

She finally spoke. 'There must be something special about you.'

'What d'you mean?'

'Well, something protected you, so you must be worth saving.'

The wind picked up, buffeting their coats and tangling their hair.

Killian welcomed the cold air whipping at his warm, damp face. It brought with it a strange clarity and numbness. Everything in his world slowly faded to grey and slid away, leaving only one question. 'So,' he said eventually, 'what're we gonna do now?'

'We head back to the island and try to work out what just happened. Then we do something about it . . . together. It looks like we're gonna be partners for a little while longer.'

'And here I was thinking life couldn't get any worse,' he said with a desultory smirk.

They sat on the hill and watched the sunset fade away, the multitude of colours giving in to the inevitable night one by one.

'Come on,' he said, standing up. 'We'd better go.'

He held his hand out and pulled Lily up.

They walked across the hill and back onto the coastal path towards Brackmouth, the cold evening wind forcing them shoulder to shoulder. The light was fading fast, and before long, the darkness of the oncoming night enveloped them.

LEARN MORE ABOUT THE AUTHOR

WWW.JODELANCEY.COM

ACKNOWLEDGEMENTS

Writing a book is often a solitary and lonely pursuit, but ironing it out and making it shimmer requires more than one person. So, without further ado, I'd like to thank the following:

Lesley Jones and Natalia Leigh, my wonderful editors. You've both taught me so much about storytelling and style and helped me to kick *The Crystal Shore* into shipshape. I couldn't have done this without you.

Thea Magerand, my amazing cover and character artist. You pulled all my visions out of my head and made them real. I still get emotional looking at your art.

Luke Harrison, for using your magical skills to recreate the cornelian glyphs.

Greg Rupel, for putting all the pages of this beast together and making it shine.

I want to give a special shout-out to:

Josie Sexton, Tess Serrano, Liam Sellars, Michela Bottin, and Hana Oni. The character commission pieces I've had from you guys decorate my writing cave. They help me to keep writing and working to improve myself.

Colin Vearncombe, also known as Black. I know tragically you can't read this, but I want it here in print: *Wonderful Life* changed my life.

I would also like to thank the below swashbuckling heroes, for helping me get through all this:

Meg Rouncefield, you've been my cheerleader for so long and believed in me when I didn't. I don't think you know how many times your texts have scraped me off the floor.

Luke 'double shout-out' Harrison, for spending quality time with Killian and Lily, and for being a burst of positivity when I'm being a Negatron. Lounge eggs are on me.

Rachel Willoughby, for sailing the seas on the *Tempest* with Lily and her crew, long before they became manageable. Now you must pick: Killian or Raven?

Lauren Spencer, for your encouragement, wise words and just being you. You're the Tracey to my Garrett.

Bibi Omar Zajtai, Daz Cook and Tom Cooper, for reading my rickety first draft many years ago. I hope you all enjoy the sparkly new version.

Ivanka Ezhova, for helping me to see who I really am, and changing my outlook on life.

Mum, Dad and Justine, for being there when it matters the most.

The Instagram writing and bookish community. You guys are awesome.

And thank you so much to my partner, Dave May. You've always been there for me and never let me give up on my dreams. Without you, Killian would still be a mere scribble in the back of a notepad somewhere.

I love all you guys.

Finally, I'd like to thank you so much for reading. Taking someone else on Killian's journey with Lily and her crew means the absolute world to me. I hope to see you on the next adventure.

JO DE-LANCEY

is a fantasy author from the UK. Even though she currently lives in a landlocked county, her Cornish blood always calls her back to the sea, so sailing away with Killian on his adventure was the most natural thing in the world for her.

She draws influences from many places, including books, movies, life experiences, her crazy dreams, and the early Final Fantasy games – IX is the best, fight her. Fun facts time: Captain Lily Rothbone's backstory came to her in a dream, and Thomas Gainsborough's appeared to her during a gong meditation session in a disused mine. If you're intrigued, pop along to her website and ask. She'll happily tell you about the mine gongs, but probably not the backstories; you'll have to wait for those.

In her free time, she likes reading, hiking, experimenting with cocktails, petting her bearded dragon like a Bond villain, and playing video games with her fiancée. She also has a bunch of tattoos and is always looking to add to the collection.

Sign up to her mailing list for free gifts, fun newsletters, cover reveals and release dates.

You can stay connected on Instagram at

@Jo.r.delancey